CW00841617

JOSH MOONFORD
AND THE LOST CITY OF CANTIA

Josh Moonford and the Lost City of Cantia

Published by The Conrad Press in the United Kingdom 2019

Tel: +44(0)1227 472 874
www.theconradpress.com
info@theconradpress.com

ISBN 978-1-911546-50-4

Copyright © James Essinger 2019

The moral right of James Essinger to be identified as author of this work has been asserted in accordance with the Copyright, Designs and Patents Act 1988.

All rights reserved.

Cover illustrations by Maria Priestley.

Typesetting and design by: Charlotte Mouncey, www.bookstyle.co.uk

The Conrad Press logo was designed by Maria Priestley.

Printed and bound in Great Britain by Clays Ltd, Elcograf S.p.A.

JOSH MOONFORD
AND THE LOST CITY OF CANTIA

JAMES ESSINGER

For Joe, Cara and Christy

And in memory of
Barbara Elsie Lammers
(15th September 1954 - 2nd January 2016)

List of illustrations

'So what are you saying, Josh?' Lindsay asked me, *'that there's a secret Roman town down here where people speak Latin and which nobody knows about in the world we come from?'*

***

Facilis descensus Averno...
Sed revocare gradum supersaque evadere ad auras,
Hoc opus, hic labor est.
Easy is the way down to the underworld...
But to withdraw one's steps and make
a way out to the upper air,
That is a task, that is a labor.

Book 6, *The Aeneid,* Virgil

1

I wanted it to be a dream, but it wasn't.

The two giant lions were scanning the arena with glowing green eyes, the spectators in the amphitheatre stomping their feet and hurling bloodthirsty shouts.

Have the Cantians always been like this, I wondered, *or only since their Godless Revolution started?*

My heart thumping, I turned to Troy. '*I'm going to try to save Carlo.* I've got my sword. That big tapestry down there that's hanging from those hooks: maybe I could use it to lower myself down.'

Troy glanced down at the tapestry and the hooks. 'You're right. It might work. You go, and I'll follow you.'

Declan stared at Troy and then at me. 'What about me? Where do I fit in?'

'Nowhere,' said Troy, 'you're superfluous to requirements, just like you said I was.'

'OK, OK,' Declan replied. 'I admit I shouldn't have said that. Listen, I'm armed and I'm coming down into the arena with you both.'

'I'm coming too,' piped up Dora, 'and so is Sam.'

I turned to her. 'No, you're not. You and Sam stay here. It's much too dangerous.'

'Oh, yes,' Dora retorted, 'and watch the coolest man in the world get EATEN ALIVE when we could try to save him?'

The giant lions roared again.

I glanced down at the tapestry, wondering if my weight would rip it. But I knew the tapestry was our only chance.

One of the huge lions, screaming and roaring, started rushing towards Carlo. Carlo quickly put an arrow in his bow and shot at the charging lion, but the arrow missed. The lion jerked to a standstill, then roared even more loudly.

I turned to Lindsay and kissed her quickly on the lips. She looked astonished, and taken aback, but maybe, just maybe, she didn't actually look cross.

'I... I need to say something to you,' I said.

'What, Josh?'

'I may get killed down there in the arena. Yes, that's very likely going to happen. But I want you to know that I really love you and I think what's happening between us - that you prefer Declan to me now - is a total nightmare.'

But she didn't even reply.

I couldn't bear to see how little Lindsay cared about me. I turned round and looked down at the floor of the arena.

Suddenly, the idea of dying didn't seem so bad after all.

2

I'd been to the old Roman museum a couple of times before it got refurbished. The museum was pretty boring in those days, with just some old broken pots, and a few models of life-sized Romans that didn't move or do anything interesting.

There was a real Roman sword there, though, which I knew the Romans called a *gladius*. This was quite a short sword, only about two feet long. The Romans used it mainly to stab people. Believe me, you didn't want to have someone stabbing you in your stomach with one of those. But the gladius at the old Roman museum was all rusted now.

That was in the days before the Roman Museum was modernized and had lots of money spent on it. My home town, Canterbury, in south-east England, is a major tourist town and so I suppose the people who spent the money expected the new museum to be very profitable.

They didn't build Cantia, though.

3

Before it all happened, we were quite a normal family really. Or at least I thought we were.

I suppose it really started when the Anglo-Saxons invaded Roman Canterbury in about 550AD. That's a pretty long time ago now, and I can't imagine that anything which happened back then will seem especially important to you. Except that the Anglo-Saxon invasion *was* really important, because the Anglo-Saxons who invaded were pagans who worshipped some really creepy gods, but the people of Roman Canterbury were Christians, and their religion was really important to them, which was one of many reasons why they were desperate to continue their lives and traditions. And so they went to live underground.

I suppose I'm sort of a Christian too; I mean, I go to church sometimes, though I don't think anyone could accuse me of being especially pious. In fact I think evolution very likely did happen, mostly, but on the other hand I also think *someone* must have started the universe going, after all, how could it have just started by accident? That's who I think God is, the person or being who started it. But you don't need to believe any of this to enjoy (I hope) knowing about what happened to all of us in Cantia.

4

For Dora, Sam and me this all began about a month ago, while we were on the train from Rye in East Sussex back to Ashford in Kent on Sunday afternoon, August the thirtieth. That was when Dora found a news story about Carlo Clancy.

At that point none of us, obviously, had any idea how important Carlo was going to be in our lives.

I mean, who'd have expected what was going to happen, to happen? Why would a huge megastar like him have been interested in us, let alone depend on Dora, Sam, Lindsay, Troy, Declan and me to save his life?

5

Dora, Sam, Mum and me were coming back from our week's annual holiday at Waddington's Holiday Camp, near Camber Sands, on the south coast of Kent in England.

We'd had quite a good time. The weather wasn't great every day but it was sunny enough on about three or four days for us to be able to swim, and at other times we went on the rides at the funfair.

Dora has curly, bushy, dark brown hair. She's basically five feet two inches tall, but her hair adds about another four inches to her height. Dora has a round, cheerful face, is a bit plump and surprisingly strong. She can't quite beat me in arm-wrestling but she almost can, which is a bit embarrassing. Not surprisingly I don't arm-wrestle her very often.

Sam looks like a male version of Dora, I mean his features are quite similar although more boyish obviously. He's slimmer than her and his hair's a lot shorter. His nose is a bit larger than hers but those are basically the only differences. He's five feet four inches tall, but definitely not as strong as Dora and when they have fights, which is most of the time, she usually wins. I don't think being regularly beaten up by his sister can be very good for Sam's mental development. Actually he *is* pretty mental, though he can be a sort of genius sometimes, too.

Dora and Sam, who are both twelve years old and about to start Year Eight at school, were sitting next to each other, strangely silent, looking out of the window at Romney Marsh, with its wide fields, its narrow canals and the sheep and lambs which are pretty much everywhere on the marsh. Mum was reading *Health Food News*, getting back into complete healthy eating mode after our holiday, when even she had had a couple of meals (soya burger and salad, and veggie sausages and brown rice) in the holiday camp canteen.

Mum runs a health-food shop in Canterbury called Food for Thought. She works there every day except Sunday. The shop has never made much money and actually it was a wonder we hadn't all starved to death, or at least been reduced to eating the shop's stock.

But somehow Mum kept Food for Thought going: how she did that was certainly food for thought. Mum's thirty-nine, and quite slim and athletic, with long curly dark brown hair. She's five foot six, basically the same height as Dora, and Mum uses a perfume called White Musk which we didn't notice any more because we're so used to it. I only mention Mum's perfume because it becomes very important later.

The fourth one of us was me - i.e. Josh Moonford. I was fifteen then but I was going to be sixteen in exactly two weeks, that is, on Sunday, September the thirteenth. I'm five feet eight, by the way. I had a book with me on the train: the second volume of the *Sacred Guardian* trilogy by the fantasy writer I. M. N. Plardot. He's French, and almost all his books have been translated into English. The first volume was called *The Brotherhood* and while in a way it was a typical fantasy book featuring lots of characters with weird names and lots of fighting and swords and girls with long hair who the heroes rescued from castles and stuff like that, oh and dragons, too, it went beyond that and was quite deep in many ways. It had a theme of how good can triumph over evil if good is courageous enough, which I hoped was true. Also, *The Brotherhood* was well written and I like those kind of books although I didn't ever imagine such things would ever happen in real life.

The last station before the train arrives in Ashford is called Ham Street. There's also a town in Kent called Sandwich and one called Deal, so if you're in Kent you can have a Ham Sandwich Deal. A guy who got off at Ham Street left his newspaper on the table which was a few tables along the corridor from where we were. As soon as he'd left the train, even before the doors started to close again, Dora grabbed the newspaper and brought it back to our table so she could read it.

A news story Dora found said that Carlo Clancy was going to be filming some of a new movie he was going to be making - it was called *The Archbishop's Anagram* - in Canterbury itself, including at the cathedral, and that Carlo was coming to Canterbury very soon to do the filming.

I'm sure you'll have heard of Carlo Clancy, the famous Hollywood actor born in my home town, Canterbury, who spent the first sixteen years of his life there. He'd actually attended our school when he was younger and after he became famous he used to come and present the prizes on Speech Day sometimes. He'd presented me with a prize once but he'd got my name wrong though of course I didn't tell him that, at least not then.

During the rest of the journey home, Dora read or rather re-read the newspaper story about Carlo about five billion times.

She's pretty much obsessed with Carlo. She's seen all his movies, including the three *Sacred Guardian* movies, which made Carlo really famous. Dora and Sam had seen those three movies but I deliberately hadn't yet because I wanted to finish reading the books first. I was still reading the trilogy's first book, which is called *The Brotherhood of the Sword.*

At that time, we all lived in a little terraced house on 55 Prospect Place, which, in case you don't know Canterbury, is quite near Canterbury East railway station.

The house was small but we were used to it and basically we all loved it. Dora, Sam and me had lived there all our lives. Mum had moved to Canterbury with Dad about three years before I was born. At first they lived in a flat above the shop, which they ran together but eventually they bought the house we lived in.

When you went into the house there was a small ground floor room on the left where Mum kept surplus stock for the shop (it always smelt of e.g. nuts and banana flakes and carob) and she would sometimes do her paperwork there at the desk. I often did my homework there if Mum wasn't working in the room as it was really quiet. At the end of the short corridor on the ground floor was a big room which was the TV room and the living-room combined. There was a big mirror on one side that covered an entire wall.

Through the other side of the room was a kitchen and through another door in the corridor was a staircase that led up to the first floor and to three bedrooms; Mum's, Dora's and the one I shared with Sam. My pet parrot, Caesar, lived in the basement of the house, which sounds pretty creepy and spidery but it was actually quite nice because Mum had arranged for a radiator to be put down there and the basement was painted some years ago by her and me. In case you were wondering, when we were on our holiday,

Caesar was given food and water by a lady who lived a few doors down the street from us.

Sam had a pet too, who was also kept in the basement although sometimes he was allowed to spend a night in our room. Sam's pet was called Bruce. He was a giant millipede. This might sound as if Bruce was very big but he wasn't, in fact he was only about five inches long, but compared to most millipedes that made him a giant. Sam had bought Bruce from a pet shop in Canterbury the previous November with his birthday money.

Bruce didn't ever do very much, at least not in those days. He lived in a rectangular goldfish tank without any water in it except for in a little saucer he drank from. The tank also contained pieces of tree bark, quite a lot of moss, a cuttlefish bone which Bruce was theoretically supposed to nibble to get calcium from but I'd never seen him touch it, the saucer of water and a clump of lettuce, which was Bruce's favourite food although sometimes he liked eating a slice of cucumber too. As you'll probably have guessed, Bruce was a vegetarian, or at least he was then. According to Sam, Bruce had 184 legs, 92 on each side. I didn't know whether Sam had counted them, but it was perfectly likely he had. That's just the kind of thing Sam would do.

Sam had named Bruce, Bruce, because of the old movie *Armageddon*, which is one of Sam's favourite movies and which he's seen loads of times. I don't want to spoil the movie for you in case you haven't seen it but all I'll say is that in it Bruce Willis basically saves the world and that was why Sam named Bruce, Bruce. As for Bruce himself (Sam's giant millipede, not Bruce Willis) he was usually curled up and looked a bit like a miniature tyre. According to Sam, Bruce had once nipped him, which seemed to me extremely ungrateful considering Sam was utterly devoted to Bruce and totally loved him. But on the other hand the fact that Bruce *could* nip under certain circumstances does actually become quite important…

I'd had Caesar as a pet for two years. He was a very intelligent parrot and I'd taught him to speak a bit of Latin, which was my favourite subject at school, I suppose because I found the Romans so interesting.

That Sunday evening, after we'd come back from the holiday camp, and after dinner, we all played Monopoly. It's not my favourite game, which is chess, but I like playing Monopoly with Dora and Sam and Mum partly because it's quite amusing how Mum, who's very good at Monopoly, always takes mercy on Dora and Sam and if they land on one of her properties she lets them borrow the money from the bank so that they don't have to be kicked out of the game and made bankrupt. She tries to let me off having to pay her too but I always refuse as I think it's a bit babyish.

Another weird thing when we played Monopoly is that Bruce took part. Sam would put him on a dinner plate on the table and allocate a metal token to Bruce. Sam made Bruce's moves for him and helped him make his property-buying decisions and he frequently lifted Bruce up to one of his ears as if he was listening to what Bruce was saying.

The next day was the first day back at school, Monday August the thirty-first. That was the day I met Lindsay.

6

Our school's named after a famous writer, Joseph Conrad, who lived near Canterbury towards the end of his life and is buried in our city. We had to read one of his books, called *Heart of Darkness*, in the spring term of Year Ten but although there are some good bits it's quite hard to understand and mostly pretentious.

The weather had changed overnight. It was drizzling that Monday morning when we left home. We usually cycled to school, though not when it was wet, so we walked the half mile or so between our home and the school itself pretty fast. I suppose we got there at about eight thirty - school started at eight forty-five. I said goodbye to Dora and Sam and went straight into my classroom and said hi to some of the people, all of whom I knew from Year Ten. Starting Year Eleven felt like a big change because we'd be doing GCSEs at the end of the year.

I went to sit at a desk not far from the front of the class and took out some of my books and put them inside the desk. There were still old-fashioned wooden desks at the school which you could put books in. Once I'd stowed them away I grabbed *The Brotherhood* and opened it at where I'd got to. Our teacher hadn't arrived in the classroom yet to do the registration and so it was all pretty noisy and chaotic in the classroom, but I'd got to a specially interesting part of my book and was just focusing on what I was reading, or at least I thought I was.

A few minutes later, I saw a girl with yellowish, almost golden, hair, that was done up at the back, come into the classroom. She had a red leather bag slung over her left shoulder. Her face was creamy-coloured. She was very pretty. She had greenish eyes and a nicely-shaped nose. Like me, she was wearing school uniform. Whatever sex you are, you have to wear the school tie, which has maroon and gold stripes. She was wearing all this, and the grey skirt girls have to wear along with black tights.

For some reason she glanced at me and this was strange because from the beginning it was like I was someone important to her, although I didn't see how I could possibly have been as I'd never met her before. A moment later she walked up to me, coming to within a few feet of me and said, quietly, in a soft sort of voice, 'Excuse me, I'm new. Where shall I sit?'

She had a nice accent, it might almost have been Irish but it wasn't quite.

I cleared my throat. I felt quite nervous. It wasn't as if I wasn't used to girls because obviously I live with Dora although Dora's hardly typical of girls thank goodness but, well, this girl with the yellowish hair was even prettier than I thought, though she looked bossy too. Though pretty girls usually are, in my limited experience.

'Well,' I said, 'it's the first day back, so you can sit wherever you want.'

'All right, I'll go here then.' She took her bag off her shoulder and sat down at the desk on my right. Somehow it felt as if she and I were kind of in a little world of our own.

'So who are you?' she asked.

'Josh,' I said, hearing my voice feeling a bit dry and hoarse which was pathetic. 'Josh Moonford.'

'Hi, Josh. I'm Lindsay Penhaligon. And… in case you're wondering, yes, I'm the new headteacher's daughter.'

The penny dropped right away in my already besotted brain. I'd heard we had a new headteacher starting that term, Dr. Penhaligon, who was from Cornwall.

'You are?' I said.

'Yes. We're from Penzance. It's actually about three hundred miles from here, *sooooo* far away. I miss my friends terribly, but I can keep in touch with them on Facebook.'

I wasn't sure what to say next, except *well, I'm on Facebook too, maybe we could become Facebook friends?* but I knew I could hardly say that. I mean, maybe she wouldn't want to become one of my Facebook friends, after all.

Then I thought of something I could say. 'Why did your dad want to come all this way to work here?'

'Oh, partly it's a promotion; he was head of science at the school where he was teaching before and so being headteacher is a big thing for him. But also his own mum and dad live in Tunbridge Wells, which isn't too far from here and they're getting old and Dad doesn't want to be so far from them as he was in Cornwall. You like *The Brotherhood?*' She was looking at the front cover of my book, which I'd closed on my desk with a finger holding my page. There were two castles on the front, a forest, and various war-elves fighting.

'Yes… it's great.'

'I've read all three in the series, and seen the movies, too. I can't believe Carlo Clancy once went to this school!'

'Yes, it's pretty amazing,' I said.

That was how we met.

I was usually pretty hopeless when I talked to girls who weren't Dora. I'd never had a girlfriend, nor even a kiss with a girl.

It's true I'd gone to the school's summer fete near the end of the summer term with Stephanie Lacey, who was believed by many people to be one of the most beautiful girls at the school and I'd been incredibly excited about that and could hardly sleep a single snore the night before. But Stephanie had never held my hand at the fete. I was nervous all the time I was with her and couldn't speak, only mutter pathetically. Then, when we were heading to the stand where you throw wooden balls at old crockery to break it, she saw John Crowther who everyone said she fancied and she basically just dumped me there and ran up to John and kissed him and didn't even turn around or anything to see how I was. It turned out later she'd had an argument with John and had only asked me to go with her to the fete to try to make him jealous. She'd succeeded.

But even though I was obviously useless at talking to girls, strangely enough I got on really well with Lindsay from the very first time I saw her. I don't mean I wasn't nervous at all: I was. But soon I found I could think of reasonably sensible things to say to her. She's only about two inches shorter than me, in case you're interested.

That first day back at school I discovered that Lindsay and I were in the same class that Monday for Ancient History, French and English. Lindsay didn't do Latin, unfortunately. During afternoon break that same day, Lindsay suggested, which amazed me as it meant she'd sort of asked me out, that after school we could go to the café at Marks and Spencer on the High Street in Canterbury, opposite Cafe Rouge where Mum has dates sometimes, though they're always a disaster because I think she still loves Dad. So after school Lindsay and I went there for macaroni cheese and salad. She paid for me. I didn't want her to but she said it was her invitation and I could pay 'next time'. I loved her saying there'd be a next time.

We walked home from Marks and Spencer together afterwards as Lindsay lives quite close to me, in a posh house about half-way down St Augustine's Road. Of course she didn't hold my hand, but we had lots to say as we walked home, especially about the Romans. I walked her to the gate of her front garden.

7

The next morning when I got to the classroom, Lindsay was already sitting there at the desk next to mine.

'Guess what?' she whispered to me as I sat down at my own desk. It was pretty noisy in the classroom, though not as noisy as the day before.

'What?' I whispered back.

'It's my sixteenth birthday today.'

'You should have told me,' I said, still keeping my voice down. 'I'd've got you a present and a card.'

'No, I didn't want any fuss. I mean, I'm not having a party or anything. I don't really know anyone in Canterbury yet; only you actually. Hey, shall we be Facebook friends?'

'Yes, yes, I'd really like that.'

By lunchtime I'd actually - yes I know it's hard to believe but I did - plucked up the courage to ask her out that evening to the cinema, and to my amazement she said yes and that it was OK as she didn't have much homework that evening. I didn't either; the term hadn't got properly going yet. After school I bought her a *Sacred Guardian* birthday card, which had a photo of Salogel on the front, the character Carlo Clancy played in the three movies. I signed the card *Happy birthday from Josh x*. I wanted to do more than one 'x' but I wasn't sure she'd want me to. I also wasn't sure what Lindsay would like for her birthday, so I bought her the biggest box of Maltesers I could find from the newsagents near the school, and we gobbled them down later at the cinema while we watched a movie called *Dragons and Warlords*, which was OK, but as it contained a talking dragon it was a bit stupid. Afterwards I walked her home again, but she didn't kiss me goodnight or anything.

So Lindsay wasn't exactly my girlfriend, but she'd become one of my best friends really quickly. She hadn't even looked embarrassed when I told her I belonged to the school chess club. I'm not an especially good chess-player, but it was a useful place to go at lunchtime if you didn't have anything much else to do. There were always some titchy Year Sevens and Year Eights there who said they were good at chess, but in fact they were easy to beat, which was more than you could say about the robot gladiators in Cantia.

8

Well, during morning break the day after I'd gone to the cinema with Lindsay, Dora got involved in a big fight in the playground.

Unlike Dora, I'm not an expert at fighting and I've always managed to avoid getting into fights, but I'm not a coward and if the fight had gone against Dora I'd have got involved and helped her. But what happened was, well you'll see.

I was in the playground talking to a couple of guys who are also in the school chess club. Lindsay wasn't there. What happened next I don't exactly know, but a few minutes after I'd gone into the playground I saw Dora fighting with a guy called Spud Lyell, the sort of guy who calls people names and swears most of the time. He had short scraggy brown hair, was missing a couple of teeth and generally had a wild, psychotic look about him. His name was really Simon but no-one at school called him that. He didn't look like a Simon anyway.

The start of his fight with Dora happened so quickly I didn't have time to run to help her, but she was doing so well in the fight that I knew she'd have been furious if I'd have joined in because she'd have said that she could deal with Spud herself. Spud was in Year Nine and so the year above Dora and he's quite a well-built guy but Dora can really fight if she wants to and isn't scared of having to fight boys, even older ones. I suppose she gets lots of practice with Sam and basically what I saw was Spud being oppressed and pushed around by the terrible tornado who was Dora and then he

was on the floor on the playground and she was pressing his face against the tarmac and now she sat on his back and was pulling his left arm behind him and lifting it up towards the back of his neck until he shrieked out in pain.

Of course by this point pretty much the entire playground was into this and everyone was standing around in a sort of circle like watching gladiators fighting in an amphitheatre. I went up as part of the circle and I saw that there was no point me having to do anything because Dora was completely in control. I couldn't see Sam: I suppose he was working in the library or maybe he was still in his classroom. I just watched what was happening.

'*Say you're sorry!*' Dora shrieked at Spud.

'No! Get off me, you cow,' Spud spluttered.

'*SAY YOU'RE SORRY!*'

'No, your mum's a loony!'

Dora pushed his arm higher up to where it must have become even more painful and at the same time she hit Spud two or three times on the back of his right shoulder which forced his face against the tarmac even tighter. He yelped like the weasel he was.

I didn't know about the background to this but it was pretty obvious he'd said something rude about Mum and that Dora was defending her.

'*APOLOGISE FOR WHAT YOU SAID!*' Dora screamed at Spud, pushing his left arm up even higher and now I was really worried it might break.

'All right, *all right*, you cow. Get off me!'

'*Say my mum's not a loony!*' Dora demanded.

'All right, she's not. She's not a loony.'

'Say she's beautiful and nice and really clever!' shouted Dora.

'She's beautiful and nice and really clever,' replied the vanquished Spud.

'*AND I'M NOT A COW!*'
'No, you're not.'
'*And you surrender!*' said Dora.
'All right, I do, I do, get off me.'
'*Say you're sorry again.*'
'I'm sorry, I'm really sorry,' said Lyell.

Dora only now got off him and stood up. Spud, bruised and battered, got hesitantly to his feet. Everyone started to clap, including a tall boy whose name, I knew, was Troy Wilson and who was in Year Nine like Spud. I'd never spoken to Troy, but you know how it is in a school: you know people by sight even if you've never spoken to them. Troy was basically the leader of the Middle School chavs. He was about six feet tall.

Just in case you don't know what a chav is, I suppose I'd better tell you but it's not easy for me to describe what they're like without me seeming like some really creepy goody-goody, which I'm not. But basically chavs don't like doing schoolwork very much, and they're into things like shoplifting and smoking and generally behaving like prats. (I assumed Troy was like that as well until I got to know him.) Spud certainly was like that. I already knew that Troy described the chavs in his gang as his 'soldiers', which I thought in those days was a pretty conceited thing for him to say and I suppose it was, but on the other hand now that I know Troy better, he probably was a reasonably good influence on them compared with what they might have been like if they hadn't known him.

Of course, I was very, very impressed with my sister at that moment. I knew she'd had fights at school occasionally but I'd never seen her have a fight in the playground, let alone in front of an audience of what must have been at least fifty people.

Spud brushed a bit of grit from the skin on his forehead. He looked at Dora and she looked at him. Dora started to cry. She sniffed back her tears. Yes, she'd beaten Spud and humiliated him, but you could see how upset she was. Her fists were clenched, as if she expected Spud at any moment to take his apology back and would have launched herself at him again if he had.

I watched Spud and wondered what would happen next. I also noticed that Troy Wilson was looking hard at Spud and I could tell that in Troy's expression there wasn't any sympathy for Spud at all. Instead, I had the very strong feeling that if Spud had taken back his apology there was a serious chance Troy would have launched himself at Spud instead and believe me, Troy was one of the tallest and strongest boys in the school and Spud would have had no chance at all against him.

I noticed Spud glance at Troy, and then Troy's glance back at his soldier was very very stern.

Troy took a couple of steps towards Spud from out of the ring that was surrounding Dora and her humiliated adversary. Now, Troy was only about five feet from Spud, who glanced at Troy in a snivelling kind of way and said:

'She took me by surprise.'

Troy shook his head scornfully. 'Even if she hadn't, she'd still have beaten you. She'd have beaten you even if she'd had one hand tied behind her back, you muppet.'

'Dora's a good fighter,' some boy called out from the ring, like a Roman amphitheatre spectator starting a chorus of approval for a gladiator whose skills haven't been fully appreciated by the crowd until now.

Troy shook his head again. 'No, you're not a good fighter,' he said to Dora. 'You're a brilliant fighter.'

Now Troy turned to Spud again.

'This ends here, understand?' Troy said.

'What d'you mean?' Spud asked.

'I mean what I said,' Troy replied. 'This ends here. You don't try to get your own back at her, and you don't say anything else nasty about her mother. Is that clear?'

Spud gave a solemn nod.

'*Is that clear?*' Troy repeated.

'Yeah, yeah, it is, man,' Spud said, sulkily. He backed away and disappeared into the ring of spectators, who parted for him a bit but not with much enthusiasm and jostled him as he hurried away through the crowd and back to the school building.

Troy walked up to Dora, whose face was red and whose eyes were bleary with tears - could see this now. Her school uniform was looking pretty scuffed. Troy reached out his right hand and shook hers.

'I didn't see the start,' Troy said. 'What happened?'

'He was rude about my mum and her shop,' Dora replied, breathlessly. 'He called her a loony.'

'In that case,' said Troy, 'he was out of order and he deserved what he got. Hey, do you want to become one of my soldiers? I'll make you a lieutenant.'

Dora shook her head slowly but politely. 'I would,' she said, 'but I don't think my mum would like it.'

'OK, I get that. Maybe see you around, OK?'

'That would be great,' Dora said, and the look in her eyes at that moment seemed to me one of pure and unadulterated admiration.

At point I heard a voice from behind me. The voice said:

'Oh please, give me a break!'

9

I glanced behind me and saw a sixth former. I could tell he was because he had a gold lapel school badge rather than the usual white one. There wasn't a crown on it, though, which meant he wasn't a prefect. He was about the same height as Troy. He had long, well-groomed dark brown hair that fell down to his shoulders, brown eyes and a haughty kind of expression. I'd never seen him at the school before and I thought that most likely he'd joined the school that week, on the first day of the new term.

'Who are you?' Troy asked.

'I'm Declan Jacques, if it's any of your business,' the sixth former said. He pronounced it *Jacks*. I didn't actually know at the time how to spell his surname: I only found out how to later, 'This is a school, by the way,' Declan added, 'not a training-ground for gang warfare, nor a branch of the international mafia. I've only been a pupil here since Monday, Wilson, but I've already heard a lot about you. Just because this young lady has dispensed what I presume was perfectly justified justice against one of the thugs you hang around with, doesn't mean you have to behave as if you're the king and you've just given her a medal.'

Troy glared at Declan. 'I don't need to listen to this, you prat.'

'I'm not a prat. And just watch it, Wilson, or I'll recommend you for detention.'

'You can't do that,' said Troy. 'You're not a prefect.'

32

'I can recommend you for a detention anyway.'

'Oh, I'm *so* scared,' Troy said. 'Anyway, I'm going back in now. Keep out of my face, OK?'

Troy, looking completely calm and sure of himself, strode away, leaving Dora with her friends. She still looked tearful and upset. The crowd was already thinning now and by the time I went over to Dora it had more or less almost dispersed so we were talking now pretty much in private.

'Did you see it all, Josh?' she asked me.

'Yes, well, at least most of it. I didn't see him insult you but I saw what happened after he did.'

'You won't tell Mum, will you? You know what she's like if we're involved in fights. She gets really cross.'

'Don't worry, I won't.'

Dora was right about Mum not liking us getting involved in fights. I think Mum was always scared we might become tearaways and have rough lives and that all her efforts to struggle to support us financially would come to nothing. I suppose she was also worried that without a dad we were all more likely to go wrong.

10

OK, actually so this is why we didn't have a dad.
His name was Paul Moonford, and he and Mum
met at university in London and got married while they were
still at uni. After they graduated they worked in London
for a couple of years, Dad for an oil multinational and
Mum in the foreign rights department of a large publishing
company. She said they were really happy and loved each
other very much but didn't enjoy the stresses of London life.

'We wanted to start a family, darling, you see,' Mum
had said to me a few years ago without Dora or Sam being
there. 'Dad and I decided to start a family outside London.'

Mum had been a vegetarian since she was only twelve after
she saw a programme about battery chickens on television.
Her dream was to start a health-food shop. Mum and Dad
had an idea that they would set up the shop together and
could run it together. One summer day when they were in
London and they went for a day excursion to Canterbury
to see Canterbury Cathedral, which neither of them had
ever seen before, nor had either of them been to Canterbury
before, they fell in love with Canterbury and decided to set
up the health-food shop there.

They moved to Canterbury and started the shop and it
did OK but not well enough to support them both and after
a couple of years they had to accept this. Dad got a job in
London again at another oil multinational. By this point I'd
been born. Then there was a recession and Dad was made
redundant and for a year or so he lived on the redundancy

payment and what the shop earned but then it was time for him to get a job again and now it became a big problem because by now Mum was about to have the twins and she couldn't work and Dad needed to make some money.

The problem was he couldn't find a job, no matter how hard he tried, because there was still a recession in the oil industry, but he knew he could get work and be well-paid if he was willing to work abroad on a contract for a minimum of six months. That was how much time you had to work in most contracts on offer.

So one day, about eight years ago, Dad came home from a visit to London to a recruitment agency and explained to Mum that he'd been offered a six-month contract with an oil company to work in Saudi Arabia on a new exploration project. Mum and Dad were both really upset about the fact that he could only get work by going abroad. But what choice was there?

A few weeks later - the day was June the third - Dad said a very tearful farewell to Mum and to me. I was seven at the time and the twins just four. Then he got a cab with his luggage to Canterbury West Station to catch the high-speed train to St. Pancras and then to go by underground to Paddington and get the Heathrow Express to Heathrow for his flight to Saudi Arabia. We didn't travel to the airport to see him off. Mum said it would be too upsetting for the twins, though I suppose she knew it would be upsetting for Dad, her and me too.

The problem was, Dad never got to the airport.

It's known that the taxi driver dropped him off at Canterbury West Station because that was something the police could easily investigate and they found the taxi driver and Dad had even paid the bill by card so the police could prove that he paid the bill and reached Canterbury West station. (There are two stations in Canterbury: Canterbury

East and Canterbury West: the east station is on the west side of the city and the west station is on the east side. I don't know why this is, but Canterbury is a weirder city than you might think, as you'll discover if you read on). Dad had also bought a single ticket to Heathrow Airport by card: the police could prove that, too.

But after Dad bought that single ticket to Heathrow Airport the trail stopped. The police had investigated the matter really thoroughly and it was a complete mystery what had happened. Dad had never used any of his credit cards or debit cards after he disappeared. He'd never used his mobile either.

On Thursday, the day after the big fight, I asked Lindsay whether she might like to go with me that coming Saturday, September the fifth, to an Open Evening at the new Roman Museum in Canterbury.

The Roman Museum had recently been refurbished, with all sorts of interesting animatronics including gladiators that fought, and now term had started there was a free Open Evening at the new museum that coming Saturday for anyone at school in Canterbury. You didn't need to wear school uniform though. Our Latin teacher Mr Kinder told the Latin class about it. You could come along by yourself or bring your parents if you wanted, but I didn't imagine many people would bring their parents. Lindsay said she'd love to come. I was planning just to go with her.

Saturday was a sunny day. When Lindsay came out of her house to meet me after I knocked, I thought she looked totally beautiful. She wasn't wearing school uniform but a green short-sleeved top, a pearl necklace (she said it was a birthday present from her Mum and Dad), black jeans and black trainers. I couldn't believe how nice she looked in these clothes.

I forgot to tell you that Dora, Sam and Troy had arranged to go to the Open Evening at the Roman Museum too. Not surprisingly, as the museum isn't all that big (it's down some stairs, at the same level as Roman Canterbury, which was about fifteen feet lower than modern Canterbury), it wasn't long before we bumped into them. After Lindsay and I arrived we decided to go to the café at the museum to have something to eat and drink before we began exploring the new museum. Lo and behold, who should we find in the café drinking Coca-Cola and eating sandwiches but Dora, Sam and Troy.

Dora looked really pleased to see Lindsay (if not me) and invited us to join them, so we did. Dora and Lindsay chatted away. Lindsay and I had Cokes too and some pastries from Ancient Rome (well, made to an Ancient Roman recipe, anyway) that were on sale at the museum and which were made from ricotta cheese and honey and tasted nicer than that sounds. I paid for Lindsay and me. I don't have much money, but I save my pocket money carefully and some Saturdays I help Mum out at the shop and she pays me ten pounds for a morning or afternoon and twenty pounds if I'm there all day.

After we left the Roman Museum's café, the five of us all started going round the museum together. There were lots of animatronic figures e.g. a *retiarius* gladiator, armed with a net and a long trident, fighting a gladiator who had a small circular shield to defend himself and who was armed with a gladius that looked real but I suppose was actually plastic. The two gladiators, enclosed in a glass case, fought in a corner of the museum on sand, with a painted backdrop of cheering spectators. The fight was ferocious, but the animatronics had been designed so that these two gladiators never actually touched each other.

I knew that a lot of skeletons from Roman Canterbury had been found a year or so ago during the excavations for the new Whitefriars shopping centre in Canterbury. They'd brought the best skeletons into the new museum and put them into a special skeleton room. After we'd watched the gladiators for a while, I said I wanted to go and look at the skeletons and I asked if anyone wanted to come with me.

Dora didn't want to go into it, which surprised me a bit; after all, why should anyone who could fight Spud Lyell and beat him be afraid of a few skeletons? But Dora said the skeletons sounded 'creepy'. As soon as she said that, I knew Sam wouldn't want to go to the skeleton room either. Lindsay told me she'd stay with Dora. I didn't protest about that, after all, Lindsay was sort of my girlfriend or at least I hoped she was, and so I didn't want to say anything that might annoy her, but I definitely thought it was a shame she didn't want to come with me to the skeleton room. On the other hand, if she had, everything might have been completely different and we might never have got to know about Cantia.

'We'll just keep on exploring the museum,' Lindsay told me. 'Don't be too long, Josh.'

I liked her saying that.

I nodded. 'I won't.' I glanced at Troy. 'What about you? You fancy coming?'

'Nah, I won't bother, mate. I've seen plenty of skeletons in my time.'

I wanted to ask him where, but I didn't. Troy's the only person I've ever known who calls me 'mate'.

So I went to see the skeletons by myself.

11

The skeleton room was long and quite narrow, maybe only about ten feet wide. To start with, I was the only person there who wasn't a skeleton.

The room didn't have any animatronics in it at all. Though I suppose that wasn't surprising really; I mean you could hardly have had pretend animatronic skeletons dancing or playing the guitar; *that* would have been too tacky. But even if they'd just been walking along that would hardly have been respectful to the real dead people there whose skeletons were on view under glass cabinets.

I thought maybe I'd find the skeleton room creepier than I was expecting, and for a few moments I did, but not for long because soon I realised that this was real history; these had once been actual Roman Christian people who spoke Latin, and who'd once lived in Roman Canterbury and who were part of the huge Roman Empire and that actually made me feel more interested and less creeped out.

I looked at the various skeletons - of men, women, young children, and also a skeleton of a cat, a little dog and a chicken - all from Roman Canterbury.

What I found most interesting of all was a girl's skull in a glass-topped cabinet at the far end of the room.

Next to the skull, under the glass, was a piece of white card, held in position by little pins. On the card it said: *skull of girl from Roman Canterbury. Circa AD 200. This girl died when she was about fourteen years old. The cause of death is unknown.*

I stared at the girl's skull and at this little white sign next to it. I couldn't help wondering what the girl had looked like, what her name was, and how she'd died. I also found myself wondering what her voice had sounded like when she'd spoken Latin, and what made her laugh, and what she spoke to her friends about etc.

Suddenly, I heard heavy footsteps behind me.

For a moment I had the weird thought that it might have been the girl's ghost behind me. I span round to see. What I saw, though, wasn't a ghost, but a man.

He was bald, with a ferrety sort of face, black-framed specs, and bushy ginger side-burns. I suppose he was about the same age as Mum. He was wearing a black suit and a black tie, like he'd been to a funeral. In his right hand he was carrying a black holdall about three feet long.

He came towards me, heading in a determined way for the cabinet with the skull in it. I moved a few feet to the right to make way for him.

As he approached closer, I saw that the holdall had a black zip, which stretched all the way along the top of the holdall, and that the zip was open about six inches on the side furthest from me.

But that didn't seem so important. What seemed to me much more important was that I could *see something* through the open part of the zip.

I didn't know what it was. It was sort of tubular, and looked like it was made of a silvery metal, which might actually have been silver for all I knew.

There were two parallel, straight raised edges of silvery metal running along the back of the tube, like railway lines.

I could only see the six inches or so of the lines, but I guessed that they ran all along the back of the tube.

What was it in the holdall? I thought maybe a musical instrument of some kind, but this guy frankly didn't look very musical to me and besides, why would he be carrying a musical instrument in the Roman Museum?

At that point he saw me looking at the holdall. He quickly reached down, zipped the holdall up all the way, put it on the floor, then in a gruff voice, he said, 'There ain't nothing in there that concerns you, kid.'

'It's OK,' I said. 'I didn't think there was.'

'Good,' he said, sharply, then right away seemed to ignore me and started staring at the girl's skull. He put both his hands, palms down, on the glass top of the case. I noticed that on the back of his left hand there was a tattoo of a red snake with big yellow fangs, and on his right hand a roaring lion with a golden mane.

Next, the man started whistling quietly, kind of to himself, before suddenly, without any warning, turning to me.

'This place is even better than the custard, ain't it?' he said, like as if I *knew* him, which I certainly didn't, nor wanted to, either.

Custard? I wondered. What was he on about? I suppose he just saw me as a random person to say something to. I wanted to get out of there and I'm sure you would have too if you'd been there. But still, I thought I'd better say something, so I muttered, 'yeah, I suppose it is,' even though I didn't actually know what I was agreeing with.

This weirdo didn't say anything else to me, but just went back to staring at the skull. But as I couldn't see the girl's skull much any more really and as the social possibilities right now didn't seem very promising, I turned round and walked quickly out of the skeleton room and back to Lindsay, Dora, Sam and Troy.

I was expecting the guy with the mysterious holdall to call something else about custard after me, but he didn't. I wondered what he was doing there, actually, because basically the open evening was for school pupils - though parents or guardians who are theoretically in charge of us could come too - and there wasn't anyone with him at all.

When I found Lindsay, Dora, Sam and Troy, they were watching an animatronic oyster-seller, a life-sized Roman in a brown toga. He wasn't as violent as the two gladiators, which was just as well; I mean, after all, if you're an oyster-seller, killing your customers isn't good for business. There were two woman customers animatronically pushing against each other, desperate for oysters, and shoving brown coins they held in their fingers towards the oyster-seller. The oyster-seller offered them oysters on a plate with his left hand and put his right hand out for money, but as this just kept happening and being repeated; the oyster-seller never got his money and his customers never got their oysters.

One thing about it made me secretly sad. I thought of Mum's shop and how often she hardly had any customers at all.

'What were the skeletons like, Josh?' Lindsay asked me.

'Sort of dead, I expect,' said Sam.

It's best mostly just to ignore Sam, though sometimes he has flashes of insight and genius.

I shrugged. 'Well, there was a girl's skull, which was sort of fascinating, because it made me think of what the girl might have been like when she was alive. Then a strange guy came into the room. He was a weird-looking bloke with a bald head, specs and bushy side-burns. He had a holdall with him.'

'What was in it?' asked Sam.

I shook my head. 'I don't know. But I did see a bit of what was inside, because at first, until he saw me noticing, a little of the holdall's zip was open. I saw what looked like a sort of musical instrument. And there's something else, too.'

'What?' Lindsay asked.

'He was looking at the skull, then he suddenly glanced at me and said: "This place is even better than the custard, ain't it?"'

Lindsay stared at me. 'The custard? What did he mean by that?'

I gave a shrug. 'I don't know.'

'Was he bonkers?' asked Dora.

Dora thinks almost everyone's bonkers. If you ever met Dora, she'd most likely think you were bonkers even if you weren't at all, or only a bit.

'Maybe,' I said.

'No, he didn't mean *real* custard,' Troy put in.

We all looked at him. The thing about Troy is that there's something in how he speaks and behaves that makes you think he knows what he's talking about. Of course, this might actually be because he *does* know what he's talking about.

'It's how some people speak in parts of East London,' Troy went on. 'They're called Cockneys. My uncle Kev, who lives in Stepney, talks like that. Like for example, when he says, "plates of meat", he means "feet" 'cause that rhymes with it. Or when he wants to say he's going down the road he says he's going down the "frog and toad".'

'Why would he say those things instead of what he means?' asked Sam.

Troy shrugged. 'It's how some people speak in East London. Still, my uncle Kev drinks about twelve pints of beer most evenings, so it's never exactly clear what he means about *anything*.'

'Yes, it's called Cockney rhyming slang,' said Lindsay. 'Troy's right. People who speak it don't say what they mean, but things that rhyme with the thing they mean.'

'Why?' asked Sam.

'I don't know,' said Lindsay.

Troy gave a nod and glanced at him: 'In the old days, some of them Cockneys were robbers, and they wanted to talk in a way the cops wouldn't understand.'

'I see,' I said, 'but then what does "custard" rhyme with?'

'Mustard?' suggested Sam.

We all stared at him. 'That's yellow too,' he added.

He was only trying to be helpful, of course. I realise Sam and Dora often sound like a pair of escaped lunatics but that's what having a younger brother and sister is like, basically.

'What Custardface meant,' said Troy suddenly, 'was television.'

'Television?' I said.

'Yeah.'

'But, Troy,' I said, '"television" doesn't rhyme with "custard".'

Troy glanced back at me. 'No, but "telly" rhymes with "custard and jelly". Sometimes it's not the rhyming word you say, and you don't need to say both words anyway, just one of them.'

'I'm totally confused,' Dora complained.

'Me too,' I admitted. 'But still, what Troy says makes sense. The guy in the skeleton room must have meant this new Roman Museum is better than what's on TV.'

'How about telling us more about Custardface?' Troy said to me.

So I explained how the man had dressed like he'd just been to a funeral, and I told them about his tattoos.

'*Awesome,*' said Sam, glancing at the backs of his own hands, and obviously wishing he had tattoos there himself.

'Was he with a school pupil?' Lindsay asked.

'No,' I said.

'Well, what was he doing here, then?' asked Lindsay.

'And what d'you think *was* in the holdall?' Dora asked me.

All the while we'd been saying this, the oyster-seller and his customers had still been animatronicking, if that's how you spell it, which it probably isn't.

And then at that very moment, the guy I'd seen in the skeleton room, the guy Troy had called Custardface, walked up in front of us, still carrying his holdall, and started staring at the oyster-seller.

12

None of us said anything. The oyster-seller animatronic doesn't actually make any noise, and suddenly it was really strange to be there in total silence next to this very weird guy with his mysterious holdall.

Custardface didn't seem to recognise me, and I got the impression he didn't find the oyster-seller very interesting, because after only about half a minute or so he started walking away from us, down the Roman street. This is a long pretend street in the museum which has Roman stalls and other animatronics along it, but not the fighting gladiators, which are in a different part of the museum, near the entrance.

I watched Custardface head off along the road. He just walked in a straight line, and at the end of the Roman street, maybe thirty yards away, he vanished to the left.

I just looked at the others.

'There's something *very* weird about that bloke,' I said. 'I'm going to follow him.'

'Why, Josh?' Lindsay asked.

'Because I want to know what he's doing here, and what's in that holdall.'

'But why not just leave him alone?' Lindsay said.

'Look, he told me off in the skeleton room for looking at his holdall. He can't just go around here walking around as if he owns the place and telling people off for looking at something weird and silvery in a bag he's carrying. It wasn't *my* fault the zip was open a bit. So I'm going to try to find out a bit more about him.'

'Josh, I really don't think you should,' Lindsay said. 'We really ought all to go home.'

'No, I reckon Josh is right,' Troy said. 'That guy looks pretty sinister. We ought to see what he's up to.' He glanced at me. 'I'll come as well, mate.'

'Troy,' I said, 'that's really good of you, but I think it'll be easier for me to stay out of his sight if I'm by myself.'

Troy shrugged, then nodded, and said, 'OK, mate. Go by yourself this time if you want. But remember, I'm Troy Wilson, and I like to be where the action is.'

'I'll remember that,' I said.

I admit I didn't take Troy as seriously then as I did later on that weekend.

That was pretty stupid of me, because without him, I wouldn't be alive to be writing this.

13

I put my phone on silent, then quickly headed up the Roman street, only glancing at the pretend Roman restaurants and shops on either side of me, and at the animatronic figures I passed on the way, which included a Roman soldier on an animatronic horse which reared up on its back legs, a Roman blacksmith hammering a *gladius* on his anvil, and a Roman girl rolling a hoop along a groove about ten feet along the street, who then turned round in a robotic way and went back to where she'd started, which was pretty creepy.

Just before I reached the corner Custardface had disappeared round, I listened hard, but couldn't hear anything.

I risked a careful peep round the corner.

There was no sign of him, but I saw a long corridor stretching maybe twenty yards before turning to the right. It had a few doors along both sides that I supposed led into offices. This corridor had a grey carpet all the way along.

I trod quietly along towards where the corridor turned right. Just before I reached this corner, I hear a voice from around the corner, so I froze.

After a few moments, I tiptoed up to the corner. Listening hard, I found I could hear what the voice was saying without needing to put any part of my head, even just my nose, round it. There was only one voice. It was definitely Custardface's. I thought he was probably on the phone, most likely a mobile, as I couldn't imagine there'd be a landline out there in the corridor.

'Listen,' he said, 'it's going to be more difficult than I expected, right?'

There was a silence, then he started to talk again. 'Why didn't you tell me about the food? It was like something from a nightmare. And what are all those cogwheel things?'

Another silence. I wondered what he meant by the food being like something from a nightmare. Did he mean what was on sale at the Roman Museum's café? He might have done, I suppose, but the food there had seemed OK to me. And what did he mean by 'cogwheel things'?

There was another silence, lasting maybe half a minute or so, before he said, 'Don't worry, Stan. I won't let you down. I like money, in case you haven't noticed. Yeah, of course I know it's important. I only wish I could understand their stupid language. Now, listen, I've something else to say. If I'm going back down, *I want my dins.* Make it happen, OK?'

A moment after he'd said that, I heard footsteps from where his voice was coming from. Was he heading in my direction? I didn't wait to find out. I ran up to the nearest door in the corridor and turned the handle. Luckily for me, the door opened. It led into a small office, and I hurried in there as fast as I could and closed the door behind me. If there'd been someone there I think I'd have told them about Custardface, but there wasn't. I stayed close by the door, listening hard. I couldn't hear anything. After maybe half a minute I opened the door a tiny crack and listened again, but still couldn't hear anything.

I was pretty sure Custardface hadn't come down the corridor towards me, which meant he must have gone on to some other part of the museum. After a while longer, I opened the door and walked back up the corridor to the corner where I'd heard him talking on the phone. There was no sound this time.

I peeped round the corner. Now, I was seeing the new corridor for the first time.

There was no sign of Custardface at all. This corridor was completely different to the other one. It wasn't very well lit, for one thing. Its walls were of red brick and looked as if they still needed to be whitewashed and painted. I thought that maybe as the new Roman Museum was so new, they hadn't got round to decorating this part yet. There was no carpet on the ground, just grey paving-slabs. I couldn't see how long the corridor was; it was too dark and spooky and seemed to get even darker as it went farther along. There were faint, flickering overhead strip lights every few yards but they didn't give much light.

I wondered where Custardface had gone.

14

'You really heard him talking on the phone, Josh?' Lindsay asked.

I nodded. 'To someone called Stan.'

Troy just stared at me. 'What did he say?'

'Well, he started by telling whoever he was talking to that "it" was going to be "more difficult" than he'd expected.'

'What did he mean by "it"?' asked Lindsay.

'I don't know. Then he said the food was "horrible". Oh, and he talked about some "cogwheel things". I don't know what he meant by those, either.'

I glanced at the others. 'He also said to Stan, "I like money, in case you haven't noticed", and then said he wouldn't let Stan down. Oh, and Custardface told Stan he wished he could understand "their stupid language".'

'Whose language?' Lindsay asked, giving me a puzzled look.

I shrugged. 'I don't know that either. Then he said, *"if I'm going back down, I want my dins."*'

We all thought about this.

'He must have meant he wanted his dinner,' Dora said, after a few moments. 'After all, if he didn't like the food they'd given him, he'd be hungry.'

'Yes, maybe,' I said.

'Or perhaps "dins" rhymes with something,' Sam suggested.

We all looked at Troy, the expert in this particular area. He shrugged. 'I dunno. "Bins", maybe.'

'"Sins" sounds more likely,' Lindsay suggested.

'But why would he want his bins or his sins?' Sam asked, suddenly being Mr Logical.

'And even if he did,' I said, 'what could he have meant when he said he was going "back down"? Back down where?'

Lindsay shrugged. 'It's very weird. Did he say anything else you can remember, Josh?'

'No, I don't think so.'

Lindsay crinkled her nose into a frown. 'I wonder who Stan is?'

I shrugged. 'Some friend of his, maybe.'

'Actually, what I think is there's a secret entrance in this museum to some strange magical place,' said Sam.

'You really are bonkers,' Dora told him.

'Sam, that's a pretty random suggestion, if you ask me,' I said. I glanced round at the others. 'I want to go after Custardface again, though, and see where he's gone. He can't have gone far, can he?'

'I'm definitely coming too, this time,' said Troy.

I looked at him. 'OK.'

'Josh,' said Lindsay, 'you can't just keep *following* this man. Maybe he simply works here, or something, I suppose. You can't keep going after him to find out what he's doing: he might call the police.'

'That's fine,' said Troy. 'Yeah, let him do that, and when the cops come he can show them what he's got in his holdall.'

That's what so cool about Troy: he doesn't put up with any nonsense, and he somehow always sees to the heart of a situation.

Lindsay shrugged. 'Troy, I suppose you're right. But I still think we should all go home. I think following that man could be dangerous.'

'Danger's fun,' said Sam. 'I want to go with Josh and Troy.'

'If you and Sam are going, Troy,' put in Dora, 'so am I.'

'No, you're not,' I told her. 'You're only twelve, like Sam. You're staying here.'

Dora scowled at me. 'You can't tell me what to do, Josh. You're not Dad. Dad's dead, most likely. I'll do what I want.'

'No, listen, Dor, your bro's right,' said Troy. 'You and Sam should stay here.'

'No way,' said Sam. So now everyone was coming with me, apart from Lindsay. So much for me trying to keep a low profile.

But of course I wanted Lindsay to come. I glanced at her. In fact, we all did.

'All right,' she said. 'I've always wanted an adventure. Maybe this will be it. All right, I'll come with you all.'

I smiled. I'd loved her more or less from the moment I met her, but I loved her even more now.

We all put our phones on silent now and headed up the Roman street, Troy and I at the front, then the twins and Lindsay.

At the end of the street, I took a peep around the corner, but there was no sign of Custardface, so we went on walking quietly, along the carpeted corridor now. I half expected someone to come out of one of the other doors.

Soon we reached the right-hand turn at the end of the first corridor.

I waved at everyone to stop, then I edged up to the corner and listened. I peeped round the corner into the dimly-lit and creepy red-brick corridor.

'Anyone not want to go on?' I asked. No-one said they didn't, so we headed onwards into the red-brick corridor with the grey paving-stones on the floor.

The further on we went, the dimmer the lights became. I

started to think there was no way I'd lead the twins, Lindsay and Troy down the corridor if it got much darker than this.

But it did, as if it wanted to scare us off. I was close to telling everyone we ought to give up, when the end of the corridor suddenly loomed up in front of us. It was a dead end. A brick wall.

I was thinking Custardface must've gone into one of the side-offices. I was still thinking that when there was a huge white flash, but without any sound.

The whole world seemed to have exploded.

15

All I could see were billowing white clouds. I couldn't hear any sound.

My first thought, hardly surprisingly, considering the way the world is today, was that Custardface was really a suicide bomber and that the thing inside the holdall had been a bomb and that we'd all been blown up. I mean, nowadays you sort of half-expect to be shot or blown up pretty much every time you go outside, and even though terrorists haven't done any massacre in Canterbury yet, (perhaps because hopefully they don't actually know exactly where Canterbury is), you never know what might happen.

But I would have had to admit that there was one basic thing wrong with my theory. This was that I didn't actually *feel* dead. Not that I suppose I'd have known what feeling dead was like, because if you're dead then surely you don't feel anything at all, unless there's an afterlife, which I'm not sure there is though of course there might be.

But I remember thinking something like this: *Maybe, because I've never been dead before I don't actually know what being dead does feel like. Maybe in fact being completely dead is like this e.g. because perhaps your brain cools down for a while before you're dead.*

Then I thought: *are Dora and Sam dead too? If so, Mum won't have anyone now. And what if Lindsay and Troy are dead as well?*

It was then that I saw grey, person-sized shapes starting

to form among the clouds - four of them. They looked like ghosts.

So perhaps this is what being dead is really like, I thought. *You see white clouds and ghosts of other people, who are dead like you are. So perhaps heaven exists after all, which probably means that God exists too. So all those people who think He doesn't exist are actually wrong.*

Slowly the grey shapes turned into Lindsay, Dora, Sam and Troy.

They were looking in my direction. *Can they see me?* I wondered.

Lindsay's lips were moving, but I couldn't hear any sound coming from them. Dora seemed to be trying to say something too.

The clouds finally started to dissolve. As they did, I stopped wondering whether we were all dead, because I could see everything around me, and it was simply amazing...

Yes, we were in Canterbury. Yes, it definitely was Canterbury. But it wasn't a Canterbury I'd seen before or even imagined. I only knew it was Canterbury at all because I could see the famous cathedral in the distance.

The difference was, the Canterbury Cathedral I knew had always been surrounded by old buildings, but here the cathedral was in the middle of a huge, white open square. All five of us were standing in the square, which was paved with an enormous slab of what looked like stone. The ground was a sort of warm, creamy colour, like vanilla ice-cream.

All around the square were enormous silvery metallic buildings, maybe two or three times higher than the cathedral itself.

The buildings didn't have any windows. As I looked, the buildings' silvery metallic colour morphed into another for just a few seconds, then changed again: white, then light blue, dark blue, light orange, dark orange, green, and back to white once more.

I saw the others looking around at all this, just as I was. There was no-one in the square. But when I tried to speak to them, I couldn't. I opened my mouth, but no sound came out. And I could see the others had the same problem. We all tried to speak, but none of us could.

Perhaps we aren't dead, after all, I thought. *Perhaps it's the world that's dead.*

The next thing I knew, everything went black - and for some time, I don't know how long - I fell unconscious.

16

When I woke up, Lindsay and the twins and Troy were all lying on the ground near me in a collapsed pile. There was no sign of Canterbury Cathedral now.

We were back where we'd been when the explosion had happened, in Canterbury's Roman Museum at the very end of the red-brick corridor.

Troy sat up, gently lifted Dora off him and laid her on the ground, then started shaking her. 'Come on,' he said. 'Wakey-wakey.'

Lindsay, Dora and Sam slowly sat up, and rubbed their eyes.

'Are you all OK?' I asked.

'I think so, but I'm not sure,' Lindsay said.

'I'm OK,' said Sam.

Dora turned to me. *That was so weird.*

I nodded. 'It was like a very strange dream.'

'Or nightmare,' put in Sam.

'Yes,' I agreed. 'The cathedral. The big open space. The incredibly tall buildings. All those colours that kept changing.'

Lindsay nodded. 'You saw that too, Josh? Yes, it *was* like a dream, or being dead.'

'I think Custardface was hiding somewhere in the corridor,' put in Sam, 'and shot us with a ray-gun.'

'Get real, Sam, please,' I said. 'Ray-guns don't exist.'

'They might do, and we don't know about them,' Sam protested.

'Well, if he did shoot us with something,' I said, 'where exactly was he hiding?'

I looked around, just as the others did. We were still at the end of the dimly-lit corridor, a few yards from the brick wall at the end. I couldn't see anywhere that might have been a hiding-place for Custardface.

There was one other thing that seemed strange, though.

This was an empty paper coffee-cup lying on its side about five yards away. I hadn't noticed it before, but there was no door or anything nearby where Custardface might have hidden, so I decided it couldn't have been him who'd left the cup, but that the coffee-cup must in fact have just been there all the time.

Suddenly I heard footsteps coming fast from down the far end of the red-brick corridor. It was too dark for us to see who was rushing towards us. It felt so spooky. I was completely creeped out, and could hardly breathe.

Was Custardface going to shoot us again?

17

Then I saw who was running towards us.

It wasn't Custardface.

No, it was someone else; Declan Jacques, the sixth-former who'd been so rude to Troy in the playground after Dora had won her fight on Wednesday.

Declan skidded to a stop like a character in a cartoon. The corridor was pretty dark, but there was no mistaking his dark brown, shoulder-length hair and arrogant expression. He was wearing black jeans, a red button-up tee-shirt and a black jacket.

He stared at us all. 'What are you lot doing here?' he asked, very bossily.

I don't think he'd seen Troy when he asked him that question. But then he did see him. 'And what exactly are *you* doing here, Wilson?'

'After the way you spoke to me in the playground, Jacques,' said Troy, 'I'm really not interested in talking to you at all.' Troy turned away from Declan and glanced at Dora. She avoided looking at Declan too.

Declan now fixed his eyes on me. 'Hold it, I recognise you. I've heard about you. You're the school's Latin star, aren't you?'

'How do you know?' I asked him.

'I just do. Isn't your name Moonriver, or something?'

'No, Declan, it's Moonford. Josh Moonford.'

'Oh, yes, that's right,' replied Declan in his drawling way, as if he were the host of a TV game show and I'd just won a point for knowing my own surname. 'Well, what are you all doing here? This is hardly the part of the museum that's open to visitors, is it?'

'No,' said Lindsay. 'In fact, we might ask you what you're doing here yourself?'

Declan glanced at her. 'Oh, hello. And who are you?'

'Lindsay Penhaligon. I'm in the same class as Josh.'

'You're not Doc Penhaligon's daughter, are you?' Declan asked.

'Yes. Yes, I am.'

'I see. Well, I'm Declan Jacques, the new genius at the Joseph Conrad High School. Frankly, I'm surprised you haven't heard of me.'

'Actually, I've only been at the school for a week,' said Lindsay, still completely calmly, 'and I haven't had time to consult the school's directory of geniuses just yet.'

Declan looked at her as if he was impressed. 'Ah, a fellow wit! There are few of us about, Miss Penhaligon.'

'Declan, what *are* you doing here?' I asked him.

'I've a part-time job helping out at the museum, Moonford.'

'But we haven't seen you here so far this evening,' I told him.

'That's because I've been helping out doing some work in one of the offices. I wasn't involved in the Open Evening. I came down here to check out the voices I heard. So what exactly is going on here?'

'Have you seen a man around here,' I asked him, 'bald except for two bushy ginger side-burns, and carrying a black holdall?'

'No,' Declan said. 'Why d'you ask?'

That was basically the first time I'd heard him say anything that wasn't to some extent arrogant.

'We were following the guy along this corridor here,' I told him. 'We think he's an intruder. We spotted him on the Roman Street and followed him down here to see what he was up to, but we've lost him. He speaks Cockney rhyming slang and said "custard" for "television", so we call him Custardface.'

'That's pretty immature of you all, to call him that,' said Declan.

'What's wrong with being immature sometimes?' Lindsay asked. Without waiting for an answer, she turned to me. 'Go on, Josh, tell the genius the rest of it, as he's so interested. Maybe he can let us know what's going on.'

I nodded at her quickly, then I turned to Declan and went on: 'Custardface must have left somehow, escaped through a side-door somewhere maybe. There's someone called Stan involved too; we've no idea who he is; Custardface was talking to him on the phone.'

'Did you all hear him?' asked Declan.

'No,' I said, 'only I did. Custardface looked really suspicious, so, well... I followed him. I mean, I was the one who did, to start with. That was when I heard him on the phone. I'd noticed him in the skeleton room earlier and part of the zip of his holdall was open and I saw a bit of a weird silvery-looking metal thing inside.'

'That's all you noticed?' Declan asked. 'You didn't see what it was?'

I shook my head. 'No, I only got a glimpse of it. So I came back and told the others about the phone call, and then basically we all followed him. We hadn't been doing that for long when something very very weird happened.'

'What?' asked Declan.

'Well,' I said, 'we were all just walking along here, looking for Custardface, when… well, everything just seemed to… *explode*. I actually thought I'd died.'

'So did I,' said Sam.

Declan glanced at Sam. 'I've seen your sister before, the little Amazon of the playground, but who are you, exactly?'

'Sam, her twin,' Sam said. 'What d'you mean by amazon? I thought that was where people buy books and CDs and stuff.'

'Never mind, Moonford Three,' said Declan. He glanced at me. '"Everything just seemed to explode?" What are talking about? How could that have happened?'

'We don't know, but it did,' I said. 'And what I've just told you isn't all of it, either.'

'So tell me the rest,' Declan said.

'All right.' When I'd finished explaining to Declan what I'd seen after the explosion, he shook his head slowly, only somehow I could tell he was shaking his head in amazement, not in disbelief.

'So… this all really happened, Moonford? This isn't some kind of adolescent joke?'

'No, of course not,' I said. 'It really happened.'

'We all saw it,' Lindsay said.

Declan nodded slowly. He seemed suddenly to have plunged into deep thought. Then he looked at me and said, 'OK, let's go to the museum's reception and tell them about this Custardface guy. You're right; him being here does sound very suspicious. Reception can call the police. When they come, though, I don't recommend any of you tell the cops about the explosion thing. I mean, I really don't want any of you to get locked up as escaped loonies.' He glanced round at all of us. All right, let's seize a chance to get out of this creepy corridor.'

And maybe we would have just headed to the reception of

the new, refurbished Roman Museum, reported Custardface to reception, waited for the police to arrive, told them what we knew, and let the police get on with the job of catching him, assuming they wanted to. Then we'd have gone home and got on with our normal lives and spent the rest of our lives being comparatively normal.

Only that's not what actually happened.

What actually happened was that suddenly the right side of the brick wall - I mean the brick wall that had seemed to be a dead end - slowly started to swing open.

18

'*What is this?*' Lindsay gasped.

The wall was hinged in the middle in a way you didn't notice until it opened. The section on the right just kept on slowly swinging backwards, revealing a dark entrance - or it might have been an exit, for all I knew - that smelt very musty. Then the section of the wall that was swinging back came to rest, with a sort of slow grinding sound, against the wall on the right.

I stepped forward to get a better look.

I took a few steps into the cavity. The dim light from the corridor was the only light reaching in there, but it wasn't strong enough to show anything more than brick walls on either side of the hole.

'I was right, you see,' I heard Sam say, calmly, from behind me.

'Right about what?' I said.

'About there being a secret entrance here which leads to a magical place.'

I glanced at him. 'Sam, it's just a hole in the wall, that's all.'

'Perhaps Custardface went in in there,' Dora hissed, excitedly.

I came back out of the cavity. It was nice to breathe fresher air again.

'It's *very* creepy inside there,' I said.

'I think the people who run the museum don't even know it exists,' said Sam. 'We should go and tell them about it.'

'Oh, stop being so bonkers,' Dora told him. 'Of course the people who run the museum must know about it, they just haven't told anyone else about it yet.'

'That's possible, I suppose,' Lindsay said.

'But why would they put this in?' I asked. 'I mean, it doesn't seem very Roman to me. And if it's part of the new museum, why didn't they tell us about it?'

'Have you heard of this, Jacques?' Troy asked Declan.

'Of course not.'

'I want to see what's in there,' said Dora. 'It's cool, this hole that's opened up. I'm going in.'

And she dashed forwards towards the entrance. Dora can really move when she wants to, and she did now. All I saw was a blur of Dora in her white long-sleeved tee-shirt, blue jeans and white trainers. I grabbed hold of her left shoulder for a moment but she wriggled out of my grasp like an eel and scampered deeper into the cavity in the wall.

For a few seconds we heard her footsteps racing away from us in the darkness before they faded away.

19

'Oh, that's just *great*,' I said.

I rushed a few yards back into the cavity. 'Dora!' I yelled. 'Come back!'

My voice echoed back to me.

'If there's an echo it goes in quite a long way,' I said. I was already starting to get really worried for Dora.

'Man,' said Troy, 'we've got to go after her.'

'I'm coming as well,' said Lindsay.

'So am I,' put in Sam.

'No, you aren't,' I said to him.

Sam glared at me. 'Yes, I am.'

'Sam, we can't all go in,' said Lindsay. 'One of us needs to stay here, so people know where we've gone.'

'Well, maybe Declan can stay,' Sam suggested.

'Me!' Declan said. 'Me stay behind? *No way*. No way am I going to be the one who stays behind! I can't have people saying Declan Jacques was too scared to follow a bunch of adolescents through a hole in a wall, can I?'

'Stop calling us adolescents,' Lindsay said to him. 'I mean, you're not exactly an Old Age Pensioner yourself.'

'Sorry,' said Declan, which surprised me a bit.

'Thanks,' Lindsay said to him, which surprised me a bit too. She glanced at me. 'Actually, now I think about it, people will spot the opening in the wall and investigate, so it should be safe enough to go in.'

I nodded. That hadn't occurred to me, but anyway it

basically settled the matter. Troy joined me up front, and I led the way into the darkness.

We trod carefully, keeping our hands in front of us so we didn't hit our heads or faces against anything we couldn't see. The musty smell got worse, and it was really very dark in there, though there was still enough light for the time being coming in from the corridor for us to see the brick walls on either side and a brick ceiling maybe a yard above us.

'Dora!' we all called out, but there was no answer, just our echoing voices dying into whispers, then silence.

I looked behind me. Everyone was in the cavity now, including Declan, who'd come in last.

And then something happened which I hadn't been expecting, I suppose because I was so focused on what had happened to Dora.

The brick door closed behind us.

20

It didn't close with a slam, nor with any noise at all, but smoothly, quickly, and completely. One moment there was a hole in the wall leading back to the world we knew, the world of light; the next second the doorway was gone. And so, of course, was the light from the corridor.

'Oops,' said Declan.

'We should have left someone outside after all,' Sam said, unhelpfully.

I tried not to panic. It was suddenly pitch black; you couldn't see a thing. How long would we be here? I wondered. Forever? My heart had started to beat really, really fast.

I stumbled back through the complete darkness to where I guessed the hole had been. When I reached the wall I knocked as hard as I could on the brick with both my hands, until all my knuckles were really hurting. I heard Troy's voice alongside mine saying 'I'm here too, man!' and I heard his knuckles rapping too. Then we both stopped knocking. My knuckles were hurting too much, and I could easily imagine Troy's were too.

We listened.

I couldn't hear anything at all from the other side of the wall.

So would we all die of thirst? Starve to death?

And where was Custardface right now? Had he found Dora and kidnapped her? Or maybe he was crouching in a corner, waiting to attack us?

'Josh, what are we going to do?' Lindsay called to me, and it was seriously spooky, hearing her voice maybe ten feet away and not being able to see her at all.

'It's OK,' I said, calling trying to be brave, and snatching out my phone like it was a gun. 'I'll phone the museum's office. I can get the number from google. My phone's light'll help too.'

The light on my smartphone was very bright, but it was very focused, too, like a searchlight. It was too focused, in fact. I shone it around at everyone, like as if to reassure myself that they were still there.

'Please don't, Josh,' Lindsay said. 'The light's much too bright. It's almost blinding.'

'Sorry,' I said, quickly pointing the light down to the ground, which had gravel on it, though this must have been real gravel.

At least I could see the colour screen of my phone, which was clearly lit by the much gentler screen light than the torchlight from the back of my phone. But as I glanced at the screen of my phone, my insides went icy.

There was no signal at all.

'Oh, no,' I whispered.

'What is it, Josh?' Lindsay asked

'I don't have any signal on my phone,' I said.

Troy and Sam had started playing the lights on their phones around the walls.

'I don't have any signal either,' said Troy's voice, out of the darkness.

'Nor me,' said Sam.

'Well, we still have to find Dora,' I said. 'Let's all switch our lights off and see if our eyes can get used to the darkness.'

The lights on their phones went off. We waited.

Maybe a minute or so later I said:

'I think I can see something.'

Peering into the darkness ahead, I could just about make out a *very* ghostly corridor ahead of us, its walls maybe ten feet wide and an arched ceiling about eight feet above it. The walls and ceiling weren't of brick at all, but were white.

'There's a really faint light ahead,' I said. 'I can't see where it's coming from, though. I think the walls are made of chalk.'

'I think so, too,' Lindsay said. 'Not that that makes me feel very reassured. I mean, blackboard chalk snaps pretty easily doesn't it? I hope the ceiling doesn't just fall down.'

'It's really creepy here,' said Sam, in a ghostly voice which of course made things feel even creepier.

'I hadn't noticed,' said Declan.

Suddenly I heard Dora call 'Josh, come over here!' out of the darkness.

I didn't think she was too far ahead, but even though I could just about see the wall of the corridor, it was too dark to see her. We walked on through what was still almost complete darkness, but then I could see that Dora was at the far end of some sort of room at the end of the corridor. The room was about the size of a kitchen. It had white walls, but that was all I could see. I thought maybe they were made of chalk too. I could just about see a Dora-shape, very faintly, at the far end of the room, but it was too dark to see what the end of the corridor looked like.

Then I heard a strange metallic sound behind me. I turned round and saw two silvery doors sliding shut behind Declan, who was maybe ten feet behind me, with Lindsay, Troy and Sam between him and me. I was amazed to see the doors; I hadn't even noticed them. They must have been housed in slots in the walls.

A moment later, and the silvery doors had closed tightly together behind Declan, trapping us all ahead of them.

Now it was completely pitch black again.

21

We stood there, in the total darkness, for about half a minute. I must admit I felt absolutely totally scared.

Then, a moment later, we actually got our first enjoyable surprise.

An overhead light came on.

It wasn't especially bright; it was the kind of brightness you get in a room that has a light with a dimmer switch if you turn the dimmer almost completely down.

I glanced up at the light for a moment. It was a strip-light. Why had it come on? But at least it let me see the room, which was a bit bigger than the previous one. It was square-shaped, and the walls were white, just as I'd seen in the darkness. I still thought the walls might have been made of chalk, but I wasn't sure.

Dora was standing on the far side of the room, maybe twenty feet away. She was staring up at a sign that I hadn't noticed before because the room was too dark. The sign was just above something else: a strange-looking black outline of a door in the white wall. At the same time I noticed that on the right-hand wall of the room, there were about a dozen black metal coat-hooks stuck into the wall. Hanging from these hooks were also about a dozen Roman-looking togas and a similar number of Roman-looking dresses, all in different colours. Arranged neatly in a long row on the floor underneath the togas were about twenty pairs of Roman sandals.

The sign had big black capital letters against a plain white background. I was about to start reading it aloud, but Sam got there first. Somehow the sign sounded even weirder than it already was when Sam read it out, though the sign was pretty weird already:

CANTIA: TRANSIT PORTAL
WARNING!!
UNDER PROVISION 8A OF THE
SECRET ENGLISH LAW *THE CANTERBURY
UNDERGROUND ANOMALY ACT 1932*
YOU MUST WEAR CANTIAN CLOTHES
BEYOND THIS POINT!!
A BREACH OF THIS LAW IS AN
ACT OF TREASON, PUNISHABLE BY
LIFE IMPRISONMENT!!
THERE IS ONLY ENOUGH OXYGEN IN THIS
ROOM TO KEEP ONE PERSON ALIVE FOR
30 MINUTES.
YOU HAVE BEEN WARNED!!

22

After Sam had finished reading out what the sign said, there was a very long silence.

'Josh,' said Lindsay, at last. 'What do you think "Cantia" is?'

I just glanced at her. 'I wish I knew.'

'And what can the "Canterbury Underground Anomaly" be?' Lindsay asked.

'I wish I knew that too,' I said.

'I don't even know what an alomany is,' said Sam.

'Anomaly,' said Lindsay. 'It means something that goes against what you expect.'

'Like if Dora gave me some of her pocket-money?' asked Sam.

Lindsay smiled faintly. 'Well, yes, if she didn't normally do it.'

'She doesn't,' said Sam.

He glanced at Dora. 'Why did you run on in here, anyway?'

'Because I felt like it,' Dora told him.

The togas and dresses on the hooks ranged from one long enough for grown-ups to ones for younger people like Dora and Sam.

'What *is* this?' Troy muttered. 'Signs, clothes, sandals... *where are we?*'

'And what *can* "Cantia" be?' Sam asked.

'Well,' I said, 'it must somehow be something to do with Rome, so I suppose Cantian clothes are like Roman ones.'

'How can it be treason not to wear Cantian clothes, though,' said Lindsay, 'and can there really only be half an hour's oxygen in here?'

'Well, that corridor we were in was pretty musty,' I said, 'and this room's only quite small now those creepy doors have closed behind us. Maybe... well, maybe the sign's serious. Maybe it's true.'

'Whatever Cantia is,' said Sam, 'if that sign's right, and as there are six of us, there's only enough oxygen to keep us alive for five minutes.'

I nodded. 'Thanks for pointing that out, Sam, and making things even scarier than they are already.'

'Josh, do people know if their oxygen's running out?' Lindsay said.

'I don't know,' I said.

Lindsay glanced at me. 'What are we going to do?'

I gave a shrug. 'I don't know, but maybe we should put the clothes on, and then perhaps somehow we can get out of here through the outline of that door under the sign. Perhaps it'll open. The sign says *beyond this point*, doesn't it? Which means there must be a point beyond here. In any case why would there be all these clothes if we weren't supposed to put them on? And anyway, we can't go back, can we?'

'There's not much doubt about that,' said Troy.

I found myself thinking: *what's it like to die from not having enough oxygen? You must gasp and choke for every last molecule of air until you go blue and suffocate, like if you were holding your breath and then couldn't breathe again.*

I nodded quickly. 'Yes, maybe Sam is right. All right, let's put the Cantian clothes on.'

'I'm not taking my underpants off, though,' said Sam.

'Sam, I don't think we need to take our underwear off

or anything weird like that,' I said. 'The sign just says we have to wear Cantian clothes - which is what these Roman-looking clothes must be. We can put them on over the clothes we're wearing. No-one could see what we've got on underneath anyway. Come on, we need to hurry up.'

Dora and Lindsay were the first to reach the clothes hooks. Dora grabbed a red dress and slipped it over her tee-shirt and blue denim jeans. Lindsay took hold of a white dress and put it on over her green short-sleeved top and black jeans. You could still see her lovely pearl necklace, but I hoped that wouldn't be a problem. After all, maybe there were pearl necklaces in 'Cantia', whatever Cantia was.

As for Declan, he was already grabbing one of the togas, a grey one that looked as if it might fit him.

'How do I put this thing on?' he said, taking his jacket off.

I wasn't sure, so I ran towards the clothes hooks. I found a white toga and took it from its hook. I'd suddenly decided I wanted to wear the same colour Lindsay was wearing. I'd expected the toga would be difficult to do up; a toga is just basically a length of cloth, after all. But as I lifted it off the hook, I saw that it was all ready for wearing.

'Three minutes!' Sam shouted. I supposed he was using his phone to check the time.

'The folds are in the right place already,' I said to Declan. 'You just slip it on.' And I quickly put mine on to show him. Declan gave a shrug, said, *'Oh, God,'* but then he put the toga on.

About ten seconds later I was wearing the white toga over my red Greenpeace tee-shirt and white Chino trousers with my wallet in my pocket. Once the toga was on, I couldn't see my tee-shirt or my trousers.

'Two minutes!' called Sam, like a prophet of doom, hurriedly putting on a dark brown toga with his left hand.

He was amazingly quick, I thought. Troy found a black toga. He threw his denim jacket to one side.

'I can't keep that on under this,' he said, 'I'll come back for it.'

'Ninety seconds!' called Sam.

'Josh, I don't feel well,' Lindsay gasped at me.

'Me neither,' moaned Dora.

I was breathing as deeply as I could, but I just wasn't getting enough oxygen into my lungs. I started to gasp. The others were all breathing deeply and gasping too.

'The sandals!' I managed to shout.

Still gasping, I pulled my black trainers off, straining for breath, then ripped my socks off. Troy, Sam and Declan pulled off their socks and chucked them onto the floor. Dora and Lindsay weren't wearing socks or tights.

I put on a pair of Roman sandals very quickly. Troy was coughing as he helped Dora, who was gasping for air. Declan, a determined look on his face, which I could see was starting to turn pale, kicked off his black shoes and managed to fumble a pair of sandals on. Sam was coughing so much, he couldn't reach for a pair of sandals, but Declan found the energy from somewhere to help him.

We were coughing and gasping just so much.

'Look!' Sam croaked, pointing to the door.

The outline of the door was opening and the doorway below the outline was sliding upwards. With a massive effort, we raced to the opening doorway and fell to our knees to gasp at what was, thankfully, mercifully, fantastically, *fresh air* coming in.

It was a few minutes before we started to speak again, and only after we'd had our fill of the world's best-ever invention: air.

'What can have made the door open?' I said.

'It somehow must know we're wearing Cantian clothes,' Lindsay gasped.

'But how can a door *know* anything?' I said.

I glanced ahead through the open doorway into another, larger room with white chalk walls and a domed ceiling that was about twice as high as Troy, so about twelve feet high. Without a word, Troy stood up, went through the open doorway, walked to the right and was suddenly out of sight. Then I heard him call back to us. 'I can see something!'

'What?' I asked.

'A hole,' he called back.

'A hole?' I echoed.

Troy appeared back in the doorway. 'Yes. With some stairs in it. They're going down.'

'Far down?' I asked him.

'Deeper than I can see,' said Troy.

23

Troy was standing by the hole and peering down into it. The hole was about six feet wide.

The hole had wooden steps that went down, and at an angle of about forty-five degrees, into what, at first, seemed like complete darkness. But if you looked hard, you could see some dim light-bulbs in the slanted ceiling above the steps. I counted seventeen steps before it got too dark down there and I couldn't see any more.

'The stairs must go down to the magical place,' said Sam, in a satisfied tone, and continuing with his theory.

Dora sighed.

'This must be what Custardface meant by "if I'm going back down, I want my dins,"' Lindsay said. 'After all, there are hardly likely to be *two* holes in the ground with stairs in them, are there?'

'No, most likely not,' I agreed.

'But if he did come down here,' said Dora, 'how did he get through the oxygen trap?'

'Maybe the thing in his holdall was breathing apparatus,' Sam suggested.

'Yes, maybe,' I said. 'After all, if he'd been here before, he'd have known he needed it.'

'And as there was just one of him,' said Sam, 'the oxygen supply would have lasted longer.'

'Well, anyhow,' said Troy, 'we'd better get going down there ourselves. Like I said, there's no way back.'

'Even if there was,' said Sam, 'I really want to know what's down there.'

'Well,' said Declan, peering down the staircase and frowning, 'if you lot are mad enough to want to check out wherever these stairs lead to, I'd better come with you, I suppose.'

I glanced at Lindsay. 'What about you? Will you come?'

'Josh, I'm not saying I want to, I mean, it looks really spooky. But Troy's right, there's no way back.'

I glanced at Troy. 'D'you want to go first? After all, you discovered the steps.'

'No, I'll follow you, mate. You're Dor's elder brother, after all. This is your gig.'

I smiled at him. 'Thanks.'

I drew a breath, and then I stepped into the hole and onto the first step. I was so glad Troy was letting me lead the way. Troy followed me, then came Sam, Dora and Lindsay. Declan was last, like before. Our sandals clattered on the wooden steps.

The walls and sloping ceiling were only a few feet away from us. They were made of chalk. Fortunately the steps weren't; they were solid brown wood. There were faint lights, dim electric candle bulbs stuck in the ceiling above us, every couple of yards or so. Even when our eyes adjusted again we still couldn't see more than a few yards in front of us.

'We could use the lights on our phones again,' Sam suggested.

'No,' I said, 'our lights didn't help before, and all we'll do is lose our night vision. And besides, there's a glow down there.'

There was, too.

It was a faint glow far below, just enough to give us some encouragement we weren't heading into total darkness.

The glow slowly became a bit brighter, but as we walked on I couldn't see where it was coming from.

We kept going down the steps for maybe another five minutes or so. Finally, I began to make out a white floor at the bottom. I hurried to reach it. When I did, I quickly moved away from the foot of the steps so everyone else had space to stand as they came down. The floor looked, and felt, like it was made of chalk, too. I lifted my right foot; even in the very dim light I could make out that there was white powder on the underside of my sandal.

'Where *are* we?' said Troy, just behind me. It was still really dark even with the glow, and Troy in his black toga looked more like a silhouette rather than a person. Now he reached the bottom too, followed by Lindsay, who in her white dress looked like a ghost.

I suppose I must have looked like a ghost too, I mean if Lindsay did. I was pleased nobody had said anything (well, at least not so far, anyway) about us both wearing the same colour clothes. I liked how wearing the same colour as Lindsay made me feel.

Dora came down in her red dress, then Sam in his brown toga. Declan, in grey, was last.

At the bottom, from the way the air suddenly felt much cooler on my cheeks, and the way Troy's voice had just sounded, I thought that the walls and ceiling (I couldn't see them because it was so dark) must be quite some way away.

I guessed we were in a long tunnel.

There were no lights except for the glow, which turned out to come from what still appeared to be some distance away, straight ahead.

'Well, we obviously need to walk towards that glow,' I said to everyone. 'But we won't be able to see where we're going.'

'Let's hold hands,' said Lindsay. 'That way, if one of us falls down a hole, we can all help.'

'Actually, I don't want to hold hands with anyone,' said Declan. 'I'd rather fall down a hole.'

Lindsay turned to him. 'Do you have to be like this, Declan?'

'Yes, probably,' replied Declan, sulkily. 'Besides, it's just common sense. If one of us does fall down a hole, anyone whose hand they're holding would most likely be dragged in as well.'

'Or might have a chance of saving whoever's falling,' said Lindsay.

Declan didn't make any reply to this.

I said, 'The important thing is, we head towards the glow. There's no other choice, after all. Of course, anyone who wants to hold hands, should.'

We all started going along in a long line. I was on the right, and Lindsay moved to walking on my left.

Suddenly Lindsay put her right hand out towards me. I took it.

Lindsay's hand felt really nice: cool and smooth and yet her fingers felt strong. She entwined them with mine. Dora came to walk next to Lindsay and put out her right hand for Lindsay to take with her left, which she did. It was too dark for me to see whether Sam was holding Dora's hand, but I doubted it. I couldn't see Troy or Declan at all. I didn't think *they'd* be holding hands, though.

As we walked, the glow gradually brightened. Slowly we began to see where we were.

We were in a tunnel, just as I'd thought, and there were rounded chalk walls maybe ten yards away on either side, and a chalk ceiling about as high as the top of our terraced house on Prospect Place, which felt a long, long way away now.

The tunnel was coming to an end. Lindsay let go of my hand now. I was very sorry she did.

But I didn't have much time to be sorry about this, because of what I was seeing when I looked ahead.

24

In front of us was a chalk wall that stretched across to the walls on each side and up to the ceiling.

In the middle of the wall were two large black gates set in an archway that sloped downwards from the top on either side. Above the gates there was just more white wall, that reached up to the ceiling. There were two black metal rings, one on each gate, where the gates met in the middle.

At the top of the gates and just above them, set into the chalk, was a glass lantern with a bright light inside.

Lindsay just stared at the gates. 'What can these be?'

'They must be the gates to Cantia,' Sam put in, in a quiet, awestruck voice.

I glanced at him. Yes, he was bonkers, but on the other hand all of his suggestions seemed to have come true so far. I suddenly thought that perhaps when bonkers things start to happen to you, you need someone bonkers to make sense of them.

Wherever the gates went to, they looked firmly shut.

'So, now at least we know where the glow came from,' I said.

'Yeah, mate, we do,' Troy said. 'But underground gates? What's going on?'

I shrugged. 'Let's try and open them, then we might know.'

'Josh, please listen to me,' Lindsay said. 'As far as our families are concerned, we could still just be out for the evening. It's only about half an hour since that weird brick wall opened, after all. If we go through these gates, though, who knows what'll happen? We don't know when we'll get back home, if we ever do.'

'I understand,' I said. 'Let's just hope we do get back home. But you know I have to try to open these gates, don't you?'

Lindsay nodded. 'Yes, I know. 'All right, let's see if we can get through the gates.'

Dora and Sam clapped.

'Just hold it a sec, though,' said Declan. 'If I'm going through, I really would rather *not* be going in the company of Wilson. I realise we can hardly expect him to go back, and I know he won't want to, anyway. But I think, before we go through these gates and find whatever there is to find, Wilson should agree not to steal anything, or cause any mayhem.'

Troy just shook his head slowly. He stared at Declan. '*Listen*, you long-haired prat. I don't want you to tag along with me any more than you want me to be tagging along with you.'

'Oh, shut up, Wilson,' said Declan.

'Who's going to make me? You, Jacques? I don't think so.'

Declan and Troy glared at each other. They were both the same height, about six feet. Declan, of course, was older; as he was in Year Thirteen I knew he must have been about eighteen. Troy was about four years younger, but he was as well built as Declan, maybe even more so, and I guessed about a million times more streetwise. If it ever came to a fight between them, I certainly wouldn't have bet on Declan.

I went up to the gates and grabbed the metal rings of the right-hand gate. I pulled hard, which wasn't enough to make it budge, so I braced my legs against the chalk ground and pulled even harder, and this time the gate slowly started to move with a grumpy squeak. I tugged and tugged at the gate, and pulled it far enough open for us to step through to the other side.

The moment I was through, I stopped again.

What I saw now was even more amazing than seeing the gated archway in the first place.

25

Three men, dressed as Roman soldiers, their bodies illuminated by the lantern, were lying motionless on their backs, obviously unconscious, on the chalky ground on the other side, close by the partly open gate.

They had grey helmets and armour, and short trousers with armoured flanges protecting their upper thighs. Each of their breastplates was decorated with a gladiator fighting a lion. Their swords - which I could see at once were obviously *gladius* swords - and long, curved shields were lying close by them.

Lindsay, Dora, Sam, Troy and Declan had followed me through the gateway by now. We circled the soldiers like hungry hyenas and stared at them.

'They're all out for the count, aren't they?' said Troy.

'Yes, it looks like it,' I said.

'I don't think they can be real,' said Lindsay. 'They must be some sort of *models* or something, you know, like in the Roman Museum.'

'Or they could be animatronic soldiers who might get up at any moment and start fighting each other,' Sam said, sounding hopeful.

I quickly walked over to the nearest soldier, knelt down and took hold of his right hand. I felt it for a few moments, then carefully lowered the soldier's hand back down onto the ground and went to feel the right hands of the other two soldiers. I glanced at Lindsay.

'No,' I said, keeping my voice quiet now as I didn't want the men to wake up, 'they aren't animatronics.'

'How d'you know?' said Lindsay, making her own voice much quieter too. I loved her even more that she'd done that.

'Because,' I said, still quietly, 'not even animatronic models have *pulses*.'

'You mean... they're *alive*?' Lindsay said, in a kind of breathless gasp.

'Why are you both talking so quietly?' asked Dora.

'Dora,' I said, in a half-whisper, 'you need to keep your voice down. These soldiers are real people, and they're still alive. We don't want to wake them up, do we?'

Troy glanced at me. In a hissed whisper - Troy always gets up to speed with situations very quickly - he said, 'listen mate, we should grab those guys' swords so they can't kill us if they *do* wake up.'

'Yes,' I said, 'you're right. Good thinking.'

Troy quickly picked up the sword of the soldier whose pulse I'd taken. The weapon was short, no more than a couple of feet long, and had a horribly sharp-looking V-shaped point.

Troy picked up the two other swords. He gave one to me. I felt the point with my right thumb. It was even sharper than it looked, and that was saying something.

Troy glanced at Declan. 'You want this?' Troy's voice was quiet but firm.

'Not particularly,' Declan hissed back. 'But I don't have any choice, do I?'

'Not if you want to be a man,' Troy replied, slowly and quietly.

'Oh, give me a break,' said Declan. But he took the sword, all the same.

I looked ahead. There were lights visible, maybe a couple

of hundred yards away. We were still in a tunnel with chalk walls and a chalk ceiling, but here, on the other side of the gates, the tunnel was a fair bit wider. Also, there was a light on this side, too, above the top of the gates. All the same, even though we could see the unconscious men well enough because of the light, we couldn't see the end of the tunnel ahead; the lights there still weren't good enough.

In silence now, we started heading towards the distant lights. Troy, Declan and me all held our swords in our right hands, the tips of them pointing forwards. I looked behind me just once, but there was no sign of the soldiers having woken up, let alone coming after us.

After we'd gone maybe fifty yards, Sam turned to me. 'What d'you think happened to those soldiers, Josh?'

I shrugged. 'I wish I knew.'

'Maybe Custardface came down here before us,' Sam suggested. 'Perhaps he knocked the soldiers out.'

'Well, it's possible,' I said.

Troy nodded slowly. 'He must be a tough devil, though, to have knocked out three soldiers.'

'Maybe he used the thing in his holdall, whatever it was,' Sam suggested.

'Yes,' I said, 'that's possible too.'

'Whatever happened to the soldiers,' said Lindsay, *where are we?*'

'I suppose we must be in Cantia,' I said.

'What's Cantia though?' Lindsay asked.

'It's probably an underground set for Carlo's movie,' said Dora.

I shook my head. 'A movie filmed this far underground? I don't think so. But even if it is, where are the cameras and movie crew?'

'Quite apart from the fact that Carlo's movie's called *The*

Archbishop's Anagram,' Lindsay said, 'which doesn't sound very Roman to me.'

Nobody, including me, seemed to disagree with that. We just kept on walking, and the lights I'd seen in the distance grew brighter.

Now, I could see that there was an open archway ahead of us, set into a chalk wall which we came closer to with every step. As we did, I could see that there were some small buildings visible through it, buildings that looked like little cottages. Further away, well behind the wall, and with faint lights on them, I could see the silhouettes of buildings that obviously were much taller than the archway.

'I think it's a sort of... *underground village,*' I said.

Lindsay turned to me. 'Josh, that really isn't possible. It really isn't.'

'I know,' I said. 'But look. What else can it be?'

'You should all put your swords away,' said Sam. 'If anyone lives here, they might not like it if we're armed.'

'People can't live down here, Sam,' I told him. 'That would really be completely crazy.'

Sam glanced at me. 'Josh, there are buildings, and buildings mean people.'

I couldn't help thinking Sam did have a point. Talking of which, I quickly experimented with the best way to hide the sword inside my toga, then I glanced at Declan and Troy. 'Look, you can stick the tip carefully down one side of your shorts and cover it up with the toga fabric.' You might think this was quite difficult but the swords were *gladius* swords, and only about two feet long.

Declan and Troy both hid their swords in the way I'd suggested, and we walked on until we reached the archway and went through it.

There wasn't a tunnel on the other side. Instead, we really

were, amazingly, we were in what was... well, basically a *street*.

It was lit by the strangest of street-lamps. Every fifteen feet or so, glowing, yellowish planks, perhaps six feet high and maybe a couple of feet wide, were set vertically into the ground, casting a yellowish glow on the houses and the street.

I looked up, but I couldn't see a ceiling overhead, just blackness once the light from the street-lamps wouldn't penetrate any further upwards.

The little cottages on either side of the street were like the backdrop of a Dick Whittington stage pantomime. They had sharply sloping roofs and white walls, and were mainly just one storey high.

We were all looking at this in complete astonishment when suddenly a man emerged from the street on the left.

He was wearing a toga.

26

Even in the yellowish light I could see that the Cantian man's toga was black, like Troy's.

Fortunately, it was obviously dark enough for the Cantian man not to notice how intently we were looking at him. He walked calmly and peacefully down the street, in the middle. One of the things I thought at this moment was *they don't have cars down here.* Of course, I didn't know that for certain, but it seemed a pretty good guess, as the man in the toga was walking in the middle of the street.

I also remember thinking *so this is Cantia, they really wear Roman clothes here. What is this place, and why haven't I heard about it before?*

I could only think that it was something to do with the refurbished museum, I mean something like a kind of amazing, ultra, and fantastic new attraction.

But even as I thought that I wondered about the oxygen trap. After all, if you're trying to attract visitors to a new tourist amenity, the last thing you want to do is to *kill* them, especially not before they've paid their entrance fee.

The man in the toga saw us now. He smiled, and raised his right arm until his palm was almost vertical.

'*Salvete,*' he said, and then continued walking down the street until he faded into the yellowish light.

'He was in a *toga*,' Lindsay said.

'Yes, I think we noticed that,' murmured Declan.

'Well, we're in togas too,' said Dora. 'This must be what the sign in the oxygen trap room meant. These really are Cantian clothes we're wearing, and people down here wear togas.'

'Just like the Romans did,' Sam commented, when as I was about to say much the same thing.

I found myself just shaking my head slowly in total amazement, surprise, astonishment, bewilderment and quite a few other emotions too. 'But what is this place?' I said. 'Until now I still thought it might be part of the museum, but now I don't see now how it can be. It would have cost a fortune to have built all this, and besides, if they did, then why didn't they announce it when they launched the refurbished museum with that TV advertising campaign and the ads in the local newspapers?'

Lindsay looked at me. 'But Josh, if this isn't a part of the new museum, what can it be?'

'It's some kind of magical kingdom, like I've been saying all the time,' Sam put in.

'Whatever it is,' I said, 'why has nobody ever told us about Cantia?'

Lindsay glanced at the oldest member of our team. 'You're being uncharacteristically quiet.'

'That's because I'm thinking,' Declan said.

I glanced around at everyone. 'Did you all hear what that man said to us?'

'It sounded like Sally Vetty,' said Dora.

'That's what I thought he said too,' put in Sam.

'Perhaps Lindsay or me reminded him of someone called Sally Vetty,' Dora suggested.

'Oh, yeah, right,' said Sam.

I shook my head. 'Listen. Listen, all of you, please. That man... he wasn't saying anyone's name. He was speaking

Latin. He said *salvete*. That means "hello" or "good day" in Latin.'

'Well, at least they're polite down here,' Troy said. 'But that doesn't necessarily mean we're safe.'

'Josh,' Lindsay said, 'how can anyone speak Latin today? It's a dead language. I know it was still used by scholars and some travellers until maybe five or six hundred years ago, but that's all it was used for. Apart from science, where a lot of things have Latin names, it's no longer spoken anywhere in the world.'

'But perhaps Latin's still spoken *here*,' Sam said.

We all looked at him.

I shrugged. 'Maybe you're right, Sam. Perhaps Latin isn't a dead language, or at least not down here. After all, that man even gave us a Roman salute.'

'So what are you saying, Josh?' Lindsay asked me, *'that there's a secret Roman town down here where people speak Latin and which nobody knows about in the world we come from?'*

'I didn't even know there was all this *space* underground,' Sam said.

'Actually,' Declan put in, promptly, 'Canterbury's built on chalk, so I suppose hollowing bits out wouldn't be difficult.'

I supposed he'd studied the subject in a geography lesson. 'But who'd take the trouble to hollow it out unless they were completely mad?' I said. 'I mean, there's not any oil or natural gas underneath Canterbury, is there?'

I'm not sure whether Declan was about to answer this or not. Before he could say anything (if he planned to), another man came out into the dim light farther down the street. He was wearing a toga too, which in the dingy yellow light seemed a sort of pale orangey colour.

'*Salvete*,' he said.

This time I said it back.

95

The man smiled faintly at me, then walked past us.

When I was sure he was too far away to hear us, I said, 'The next person I see, I'm going to try asking them in Latin where we are.'

'Are you sure you should do that, Josh?' said Lindsay. 'How do we know they won't get hostile to people down here who aren't from here?'

'They might not even know our world exists,' Dora said.

'Oh, come on,' said Sam. 'How would they not know about our world?'

'I think Lindsay's right,' said Troy. 'I think Dor's right too. I reckon we shouldn't assume anything, not if we want to stay alive.'

27

J ust standing there quietly and thinking about things for maybe ten seconds, which is after all plenty of time to do some serious thinking, I suddenly thought that maybe what Dora had just said about the people of Cantia not knowing our own world existed really might be true.

I glanced round at all the others and then shrugged. 'Maybe Dora *is* right. Perhaps they don't know about our world. And I agree with Troy, we can't assume anything. So let's not talk English while they can hear us. Let's not give ourselves away.'

Lindsay nodded. 'And Josh, only you must speak to anyone. And you must only speak to them in Latin. We're just so lucky you're the school's Latin star. OK, let's go.'

So we did. It also struck me as lucky that we were wearing clothes that harmonized with what the Cantians preferred to wear. But of course it wasn't really luck; the sign in the oxygen trap had given us no choice. But then who had created the oxygen trap in the first place?

It all seemed to me a big puzzle, but there wasn't really any time to think about it anymore. The reason was that we obviously had to decide which direction to go in. After thinking about this for a few moments, I suggested we went in the same direction in which the first man we met had gone.

The street we were on went along for about another hundred yards in the same yellowish semi-darkness from the weird lights. Then we saw more houses, like chalets really, of just one storey and maybe about twenty feet wide and without any windows in the front at all but just doors that looked as if they were made of tree bark or something like that.

I wasn't sure what the houses themselves were made of. They were white and looked as if they'd been whitewashed all over. I wondered if they were made of chalk like the surrounding of the stairs had been, but I couldn't really imagine a house being made of chalk. I wanted to say to the others that it would be good to knock on a door and ask where we were, but then I realised that would give away that we were strangers. Also, there were more Cantian people in the streets now, walking along, some going in our direction and others going opposite and some crossing from one side of the street to the other and going down little side streets which went off to the left and the right. I looked up ahead and just saw nothing but blackness. I couldn't see a ceiling or a roof or anything like that, but of course it was night-time now. Then I thought, *maybe they never have any proper daylight here,* and I thought how awful it would be down here if the only light they ever had was this yellowish one.

I noticed that quite a few of the Cantians were young people of about our own age. I thought they might have come up to talk to us, but they didn't. I did hear some young people talking in a group about ten yards away and they were definitely talking Latin and it struck me that it was great that some of the people there were of our own age because it meant we weren't likely to be too noticeable.

There were other plank-lights glowing gently in the street now. I saw a boy and a girl of about my age holding hands and walking towards us. I listened hard as they passed us.

'Yes, it's really is Latin they're speaking,' I whispered to everyone.

'What are they saying?' asked Declan.

'Something about going to see a show in the amphitheatre tomorrow afternoon,' I told him.

The moment I'd said the word 'amphitheatre' I regretted doing the translation.

'An amphitheatre?' said Dora and Sam, pretty much together.

'That's crazy,' said Lindsay. 'How can an amphitheatre fit down here?'

'We've got to go to the amphitheatre!' Dora whispered loudly, completely putting us all at risk.

I looked round to see if any Cantian had heard her.

I don't think anyone had.

And that was when I saw something even scarier than anything we'd seen so far.

28

Bathed in the strange yellow Cantian street-light, and looming up on the left-hand side of the street, between two of the pretty much identical Cantian chalk houses, we saw a sight that made me feel dizzy and sick.

It was a sight I'd seen often enough in books in religious lessons at school e.g. the Bible, but that was just in books, and now here we were seeing it in reality.

What we saw was an old man, with a white beard and wearing a toga that looked like a grey one, hanging, obviously dead, on a cross.

29

The vertical spar of the cross was, maybe, I don't know, five yards high, the shorter horizontal spar perhaps two yards wide. As we got closer, horribly fascinated by what we were seeing, I saw that the old man hadn't been nailed to the cross but that his arms and legs had been tied to it with some kind of black rope.

What was certain was that he was dead.

In the ghostly street light which illuminated him in a ghostly way, making him seem like a spectre from a nightmare, I saw that his head was lolling down, his tongue protruding slightly from his mouth.

I glanced at Lindsay. Her mouth was wide with horror. Troy, his arms folded as if he were trying to keep calm, just looked up at the body on the cross. Declan appeared frozen with shock. The twins had looks of bewilderment on their faces, as if they couldn't quite believe that what they were seeing was real.

I hoped it wasn't.

I mean, I really really hoped it was a model of some kind, like the ones in the Roman Museum.

The man being on the cross at all was terrible enough, but what was even worse was that the Cantian people who walked past us in their togas and dresses didn't seem at all surprised to see the man on the cross. I mean, they all looked calm about him being there.

Why was this? Why did none of them pay any attention

to what we were seeing? What was wrong with these people? Were they in fact, as I still thought they might be, actors in some strange new underground theme park which the company that had refurbished the Roman museum had installed down there? Did they know that the man wasn't really dead? Was he simply a model?

But if that was the case, then what exactly were they all doing down here? I mean, if this *was* a theme park, then why were they all going about their business as if they would never have any visitors or certainly weren't playing a part in a new tourist attraction designed by the people who'd funded the new museum?

There were Cantians quite close by so I went up to Lindsay and as I did I beckoned Dora, Sam, Troy and Declan around us. Now I whispered, feverishly: 'I hope so much that this is all an underground theme-park connected with the museum. But we don't know it's that and we can't risk the consequences of being wrong about it. We've got to keep walking, OK? I know this man on the cross is awful, but *we've got to keep walking*. We'll just draw attention to ourselves if we stay here gawping.'

Lindsay gave a nod. Obviously she was too horrified to say anything. The twins nodded, too. Troy whispered 'OK, mate, I agree.' Declan said nothing. Then we all broke out of the huddle.

I headed down the Cantian street, trying hard not to cry, which I actually did want to do, I was feeling so sick and upset. Somehow I managed not to, though. I'm sure one reason why I didn't was that Lindsay ran to catch up with me and slipped her right hand into mine as we walked along, she in her white dress and me in my white toga. It was like how she'd held my hand when we'd been walking in the gloom towards the glow, on our way into Cantia. I was amazed how cheered up I felt with one of Lindsay's hands in mine, though I really shouldn't have been amazed about that, as after all I loved her a lot even though I didn't dare tell her I did.

There were no Cantians near us at that moment, so I winged it. 'Do you think the guy on the cross was real, or pretend?' I asked her in a hissed whisper.

She shook her head. 'I don't know,' she whispered back.

'I just hope it's not real,' I said. 'But either way, we need to find a way out of this terrible place. I mean, there must be a way out, surely? But it has to be a real way out: not one that ends in steel doors or in a brick wall. People can't spend their whole lives down here, can they?'

'Maybe they do,' Lindsay said, quietly. 'Or until they get crucified, anyway.'

I glanced behind at Dora and Sam, who were walking along, and now I noticed that they were holding hands too, which they sometimes actually do when they're walking together but normally only when they're certain nobody can see them; I mean this is something I noticed when they weren't aware I was watching them. But now they saw me watching them and they didn't stop holding hands. Sam was on the left-hand side and Dora was next to him on his right. Troy was walking next to her, although he wasn't holding her hand. Seeing the twins with Troy next to them made me feel very reassured.

Declan was walking behind the twins and Troy. It was difficult to read the expression on Declan's face, partly because as he was a little way from me and the light quality was still so peculiar and yellowish, it wasn't that easy to see him very clearly, but as far as I could guess his expression was a kind of anxious determination, that he wanted to go ahead and keep walking with us but had no idea what he would be likely to find. That, I suppose, was basically what I felt about everything too.

So there we were, a kind of impromptu team, trying to make sense of where we were and what we were doing. It wasn't easy. As we kept on walking, we saw more Cantians coming into the street from the side-roads as if they were going somewhere. I still had no idea what exactly this place Cantia was, and whether it was real or not, but I agreed with Lindsay, that the more I was there the less likely it seemed to me that it was a theme-park. And besides, if there was no-one to watch them, I mean if there were no visitors, then why didn't they just all go and have e.g. a cup of tea and wait until some visitors arrived, rather than just going about their lives? That seemed a very reasonable question.

Boys and men in togas, and girls and women in Roman dresses, passed us and often said '*Salvete*' to us, so I said '*Salvete*' back. I felt sick doing it. How could they all be so calm? Didn't they know that people were getting crucified?

Would we see any more crucifixions?

But what we next saw was... *no, surely not*, I thought.

It was an underground church.

A beautiful underground church, made of grey stone, with small oval windows. I knew it was a church because it had a pointed steeple, also made of what looked like grey stone, though I couldn't see the top of the steeple because it was too dark above us.

A dozen or so Cantian men in togas and women in dresses - some of the togas and dresses were in colours that looked quite bright even in the yellowish light - were walking in a stately way towards the church. We waited until the people had gone in.

I felt reassured that there was a church down here. I mean, everything was otherwise so unfamiliar and scary.

The terrible sight of the crucifixion - whether it was real or not - had totally spooked me. But knowing there was at least one church down here, well, that felt really comforting and reassuring.

Then I noticed that there was someone lagging behind the people who were heading to the church. His toga was black, like Troy's, but he had a hood, and the hood was up. I thought maybe he was a monk.

Then I looked harder, and realised suddenly who it really was.

30

It was Carlo Clancy, our school's most famous ex-pupil.
Seeing Carlo there in Cantia, my first thought was, of course, total relief.

Obviously Dora was right after all, and this weird place we'd come to must be an underground set for Carlo's movie. So the crucifixion we'd seen wasn't real; it was only pretend, and the apparently dead man must have just been a model made for the movie set.

Sam had recognised Carlo as well, and you bet Lindsay had, from the way she was gazing at him in amazement. Well, I mean, even if not everyone's seen *The Guardian of the Sword* movies, who hasn't seen *Pirates of Montego Bay* and *The Odyssey?*

As for Declan, he looked even more astonished at seeing Carlo than Dora and Sam did. Troy was the only one among us who looked fairly laid back about seeing him. You might in fact have thought that perhaps Troy hadn't actually *recognised* Carlo.

As for Carlo himself, he was staring as hard at us as we were at him.

'Is it really you, Carlo?' Dora murmured.

He glanced at her, then again at the rest of us. His eyes opened wide and he waved his right hand frantically, then touched his lips with it, as if to shush Dora. A moment later, in an urgent, hissed whisper, he said: *'Are you lot English?'*

31

It seemed a pretty strange question to ask, but I thought I'd better answer it, so I said:

'Yes… yes, we are English, Mr Clancy.'

Carlo just stared at me. 'You know my name.'

'Of course,' I said. 'You're world-famous.'

I nearly said *I met you at our school prizegiving and you got my name wrong.* But I didn't say that because it didn't seem a very polite thing to have said, and besides, there were obviously far more important things to think about at the moment.

'Yes, maybe,' said Carlo, 'but that isn't helping any of us at the moment, is it? Do any of you know where we are?'

I looked round. I was obviously very nervous about speaking English but fortunately there weren't any Cantians nearby.

'Well, Mr Clancy,' I said, 'we all think this is a set for your new movie.'

'Believe me, it isn't. And by the way, please call me Carlo. Time's not on our side. And it's good you're keeping your voice down, because I don't think they speak English here.'

'No, they speak Latin,' I said quietly.

Carlo just stared at me. *'Latin?'*

I nodded. 'Yes.'

'That's not possible,' Carlo said.

'Oh, please stop acting, Carlo,' said Dora, fortunately

remembering to keep *her* voice down. 'Please. This place can't be real, you're scaring us.'

Carlo looked round at all of us. 'Listen, I'm not acting, OK? I don't know where we are or how I got here, but I'm nothing to do with this place. All I know is I was kidnapped last night when I was alone in Canterbury Cathedral, scouting out a location - with the permission of the Dean - for my movie *The Archbishop's Anagram*. So let me say this again: we're not in a movie set. We really aren't. We're somewhere real.'

I glanced round at everyone. 'So the crucifixion really happened,' I murmured. 'Oh, no.'

'Yes,' Lindsay said. She glanced at Carlo. 'We saw a crucified man about five minutes ago.'

Carlo nodded grimly. 'Yes, so did I, and I think the guy really is dead. Do any of you know anything about this place at all apart from that people get crucified? Do you even know what this place is called?'

I drew a breath, trying hard to stay calm. I knew I had to answer Carlo's question.

'It's called Cantia,' I said.

32

'Cantia?' Carlo repeated. 'C-A-N-T-I-A?'

I nodded.

'But where exactly are we?' Carlo asked. 'I've travelled to lots of parts of the world, but never heard of any place called Cantia. I was unconscious when I was brought here, so I didn't see how I came here. Obviously it isn't in England, or for all I know even anywhere in Europe, or in North or South American or I think I'd have heard of it before.'

It was only now, after Carlo had said this, that I realised that as far as he was concerned, Cantia really might be anywhere in the world. He hadn't given me any indication of how long he thought he'd been unconscious, but of course with modern jet travel you can get to, or be taken to, many remote places in only a few hours really, or only a few hours more if you want to go a really long way.

'Mr Clancy, Carlo... Cantia... well, it's *underneath* Canterbury, you see,' I said.

Carlo blinked, then glanced round at the others. I think he expected at least one of us to burst out laughing. None of us did, though.

He turned to me again. '"Underneath Canterbury?"'

I nodded.

'Listen,' Carlo said to me in the same hissed whisper, 'I've had a really bad day, OK? I don't need any nonsense from... no disrespect... a bunch of teenagers. I've been kidnapped.

I'm on the run. I'm in danger. Very likely you all are too. So please, cut the nonsense and tell me *where we are.*'

'Carlo,' Lindsay said, 'Josh is telling you the truth. Canterbury really is above us, just like he said.'

Carlo looked at Lindsay, and then at me. 'So your name's Josh, right?'

I nodded. 'Yes, and we've met before, Carlo. We met last year, you see, at a prizegiving at my school. You were once a pupil there, at the Joseph Conrad High School in Canterbury. Lindsay's in my class, this is her. And here are Dora and Sam, my younger brother and sister - they're twins. And this is Troy, and that's Declan.'

Carlo looked hard at me, then he said, 'You know, I think I remember you.'

'I won the prize for Latin. You called me Joe.'

'I'm sorry about that, Josh,' Carlo said, 'Maybe I didn't hear the name properly when the headmaster said it, or perhaps I was being inattentive. So you won the Latin prize... does that mean you can speak any Latin?'

'Yes. Yes, I can.'

'And understand it?' Carlo asked.

'Well, I think so, yes,' I said, though more hesitantly. 'I mean, I've heard what some of the people here are saying, and I can understand that.'

Carlo nodded. 'Great. That's going to really help us. But how can anywhere be *underneath* Canterbury? And why are they crucifying people?'

'We don't understand that either,' said Lindsay.

'And why are you all wearing Roman clothes?'

'That's a long story,' I said.

'I bet it is,' Carlo replied, 'and the longer we stay out here speaking English, the more likely we'll get noticed and goodness knows what'll happen to us then. Maybe, just maybe, we can find somewhere to stay. Also, there's someone down here I have to rescue. I just hope we're in time to stop them crucifying *her*.'

Across the street, a woman in a chocolate brown dress stopped and looked at us and, I imagined, realised there was something odd about our group. For a silly moment, I wondered whether this woman was who Carlo was determined to rescue, but I didn't imagine she could have been. Then she walked on.

'Josh,' said Carlo, when she was out of earshot. 'I'm sure I saw some of your faces on the TV news a few days ago. Have you been on TV this week?'

I shook my head. 'Carlo, it must have been some other people you saw. We're just school pupils from Canterbury. We've never been on the TV news. I'm really worried we're starting to be getting noticed down here, though.'

'Yes, and so am I,' Carlo said. 'We badly need to find somewhere down here where we can talk in private. Let's head on down the street and keep our eyes peeled. They mustn't know we're strangers, so no-one's to speak English if we're near any Cantians. Come on, let's go.'

Only now, I saw that the woman with the brown dress had stopped a passing man wearing a black toga, and both were looking in our direction as they talked. Yes, it really was time to find somewhere to stay, if we could.

Carlo pulled his hood round his face, turned and headed along the street. A moment later I caught up with him and then I walked alongside him. Despite the incredible danger we were in, being with him felt great. I also felt much safer now I was with him, and I imagined Dora and Sam felt the same, too. Well, who wouldn't? After all, he was a great hero, wasn't he?

After about half a minute I glanced behind me. The Cantian man and woman I'd seen weren't following us.

The street seemed as strange as it had before, with its Dick Whittington houses, the lamps shedding dim yellow light, the people in togas.

We'd gone about a hundred yards beyond the church, when the street opened up into what was basically a town square. Of course the town square was dark but I could make out the dim silhouettes of the buildings on the far side with their faint lights.

Carlo glanced at me, shrugged, and then began walking around the square on the left side of the square, as if he thought that was as good a direction to go in as any. There were the same dim yellowish lights here and there.

Soon we reached a two-storey, grey stone building. I couldn't tell in the dark whether the front door was dark brown or black. Above it was a sign that said, in spidery black letters:

DOMUS SANCTA.

I knew what the sign meant. There were no Cantian people nearby, so I quickly said, 'It means *holy house.*'

'What d'you think a holy house is, Josh?' Carlo asked.

'I'm not sure. Maybe it's for pilgrims.'

'Pilgrims to where?' Carlo asked.

'I don't know. To the church, perhaps.'

'Or maybe this whole place is a secret underground village you make a pilgrimage to,' said Lindsay.

'Yes, maybe,' I said, 'though if they're crucifying people, something's obviously gone seriously wrong.'

'You bet,' said Troy, 'and anyway, where would people be making the pilgrimage from? I mean, no-one's ever mentioned this place to me. I think it's possible no-one from our world even knows about it.'

'Except us,' said Sam, brightly.

'Well, whatever a holy house is,' said Declan, 'perhaps we might be able to stay the night at it.'

I glanced at him. 'What makes you think so?'

Declan shrugged. 'Just a hunch. What have we got to lose by trying?'

Carlo nodded. 'I agree.'

'I suppose I could ask, in Latin, if we can stay here,' I said. 'But if they say yes, I wonder how much it'll cost.'

'If they take English money,' said Troy.

'Even if they do,' Carlo said, 'I don't have a penny on me. Whoever kidnapped me took my wallet, my normal clothes and my iPhone. I woke up wearing only this toga, though they left my underpants on.'

'Thank goodness for that,' said Dora.

'We've some English money, Carlo,' I told him.

It seemed strange hearing myself say 'English money', when we *were* in England, sort of.

'Good,' said Carlo, 'but I don't think you should show your English money to anyone down here. After what you told me about that crucifixion, I'm really uneasy about us letting the Cantians know we're not from these parts.'

'The man on the cross looked like a local to me,' Troy said.

'Maybe people who aren't from here have an even worse death,' Dora suggested, as if she was quite interested in what that worse death could be.

'What could be worse than being crucified?' Sam said.

Carlo glanced at me. 'Josh, if anyone answers that door, don't speak to them in anything but Latin. Earlier today, I met an extremely weird guy called Tiberius, in fact I woke up in his house in some sort of guest room. He was obviously somehow involved in kidnapping me, but he hardly spoke English at all. Tiberius is probably looking for me by now, and he might have warned all the Cantians to be on the lookout for someone who speaks English.'

'Assuming they know what English is,' I said.

Carlo nodded. 'Good point. And there's something else I need to tell you about. When I was in Tiberius's house, basically as his prisoner, I saw he had a TV in it, in the living room. There were some DVDs of my movies on a table next to the television. There was a Harry Potter book on the table, with the red Hogwarts train on the front. I didn't recognise the title, though: it was in a foreign language.'

'Was it *Harrius Potter et Philosophi Lapis?*' I asked him.

'I don't know, Josh, it might have been, yes, now you mention it I vaguely think that might have been the title.'

Lindsay gave me a puzzled look. 'What are you talking about, Josh?'

'That's the first Harry Potter novel in Latin translation. The publisher commissioned a Latin translation as a gimmick, but it actually proved quite popular. I wonder how it got down here?'

'Or maybe the Cantians commissioned it?' Lindsay said.

I shook my head. 'I don't think so. They must have got it from our world somehow, but I can't imagine how.'

'Well,' said Carlo, 'whichever way it got down here, it obviously did. Also, we have to assume that the Cantians have television, which means that I might be recognised. Frankly, it's a good job none of you lot *were* on TV earlier this week or you'd be in danger of being recognised too. So, Josh, when you talk to whoever opens that door, I'll stay well in the background.'

'OK, Carlo,' I said. 'I understand.'

As I went up to the front door, I wondered again who'd kidnapped Carlo.

I gave the door two quick knocks.

Nothing happened for maybe a minute.

I gulped, and tried not to look as creeped out as I felt.

Then the door creaked and slowly started to open.

33

Peeking out at us from the doorway was a small grey-haired old lady, bathed in a dim, whitish light. She looked us over with dark, piercing eyes and scratched her little nose, which was quite small and shrivelled. I thought maybe someone had bashed it hard with a hammer some time ago and the nose had never quite got over it. Her face reminded me of a Pekinese dog. Her Roman dress was grey and scruffy.

I raised my right hand, making my palm vertical like I'd seen the Romans doing it in my school books.

'Salvete, sumus peregrinatores,' I said, my heart beating fast. I knew saying 'Hello, we're pilgrims' to the old lady, was a pretty sneaky try, but I couldn't think of anything else to say.

The old lady stared at me, then at Dora and Sam.

'These children should be in bed and asleep,' the old lady said back to me, in Latin.

'We shall all sleep well in this holy house,' I replied, in Latin of course. My heart was beating fast; I expected at any moment that she'd tell us all to get lost, or even worse, call whatever police they had down here. Actually, I was surprised she hadn't already.

The old lady looked at me and the rest of us doubtfully, as well she might have done. I was still expecting her to tell us to get out of there. But then she raised her right hand, and beckoned us inside.

'Who's he?' she asked, pointing her wizened right forefinger at Carlo as he, the last one of us in, approached the entrance.

'Monachus,' I told her. I knew that meant 'a monk', and I was hoping she wouldn't turn a monk away from a holy place. Oh, and in Latin you don't have to use words for 'a' or 'the': you just say the word. I suppose this makes Latin easier than English, in a way.

'Monachus?' she repeated.

'Ita vero,' I said. Latin doesn't actually have words for 'yes' or 'no'. Ita vero is supposed to be what the Romans used for 'yes', although since no-one from today was around then to check, it's totally impossible to know this for certain. 'No' in Latin, by the way, is non est, or at least that's what it's supposed to have been.

The old lady gave a reluctant nod. Maybe she was taken in by my Latin, or maybe she didn't feel comfortable about turning away a monk and his friend.

Carlo closed the door behind us, moving in a slow, monk-like way. He was certainly a good actor. Then we were all inside the holy house, in some sort of reception area. There was just enough light for us to see each other and where we were. The light came from several small circular flat lamps glowing white and looking like lit-up dinner-plates, hanging about halfway down the walls all round the room.

The only pieces of furniture were a long, brown bench set against the left wall, and - on the far right - a semi-circular counter made from pieces of gnarled old-looking wood. The walls were made of some kind of white stone with black veins in it, like that posh French cheese which smells rank but tastes quite nice, even though some people find it yucky. Behind the counter was a brown door, and another one in the far wall straight ahead.

The old lady went to stand behind the counter, still

peering hard at us with her beady eyes. She didn't look too friendly, I can tell you.

There was a very strange thing on the counter. I didn't know what it was. It was a cube about a foot long in each direction, consisting of a silvery-coloured metal plate at the bottom and a similar plate at the top, with the top plate connected to the bottom one by four metal rods in all four corners of the cube. Within the cube was an amazingly complicated array of cogwheels, each maybe an inch in diameter, that were mostly on top of each other in vertical columns.

Trying not to be distracted by the strange cogwheel cube, I walked over to the old lady, hoping I could remember enough Latin not to give us all away. I can't say I felt confident; I mean, our teacher Mr Kinder encouraged us to speak Latin in class, but this was, to put it mildly, different. I'd never spoken Latin to anyone whose actual *language* was Latin. Well, how could I ever have imagined I ever would?

I went up to the counter. I was about to say '*salvete*', but the old lady spoke first.

'*How many rooms do you want, young man?*'

I thought quickly, then said, '*A room each, please.*' Of course, I felt very relieved she was open to the idea of people staying there *at all*.

The old lady counted Lindsay, Carlo, Declan, Troy and the twins under her breath, in Latin, with her right forefinger, *unus, duo, tres, quattuor*. Then she reached under the counter and jangled large, old-fashioned-looking, metal keys down on the counter one at the time. She went on doing this until there were seven keys there. She slid them noisily across the counter towards me.

I picked up a handful of keys and looked at them. There was a sort of little flat piece of metal about halfway down each key's handle, and this flat piece of metal had a number embossed on it. The numbers weren't one, two, three and four etc but instead I, II, III, IV, and so on.

These people really are like the Romans, I thought.

'*The rooms cost ten denarii per night,*' the old lady said. '*I'm going to bed; it's late. Pay tomorrow morning. And remember, this is a holy house.*'

The old lady gave a grumpy nod, a grunt for good measure, turned round and disappeared through the door behind the counter. With the large bunch of keys in my hand, I joined the others.

'What was that all about?' Sam asked.

'She said we had to remember this is a holy house,' I explained.

'Yes,' said Dora, 'it is holy. It's *wholly bonkers.*'

Carlo looked reproachfully at Dora, but I saw a faint smile in his look, too, as if, despite all the fear and terror we were in, he appreciated Dora making that silly comment. Dora went pretty red, though. Carlo glanced around at the rest of us and whispered: 'Listen, just because that old biddy's vanished doesn't mean it's safe for us to speak English. Josh, those are our room keys, right?'

'Yes, they must be. She said it's ten *denarii* each a night, and that we don't need to pay until the morning.'

'Great, at least we won't get arrested and crucified until then,' said Troy gloomily.

'Josh,' Lindsay said, 'how does she know we aren't going to sneak out in the morning without paying?'

I shrugged. 'I don't suppose she does, but there can't be too many people living down here, can there? So maybe anyone who sneaks off without paying wouldn't have much chance of getting away with it.'

'If there are only a few people in Cantia, though,' said

Lindsay, 'all the Cantians would be able to recognise each other and the old lady would have realised we're not from here the moment she saw us. So there might be more people living down here than we think.'

'Maybe somehow we'll find out how many,' Carlo said.

'Josh, what do you think that strange cube thing on her table can be?' Lindsay asked me.

'I don't know,' I said. 'I wish I did.'

'I really think we should get to the rooms now,' said Carlo. He pointed to the door on the far side of the reception area. 'They must be through there.'

Carlo, Declan and Troy, all being about the same height, had to duck to get through the door. The doorway led into a smaller version of the room we'd just been in, and was lit by the same kind of whitish light, except that this smaller room didn't have any furniture in it at all. There was an open doorway on the opposite side. This led to a flight of brown wooden stairs.

I trod carefully on the first stair. It didn't break, so I stepped onto the next one. The staircase went up to a dimly-lit corridor.

On the left side of the corridor, which was made of the same black-veined stone the rest of the holy house was made of, I counted eleven black doors, with I, II, III etc. on them. I supposed the ones farther down went IX, X and X1, though I couldn't see the numbers that far along. On the right-hand side of the corridor was another door, which was also black but which didn't have a number on it.

'Maybe some of the other rooms have pilgrims in them, too,' I whispered.

'All the more reason for us to get into a room right now,' Carlo said quietly. He pointed to the closest door, the one with a Roman 'I' on it. 'Josh, d'you have a key for this one?'

I nodded, selected the key with the number '1' on it, and stuck it into the lock. The lock was stiff and I had to turn the key so hard it hurt my fingers, but the lock finally moved. I opened the door and stood back to let everyone in, Carlo first.

Sam stayed in the corridor next to me. 'Josh,' he whispered, when everyone but him and me were in the room, *'I've absolutely got to have a wee.'*

I glanced into the room everyone else had gone into. It was about the size of our living-room at Prospect Place. In one corner of the holy house bedroom was a narrow bed with a couple of grey blankets folded on top. There were also two stumpy grey stools. A small yellow light on one wall cast gloomy shadows in the corners. There was a quite large window on the far side of the room which seemed, from where I was standing, to be overlooking just darkness. There wasn't a bathroom in the room, nor a door that might've led to one.

I shrugged at Sam. 'All right, let's try that door over there on the other side of the corridor. There might be some kind of bathroom around here. After all, everyone needs a wee sometimes, even Cantians.'

Sam followed me along the corridor, to the black door on the right. Was anyone in there already? I wondered.

I knocked on the door, nervous but ready to talk Latin if anyone came out.

But no-one did, so I gave the door a push, and it opened.

This room, which was lit fairly well by two dinner-plate white lights on the ceiling, and which was about three times as big as our Prospect Place living-room, had walls made of the holy house's black-veined white stone.

On the far side of the room was a strange-looking row of six pipes, each about three feet from the next one. At floor level the pipes were narrow, but they opened up at the top like trumpets, or like some strange plants from an alien world. On the left side of the room, next to each other, were two cubicles without any doors. Inside each cubicle was a wooden seat with a large hole in the middle, but no lid. I went into one of the cubicles and looked down the hole in the seat. It was so dark through the hole you couldn't see anything at all.

Sam went up to one of the trumpet-pipes. 'I think those must be for, you know... weeing in, Josh.'

I nodded. 'Yes, I think so.'

Sam went and had a wee into the pipe he was nearest to, then washed his hands in a brown bucket of water near the pipes. I expected the water to be stagnant and smelly, but to my surprise it looked clear and even drinkable. On the floor by the bucket was a lump of some kind of soft red clay. When I grabbed a bit and sniffed it, it smelt of carrots.

Sam broke off a piece, dipped his hands in the water and experimentally swirled the carrot clay around a bit. The moment he did, large bubbles appeared in the water, which now began to smell of spearmint.

'That must be their soap,' said Sam. 'It's very weird.'

Look who's talking, I couldn't help thinking.

There didn't seem to be anything like a towel there, so Sam dried his hands on his toga. I thought I might need a wee myself, but decided I didn't.

Sam and I went back to room number 'I'. I knocked, then explained quietly through the door that it was me and Sam and we got let in. Once we were inside and the door was shut, Sam excitedly told everyone about the lavatory arrangements, such as they were.

'Is there a toilet for girls?' Lindsay asked.

'It doesn't look like it,' said Sam, in what sounded to me like a sort of satisfied tone.

Lindsay glanced at me. 'Josh, is the bucket the only way of having a wash?'

'I think so.'

'There wasn't a shower or anything?'

'Sam and I didn't see one.'

'There are no doors on the cubicles, either,' said Sam.

'Are you serious?' said Lindsay.

Sam nodded.

Lindsay gave a nod. 'Well, at least we're safe and indoors and alive, unlike that poor man we saw on the cross.'

'I think maybe the toilets here in holy houses are made creepy deliberately, to put people off coming to stay,' said Sam.

'Well, let's hope it's worked and no-one else is,' I said.

I took the key out of the keyhole, closed the door, and locked it from our side, so we were all in the bedroom now.

'If there are any other people staying here,' I said, 'the old lady downstairs would probably have given them the lower-numbered rooms first. The key to this room, for example. So maybe there's no-one else staying.'

'You may be right, Josh,' said Carlo, 'but we still have to be very careful. We can't assume there aren't any other people in here, we really can't.'

He looked round at each of us. 'All right, so now we need to talk.'

34

'Let me tell you what happened to me,' Carlo went on. 'Like I said, I was kidnapped yesterday evening and brought down here. All the preparations for starting to film *The Archbishop's Anagram* have been going pretty well. I was in a great mood when I was wandering inside the cathedral yesterday evening. I was by the St Thomas à Becket's memorial, the one with the pointed swords that have red paint on them to look like blood, when suddenly everything went dark. Whoever kidnapped me must've put something over my face, chloroform or something, maybe. When I woke up I got the sense I'd been asleep for a long time. I think I was out all night, and for much of today too.'

'Where were you when you woke up?' Dora asked.

'In a small, dark room, that was a bit like a large cupboard. I didn't know when this was, but I was pretty sure it must have been the next day, so it must definitely be Saturday now.'

'Yes, it is Saturday,' I reassured him.

'Well,' said Carlo, 'at least I'm right about that. OK, well, the next thing I remember was being marched along a corridor by a very muscular guy who looked a bit like a gorilla. He had a purple toga on. And listen, I remember getting a glimpse of someone else, too.'

'Who?' I asked.

'A lady: I'd say she was in her thirties. She was being marched down the corridor ahead of me. At one point she turned round quickly and our eyes met. She's very beautiful. The strange thing is, I'd seen her before.'

'Did she recognise you?' Dora asked.

Carlo shook his head. 'No, I don't think so.'

'So they kidnapped someone else from up above too, and you know her?' I asked.

'I wouldn't exactly say I know her, Josh, but yes, I have seen her before. I was really groggy with whatever they'd drugged me with, or I'd have done all I could to rescue her and escape. But I had almost no strength. I remember being pushed through a doorway into a windowless room. It was only then I realised I was wearing this black toga with a hood.'

'So whoever kidnapped you must have dressed you in the toga?' I asked.

'I suppose so, and then about half an hour later, an incredibly small guy - he can't have been more than about three feet tall - came into the room through a door I didn't think was there until he came through it. I know that sounds crazy, but that's what it was like. He brought me an extremely strange meal on a tray.'

'What was the meal?' asked Sam, at once. He always likes to know about food.

'You don't want to know,' said Carlo.

'Oh, I definitely do,' said Sam.

'OK,' Carlo said, 'if you insist. Well, a nine-inch roasted slug was one of the more mentionable things. As you might imagine, I didn't bother sampling that. I did eat a bit of what reminded me of a turnip, except it was pink and tasted like a mushroom. Everything else looked much too weird and disgusting to eat.'

'Sounds like school dinners,' said Sam.

'Sam,' said Carlo, 'I assure you that if it had been a school dinner I'd've wolfed it down, I was so hungry. Actually I seem to remember that the school dinners at the Joseph Conrad High School weren't bad at all.'

'Then they must have got worse since when you were there,' said Sam.

Carlo shrugged. 'Maybe. Well, anyhow, I tried talking to the little guy in English, but it was obvious he didn't understand a word I said. Then suddenly he cleared off through a large hole that appeared in the wall. The hole closed up again almost before I noticed he'd gone.'

'That's weird,' Sam commented.

'Yes,' said Carlo. 'Oh, and when I needed to use the bathroom, the outline of a door appeared in the wall, and the door opened into a strange little bathroom. I know this'll seem very crazy but the door *seemed to know* when I needed it.'

'It did?' I said.

Carlo nodded. 'Yeah. Pretty strange, eh? Then, about an hour later, another chap came into the room, through the same door the little guy had used. He was about as tall as me. He looked like a Mafia gangster from a Hollywood movie. His skin was olive brown, as if he were tanned, though I don't imagine there's much sunshine down here in Cantia, at least if it really is beneath Canterbury as you all say it is. He looked Spanish or Portuguese, I thought. Then he stared at me, smiled very creepily, and said, "my name - Tiberius".'

'So he could speak English?' I asked.

'Yes, but not too well. He only knew a few words. He kept saying "no problem", in reply to practically anything I said, and I said actually it was a pretty big problem that I'd been kidnapped and brought down there, but I don't think he understood what I was saying. Then he said he had, as he put it, an "important job" for me. I asked him what job, but he didn't answer; he just left by that weird door, which only opened when he went up to it. Well, about an hour ago, I was wondering whether I was going to be in that room for the rest of my life, and I was standing by the door outline, feeling really desperate to get out, when the door suddenly opened and I found myself in a long corridor with another door at the end. I ran along the corridor, opened the door again by trying to feel that I really *wanted* to get out, and I found myself in that street where I met you all.'

Carlo was silent for a moment, then said:

'Now I need to tell you all about the lady I recognised. It wasn't only the glimpse I had of her face that made me sure I'd seen her before. It was her perfume too. In that corridor it was powerful stuff. It's called "White Musk". I used to have an Australian girlfriend who wore it.'

I smiled. 'As a matter of fact, our mum - I mean, mine and Dora and Sam's - wears that perfume too. It's her favourite. We sometimes even tease her a bit because she wears it practically all the time. Maybe the lady you saw is from down here, and the Cantians have White Musk too?'

'Maybe they do, Josh; I don't know. But the lady I'm talking about is definitely not from here. She runs a shop in Canterbury. It's called Food for Thought. It sells health food, as you might guess from the name. I saw her there and we spoke a bit when I paid for my stuff: muesli and energy bars I think it was. Actually, I don't think she recognised me, which was a nice relief compared to what usually happens when I go into a shop.'

I just stared at Carlo. So did Dora and Sam.

'Carlo,' I said, 'is this some sort of joke?'

'Josh, believe me, the last thing I'm in the mood for right now is cracking jokes.'

'Carlo,' I said, 'I'm sure whoever you saw needs rescuing, but you've definitely made a mistake about who she is. You say you saw her last night?'

'Yes.'

'Then - I'm sorry to say this - but you're wrong about who she is. The lady who runs Food for Thought... *she's our mum*. Well, mine, Dora's and Sam's mum. And she was at home with us last night.'

Carlo stared at me. 'She was? Are you sure about that?'

'*Yes*. Her name's Isabella. It's not too weird she didn't recognise you... Mum isn't as keen on movies as Dora, Sam and me are. But Carlo, it can't be our mum you saw down here. *It just can't be.*'

'Why not?' Carlo asked.

'Because Dora, Sam and me had tea with Mum about three hours ago in our house in Canterbury before setting off for the Roman Museum. Mum was in her shop all day today, and we were at home yesterday evening, and Mum was there all the time. So you see, *she can't have been here.*'

'Josh, listen, I tell you, it was her. I really did recognise her.'

I just knew he had to be wrong. I just knew he must've mistaken her for someone else. My head was spinning. I thought I was going mad.

Then Lindsay turned to Carlo. 'I've a question.'

Carlo nodded at her. 'Ask away.'

'What date is it?'

35

'What date is it?' Carlo said, 'You mean today?'

'Yes,' said Lindsay. I could hear the tension in her voice.

'Well,' Carlo, said, 'I came to Canterbury yesterday, Friday the eleventh of September. So, today must be the twelfth.'

'No,' I gasped. 'No, that can't be right.' My brain felt like it was going to explode. 'That's not possible. Today's Saturday the fifth of September. The fifth. It's not the twelfth until next Saturday. And next Sunday, the thirteenth, is my sixteenth birthday.'

September the thirteenth, the Roman Ides of September, I thought. *In the Roman calendar the Ides of March is the fifteenth, the day Julius Caesar was stabbed to death. But the Ides of September is on the thirteenth.*

'Excuse me, sir. My name's Declan Jacques by the way. Moonford… this kid here… only told you my first name. I'm a sixth-former. I'm a great admirer of your movies.'

'Thank you, Declan.'

'I need to say something to Moonford, please, sir,' Declan added.

'Declan, please don't call me "sir". I'm Carlo. But, yes, go ahead.'

Declan turned to me. 'Moonford, I'm afraid you're completely wrong. It's September the twelfth today, Saturday the twelfth.'

Carlo shook his head slowly and looked hard at Lindsay,

Troy, Dora, Sam and me, then he said, 'It *was* you all I saw on the TV news a couple of days ago, I mean apart from Declan, anyway. I knew it was. You're missing, aren't you? You've been missing for a week.'

Lindsay stared at me. 'Josh, what can have happened?'

I shook my head. I was sure I was going mental. 'I don't know, I just don't know.'

'I suppose we've travelled a week forward in time,' said Sam, calmly.

'Sam,' I said, 'Listen. *People can't travel in time.*'

'Well, obviously they can,' replied Sam, just as calmly. 'Carlo must be right. We thought we were still in our own time after we had that weird experience earlier, but obviously we weren't. We came back a week later. Declan didn't have the weird experience we did, and that's why he wasn't on the news. We've missed a week, Josh.'

'But that's impossible!' I said. 'How can anyone travel through time?'

Sam shook his head slowly. Not even he could answer that question.

I looked at everyone. 'I think I am going mental,' I said.

'Try to stay sane, Moonford,' Declan advised me. 'This is no time to be going into meltdown.'

Dora looked hard at me. 'Declan's right. Josh, you can't go mad. You're our leader. We need you. It's bad enough having one brother who's bonkers, I don't want another one.'

'Josh,' said Carlo, 'I don't know what's going on. All I know is that you seem to have gone forward a week somehow, impossible as that sounds. You need to tell me about that weird experience you had. But let's make no mistake. This place, Cantia, and what we're all going through, this is all happening *today*. It's not the result of some time travel to the past. *It really exists today.*'

132

'Yes,' I said, 'you're completely right. Cantia exists today. But I still don't know why anybody would bring Mum down here, I don't know that at all. It's driving me crazy, just like the idea that we've gone forward a week.'

'Josh,' said Carlo, 'tell me about the weird experience Sam was talking about.'

So I quickly explained to him what had happened to us, how we were caught in the explosion and how, after the flash vanished, all I could see were billowing white clouds, and then Canterbury Cathedral with strange, gleaming silvery buildings around it, and the giant pavement with stones the colour of vanilla ice-cream.

'Actually,' said Sam, sounding a lot calmer and less mental now, 'I've been wondering whether before we ended up a week later than we started, we first got catapulted into the distant future.'

'Well, something pretty wacky happened to you, that's for certain,' said Carlo, 'but no matter how bizarre or extreme it seems, we have to deal with it.'

'Actually I was sure time travel would be possible before long,' Sam put in, knowingly. 'Maybe the Americans have invented it already, but just haven't told anyone about it yet.'

Lindsay snapped her glance in Declan's direction. 'You must have seen us on the TV news. Why didn't you tell us?'

'Because I don't watch the news, on TV, on my phone or anywhere else,' Declan replied at once. 'Massacres, bombings, revolutions, flooding, crime, pets who can read minds, smirking celebrities - it's all too depressing.'

'All right, but even if you don't watch TV,' Lindsay said, 'we've been missing from school. There must have been a huge panic there about us.'

'Well, maybe there was,' replied Declan, 'but you see, I haven't actually been at school this past week. I got permission to take a late summer holiday to visit my mother, who lives in the South of France.'

'OK, OK,' said Lindsay, 'but you told us you were working here at the museum earlier this evening.

'Well, I was,' Declan replied.

'But then why wasn't the museum just totally concerned about our disappearance?' Lindsay asked.

'Of course they were concerned about it,' Declan said, 'but how were they supposed to know you'd vanished here? They assumed you'd all left the museum and disappeared later on.'

'Yes,' I said, 'that's what they would think. They must have searched the museum really thoroughly, and how many places can there be to search there? They'd have assumed we'd left the museum. The trouble is, they wouldn't know about the brick wall which opened and then closed.'

'My poor dad!' Lindsay said. 'He must be so, so worried.'

I wondered why she didn't say her poor mum, too.

'*My* dad'll be so mad with me,' said Troy.

'I'm sure he'll just be glad to know you're OK,' I told him.

'You don't know my dad. Besides, we're not home yet.'

Lindsay glanced at me, 'Josh, I absolutely have to find a way of letting my father know I'm all right.'

I nodded, reached inside my toga and took my phone out of my trouser pocket. There were no bars showing a signal. There was just the time and the date.

'Maybe our phones don't work down here,' I said. 'The Cantians either don't have mobile service or wi-fi or use different systems to the ones we do. Oh, and, my phone thinks it's still September the fifth.'

'Well, it would, wouldn't it?' said Sam. 'We travelled through time so quickly, your phone's clock didn't notice.'

Declan pulled his mobile from his pocket, and showed

us the date and time. It backed up what Carlo and Declan said: somehow, by some crazy technological miracle, we'd lost a week of our lives. Declan's phone showed the twelfth of September.

'Maybe... maybe I can phone Dad from a landline,' said Lindsay, 'or email him.'

'Actually, we don't know if they even have landlines here,' Carlo put in, 'or computers. Though there was a TV in Tiberius's living-room, so maybe they do have technology of some kind.'

Glancing at Lindsay, I said, 'I promise, if we do find any working telephone down here, you'll get the chance right away to tell your parents you're safe.'

'Thanks.' Lindsay gave a brave smile.

'Well,' said Dora, 'if Mum really is down here, we can rescue her, and then she'll know we're here and she won't need to worry about us.' Dora's often surprisingly practical about things. 'So we were *really* on TV, Carlo?'

'On Wednesday, yes,' said Carlo. 'I was on the same evening TV bulletin you were. They showed a recorded interview with me about my movie, *The Archbishop's Anagram*. I was interviewed by a movie reporter called Emma Crucifus. I remembered her surname because she has the same surname as my great-grandfather William Crucifus on my mother's side. I even mentioned that to Emma on the air. Of course, William's been dead for quite some time.'

He was rambling a bit. I guessed even Carlo was getting rattled at what was happening.

'Poor Mum must be terrified,' I said.

Dora shrugged. 'Probably not. Knowing Mum, she's being brave.'

Carlo glanced at me. 'Rescuing Isabella is our top priority.'

'Dead right it is,' said Troy. 'No one's going to be

135

crucifying her or any of us, not if I can help it. It's time to kick some Cantian butts.'

'*Yes!*' Dora exclaimed.

'Well, I'm not a brilliant fighter like Dora,' Sam put in, 'but I'll do my best.'

'I hate violence,' said Lindsay, 'but I'll do my best too.'

'So will I,' said Declan.

I turned to Carlo. 'OK, we're all ready.'

Carlo stared at us all. 'Hold it, hold it. You don't think you're all coming *with* me, do you?'

'Of course we do,' I said.

Carlo shook his head. 'I'm sorry, no. I have to go by myself. I can't risk you young people getting hurt, can I?'

'We want to go with you, Carlo!' I pleaded.

'No, Josh, I need to find your mother and rescue her. It'll be easier on my own, without me having to worry about the safety of you young people as well. How big can Cantia be? If Isabella's here, I'll find her.'

'*But you need our help,*' I told him.

'You're all very brave,' Carlo said, 'and I really admire that, but you all need to factor something into your thinking. How would it look if news got out that Carlo Clancy risked the lives of six young people? People would think I was too scared to do what needed to be done myself. I'm sorry, I have to go alone. Actually I'm only an actor, but my fans think I'm a hero. Well, now it's my moment to try to *be* a hero.'

'Carlo, you'll need us when you get there,' I said.

'Especially,' said Troy, 'as we've got three of these.'

And, reaching into his toga, he took out his sword in a very cool, heroic, dramatic way.

Carlo just stared. 'Where did you get that sword?'

'That's another long story,' said Troy, and I knew he was saying this so Carlo wouldn't ask us about the soldiers.

'I've got one as well,' I added, carefully drawing mine.

'And me,' said Declan.

Carlo looked hard at Troy's sword, then went over and felt its needle-sharp tip. 'This is a serious weapon. Troy, you shouldn't be wielding it unless you're prepared to use it.'

'Believe me, I am,' said Troy.

'We want to come with you, Carlo,' Dora said, tearfully.

'You're all very brave, but I'm sorry - I just can't allow it.'

My stomach began to churn, just like the butterflies feeling you get before an important exam or if you're going for e.g. coffee with a girl you really fancy. 'At least take one of our swords,' I pleaded. I was close to crying too, but I wouldn't let myself show it. 'After all... we know from your movies you know how to use a sword.'

'They're only movies, Josh,' Carlo said. 'Still, I did get some training in sword-fighting when we were making *Pirates of Montego Bay.* So OK, I'll take the sword.'

'You can have mine,' Declan said. 'I never fancied myself as a sword-fighter. I'm more brains than brawn.'

'Sometimes, Declan, we need to have both,' Carlo said, as Declan very carefully pulled out his own sword from inside his toga.

'Thanks,' Carlo said to him, with a smile. Declan went red. Troy showed Carlo how to hide the sword.

Carlo looked round at us all. 'You... just all stay here, where it's safe.'

'Please come back soon with Mum,' said Dora tearfully.

'I'll try, Dora, I really will.' He went over to my sister and patted her lightly on top of her head.

Dora looked up at him. 'I've seen all your movies. You're *wonderful.'*

'Dora... I'm just an actor, that's all. The magic's in the movies, not in me.'

'Oh no, Carlo, you're much more than an actor,' Dora whispered, adoringly.

Carlo smiled. 'Dora, I'll try to live up to... whatever I need to.' He gave her a big smile, pointed at her in a friendly *you're cool* kind of way, then quickly turned and left the room.

We listened to his footsteps retreating down the corridor outside, then dying out.

'I so hope he'll be all right,' said Dora.

Troy slowly shook his head. 'He should've let us go with him.'

'I don't get it. How can we have travelled in time?' said Lindsay.

'I don't know,' I said. 'I just don't know.'

36

We all stood there looking at each other and feeling totally stressed out.

'He was crazy not to let us go with him,' Troy said.

'Yes,' I agreed, 'but there was no way Carlo was going to do that. Now he's gone, though, why can't we all go out into Cantia and try to find Mum ourselves?'

'Yeah, we have to do that,' agreed Troy.

'Let's,' said Dora. 'We've got two swords left, after all.'

'I'm game for that,' put in Lindsay. 'Anything's better than being stuck in this dreadful holy house where there isn't even a door on the loo cubicles.'

'I'm coming as well,' said Sam.

Declan shook his head. 'Are you all crazy? There's no way I'm going out there. I'm sure it's incredibly dangerous. Besides, what if Mr Clancy comes back with Mrs Moonford and we're not here? They wouldn't leave without us, would they? The delay could be fatal... for all of us.'

There was a brief silence.

'I suppose Jacques is right,' said Troy. 'Cowardly, but right.'

'I'd rather be a live coward than a dead hero, Wilson, if you don't mind.'

'We all would,' Troy replied. 'But sometimes there isn't a choice.'

'Oh, for goodness' sake, Wilson, spare me your macho clichés. Who d'you think we are, some elite force of the army? We're just a bunch of school pupils stuck in a weird underground place. We're not heroes.'

'You mean *you're* not,' Troy retorted.

'Oh, shut up, Wilson.'

'Listen you two,' I said, 'this isn't helping. Maybe just a couple of us go out. Troy and me, for example.'

'What a great idea, Moonford!' Declan exclaimed. 'That would make things even worse, wouldn't it, because if Mr Clancy comes back with your mum, we'll have to wait for you and Wilson to return before we can all leave.'

'So,' said Lindsay, 'what exactly are you suggesting we do, Declan?'

'There's not much we can do,' Declan replied, 'wait here, get some sleep, and see if Mr Clancy comes back with Mrs Moonford.'

Lindsay glanced at me. 'What d'you think?'

'Well,' I said, 'it's not much of a plan, but I suppose Declan has a point. If Carlo comes back with Mum... Isabella, I mean... and some of us aren't here, that would be a disaster, as we've no way of contacting each other. Still, I really wish Carlo had let us go with him.'

37

I said I'd stay up, keep watch and try not to fall asleep.

Soon afterwards I was sitting in my room on the bed. Everyone else had gone to their own rooms now. I had the room we'd all been in, number 'I', while Dora was in 'II' next to mine, Sam in 'III', Lindsay in 'IV' and those two dear chums Troy and Declan in 'V' and 'VI', respectively.

What I'd thought was merely a plank of brown wood turned out to be a fairly soft substance, surprisingly comfortable to lie on. I couldn't work out whether it was wood or plastic.

The corridor outside was quiet now. I'd stowed my sword under the bed and taken off my white toga and my sandals, so I was only wearing my red Greenpeace tee-shirt and my white Chinos trousers. I'd discovered that quickly touching the dinner-plate lamp twice dimmed it.

So now I sat there in the half-darkness and thought about things.

Was Mum injured, knocked out or drugged? What if she was all those things? *Or what if she's been crucified?* I felt sick when I thought of that, so I tried not to.

I wondered whether Carlo had managed to rescue Mum yet; what exactly Cantia was; and why no-one back up above in Canterbury ever talked about it.

Suddenly there was a knock at my door.

A chill pulsed through my body. What if it was

Custardface? What if he'd been involved in kidnapping Carlo... and Mum... and had found us?

'Who is it?' I called out softly.

'Me,' Lindsay's voice said through the door. 'Can I come in?'

I suddenly felt really really happy. I got up and pretty much ran to the door. Lindsay was standing there in her white Roman dress.

'I know it's a bad time,' she said, 'but there's something I want to say to you.'

'What's that?'

'Happy Birthday.'

'You mean it's...?'

'Yes, just gone midnight on my phone.'

Actually I'd completely forgotten it was my sixteenth birthday. I went to sit down on the bed, then glanced at Lindsay.

'I don't *feel* sixteen. I keep thinking about Mum and what's happening to her.'

'I know, Josh. I'll try my best to help you rescue her tomorrow. As for my dad... I can't bear to think of what he's going through. He must be so worried about me. I don't care about my mum, though. She's such a stupid, selfish cow!'

I just stared at her. I'd never heard Lindsay talk like this before. 'Why're you saying that?' I asked.

'Because she is,' Lindsay said.

She started to cry, using a corner of her dress to wipe her eyes. In a strange way, I liked that she did that in front of me without feeling she had to apologise. I wanted to hug her, but I was pretty sure she wouldn't have wanted me to.

Lindsay sniffed back her tears. 'Josh, can you keep a secret?'

'Yes, of course.'

'Really?'

'I promise.'

Lindsay came to sit next to me. I shuffled along a bit, but she sat quite close to me anyway.

'Josh, my parents are getting divorced. It's just so awful. We've had an absolutely horrible summer.'

I just sat there, feeling stupid because I didn't know what to say.

'Dad got the job at your school last spring,' Lindsay added. 'It's his first one as a headteacher, and a much bigger school than the one at Penzance, where he was head of science. Of course becoming headteacher was a big chance for him. But about four months ago... well, Mum began dating her fitness instructor. She goes to a fitness class. She's having an affair with him. His name's Craig. It's absolutely ridiculous. He's twelve years younger than she is. He's moved to Kent already, to a town near Canterbury called Havisham... or something.'

'Faversham. It's about ten miles away.'

'That's the place. Mum came with Dad to Kent, because I said I was going to come with him whatever Mum did, and she wants to be near me. Oh, Josh, it's been so terrible! Mum's still living in our new house, though she sleeps in the guest-room now. And before long, I know she'll be leaving Dad and expecting me to visit her at Craig's place. Well, I've told her I'm not going to. I haven't met him but I'm sure he's awful.' She breathed fast, still crying some more as she did. 'Josh, please keep everything I'm telling you about my mum secret.'

'Of course... of course I will.'

Lindsay looked hard at me, cried a bit more, wiped her eyes on her dress again, then, to my surprise, started to smile.

'Oh, Josh, I'm so worried about everything, and so scared, and you really cheer me up.'

'I do?'

'Oh yes. You're so brave.'

'I don't feel brave,' I said.

'Well, you are, anyway. As for my mum, I'm *glad* she'll be worried about me. It serves her right. At least she won't be in the mood to see that idiot Craig and kiss him and stuff.'

She was leaning against me now. I could feel her white dress against me and I could smell a faint scent of oranges from her hair. I suppose that was her shampoo from the day before, or I mean from a week and a day before. After all, I imagined you were about as likely to find orange-scented shampoo down here in Cantia as you were to find a pink hippopotamus.

'There's something I want you to tell me, Josh.'

I wondered if she might be about to ask me if I'd ever kissed a girl.

'What... what's that?'

'What exactly happened to your dad? You told me at Marks and Spencer on the day we met that you thought he was dead. That seemed a strange way for you to put it. I didn't want to pry though so I didn't ask any more about him. But you and I know each other much better now even though, really, our trip to M and S was only last Monday... I mean the Monday before last... oh God, this is all so complicated! Josh, if you want to tell me what happened to your dad, I'd like to know... but I understand if you don't want to.'

I coughed, then cleared my throat. 'Well, basically... Dad vanished.'

Lindsay just stared at me. 'Vanished?'

'Yes. His body was… well, it was never found. That was eight years ago now, so… I suppose he must be dead.'

Lindsay leaned a bit more on me, and now I could feel all of her against me.

'What happened?' she asked.

'He disappeared on his way to Heathrow airport. He was flying to Saudi Arabia to work on a six-month contract. We all said goodbye to Dad one May morning. He set off to Heathrow airport by train. But he never got there. He just… he just disappeared. He didn't get on the plane, we know that. They never found any trace of him at all.'

'You poor boy.'

I didn't know what to say.

'You poor boy,' Lindsay said again. 'What… what does your mum think happened?'

I gave a shrug. 'She doesn't know. None of us do. The police checked Dad's bank accounts, to see if he used them after he disappeared. They monitored his accounts for more than a year. He never touched them.'

Suddenly a knock came on the door.

I looked at Lindsay and she looked at me.

'What if it's Custardface?' I said.

Lindsay smiled faintly. 'Then you have a chance to ask him what's in his holdall.'

I loved how brave she was. I wished I felt as brave as she obviously did.

Because Lindsay was being so gutsy, I wasn't as scared when I went to open the door as I'd most likely otherwise have been. In fact, I was actually pretty calm as I opened it.

When I opened the door, I saw that it was Dora and Sam.

'We want to come into your room, Josh,' said Sam. 'We're just so worried about Mum, and about Carlo, and we're *reeeeaaaally* scared.'

145

Dora glanced at Lindsay, who was a few feet behind me. Before Dora could say anything cheeky, Lindsay explained, 'I just popped in here to say hello to Josh, I knew he'd be really worried about his mum, you see.'

Dora gave a quick nod. 'And are you going to stay here with Josh?'

'I don't imagine so, no,' Lindsay replied. I thought she could have also said *that's none of your business, Dora*, but I suppose Lindsay's too polite and good-natured to say that kind of thing.

A few moments later Dora and Sam left the room after saying goodnight to us.

After I closed the door behind them, and before I could say anything, or do anything, Lindsay came up to me and kissed me on the lips.

It was amazing, and even more so because she'd completely taken me by surprise.

I didn't really know what to do, so I just let her go on kissing me. She started to sit down on my bed, still kissing me, and so that our mouths could stay together I sat down still kissing her. We must have gone on kissing for at least two or even three minutes. Then, when Lindsay did finally stop, I thought her ending the kiss was the most terrible thing that had ever happened to me.

I'd forgotten she could easily start again.

38

The first time I woke up that morning it was still dark. I listened carefully. I could hear Lindsay's faint breathing. She was sleeping on my bed. I was sleeping on my blanket on the floor. I was still drowsy, and my thoughts weren't really focused and in fact it didn't even sink into me that we were in a place which was incredibly dangerous. All I could think, when I stopped being completely asleep as I lay there, was how wonderful it had been to kiss Lindsay and to be kissed by her. That's all we'd done, kissed for maybe about half an hour altogether. It had been absolutely marvellous.

I must have just been there for ten or fifteen minutes, thinking about our kissing. Then I fell asleep again.

When I woke up the next time I think maybe two hours or so had passed because now there was proper light in the room, or at least it was the kind of light you get on an overcast autumn day: that is, it was light, but it wasn't especially bright. I had no idea where the Cantians got their light from.

I didn't feel so sleepy now, and so I sat up on the floor and looked a bit more at Lindsay. Her blanket, which had covered her when I'd woken the first time, had slipped off her almost entirely. She was sleeping in her green tee-shirt and black jeans. She looked really really pretty and I could hardly believe that she was my girlfriend, as now I supposed she was as we had done so much kissing.

I just sat there looking lovingly at Lindsay for a few

minutes I suppose, until I realised that it was a bit weird and perverted just staring at her while she was sleeping so instead I looked around the room, which was of course as it had been the night before only now there was the Cantian sort of daylight there.

I listened for any sounds outside our door, but I couldn't hear anything apart from Lindsay's quiet breathing.

I wondered if Carlo had come back yet with Mum.

But if he had, why hadn't Mum come and knocked on my door? Or maybe Mum had come back but didn't want to wake me. On the other hand, how would she know I was asleep anyway?

I looked back at Lindsay again. She was starting to wake up slowly, as if she was waking up just because she knew that I was already awake. I watched her as she stretched a bit, then yawned, blinked several times at the ceiling, then turned her lovely head and looked over at me.

When she saw me, she smiled, although I wasn't sure if it was a smile of niceness or embarrassment at her remembering what we'd got up to the previous evening.

When she spoke, though, I couldn't hear any embarrassment in her voice, just a sort of quiet happiness, or at least that's what I think it was.

'Hello, Josh,' she said.

'Hello.'

'How did you sleep?'

'Pretty well. Much better than I thought I was going to.'

Lindsay sat up on her bed in her tee-shirt and jeans.

'Well,' she said, quietly, 'kissing does tend to make people sleep really well. It's easy to sleep if your heart is full.'

That seemed to me a lovely thing for her to have said. I decided to try to think of something romantic to say myself, although that wasn't very easy because I'm not really very good at saying that kind of thing. While I was still thinking, Lindsay got off my bed and came to sit next to me. We kind of began hugging, although not kissing this time but just hugging and it was really nice. Then Lindsay slowly got up and went over to the window to look out. I got up too and went to stand next to her. As I got next to her, and before I'd looked out of the window properly, I heard her give a shriek.

'What is it?' I said.

'Josh, look!' Lindsay pointed out through the window into the square.

I looked. What I saw were more crosses.

There were six of them, all quite close to each other in a line. The crosses were the same size as the one we'd seen earlier. Two of the crosses were empty, but four had people on them.

The crosses were maybe a hundred feet away, but I could clearly see that the four people were all old men with beards. Two had been tied to the cross like the dead man we'd seen before, but two, I could see, had been nailed to the crosses through their hands and feet.

The four old men were, as far as I could see, obviously all dead.

Lindsay took my left hand in her right and entwined her fingers in mine, just like she had the last time we'd held hands.

The worst thing was that no-one in the town square gave any indication they'd noticed the people on the crosses. That was the toughest thing, the really hard thing, the thing that made you feel creepy all over. No-one had noticed. Cantian men and women, and quite a lot of younger people, were hurrying across the town square, which was paved with terracotta paving-stones. Cantian people were standing in little groups talking.

What I saw now, by the way, for the first time was that while most Cantians were white, other Cantians came from all types of ethnic backgrounds. Some were Africans, others looked as if they came from India and some looked Chinese and Japanese. This puzzled me a great deal. I mean, why would Cantia have people from different nationalities in it?

The light of the Cantian day cast the white skin of the bodies on the crosses in a sort of sickly light.

I half-heartedly noticed the 'sky' above the square. I couldn't work out how high it was, but I suppose it must have been about five times the height of our house in Prospect Place. There were no clouds; it was just a kind of grey-blue colour.

How can the Cantians make an underground sky? I wondered. *And how can they live down here anyway?*

But a question that was far more important than this was: *why were people getting crucified down here?*

By now I'd seen the soldiers too. They wore the same kind of uniforms we'd seen on the unconscious soldiers when we first came to Cantia. Some carried spears or swords, and oblong shields. Others just walked about, looking peaceful enough, but armed, all the same.

What exactly is this place? If Carlo's right and Mum really is down here, what's happened to her? And where's Carlo now, anyway?

'I think we're in hell,' Lindsay murmured.

'Or somewhere even worse.'

'I wish I was dreaming,' said Lindsay.

'Me too.'

I put my fingers to the window, maybe to try to blot out the sight of the dead men on the crosses. But as I touched the window... my finger went all the way through it.

'Now I really do think *I'm* dreaming,' I said. 'What can that glass be?'

'I just don't know. There's too much happening that I don't understand. Why would anyone have invented glass that does that? And how could glass be *made* to do that?'

I nodded slowly. 'I agree, there are too many mysteries. I'm in mystery overload. This glass is just too crazy for words.'

We stared at the hole I'd accidentally made in the glass - if that was what the window was made from. We began putting our Cantian clothes on. As we were finishing doing this, there was a knock on the door.

'It's us!' said Dora, loudly, through the door.

I quickly opened the door. 'Come in quickly, both of you,' I said. They hurried in, and I closed the door behind them right away.

Dora glanced at Lindsay. 'Did you sleep here?'

'That's actually none of your business, Dora,' I said.

'So that's a yes, I suppose,' said Dora.

'Have you and Lindsay seen the crosses in the square through the window?' Sam asked.

'Yes,' Lindsay said, 'it's utterly horrible.'

'I know,' said Dora. 'This is a completely evil and bonkers place.'

'Never mind what's outside,' I added. 'This corridor could have loads of psychotic Cantians staying on it. Dora, you and Sam need to stop running around in the corridor.'

'Actually,' said Dora, 'there aren't any other people here but us.'

I looked hard at her. 'How d'you know?'

'Because Sam and I knocked on each of the doors,' Dora told me, 'and no-one answered.'

'You're both crazy!' I said, louder than I should have. 'What if someone had answered? What if the people getting crucified are people from our world who've stumbled into Cantia? Don't you realise the danger we're all in? I mean, just what would you have said if someone had answered the door?'

Dora looked at Sam, and he looked at her, and then they both turned to me.

'We'd have said Sally Vetty, of course,' Dora replied.

I gave a loud sigh. 'Well,' I said, 'let's just be grateful there were no people in the rooms to realise that *salvete* is the only Latin word you two know.'

'By the way, I think Bruce is eating his lettuce right now,' Sam said, suddenly.

'Who's Bruce?' Lindsay asked.

'My pet giant millipede,' Sam explained.

'Sam,' I said, 'please just shut up about Bruce, OK? I don't know why you're talking about him anyway, when he's safe at home and we're anything but safe down here. And besides, I don't see how you can know what Bruce is doing at home anyway.'

'Carlo hasn't come back, has he?' Dora said.

'No,' I said, 'and I'm sure he'd have woken us up if he had, especially if he'd got Mum with him.'

'Happy birthday, Josh,' said Sam. 'I know it's the wrong time and place to say it, with the crucifixions out there and Mum and Carlo not being here. I got you a card and a present, but they're at home.'

'So are mine,' added Dora.

I nodded slowly. I was impressed by how easily the twins had adjusted to everything: us skipping the week, the crucifixions, Carlo being down here, Mum being down here. Maybe the twins really were just completely mental, or… maybe right now, down here, they were the only even slightly sane ones.

'Thanks,' I said. 'I'll have my birthday when we get home. As you can probably imagine, I'm not in the mood for it right now.'

I was careful to say 'when we get home', not 'if'. I tried to sound really confident we'd get back, but 'home' seemed about a billion miles away right then.

There was another knock on the door now, followed right away by Troy saying, in a hissed whisper, *It's me. Open up.*

I did. It was getting like Piccadilly Circus in my room. Troy, by the way, was only wearing a pair of black underpants, and his Roman sandals.

'Come in quickly, Troy,' I said.

He did. 'You seen the crucifixions out in the square?' he said. 'They gave me serious heebie-jeebies. I was getting dressed when I saw them.'

'Yes, I'm afraid we have seen them, Troy.'

'This place is just so sick,' said Troy. 'We have got to get out of here. What about the glass? Have you noticed that too?'

'Look at the window. Josh accidentally put his finger through it,' Lindsay said.

Troy glanced at the window. 'That glass is wacky,' said Troy.

'How can glass be like that?' Dora asked.

'We don't know that either,' Lindsay said, with a shrug. She glanced at Troy. 'Have you seen any sign of Carlo or Mrs Moonford?'

'No, I wish I had,' said Troy. 'But I did spot all the soldiers out in the square and all the people from different places in their different-coloured togas. Makes you wonder how they got here. But the weirdest and worst thing's the crosses.'

'I think there's some kind of revolution going on,' said

Sam, 'and that the new leaders are crucifying the ones who were in charge before.'

'Maybe you're right,' I said. 'And by the way, they might still crucify us too.' I gave a shrug. 'Well, obviously Carlo hasn't come back. I'm going to go out now and try to find Mum myself.'

'I'm coming with you, mate,' Troy said. 'These Cantians are starting to irritate me. I want to kick some Cantian butt even more than I did yesterday.'

'That's great to know,' I said, putting my sandals on. I looked at the others. 'We'd better go and see Declan and tell him what we're going to do.'

'I suppose we should,' said Lindsay.

'Yeah, we ought to,' said Troy, grudgingly. 'He may be a prat but he's one of the team, I suppose.'

'Actually I think Declan's cool,' said Sam. 'I'd like to be like him when I grow up.'

'Well, I did say you were completely bonkers,' Dora told him.

39

I went to my bedroom door, quietly opened it a bit, listened, then, hearing nothing, stuck out my head. I didn't see anyone, so I headed for Declan's door. I could hear by the footsteps behind me that the others were following me. As soon as I reached the door to Declan's room I gave it two quick knocks (I was actually grateful now for the research the twins had done along the corridor) and, keeping my voice as quiet as I could, I hissed through the door, as quietly as I could, 'Declan, it's me. Can you open the door please?'

Nothing happened.

I knocked again.

This time I heard Declan's exhausted, groany and sleepy-sounding voice. *'Go away, Moonford.'*

'He sounds sauced,' muttered Troy.

I wasn't quite sure what that meant, but I think it meant he thought Declan was drunk.

'Declan,' I said, a bit more loudly. 'Carlo hasn't come back. We have to talk.'

'Go away, Moonford, you little dweeb.'

I wasn't even sure what one of those *was*.

'I'm not going anywhere, Declan,' I said. 'Nor are any of us. You need to open up.'

There was another silence. Finally he grudgingly opened the door a bit more. I could see just about a fifth of him. I thought Declan had slept in his toga, which looked seriously crumpled. So did he. His face was pale and sleepy, his hair almost as wild as Dora's, his eyes bleary.

'Are you OK?' I asked.

'Moonford, why don't you and the rest of the Famous Five just leave me alone?'

'Who are the Famous Five?' Sam asked.

'It's retro, Moonford Three,' Declan explained, with a glance at him.

'We'd like to leave you alone, Declan, but we can't,' I said. 'We need to talk to you. Are you OK?'

'Stop asking me that. But... well, I think I am, more or less,' he added in a groany kind of way.

'You look rather... tired,' I said.

'Well, if you must know, Moonford, I found an almost full bottle under my bed of what I presume is Cantian wine. There's a weird kind of stopper you prise out with your thumbnail. The wine was revolting - it tasted like it was made of parsnips or something. Still, it had a kick.'

'Declan, we shouldn't be talking out here in the corridor,' I said.

'OK, OK, OK, come on in then, all of you.'

We did. Troy shut the door behind us. Declan's room smelt fusty. He gave a groan, sat down on his bed and buried his head in his hands.

Lindsay went to the window and calmly put her right fist through it to let in some air. Declan looked surprised, though somehow not quite as surprised as I expected.

'So, basically,' Lindsay said to Declan, 'you got drunk and now you're nursing a hangover, is that it?'

Declan gave her a grumpy stare. 'Oh, sorry, I forgot that Miss Perfect of Penzance was in the room.'

'Declan,' I said, pointing to the window, 'there are six

156

more crosses out in the town square, and four have got dead bodies on them.'

'Two of them are nailed on rather than tied on,' Sam added.

Declan glanced at Sam. 'Please, Moonford Three, spare me the horrible details.'

'Haven't you seen the crosses, Declan?' I asked.

'No, and I don't want to, either.'

'And like you've just seen, you can put your hand through the glass, and it doesn't even break,' said Troy.

'Yes, I've noticed that too, Wilson,' Declan replied.

'Declan,' I said, quickly, before he and Troy could start arguing, 'we have to assume Mum's trapped or stuck somewhere out there. Very likely Carlo is as well by now. After all, he hasn't come back, has he? We're their only hope. We know only too well what the Cantians are capable of. We need to find Mum and Carlo as soon as we can and then get everyone home and tell the police what's happening and they'll send in the army and close this place down and arrest all the leaders.'

'Carlo said he was going to try to get back to Tiberius's house,' said Lindsay. 'Maybe we'll find Isabella if we go there.'

'Bad idea,' Declan said. 'If Carlo's gone there and been captured, most likely we would be as well. And in any case, we don't know where Tiberius's house *is*.'

'Josh could ask someone, using his Latin,' Lindsay said.

'Yes,' said Dora.

'I agree,' said Sam. 'And actually, I think it was all right for Declan to get drunk if he wanted to. After all, it takes his mind off our stressful situation for a while.'

Declan glanced at him. He looked surprised, and impressed. 'Well, thanks for your vote of support, Moonford

Three. So, what exactly did you do to take your great mind off things last night? Do your eighty-nine times table? Discover a new sub-atomic particle?'

'Actually, no,' replied Sam, 'though I think I'd have enjoyed doing both those things. I slept in Dora's room because I was so scared. We just talked until we fell asleep. Lindsay must've been scared too, because she slept in Josh's room.'

There was a sudden big silence.

I wasn't annoyed with Sam, because I knew he'd said what he'd just said completely innocently, in his own strange way, and he was my brother after all.

Declan folded his arms and glanced at Lindsay. '*So...* you stayed in Moonford's room, did you?'

'Yes,' said Lindsay defiantly.

'What d'you think this is,' Declan demanded, 'the Joseph Conrad High School's annual underground kissing party?'

'Oh, do be quiet, Declan,' Lindsay told him. 'Yes, Josh and I did some kissing, and it was lovely, but what happened between Josh and me is actually not your business. Besides, look outside! People are being crucified! We need to find a way of rescuing Isabella, and Carlo too, and then of getting out of here, before goodness knows what happens to us!'

Declan gave a loud groan, then went to sit down on his bed. He buried his head in his hands again.

'Just how much wine did you drink, anyway, Declan?' Lindsay demanded.

Declan suddenly lifted his head away from his hands, then looked up at Lindsay. 'Oh, do stop trying to take the moral high ground,' he said to her. 'We're having the most terrifying experience of our lives, in case you haven't noticed. We're worried about Mr Clancy and Mrs Moonford, and what do you do? Get all lovey-dovey with her eldest son and spend the night with him!'

'Leave her alone, Declan!' I snapped.

'Oh, so now the boyfriend has a go at me too,' said Declan. He glanced at me. 'Listen, Moonford, I'm trying to focus on our mission of rescuing your mother and Mr Clancy, not just using being down here as a big opportunity for doing some snogging. And by the way, Moonford,' Declan added, 'whatever did happen between you and your paramour, can someone please introduce Wilson to the concept of *getting dressed?* It's much too early in the day to have to look at his adolescent hairy chest.'

'All right, Jacques, I'll go and get my toga, so keep your wig on,' Troy said.

'You could try putting your toga on once you've got it,' Declan suggested.

'And you could try not to be a jerk for a day,' replied Troy, under his voice but pretty audibly, all the same.

Troy hurried off to his own room. Lindsay, the twins and I just looked at Declan, who stared back at us with grumpy defiance. None of us said anything at all, not even the twins. Troy hurried back a minute or so later. I got the feeling he hadn't wanted to miss anything.

'Never mind about Josh and me, Declan,' Lindsay said. 'Why did you have to get drunk?'

Declan glanced at us all through bleary eyes. 'Because I wanted to forget about this place Cantia. It always gives me the creeps.'

40

I heard what he'd said, but it didn't register with me right away, because I was still thinking about Mum and Carlo. Then I heard the sudden really intense silence in the room.

41

Lindsay took a couple of steps towards Declan.

'What... did.... you.... just... say?' she asked, my lovely girlfriend sounding at that moment like a sort of girl/robot hybrid.

Declan looked even paler now than he had when we'd come into his bedroom. 'Er... I said Cantia gives me the creeps.'

Lindsay shook her head. '*No, you didn't, no you didn't.* You said just now it *always* gives you the creeps.'

'Yeah, what did you mean by saying *always*, Jacques?' Troy demanded.

We all looked hard at Declan. I was trying to think of an innocent reason why he'd have used that word *always*.

I couldn't.

'Well?' Lindsay said.

'Well, what?' Declan muttered, looking up at her.

'Why did you say that?' she demanded. 'Have you been here before?'

Declan got to his feet, stood up and stared down at Lindsay.

'You're very pretty, aren't you?' Declan murmured. 'No wonder Moonford's nuts about you.'

Lindsay gave a loud sigh and shook her head slowly.

'But even more to the point,' added Declan, and now suddenly his voice was completely different - sort of serious, focused, businesslike - compared with how it had been before, 'Moonford's nuts about Latin, and that's what this is all about.'

'What... what d'you mean?' I said.

'What I mean, Moonford, is that the reason we're down here is because I planned it.'

'Planned it?' I gasped, just staring at him in astonishment.

'Yes, I planned it. And because of the missing week, I had the time I needed to do what I had to do. It's all because you're so into Latin. Otherwise, none of this would be happening.'

'It w... wouldn't?' I stammered, hearing myself and thinking I sounded like a total prat.

'You see, the truth is, you were selected.'

I just stared at him. '*Selected?* What for?'

'For candidate membership of CAESAR.'

'What's that?' I asked.

Declan cleared his throat then said: 'The secret committee that liaises with Cantia. I've been an associate agent since I was fifteen. That's the minimum age for membership, at least so far. Also, you live in Canterbury, and you're a brainbox, you speak Latin and you were soon going to be sixteen, on a rather special day for Cantia. In fact, some people on CAESAR thought you were just too good to be true.'

I felt stunned and shocked and totally amazed. I went to sit down on the Cantian stool in Declan's room. I sat and let the horrible truth of what had happened sink into me. The twins looked at me, and so did Lindsay, Troy and Declan.

Finally I looked at Declan. 'But... but if you want me to be part of this weird organisation, why have you involved Lindsay, Troy and the twins and have put them in danger too? And why's my mother been kidnapped?'

Declan was still sitting on his bed. Now he looked more

wide-awake than he had before. I suddenly wondered whether him keeping the secret he'd now revealed to us was what had caused him most stress of all.

He shook his head slowly. 'Moonford, believe me, I've no idea why your mum's been kidnapped. I wish I did. As for why I involved the rest of you, I didn't have any choice, did I?'

'What d'you mean?' I asked him.

Declan stood up. His toga still looked crumpled, but he didn't, not any more. He smoothed his hair down over each side of his head and at the back, then looked round at everyone before turning to me.

'OK,' said Declan, 'I'll tell you what I mean.'

42

' Let me start by telling you more about CAESAR. It was founded in the year 1749, when Cantia was discovered by a Canterbury Cathedral churchman, who reported its existence to some clerics high up in the cathedral hierarchy, including the Archbishop of Canterbury himself. They never revealed the secret of Cantia to the wider population but they did reveal it to some people in the government. A highly secret organisation was founded to communicate with Cantia. It wasn't called CAESAR in those days but *Sodalitas Clandestina*.'

'That's Latin for "Secret Society,"' I murmured.

'Give the man a prize. I don't know Latin like you do, but I do know a few words, and those are two of them. At first, *Sodalitas Clandestina*, or S.C. as it soon became known, was interested in trying to convert the Cantians to Christianity, but the more they discovered about Cantia, the more they discovered that it was already a very religious community. It is too, or at least it was, before whatever's going on right now started.'

'What do you mean?' I said.

'OK, Moonford, quick history lesson. Fact: the Roman emperor Constantine converted to Christianity on his deathbed on May the twenty-second, 337 AD, but by that time he'd already made Christianity the religion of the Roman Empire. Fact: the Cantians are the last survivors of the Roman Empire. They're not only Christians, they're also Catholics, because the people of Roman Canterbury were Catholics. *They're* the ancestors of the Cantians, you see. OK, so in the year 550AD - by which time the Roman Empire in Rome had basically collapsed due to the barbarians invading it and so the Romans couldn't do anything to help - Britannia, which was the Roman name for Britain, was invaded by pagan Anglo-Saxons from the European continent. The Anglo-Saxons became Christians themselves in 601AD, which was when the first Anglo-Saxon king, Ethelbert, was converted from paganism to Christianity. But that happened more than half a century after the Anglo-Saxons first invaded Britain. To start with, they were a bunch of violent and bloodthirsty pagan scumbags, basically.'

My imagination was back in Roman Canterbury, and I imagined pagan Anglo-Saxons sticking their swords through any Roman Canterbury people who resisted, and then burning their houses down.

'All right,' Declan went on, 'now, many of the conquered people of Britain would have been happy to accept the Anglo-Saxons as their new masters, but back in 550 AD the Anglo-Saxons were much too bloodthirsty to allow that to happen. They drove the Roman Catholics to the west of Britain, to Cornwall, Wales, the Isle of Man, and to the far north, into Scotland. The languages those Roman Catholics spoke, Celtic and Latin, went with them. Celtic evolved into Cornish, Welsh, Manx and Gaelic. Latin died out in Britain completely. But never in Cantia.'

'No?' I said.

'Yes,' said Declan. 'Cantia's the only place left in the entire world where Latin is the vernacular.'

'The what?' asked Dora.

'The everyday language,' I explained.

'Correct,' said Declan. He glanced round as us all. 'Kent is mostly built on chalk. Hollowing it out was easy enough. The people of Roman Canterbury knew that the Anglo-Saxons had already invaded further north, so they made preparations to escape from the invaders in another direction. They went underground, starting in the catacombs of their beloved Canterbury Cathedral. But soon they dug deeper, and deeper, and over the years they created this weird but in principle fundamentally good, holy place called Cantia.'

'But how could they have had any food?' I asked.

Declan gave a quick nod, as if he'd been expecting this question. 'In the early days of Cantia, the Cantians managed to grow their own crops in secret fields - the Anglo-Saxon population of Canterbury was quite small - and then take their harvest underground. Eventually they came to prefer root crops, which they could grow themselves. Oh, and before long they herded sheep underground too, though they were already getting adept at making meals out of creatures we'd consider creepy-crawlies, though after all people from our world eat snails, fish eggs, insects and even scorpions - they're very popular in China, for example, so I don't really see the difference.'

Declan fell silent. I wondered what eating a cooked scorpion would be like, and whether you'd hold the stinger underneath its tip and not eat that poisonous part.

'Fact,' Declan said again. 'In 1534, just under a thousand years after the Anglo-Saxons invaded, the English king Henry the Eighth wanted to get divorced from his wife, Queen Catherine, because he was totally smitten by a lady called Anne Boleyn. England was a Catholic country in those days. But the Bishop of Rome - the Pope, that is - wouldn't allow him to divorce Catherine, so the king decided to start his own church, the Church of England, and that was basically the end of Roman Catholicism being the official religion of England. But down here, in Cantia, the Church of England never happened. The Cantians have always been Catholics, and still are. They're deeply religious.'

'Listen, Jacques,' said Troy, 'if they're so religious, why are they crucifying people?'

Declan shook his head slowly, and for once didn't seem to be doing so ironically. 'I don't know, Wilson, I just don't know. Obviously, something's gone seriously wrong down here.'

'Well, you're certainly right about that, Jacques.'

'Yes, I'm afraid I am,' said Declan. He glanced around at us. 'I need to tell you all a bit more about when Cantia was discovered in 1749. What they also discovered was that Cantia had science that was well in advance of what was available in our world ourselves in those days. Not that the clergymen, who discovered Cantia, understood anything much in any detail about the Cantia technology they saw. In our world the year 1749 was, after all, the very beginnings of the Industrial Revolution and frankly, technology didn't even really exist in Britain in those days. But gradually S.C. got to know Cantia better. S.C. realised slowly, in its clumsy, inept, mid-eighteenth-century way, that the science which the Cantians had was amazing. The Cantians had made all sorts of interesting inventions.'

'What kind of inventions?' Sam asked.

'One example was the steam engine,' Declan replied.

The steam engine? I said. 'But everyone knows James Watts was responsible for developing that!'

'Well, yes,' said Declan, 'that's the story we're supposed to believe. James Watts certainly had a hand in improving the steam engine and in manufacturing many hundreds of them

167

for practical use in our world. But the idea was pioneered in Cantia. S.C. bartered the invention with the Cantians for lots of luxurious eighteenth-century food - roast pheasant, for example, and top-notch wine. As for the name *Sodalitas Clandestina*, it was discontinued at around the start of the twentieth century. The name CAESAR was chosen, instead. It's an acronym, you see.'

'What for?' I asked.

Declan cleared his throat. 'At first it meant *Clandestine Administration Executive for Subterranean Anomaly Research*. The name was changed a bit in about 1950 to make the whole thing sound more dynamic. CAESAR now stands for *Clandestine Action Executive for Subterranean Anomaly Research*. But despite the change of the name, the basic aim of CAESAR has never changed. It still sets out to barter Cantian technology for consumer products, including food the Cantians want from us. For example, nowadays CAESAR offers Cantians TV and DVDs and foods they really like - including smoked salmon, milk chocolate, Marmite and extra-crunchy peanut butter - in exchange for some of the more basic Cantian inventions, which we then pretend were invented in Britain or in the United States.'

'CAESAR obviously offers the Cantians Harry Potter novels in Latin too,' I said.

Declan nodded. 'Yes. In fact a lot of Cantian technology is very much like magic anyway. As for the food Cantia barters with us, most Cantian food is actually pretty revolting, which is why they love ours. The Cantians haven't farmed sheep for a long time, though they do grow their own underground crops.'

'How did *you* get involved with this weird CAESAR organisation, Jacques?' Troy asked.

'Through a contact my mum's current husband - he's her

fourth - has in the Government. My mum and her husband have no idea about the nature of what I do though.'

'What exactly do you do at CAESAR?' I asked him.

'I mainly help people from Cantia who want to leave and come and live in our world.'

'There are such people?' I asked.

Declan nodded. 'Yes, but not many. Only two or three a year. The point is that Cantians are by and large very happy with their lives and don't want to leave their world. Occasionally some do, though. For people who want to leave, the downside is that before they leave Cantia, they're subjected to a special treatment in Cantia which makes them think that their memories of their life in Cantia are all a dream.'

'How can that be possible?' Lindsay asked. 'How can medical science do that to anybody?'

'Our medical science can't,' Declan replied calmly. 'But the Cantians' medical science can.'

'What exactly do you mean,' Sam asked, 'about the Cantians being two hundred years ahead of us in technology?'

'Exactly what I say. The Cantians people had their own industrial revolution about two hundred years before we had ours. Their technology is immeasurably more advanced than ours is. But only the ruling class in Cantia - and a sort of priestly class of people who develop their technology - have access to all the technology which Cantia has developed. Most Cantians don't have access to it. The Latin for "science" down here is *sapientia sancta*, by the way.'

'"Holy Wisdom"', I murmured.

'Declan,' said Sam, 'is whatever we got shot with, if we were shot, that state-of-the-art technology you're talking about?'

Declan nodded. 'I think it may have been. But I don't

know exactly what you were all shot with, except that it definitely catapulted you a week into the future. So it must be some kind of a time weapon. But anyway, I was also given the job of investigating you as a candidate for CAESAR membership, Moonford. Obviously CAESAR has to recruit young people, or when the elderly people at the top of CAESAR die, CAESAR would too. Even before I started at the Joseph Conrad Kissing School at the beginning of this term, I monitored you through your Facebook account - CAESAR can get access to even though you and I aren't Facebook friends and your account isn't open to the public, through surreptitious visits to Canterbury and filming you with a telescopic lens. I know that as far as you're aware I've only been at the school a week, and that's true, but believe me, I know you pretty well. I have access via CAESAR, to top-quality information-gathering resources.'

'OK, I get this,' I said, 'but Declan, if you only wanted me to be part of CAESAR why did you involve Lindsay, Troy and the twins?'

'I didn't have much choice. They were all with you at the end of the red-brick corridor at the museum. I already knew from tapping your phone messages that you and your girlfriend were going to the Open Evening at the Roman Museum. I thought that was a great chance for me. My plan was to find a way of getting you, just you, down into Cantia and giving you an initiative test there to see how you could cope with it. If you succeeded, fine, I would tell you who I was and you could join CAESAR if you wanted. CAESAR likes recruiting young people, who so often have an instinctively sharp knowledge of technology. They haven't so far ever recruited anyone younger than sixteen, though, so recruiting the twins would create a precedent, but what had CAESAR got to lose? After all, if you failed the initiative test, no problem, CAESAR would wipe your memory of what happened.'

'CAESAR can do that?' I asked.

'Yes,' said Declan. 'CAESAR can do that and many other things. We borrowed the technology from the Cantians. So don't mess with CAESAR. I followed you and everyone else here, hoping there'd be a time when you got separated from everyone else, but it basically never happened. As I was following you, I saw a guy I'd never seen before close by you. It was the guy you call Custardface. He must have shot you with something, but I didn't see it, all I saw was his holdall. I think he must have kept it in the holdall. After he shot you all, you all basically disappeared. That was when I went up to him and at gunpoint - I'm issued with a Glock pistol, and it's loaded, although I hate using guns and I don't think I'd have shot the guy even if he hadn't been helpful. But I scared him enough, and I asked him who he was and what he'd just done to you all. He told me it was none of my business and that he couldn't tell me even if he wanted to, because it was all so secret.'

Declan drew a quick breath, then went on:

'At that point I thought that he was obviously using some very advanced kind of technology, so I asked him if he was anything to do with CAESAR. The moment I said that, he seemed to warm towards me somehow and he said that he wasn't a member of CAESAR but that he was working for someone who was. I asked him who, but he said he couldn't tell me because if he did he'd be killed. He also said that he doubted I was willing to fire the gun. I told him not to be so sure about that, and I pointed the thing at him. At that, he told me that he'd just sent you all one week into the future to get rid of you. I told him he was crazy for doing that because obviously you'd all wonder what had

171

happened to you and you'd probably work out before too long that you were now a week in the future. At that point he said, something like, "Listen, mate, whoever you are, I need to get down to Cantia again. As you're involved with CAESAR, you know what Cantia is. If you want to follow me, I'm not going to stop you, but I don't advise it, because when I get down there there'll be Cantian guards and if I tell them you're not wanted, they'll kill you. They've got better weapons than that popgun you're holding." I told him that I was really happy for him to go down to Cantia by himself and that I wasn't exactly crazy about spending any more time with him. That was the point where I had my brilliant idea.'

'What idea was that?' I asked Declan.

'I realised, in a flash, and by the way CAESAR is always asking me to use my initiative, so that's precisely what I used, that I could extend the initiative test to all of you and that if you, Moonford, and Miss Penhaligon and your brother and sister all came through the test then maybe I could propose to CAESAR that we had four new recruits rather than just one. That's the kind of idea CAESAR like people in my position to have, as I say they like initiative.'

'What about me?' Troy said.

'Oh yes, you, Wilson,' Declan replied. 'Well, basically, you're superfluous to requirements. But don't worry: when we get out of here you'll get your memory wiped and you won't be any the wiser.'

'No-one's going to wipe my memory,' Troy said.

'Well we'll see about that.'

'Oh, stop arguing, you two,' Lindsay said. 'We're a long way from getting out of Cantia, and now things have got even more complicated and difficult, in case you haven't noticed. But. Declan, who exactly is the guy we call Custardface?'

'I don't know, but I think one of the CAESAR members - I don't know who, and that's the honest truth - has been using Custardface to do some very dodgy stuff down here, though I don't know what. I reckon when Custardface shot you all he didn't know how to use the mechanism properly. Maybe he sent you momentarily into the distant future but didn't know how to use the gun or whatever it was and after you'd made your trip into the far future he pressed another button and you ended up just a week into the future. I don't know. I think you're all very lucky you did end up just a week after when you were sent. As you all know, advanced technology isn't always very easy to use.'

'If they're so advanced here,' Sam asked, 'do they have really amazing computers?'

'No, they don't,' Declan replied. 'You see they invented *their* computers about two hundred years ago, from mechanical components and cogwheels, and the Cantians still use those mechanical computers, which suit their purposes beautifully.'

'So you're saying that the Cantians still use mechanical, cogwheel-based computers?' asked Sam.

'Yes,' said Declan, 'and in fact the woman who runs this ghastly holy-house dump has one on her counter. They're actually quite advanced machines; don't be fooled by their cumbersome appearance. The Cantians are very happy with these mechanical computers and haven't ever troubled themselves to try and invent more sophisticated ones. You must remember that they don't have the same demand for international networks that we have because they're a small community and are quite happy to go visit each other when they want to be in touch. They're a strange mixture of advanced technology and almost primitive ways of living, although I shouldn't say primitive but just more communal, in their small world.'

'How many Cantians are there?' Lindsay asked.

'About three thousand. So there are plenty of Cantians down here, which is why strangers aren't immediately recognised.'

'Fortunately for us,' Troy put in.

Just for once, Declan gave a nod of agreement with Troy. 'Yes, fortunately for us, or we'd all probably have been crucified by now, for all I know. And before you ask me about *that* I need to tell you that I don't know why it's happening. I don't know what's going on down here. There's never been any record of crucifixions happening in Cantia before. This is all new. My guess, though, is that there's been some sort of revolution. After all, revolutions tend to involve stupid violence being inflicted on innocent people. And I suspect Tiberius is behind it somehow. He's a very ambitious senator, he's white, unlike Augustus, the Proconsul for Cantia, who's a really great guy, an elderly Cantian of African origins. I don't know what's happened to Augustus. I just hope he's not been killed. Basically, you now know most of what I have to tell you. There isn't much more for me to say really.'

'What about the coffee cup?' I asked Declan.

'What coffee cup?'

'When we came back into the corridor after our weird experience of seeing Canterbury Cathedral in a very strange kind of futuristic town square, I noticed a coffee cup that I hadn't seen before.'

He nodded at me. 'I guess I must have forgotten to clear it up after I had a coffee. After I worked out my plan, I phoned CAESAR's control team and asked them to close the museum for a week. CAESAR can do that easily enough.

The museum's always been one of the two secret routes down to Cantia even before it was refurbished.'

'What's the other one?' Lindsay asked.

'A hidden passageway at the back of the crypt of Canterbury Cathedral,' said Declan.

'Are there any other routes apart from through the museum and the cathedral?' I asked him.

'Not as far as I know.'

'Declan,' I said. 'when I overheard Custardface talking on his phone, he was speaking to someone called Stan. Any idea who that might be?'

Declan shook his head slowly. 'No. I wish I did. He didn't mention Stan's surname?'

'No, definitely not,' I said.

'Well, we'll just have to see if we get any more clues to who Stan might be,' Declan replied.

'Yes,' said Lindsay. 'But Declan, I still don't understand how you made things happen like you say you did. In particular, the door in the brick wall at the end of the corridor didn't open because you *made* it open, it just opened.'

'No,' said Declan, 'I said the password to make it open. But of course, I didn't want you all to know I'd said it.'

'I don't remember you saying any password,' said Lindsay.

'Well, strictly speaking I didn't,' said Declan. 'The password, as you might expect, is "Caesar". So I made up a sentence with "seize a" in it, which did the trick.'

'You said, "let's seize a chance to get out of this creepy corridor,"' Sam reminded him.

'Yes. Well remembered, Moonford Three.'

'Oh, very clever, Declan,' said Lindsay. I couldn't tell if she was being sarcastic or not.

'Yeah, and very creepy,' said Troy.

'So, Declan, was the room with the oxygen running out fake as well?' I asked.

'No, that was real enough. I needed you all to want to put Cantian clothing on. The oxygen really was running out. I know where the secret emergency button in the room is located - I could have pressed it and given us an oxygen flood, but I wanted to see how you all coped. The togas, dresses and sandals have micro-sensors built into them; when the sensors are triggered by proximity to warm bodies, and when the system knows that all the bodies it can detect are activating sensors, it sends out an electronic message and the door on the far side of the room opens.'

'I see,' said Lindsay.

'I can't believe the lengths you've gone to,' I said to Declan.

'Well, there's a lot at stake,' Declan said. 'Being considered for membership of CAESAR is a pretty major thing. And right now, there's even more at stake. Things aren't going according to plan at all.'

'I've noticed,' muttered Troy.

'So, what about Carlo?' I asked Declan, 'Is he in on all this too, and using his acting skills to pretend he isn't?'

'Absolutely not,' said Declan, 'He's for real. Everything's real, including the crucifixions... unfortunately.'

Lindsay nodded slowly. 'When were you planning on telling us the truth about your involvement?'

'Soon,' Declan muttered, quietly. 'Some time today. But I really did get drunk last night on that horrible wine, and when you all came in here I wasn't as cautious as I should have been.'

'What about that stuff about you never watching the TV news?' Lindsay demanded, 'and being in France last week?'

Declan shrugged. 'What I said about never watching the TV news was basically true, but what I said about me being

176

in the South of France last week wasn't. I was in Canterbury all week.'

'Declan, you shouldn't have lied to us,' I said. 'As for us having been on television, that could make things even more difficult for us, if any Cantians saw us on the TV news.'

'Don't worry about that, Moonford. As I've said, only the ruling class in Cantia, which is in practice just fifty or so people, have TV; most can't be bothered. Believe it or not, they don't find our world very interesting; they're more interested in theirs. Tiberius really does likes TV, though. He's even learnt some rudimentary English from watching it.'

'I see,' I said. 'So do you think he might have seen us on TV?'

'Well, it's possible,' Declan said, 'but not very likely. I really wouldn't worry about it.'

'Declan,' said Lindsay, 'why are so many Cantians from other races and cultures?'

'As I said, Cantia is the very last outpost of the Roman Empire, and the Roman Empire had people in from many different ethnic origins; it was actually a very successfully integrated society. The Cantians are the direct descendants of the Romans who lived in what we now call Canterbury. But you see, most of the Romans who lived in Britain at the time weren't actually from Rome. The Roman Empire included people from all the countries that were in the empire, and that included parts of North Africa, and even some Asian people who had made their way west to the Roman Empire. These people from Africa and Asia who'd heard how rich and successful the Roman Empire was, braved all sorts of adventures and hazards to travel north to get a job in it. Many of them settled in the farther outposts of the empire, like Britannia - I suppose they got stared at too much in Rome, and very likely there was racial prejudice there - so quite a few Africans made their home in Roman Canterbury. They must have found it cold, yes, but my guess is, they found it friendlier than Rome.'

Declan fell silent.

'OK,' Lindsay said to him, 'you're obviously the Mr Wikipedia of Cantia. Maybe, just maybe, that'll help us rescue Mrs Moonford and Carlo. All the same, what it all boils down to is that ever since we met you yesterday evening, you've been lying to us.'

'No,' Declan replied. 'I'm not a liar, just a good actor. Besides, your boyfriend, or whatever he is, should be grateful.'

'Grateful, me?' I said, *why?*

Declan looked intently at me. 'Because, Moonford, I'm trying to give you all a chance - only a chance, but one chance is better than no chance - to be part of something... something almost too amazing to imagine, something that could change your lives for ever...'

43

'What if we don't want our lives changed, Declan?' I said. 'What if we were all perfectly happy with our lives before we came to the Roman Museum this evening?'

Declan nodded slowly. '"Perfectly happy?" Let's look at that, shall we? You and Dora and Sam don't have a father. He disappeared eight years ago; no-one knows what happened to him. Maybe he's dead, or maybe not. Your mother runs a health-food shop that hardly makes any money; she has difficulty feeding you all and clothing you all properly, but somehow she just about manages. You live in a cramped little terraced house, and you and Sam have to share a room because there are only three bedrooms.'

I just stared at him. 'How... how do you know all this?'

Declan shrugged. 'CAESAR knows it, so I do.' Now he glanced at Lindsay. '"Perfectly happy?" Your mother's having an affair with a guy called Craig Smith. He makes his living as a fitness instructor, but for some years he's had a significant extra income from easily tricked middle-aged women who fall in love with him.'

Lindsay just stared at Declan. 'But Declan, how d'you know this?'

'Remember I've had a week to find out about you all, and CAESAR has access to all the information that MI5, the British secret service, does. Frankly,' he glanced at Troy, 'I didn't bother to find out more about you, which was probably just as well.'

'Give me a break, Jacques,' said Troy. 'And by the way, just because you're in on this doesn't impress me. Do something to help us, and then I might start to feel a bit more impressed.'

'Declan, you could start,' I added hastily, before he and Troy had a chance to start arguing again, 'by telling us about the weird glass.'

'OK,' said Declan, 'well, like I said, I don't know too much about Cantian advanced technology. But I know about that glass they use. The Cantians call it *fenestrum*. You can put your finger or hand through it, but *fenestrum* doesn't buckle if you lean on it, because it's got a really high tensile strength. It doesn't shatter, either. It's something we're currently trying to barter with the Cantians. Now listen: Cantian scientists haven't only invented new materials, they also have ways of *altering* materials too. There'll be surprises down here for me, too; I still don't know much about Cantian technology.'

'You're not really too helpful, are you, Jacques?' Troy said. 'I mean, OK you know about the history of this place, but you're not exactly clued up on how we can get out of here, are you?'

'Also,' said Sam, 'I'm really hungry.'

Dora looked at him. 'Oh, shut up.'

'All right, but if I shut up, I'll still be hungry.'

'I'm ravenous,' said Troy.

'Actually so am I,' said Dora, as if she felt that now Troy had admitted to being hungry she basically had permission to admit this herself.

I was hungry as well, but I didn't want to say I was, as leaders have to be tough. So instead of telling everyone I was hungry too, I said: 'All right, so we'll rescue Mum and

Carlo, then we'll get out of Cantia, and go for a nice burger and chips somewhere.'

'Listen, mate,' Troy said to me. 'We've got to get out of this place first, without being crucified. Anything might happen today. How can we be at our best if we're starving?'

'I agree,' said Lindsay. 'Josh, just because no-one ever seems to eat anything in the *Sacred Guardian* books and movies doesn't mean we don't need to eat here.'

She turned to Declan. 'D'you have any Cantian money?'

Declan shook his head. 'I wish I did. I had some earlier, but stupidly I left it in the dressing-room. I left my wallet in my jacket, with the gun. It's forbidden to bring weapons down into Cantia; I would have got booted out of CAESAR if I'd brought it down here. I did intend to leave the gun there, though. But it's a state-of-the-art personal Glock that only works using my fingerprints, so no-one else can use it. I knew I had to leave my jacket back in the dressing-room with the gun in; I just forgot I left my wallet there too.'

'How do we know you didn't leave your jacket in the dressing-room deliberately?' Lindsay asked.

'Why would I do that? It was an accident, OK? It was, after all, a pretty stressful time. Anyway, I never said I was perfect.'

'Don't worry, Jacques,' said Troy. 'No-one thinks that.'

Declan just glared at him.

'I'll go downstairs,' I said, quickly, 'and ask that old lady what the food situation is. Declan, d'you think the holy house might provide breakfast free for pilgrims?'

'No idea. You'll have to ask. Just be really really careful: don't give away that we're not from here.'

'I'll try my best not to,' I said.

44

Downstairs I found the old lady standing behind the counter in the reception room, reading from a rolled-up papyrus she'd laid out on the counter. On the other side of the counter was the same weird cube that Declan had said was a Cantian computer.

For obvious reasons I was pretty nervous.

'*Salvete*,' I said.

She fired her answer back at me. '*What do you want, young man?*'

'*I'd like to know,*' I said, speaking Latin slowly, '*if breakfast is provided for pilgrims.*'

My heart was beating fast. I still dreaded giving away that I wasn't from Cantia. But the old lady didn't seem suspicious, only grumpy. She said that a '*prandium simplex*', which was pretty sure was Latin for a 'simple meal', was available at the price of five denarii per person.

I wondered whether telling her we had no money might make her want to give us something to eat for free, but I didn't as I realised saying that would have probably made her even more suspicious about us than she must have been already.

'*Thanks,*' I said to the old lady, in Latin. '*My friends and I will go out to eat.*'

'*Don't forget to pay for your rooms before you leave the holy house.*'

I tried my best to look honest, and rich too. '*We'd like

to pay for our rooms after we come back from eating,' I said, thinking this would give us more time to work out how we were going to get some money.

'Very well,' she said. But after she'd said that she stared hard at me and added, *'Remember, young man, if you and your friends leave without paying, I shall report you to a policemonk.'*

What she'd said, in Latin, was *'vigil monachus'.* I knew *vigil* meant 'policeman', so yes I supposed *vigil monachus* could only mean 'policemonk'. What were Cantian policemonks like? I wasn't sure I wanted to find out.

Suddenly, my eyes were drawn to the large, upside down headline of the papyrus the old lady was reading, which was in big black letters, and in Latin. I could just about manage to read it upside down. In Latin it said:

IN MATRIMONIUM
HOC DIE FESTO ATQUE SOLEMNI BRUTUS

Which in English is:

BRUTUS IS GETTING MARRIED
ON THIS SPECIAL DAY

I didn't know why today was so special for the Cantians. I remembered now that Declan had mentioned that my birthday was on a special day for Cantia. *'Who's Brutus?'* I asked the old lady.

She glared at me. *'Don't you know about the glorious changes in Cantia, young man?'*

'Sorry, no. I've been busy with my studying.'

I thought that was probably a safe thing to say, as surely they had schools of some kind down here, creepy as the schools probably were.

The old lady folded her arms in front of her, and went

on glaring at me. *'Brutus is a member of our glorious new triumvirate. He's getting married on this special day at the Games. The Games begin at the eighth hour.'*

I wanted to ask her more about the triumvirate, but the last thing I wanted was to let on how micro my knowledge of Cantia really was. So I thanked her, trying to sound polite as I did, then hurried back upstairs and told the others what the food situation was, or rather wasn't, and that the old woman had said there had been 'glorious changes', and that there was a triumvirate in charge of Cantia now.

'What's a triumvate?' Sam asked.

'It's a triumvirate,' I explained. 'It means three people who rule together.' I glanced at Declan. 'What's this "special day" the old lady was talking about? You mentioned something about this before, but I didn't ask you what you meant.'

'She means today's the Ides of September,' Declan replied. 'The fact that today's your birthday's one more reason why some people at CAESAR thought recruiting you was a no-brainer. For the Cantian people, the Ides of September is the day that marks the founding of Cantia. I think in Latin they call it "Celebrity Sanctuary", or something like that.'

'Sounds like a reality TV show,' Lindsay said.

I nodded. 'It might be *Celebritas Sanctuarii*. That would mean "the Celebration of Sanctuary."'

Declan nodded. 'Maybe. I've never studied Latin myself, though I've picked up a few words working with CAESAR.'

'So is the Celebration of Sanctuary a bit like Independence Day in America?' I asked him.

'I think so,' replied Declan.

'I see,' I said. 'Well, I suppose I should feel privileged about that. Have you heard of people called policemonks?'

'Afraid not, Moonford. I'm glad I haven't. They sound pretty sinister. What worries me is what the old crone downstairs meant exactly when she spoke about the "glorious changes" in Cantia. This revolution is totally horrifying.'

'When's the eighth hour?' asked Sam.

I glanced at him. 'The twenty-four-hour day was invented long before the Romans, but they made it popular. The Roman day started at six hour-glasses after midnight, or six o'clock in the morning our time. So perhaps the Cantian day is divided into hours like ours is. If it is, the "eighth hour" must mean about two in the afternoon. OK, it's seven minutes to nine on the morning of Sunday, September the thirteenth, the Ides of September. I'm sixteen; not that it feels very different from being fifteen. Today's the Cantians' Celebration of Sanctuary. So let's go out and see if we can find Mum or Carlo. Remember not to speak English. We mustn't let the Cantians know we're not one of them.'

'If we find some money, can we have breakfast, please?' asked Sam.

'I hope so,' I said.

'Just tell me something, Mr Big,' Troy said to Declan. 'Why all the James Bond stuff, anyway? Why doesn't CAESAR just come down here and take Cantia over, especially now these Cantians are crucifying people? I mean, we've got weapons that are a whole lot better than the ones people had in the eighteenth century.'

'Cantia isn't politically part of the United Kingdom, Wilson. If we did what you suggest, we'd be invading a foreign country.'

'So what?' Troy retorted. 'Who are the Cantians going to complain to - the London Underground? Why don't your buddies at CAESAR just send commandos with some serious fire-power and steal this amazing Cantian technology you've been telling us about? And just how good is it, anyway? All I've seen so far is a pretend sky, a crazy window you can stick your finger through and a bunch of prats dressed in different-coloured togas. And if these Cantians are so high-tech, why do they have swords?'

'They don't only have swords,' said Declan. 'But, yes, the Cantians are proud of their traditional weapons, and of their Roman ancestry and heritage. Why shouldn't they be? But don't be deceived, Wilson. You're in a world whose technology makes Microsoft's most sophisticated software look like a flint axe.'

'What, am I supposed to be, Jacques, scared? I'm not.' Troy held up his hands in mock horror.

'Well, maybe you should be, Wilson. You don't want to get overconfident down here and wind up getting crucified, do you?'

'Hey, listen,' said Troy. 'No-one is going to crucify me, OK? They'll have to kill me first.'

'And me,' said Dora.

'And me,' said Sam.

'What Troy said about CAESAR makes sense, though, Declan,' I said. I didn't feel inclined to add to the offers to die. 'Why *doesn't* CAESAR just come down and invade Cantia?'

'Yes, CAESAR has the power to do that,' Declan said, 'though the Cantians have resources of their own, and it wouldn't be such a one-sided fight as Wilson obviously imagines. But the real reason CAESAR doesn't do that is this: Cantian scientists are the only ones who completely understand their own technology. If we were to just burst into their labs, it would be like... well, like nineteenth-century soldiers taking over Microsoft's offices today and expecting to understand the work being done there. We'd learn nothing, and we'd lose the Cantians' trust for ever.'

Troy gave a shrug. 'OK, I suppose that makes sense. It's pretty well the first thing you've said that has.'

'Declan,' I said, 'isn't there *anything* you can do to help us get some food and find Mum and Carlo?'

'Sorry, there isn't. Everything I planned has been completely screwed up by what's happening now.'

'But you're an important cog in CAESAR,' I said.

'Yes, but down here in Cantia I'm relatively powerless, as anyone in CAESAR would be. Of course I'll help as much as I can, but I'm not a trained fighter.'

'Really, Jacques?' Troy said, 'we'd never have guessed if you hadn't told us.'

'Very funny,' said Declan. 'Listen, Wilson, while you're down here, just try to behave yourself, OK? Don't steal anything, and don't try to chat up any Cantian girls, or you'll get us all arrested.'

'Anyone who wants to arrest me,' said Troy, 'would have a fight on their hands.'

I'll bet. I was glad Troy was on our side.

'Oh, Wilson, you're so tough,' said Declan.

Troy glared at him. 'For all this about you being part of CAESAR, you're a coward, if you ask me.'

'Well, at least I'm not a criminal.'

'*Neither am I.* My dad, my kid sister Phoebe and me don't have much, but what we do have, Dad and me have done honest work for.'

'And your mother?' Declan said. 'What kind of honest work does she do, may I ask?'

'Oh, not a lot.'

'So she's one of the idle unemployed, is she?'

'No, Jacques. She's dead. She died of lung cancer when I was eight.'

There was a long silence.

Finally, Declan cleared his throat. 'I'm sorry to hear that, Wilson,' he said, speaking very quietly. 'I'm really sorry. I mean that.'

'Yeah, sure you are, Jacques.'

I glanced at Troy. 'I didn't know about your mum. I'm sorry, Troy.'

'Thanks, mate.'

I shuffled my feet, then looked round at everyone. 'Come on. Staying here isn't going to help us. We've got to do something. We'll keep the swords with us for protection, but hidden like they've been since last night. We'd better hide our phones here, though. The last thing we want is for those creepy policemonks to find them on us.'

'Josh, listen,' said Lindsay, 'what about Dora and Sam? Should they be coming with us? They're only twelve. Things could get very, very dangerous.'

'But we like danger,' said Dora. 'It's fun.'

'Yes!' Sam exclaimed, hitting his right fist into his left palm with a smack.

'We can't leave Dora and Sam alone here, anyway.' I glanced around. 'Please, whatever you do, don't look at the crosses and the dead people on them as if you're surprised or shocked. I know it's tough but we have to ignore them, just like the Cantians do. We absolutely have to blend in. Come on, *let's go.*'

45

Hardly a minute later, we slipped out past our friendly hostess. Then, for the first time, we were 'outside' in the town square in the strange Cantian daylight.

The twins were both gritting their teeth, as if they knew that avoiding looking at the terrible sight of the crosses with the dead people on them would be about the most difficult thing anyone could possibly ask of anyone.

Cantians were all around us: men and boys in togas, women and girls in colourful Roman dresses. European-looking people and African and Asian people too. Most of the Cantians even looked genuinely happy, as if today was, indeed, a really big and exciting day for them, like Christmas is for us. That was what was so bad. I knew the crosses were still there because I could see them out of the corner of my eye. So did the Cantians somehow think crucifying people was normal? But hadn't Declan said that crucifixion was a new thing in Cantia and that the Cantians were religious? So, what on earth - or *under* earth - had happened down here?

Somehow, I don't know how, we all managed to walk past from the crosses without staring at them too much.

A smiling and beautiful African Cantian lady, maybe about the same age as Mum, in a dark green dress, her very black hair done in an ornate style, suddenly walked up to us. She carried a tray made of tree bark, supported in front by a brown cord round her neck.

The tray had loads of black armbands on it. Each armband had two jagged letters on it, bright red against the black background.

The letters were 'SS'.

I'd felt sick before when I'd see the crucifixions, but those letters made me feel almost as sick. They reminded me of the Nazi death squad - the SS.

Lindsay, Declan, Troy and the twins had seen the armbands too.

'Salvete,' the lady said to us. She smiled. She had very white teeth.

'Salvete,' I said back to her. The lady's smiling face seemed to me to make her even spookier. Somehow it would've been better if she'd looked stern and nasty, like a Nazi concentration death-camp guard. She handed each of us a black armband, then stood looking at us expectantly, waiting for us to put the horrible things on. I had just one hope - that maybe the symbol on the armband didn't mean down here in Cantia what is meant up in our world.

I told her in Latin we'd come out without any money and couldn't pay for the armbands. But she replied they were *'Triumvirorum donum'* - 'a gift from the Triumvirate' - and that wearing them was *Triumvirorum iusso* - 'by order of the Triumvirate'.

An order enforced by the military and the policemonks too, I bet.

The lady went on staring at us. She really meant business about us wearing the armbands.

I looked at Lindsay, my eyes asking *what choice do we have?* Then I accepted armbands for all of us, and the woman went off, wearing a satisfied expression.

'I absolutely *do not want* to wear mine,' Lindsay muttered, her voice very quiet and firm.

'You have to,' Declan said. 'We need to fit in. Of course I don't want to wear this horrible armband, but what choice is there?' And he put it on.

I knew I should set an example, so I hesitantly put my armband on too. The others did too, just as unwillingly. Keeping my voice right down, I said to Declan, 'Maybe the Cantians don't know about Hitler. Perhaps these armbands have nothing to do with the Nazis. I mean, can we assume the Cantians know anything about the history of our world?'

Declan gave a shrug. 'The briefing I got about Cantia is short of that kind of information.'

'Well, have you heard of these armbands being worn in Cantia before?' I asked him.

'No, never. Maybe they're to do with the revolution. Crucifixions, Nazi armbands. It's all a total nightmare. This is supposed to be a deeply religious community.'

'Well, it certainly doesn't seem to be one right now,' said Lindsay.

Declan gave a nod, then suddenly beckoned us around him. 'Now listen,' he hissed, when we were all in a huddle. 'I've an idea that might just help us.' He looked at me. 'You play chess, don't you?'

I stared at him. 'Chess? Yes, I do. How d'you know?'

'It's in the briefing CAESAR gave me about you. Doesn't surprise me, a brainbox like you. Well anyway, the Cantians play chess for money in the town square. We could bet against them. That's something I do know about the place.'

'Would I have a chance?' I asked. 'I mean, is Cantian chess like ours, Declan?'

'Sorry, but I just don't know.'

'But how can I bet against them even if I think I can beat them?' I said. 'We don't have any money for a stake. And if we did, we'd use it to buy food now rather than risk it on chess anyway.'

'Actually,' Lindsay said, 'it's just occurred to me that in fact we do have some money.'

I glanced at her. 'What do you mean?'

She pointed at her pearl necklace. 'I mean this. It's not exactly money literally, no, but maybe we could sell it to get food.'

Declan nodded slowly. 'That's an idea, but there's a serious danger that trying to sell your necklace is going to draw attention to us. In fact, I should have suggested you hide it before. I don't imagine the Cantians have pearls, though maybe they have things that look like pearls, otherwise the necklace might have drawn attention to us already.'

As we crossed the square, we got closer and closer to the tall buildings on the far side. They weren't tall by the standards of the world above, but they had three, and sometimes even four, storeys, which was pretty tall by Cantian standards. I saw that one of the bigger buildings had huge panes of window glass - I mean *fenestrum,* I suppose - and stumpy black tables surrounded by smaller black stumps for seats, most with Cantians sitting on them in their brightly-coloured togas and dresses. As far as I could tell, each table had little ornaments on it, though I couldn't see from this distance what the ornaments were.

As we got closer, I saw that the building was made of the same black-veined white stone as the holy house. It had a brown door that might've been made from tree-bark, and above the front door a sign, which said, in spidery black letters against a yellow background, *Pinguis Vermiculus.*

I knew that *pinguis* meant 'fat' in Latin, but I didn't know what *vermiculus* meant.

Other shop fronts had signs such as *Pistor* - 'baker' - and

Herbae - 'herbs'. So maybe *Herbae* was a chemist's shop, with herbs being used like medicine. Both these shops had queues outside. The shop with the sign *Titulae Ludorum* had the longest queue. I wondered how much tickets to the Games cost.

There was another sign, too, one I also hadn't seen before. It said *Taberna Lusoria*. Underneath was a colour drawing of a Cantian girl and boy playing with what looked like a big crystal. They were smiling in a fairly silly kind of way, the way kids do in old adverts, all gleaming teeth and rosy cheeks.

46

S am hurried up to me. 'What does that mean, *Taberna Lusoria*?' he whispered to me.

'"Toy-shop",' I said, quietly, before I could think of pretending it meant something else, so the twins wouldn't want to go in.

Needless to say, the twins instantly headed for the toy-shop. So, despite all being so hungry, we followed them.

Well, inside the toyshop it was kind of weird because it was a combination of Roman decor and very strange toys. The decor itself did look very Roman. There were white marble tiles, each maybe about a foot square, on the floor. I had no idea where the Cantians would have got marble from. I even wondered if maybe they had some in the old days which had been shipped from Rome before they'd gone down into the underground world and they'd brought the marble with them.

There were about a dozen Cantian children inside the shop, which was rectangular and maybe about twenty yards long and maybe ten yards wide. There were loads of display cabinets with toys underneath the glass. What you had to do, I noticed, was go to one of the three Cantian women assistants who were behind the counter and point to what you wanted if you wanted to buy anything.

Well, we weren't going to buy anything, obviously, because we hadn't any money, but it was quite interesting to see the kind of things they had there. There were lots of small Cantian cogwheel cube computers, each one about six inches square. On the other side of the shop I noticed there were dozens of models of ants, the ants all being about six inches long. I went and looked at the ants under the glass, expecting them to start moving, but they weren't moving ants. They were very good models though, I had no idea what they were made of. They looked pretty spooky.

Under another display cabinet on the left hand side of the shop, the glass was lifted up, and an assistant was showing a girl and a boy, each aged maybe about fourteen or fifteen, small, red hearts. They looked like the kind of hearts you get on Valentine cards. The little hearts were maybe about two inches wide. I had no idea what they were made of. I also wondered what they were supposed to do, but the assistant saw me looking at them and for some reason she closed the glass cabinet quite abruptly. I didn't know why. I noticed that Declan had seen the hearts too and he seemed interested in them and went over and glanced at them where they were now under the glass.

The boy was holding a heart in his hand and he took it to the counter and paid some money for it, not very much I think; he gave about three copper coins for it. By now Declan was looking at us all and nodding towards us, (of course it would have been far too dangerous to have said anything in English in that little shop) and we all knew that he wanted us to leave. The twins, rather reluctantly as they were still viewing the ants, left after Lindsay, Troy and I did. I noticed that Declan didn't come out of the shop immediately but stayed behind for about a minute or so.

When Declan did come out of the shop and we were far enough away from other Cantians for me to be able to whisper this question to him without incurring any obvious risk, I asked him quietly how the hearts worked.

'Oh, they're just little ornamental hearts. Cantians give them to someone they care about. It's a tradition, like giving Valentine cards on Valentine's Day.'

'Oh, I see,' I whispered back. But I didn't feel he was telling me the complete truth about the red hearts, even if he was telling me the truth about Cantia.

I looked again at the building made of the black-veined white stone that the holy house was made of. I looked once more at the sign in spidery black letters above the yellow background which said, *Pinguis Vermiculus*. I tried really hard to try to think if I knew what *Vermiculus* meant.

We all headed up towards the building that had the mysterious sign outside. When we were about twenty yards from the first tables outside the building, I saw that I had been wrong about the little things on the tables being ornaments. At the same moment I realised that Declan had been right about the Cantians and their enthusiasm for chess, because those things on the tables weren't ornaments. They were chess pieces, and coloured red and blue, instead of white and black.

47

The Cantians were obviously very keen on chess, and loved eating and drinking while they were playing it. Many of them had plates of food - mainly hunks of what looked like coarse brown bread with some kind of black stuff sticking out from inside - and grey cups on the tree-stump tables next to the boards.

You would never have guessed that about two hundred yards from where this was all happening, four dead men were dangling from crosses.

But I knew I had as best as I could, at least for the time being, to forget about that and focus on trying to win some chess games so I could get some money and we could eat. I was pretty hungry myself by now.

As we got near the tables, I noticed at once that the chess-boards had more squares than in our chess. The boards in Cantian chess had ten squares on each side instead of eight. Also, most of the chess pieces looked weird and very different from our chess pieces.

In front of each player were little piles of brown coins.

We were too close to the Cantian players to speak English now. Declan grabbed me by the sleeve of my toga, gave me a meaningful look and nodded at the chess-players.

I thought of Mum and Carlo out there somewhere and needing to be rescued. I also thought of Troy saying how we couldn't be at our best if we were starving.

Could I win any money at chess? I knew I wasn't too

great a player, but I hoped maybe the Cantians weren't that great at it either.

I watched two boys - European Cantians - playing. They were completely absorbed in their game and an older boy, an African Cantian, sat at a separate table keeping an eye on the game. He noticed me and gave me a friendly smile. They all wore SS armbands.

The third boy, the older one, was about my age. He had a cheerful expression and curly jet-black hair, and wore a brown toga like Sam's.

Leaving Declan and the others, I went over to the boy. *'Salve,'* I said. He said *'salve'* back that's the friendly version of *Salvete*.

We swapped names. I told him my name was 'Josea', which is my name in Latin class at school. He said his was Marcus.

I sat in the empty chair opposite him. There was a chess-set between us, with some pieces I recognised and others I didn't.

'Marcus,' I said, in Latin of course. *'I'm from the countryside. I'm here with friends. We're trying to find a beautiful lady who has long, dark brown curly hair. She's from the countryside too. Have you seen anyone like her?'*

Marcus slowly shook his head, then said, rather sadly.

'I'm sorry, Josea, I have not.'

I thought of adding a description of Carlo too but realised that too many questions about missing people might make Marcus suspicious, assuming he was a suspicious kind of person. So I asked him about Cantian chess instead.

'But surely everyone knows how to play chess?' Marcus replied, looking puzzled.

He called chess *ludus latruncularius*. I knew *ludus* meant 'game', but not what *latruncularius* meant.

'No, we don't play this kind of chess in the countryside,' I said.

Marcus seemed to accept this feeble and risky explanation, and began to explain the moves and the Latin names of the pieces to me.

Cantian chess turned out to be a strange mixture of the chess I knew and something completely different. There were ten pawns on the second row of each player. The king - which Marcus called the 'Proconsul' - moved like our king did, just one square in each direction, and there was also a piece in the shape of a tower, which moved like the rook did in our chess, that is, squareways along ranks and files. Another piece was called the *nuntius*, Latin for 'messenger'. The *nuntius* was the equivalent of our bishop: that is, it moved diagonally. There were also horses, or knights, as of course they're called and they moved like our knights did.

One piece, which was completely unknown and foreign to me, Marcus called the *stultus*. It was in the shape of a little man with a pointed nose and a toga. In our chess the rooks are in the corners, but in Cantian chess the *stultuses* were in the corner and the rooks next to them. The *stultus's* move was very weird: it went three squares along any rank or file, then one square diagonally forwards in either direction.

Cantian chess had a queen, but it wasn't like ours which can go as many squares as it wants along a rank, a file or a diagonal. The Cantian queen could only travel a maximum of four squares.

Once Marcus had explained how the pieces moved, it seemed the obvious thing to do to play a game together, so we did. He didn't seem bothered about us playing for money. Phew! Just as well.

That game was a total disaster for me.

I lost horribly quickly, mainly because of course I was still

199

learning how the pieces moved, but mostly because I hadn't realised that the *stultus* was so important in Cantian chess. Also, because of the bigger board and the larger number of pieces, Cantian chess was even more difficult and more complicated than ours is.

We changed colours and played again. This time I did better. I felt a bit more relaxed now, and a whole lot more confident. I managed to win the next game, using my *stultus* to deliver a sneaky checkmate to Marcus's king. I expected Marcus to be annoyed I'd beaten him, but instead he smiled.

'Josea, you play well. You should play Senator Antonius now and bet against him. He is fat and rich and he does not play me because I always beat him. But he does not know how well you play.'

'But Marcus, I don't have any money.'

'Josea, I know that people from the countryside are poor, so if you play him I will give you a stake, and if you win you can give it back to me.'

I didn't know what to say except, *'Thank you'.*

Then Marcus said a very strange thing to me. *'When you play Antonius, you must use the Mouth of Wisdom.'*

I just stared at him. *'The what?'*

'The Mouth of Wisdom. You didn't use it when you played me, but you must use it if you want to defeat Antonius.'

The Mouth of Wisdom? Not only hadn't I used it, I didn't have the faintest idea what it was.

'What's the Mouth of Wisdom?' I asked, quickly adding, 'We don't have them in the countryside.'

Marcus pointed to a neat little hole a few inches below the top of the stump.

'When the game starts, put your finger in there.'

'Which finger?'

He shrugged. *'It doesn't matter. Any one. But not yet. Wait until the game starts.'*

'All right, I will.'

Marcus smiled, then stood up and hurried over towards a big fat white man in a purple toga who was watching chess about six tables away. Marcus said something to the man, who stood up, looked over in my direction, and headed towards me. Three men and one lady - the men were white like Antonius and the lady was black and very beautiful - who'd been sitting close by Antonius got to their feet and followed him.

Oops. So much for not getting noticed by the Cantians.

I glanced at Lindsay, Declan, Troy and the twins, who were hanging back in the square, looking hungry and stressed.

Antonius turned out to have a serious ego problem, to put it mildly. His sidekicks hung onto every word he uttered. Like him, they all wore SS armbands. He talked loudly and arrogantly, as if he were one of the most interesting people who'd ever lived.

I was worried Marcus might ask Antonius about Mum, but instead, he simply introduced me to the man as *'a brilliant chess-player from the countryside'.*

'Oh, I shall defeat him,' said Antonius, waving airily in my direction as if he thought I was about as important as a dead woodlouse. The beautiful black lady, who was wearing a bright red toga and had lots of curly hair all tied up high above her head, took out a brown leather money-bag from inside her dress and handed it to Antonius. He tossed it onto the table in front of us.

'I will wager all this that I can defeat this boy from the countryside,' said Antonius.

Marcus put three silver coins down on my side of the table.

'He wagers these,' Marcus said.

Antonius glanced at me. *'My stake is much greater. If you win, you take all the money. If you lose, I take your friend's stake and also you shall work in my house for seven days, without any wages, on unpleasant tasks.'*

I wondered what *they* would be. But what choice did I have but to agree?

'All right,' I said. I felt totally nervous.

The game started. Antonius played blue, and I played red.

Now, I reached down and put my left forefinger inside the Mouth of Wisdom, or Wisdom Mouth, leaving my right hand free to move the pieces.

Antonius reached down and put his finger inside the Wisdom Mouth on his side. His finger was so fat, I was surprised it fitted.

When I put my finger in the hole, I didn't feel anything, so I kept pushing it in, until it hit a sleek, rounded metallic surface.

The moment I touched that surface, I felt like I'd been plunged into a dream.

48

This was my dream, if it *was* only a dream. I'll never really know.

I was on a great wide open plain, with the sun blazing down from above.

The landscape was like I'd read about in books about Ancient Romans: hot sun overhead, olive-trees in the distance, red-roofed houses and a beautiful old temple in the distance on a hill. Between here and the hill stretched a great wide plain and . . . an army of maybe a thousand soldiers was spread out over it.

Each soldier in my army was red from head to toe, including his uniform and weapons. There were red men riding giant red woodlice, red men with red javelins, red infantrymen... and red war-earwigs the size of large dogs.

A second or so later I realised what all this was. I realised that this was my army in the game of chess I was playing with Antonius. I knew that I was playing red in the game and that these red pieces were mine. Except somehow, the Wisdom Mouth was making me think I was commanding a real Roman army.

I could see the enemy army, the pieces in dark blue, on the far hillside. I looked back at my army. I knew it was time to attack. But how could I make them move forward? I had to do something, because I saw that all my soldiers of war-animals, including the giant red woodlice, and the red war-earwigs, were looking at me for guidance.

So I hurried quickly towards them. I shouted, '*Adorite!*' which I knew was Latin for 'Charge!' as loudly as I could. I remembered the word from a passage in a Latin textbook from school about the Romans fighting the people they called barbarians. Well, me saying that word did the trick, it really did. My red army - men on horseback and on the back of woodlice, all the men were armed with deadly iron-tipped lances, by the way - wheeled towards the dark blue army on the hill and they charged. The blue army seemed to have been taken by surprise. It was as if they were still trying to decide what to do.

I stayed with my army, yelling words of encouragement, running alongside them and calling out to them to charge even faster, and I somehow managed to keep up with them, even though they seemed to be running faster even than the wind. Soon we were close to the hillside and I accompanied them as they raced even faster towards the dark blue army.

Somehow, suddenly, I remembered that someone had once told me that when two cars crash into each other head on, it was always the slowest car that came off worst. I didn't join my soldiers in the fight, not because I'm a coward but because there was so much obliteration and smashing and destruction and death, and sharp weapons smashing into flesh that I knew that I'd be killed if I did that, or at least I would be killed if this dream became any kind of reality, so at the very last moment I slowed my pace, but I still kept screaming out to my soldiers to fight hard and to charge, and I dodged dark blue soldiers who were coming towards me. I don't know why they didn't stab me with their weapons. Perhaps it was really a dream and so they couldn't actually do that. But I knew that I was running round and shouting like a madman, roaring at my soldiers to smash down the enemy.

I suddenly realised that I was really 'feeling the game' as Marcus had put it and that my army was creating total murder and mayhem. The battle seemed to go on for a long time. Both the armies were fighting completely mercilessly and I thought it perfectly possible my army would be defeated. But maybe the completely desperate situation we were in there in Cantia gave me extra energy for the game or maybe my finger was pushed further into the Wisdom Mouth than Antonius's was, but anyway, my army slowly began to get the better of Antonius's.

Masses of dark blue soldiers had been crushed, beheaded and chopped into pieces in the first wave of my army's attack. My red soldiers and their war-animals now outnumbered the dark blue army and its own war animals. There they lay on the battlefield, hundreds of Antonius's dark blue soldiers, like blue snow-drifts on the hillside, crimson blood pouring out of their still-trembling bodies. There were hundreds of their own giant woodlice and giant earwigs that were dead as well. My own army's giant woodlice and giant earwigs were mostly unscathed, and were rearing up, with their soldiers on the backs of them, triumphant over their fallen enemy.

I looked with pride at my army and how well they had done. We had some casualties, some men and their animals were slaughtered, but far fewer than the blue army had.

I wandered amongst my victorious troops, shaking them by the hand and I even dared to stroke the deadly-looking rear pincers of my army's terrifying giant war-earwigs.

49

I don't remember taking my finger out of the Wisdom Mouth, but I must have done.

Antonius got to his feet. He stared down at the chess-board in total horror. All his blue pieces, except one, were off the board now, lying toppled on the ground. The only blue piece still on the board was the proconsul, the most important piece in Cantian chess.

Antonius pointed at Marcus with the fat right forefinger which Antonius had used in the Wisdom Mouth. *'I shall have my revenge on you, boy!'*

Marcus shrank back from his finger.

I stood up and looked at Antonius. *'Why swear revenge on him, when I was the one who beat you?'*

Antonius glanced at me. *'You are from the countryside and do not know how to behave, but this fool Marcus is from the town. He should respect me! I shall have my revenge!'*

Antonius strode off angrily, followed by his hangers-on. Antonius's money-bag still lay on the table.

Marcus didn't have to tell me these were my winnings, I knew. I was just so excited I'd won.

I loosened the cord of the bag and looked inside. The bag was full of silver and bronze Cantian money. I was pretty sure we'd have enough to pay for our rooms at the holy house, and probably for breakfast too. I gave Marcus three silver coins across the table, then added an extra silver coin as a gift. Marcus waved his right hand as if to say he didn't want to take it, but I told him he must.

Marcus smiled and thanked me. I was totally delighted. Finally, I could buy food for the twins, Lindsay, Troy and Declan. I was about to run off to them with the money, but at that point a lean, fair-haired white man, in a grey toga and black armband, hurried over to me. He introduced himself as *curator* - which I knew meant 'manager' - of the *Pinguis Vermiculus* restaurant. He said he didn't like Senator Antonius and was pleased I'd beaten him. Then he offered me breakfast, featuring the *'most delicious delicacy'* the restaurant offered, at the restaurant's expense.

'What delicacy is that?' I asked.

The manager looked in obvious amazement at Marcus. *'Why doesn't he know?'*

'He's from the countryside,' Marcus explained.

I was still no wiser, but my hunger pangs were kicking in, and I knew that now I had some money we could all have some food soon and wouldn't be hungry any more and could be at our best and could try really hard to escape. I didn't think it would be a very good idea to ignore the manager and go off to see the others, so I decided I would simply take some of the food to the others after the manager had brought the 'delicious delicacy' and cleared off. I also thought it was weird how, after all that stress about how we were going to get money for breakfast, this wacky guy was giving me breakfast *for free!* That's the strange thing about money; when you have lots of it, you often don't need to pay for things anyway.

'I must go now, oh wizard of chess,' Marcus said. *'I hope to see you again.'*

'I hope to see you again too. Beware of Antonius.'

'I shall,' Marcus said.

I really liked Marcus, and thought he could maybe help us find Mum or Carlo, but I also knew I couldn't introduce him to the others without him realising we weren't from Cantia.

Marcus gave me a Roman salute, and I returned it. Then he rejoined his friends.

The manager was still standing close by. *'I shall bring the delicacy,'* he said.

I smiled. *'Thanks.'*

A few moments he brought it to me, all hot and steaming on a large plate. I could only imagine that the delicacies got cooked in advance.

I stared in horror.

There, in front of me, was a huge, dead, roast *maggot*.

50

I thought, *those enlarged insects in the Wisdom Mouth dream or whatever it was were somehow real; the Cantians really can enlarge things.*

The maggot was about a foot long, and maybe four inches wide. I sort of knew that maggots were a creamy-white colour, but this one was well-cooked and light brown all over. It had a sharp end and a blunt end. There were two small, bulging circles like eyes at the blunt end, which made me think that must be the head.

In an instant, I realised what *vermiculus* meant: some sort of worm.

So the name of the restaurant is the main eating experience you get here!

Staring at the plate, my first feeling was that I might be sick. But that feeling actually passed quite quickly, because the giant maggot smelt delicious like roast chicken fresh from the oven, mixed with the taste of crispy bacon. It certainly wasn't a vegetarian experience; Mum wouldn't have approved. It was garnished with a few slices of brown bread. Some slices were smeared with what looked like Marmite; others had crunchy peanut butter on them.

So what Declan said about Marmite and peanut butter being two of the things CAESAR bartered with Cantia is true, I thought. There were also some wacky-looking vegetables: green carrots, white tomatoes and large spiny yellow pods.

The manager smiled at me and said *'Bene tibi sapiat'*. I'd

never heard that expression before. I suppose it was Latin for 'bon appetit.'

I went back to wondering how to get some of the giant roast maggot to the others.

That was when I spotted the chariot.

51

The chariot was rattling in my direction from the side of the square that led to the church. It was maybe a hundred yards away now, but getting closer all the time. At first I could hardly believe my eyes, but then the chariot came nearer and I didn't have much choice.

The two soldiers standing in it were wearing Roman-type Cantian military uniforms. One soldier had a spear strapped across his back, the other carried a sword. Both soldiers grasped the armoured front of the chariot with one hand to keep their balance, while each holding on to the shoulders of a lady prisoner who stood between them.

Her long dark brown hair was done up in a fancy style bunched high on her head. She wore a beautiful yellow Roman dress and some kind of necklace with blue stones.

I hoped very much it wasn't who I thought it was. When the chariot was still quite a long way away I could keep that hope, but the hope kept on vanishing the closer the chariot came, and finally I had no choice at all but had to believe the truth.

The lady was Mum.

52

I'd have expected Mum to be completely furious and mental about what was happening to her, but she wasn't. Instead, she just stared weirdly in front of her, like she'd been drugged.

I saw all this, and of course I was desperately worried to see Mum there. But it was hard to focus only on her, because the chariot was being pulled along by... three giant earwigs.

They were even bigger than the ones I saw when I played Wisdom Mouth chess. These earwigs were each at least ten feet long. Their curved rear pincers were as long as full-length swords, and it was pretty obvious that, if the earwigs were to stab you in the stomach with those pincers, your guts would be ripped out. My head span, I felt sick and I couldn't swallow, my mouth was so dry. I knew that somehow I had to try to keep focused or I'd end up completely mental and no good to anyone.

By now, the giant roasted maggot was cooling on the plate in front of me. My mouth was open, not to eat the maggot but because I was so amazed to see Mum like this.

Lindsay and the others had seen the chariot too. Lindsay and Troy didn't know what Mum looked like, unless they'd seen her in the shop, which they'd never mentioned doing. But I was sure Dora and Sam would have hissed to them who it was there in the chariot. As for Declan, he knew so much about me that I could only assume he also knew what Mum looked like, though of course I didn't know that for certain.

Dozens of Cantians were heading in the same direction as the chariot. The chariot moved fast, so the Cantians following it had to more or less run to keep up with it. The chariot quickly passed by me maybe fifty yards away. I jumped up from my seat, keeping hold of my money-bag, quickly crossing the stream of Cantians following the chariot. A few moments later, I'd reached Lindsay and the others.

When I got to them, Dora was crying. I knew that meant she'd seen Mum. Lindsay had her right arm around Dora and her left arm around Sam.

I realised that if I was going to be a leader, it was now or never.

'I won this bag of money at chess,' I panted. 'My guess is we've probably got enough money for food and to pay for the holy house rooms. Obviously we need to follow the chariot. But if we don't pay the old lady at the holy house, she'll tell the policemonks to start looking for us. So Troy and me will go back to the holy house and pay her and get all our phones. We'll be back in a minute or two and then we'll go after the chariot, all right?'

Lindsay, Declan and the twins nodded.

'They gave me a giant roasted maggot to eat,' I said to Declan. 'How do things like earwigs and maggots get to be so big down here?'

'The Cantians... they have a special machine,' Declan replied, quickly. 'It's called a *Bio-Amplificator*. Really important for their food production. It has...well, it's got various settings.'

'You mean,' gasped Lindsay, '... it *enlarges* things?'

'Yes, basically,' said Declan.

213

'How does it do that?' Lindsay asked Declan.

'How am I supposed to know? I didn't build the thing.'

'Oh, I expect the machine makes small increases in the spaces between the atoms and molecules,' said Sam.

'Maybe you're right, Moonford Three,' Declan said. 'You're certainly a genius. Still we know that already.' He turned to me. 'Well done for winning at chess, Moonford.'

'Thanks,' I said. 'Actually, I only played one game for money, against a senator called Antonius. I beat him. I'll tell you more about it if we ever manage to rescue Mum and Carlo and get out of here. I made friends with a Cantian boy called Marcus. Antonius doesn't like Marcus at all.'

'Marcus sounds like a good bloke then,' said Troy.

Troy and I walked quickly to the holy house to pay and collect our phones. We said an insincere friendly goodbye to the old lady who ran the place. We hurried to join Lindsay, Dora, Sam and Declan, and the six of us, walking fast (not running so as not to be conspicuous) soon caught up with the people following the chariot, though we still couldn't see it. After maybe half a mile we left the town behind (I could hardly imagine how big Cantia could be), and now we were among the Cantian crowd, so we absolutely couldn't speak English to each other. We followed them through another archway.

The amphitheatre, with its walls of grey stone, towered in front of us. We walked even faster and were now only thirty yards behind the chariot, close enough for us to call out to Mum, if that hadn't been such a suicidal thing to do.

Mercifully, there weren't any crosses outside the amphitheatre. But would there be any inside, in the arena, with people on them or people *waiting* to be hung on them?

Suddenly, a large square hole opened in the wall of the amphitheatre. The chariot and the giant earwigs pulling it disappeared into the gap, and a moment later the wall closed over the hole.

Mum was gone again.

53

I knew we had to get to our seats, but there was no way I could just sit and wait to see what happened. I had to find Mum and rescue her.

Somehow I felt sure Mum was going to be on show, in the amphitheatre. So how could I stop it?

At least I'd won enough money playing chess to buy tickets for a *cubiculum*, according to the list of ticket prices on the wall next to the ticket office. I didn't know exactly what *cubiculum* meant, but it sounded like 'cubicle', so I hoped it might give us some privacy.

A *cubiculum* for the six of us turned out to cost all our silver coins, but we had enough bronze ones left to buy some amphitheatre food and, while I don't suppose any of us felt much like eating, sometimes you get so hungry that even if you don't *feel* like eating, you don't have any choice but to.

Near the ticket office were three women about the same age as Mum, all wearing grey Cantian dresses, and selling snacks that, a day ago, I'd no more have eaten than I'd have tried to eat Sam. But I was getting used to Cantia by now, and I wasn't too grossed out that the snacks were basically roasted and enlarged maggots, though not enlarged as much as the one I'd been served in the restaurant. These smaller maggots were about eight inches long, so each one was about the size of a large hot dog, and came inside a folded piece of black bread (I couldn't imagine what it was made from), though not smeared with Marmite and peanut butter this time.

I paid for twelve roast-maggot-in-bread snacks, two each, along with six clear bottles of pink juice. I wondered if the bottles were made of *fenestrum*. I hoped not. With all of us carrying our food and drink, I showed our *cubiculum* ticket to a Cantian official in an orange-coloured toga.

'What's happening here this afternoon?' I asked him.

'Great celebrations for this great day,' he replied.

Of course, what I really wanted to ask him was why exactly they wanted Mum in the celebrations, and if he'd seen the movie star Carlo Clancy anywhere, but I knew I could hardly ask him that.

This official led us along a passageway, down a corridor with walls of brown tree-bark, and about twenty rough wooden steps that led up and out into the open air. Loads of noise coming from the crowd already inside. I saw the weird Cantian overcast sky again and had my first view of the arena.

No sign of Mum or Carlo. Mercifully, no crosses either. Yet.

The official showed us into the *cubiculum*, whose side walls turned out to be about two yards high, although of course the *cubiculum* was open at the front. It was like being in a large bus-shelter or one of those wind-shelters you get on promenades at seaside resorts, for people enjoying a windy holiday. The nearest other seats were maybe twenty yards away, which was good. If we didn't speak too loudly, we wouldn't be overheard.

The moment we sat down, we wolfed down the food. The speed Sam ate his two maggots-in-bread, you'd have thought he hadn't been given anything to eat since the day he was born. I have to admit the Cantian version of a hot dog was surprisingly delicious, like eating a really nice and well-cooked sausage, at least if there was ever a sausage that tasted of bacon, with a hint of chicken.

When we'd finished stuffing ourselves, we swigged the weird drink. It tasted like a mixture of carrot-juice, parsnip-juice and liquorice, if you can imagine that, or indeed if you *want* to imagine it. But I was really thirsty, as everyone was, and the bottles of juice were the only drinks on sale.

'It's OK, but I wish it was lemonade,' said Dora.

'I wish it was Kentish ale,' said Declan.

Below us was the arena, with a high stone wall surrounding it. The spectator seats started close to the top of the wall and went up in staggered rows into the wide, horseshoe-shaped auditorium. There were hundreds of seats. Most were occupied, but there were still people coming in. It was all very noisy.

On the far side of the arena, opposite the parapet but at ground level, was a gateway with black metal bars.

I turned to Declan. 'I'm going to try to find Mum.'

'Don't be crazy, Moonford. There're soldiers everywhere. You might get arrested, and then where would we be?'

'Declan, I have to go. I'll try not to get arrested,' I said, heading off.

The arena was still filling with people. I left the cubiculum and went back the way we'd come. With the ticket in my hand - it looked like a small white bus ticket with the words *Ides Sept: cubiculum* in black - so that I could get back to my seat, I managed to find my way back outside to the strange door where the chariot had disappeared. I gave the door a discreet push, but it didn't open, so I went round the back of the amphitheatre to see if I could find another way in. By now, most of the seats in the amphitheatre were occupied.

Where's Mum? I wondered. *Where have these Cantian*

psychos taken her? I realised that, inside the amphitheatre, there must be a secret part that you couldn't get to from the aisles and walkways. But how could I get in there? For the first time since the brick wall had closed behind us, I felt like crying.

I hurried around the amphitheatre looking for a clue as to where Mum might be but there wasn't another door leading into the heart of the amphitheatre.

What would happen if I went up to a soldier and asked about her? I wondered. I'd most likely be arrested.

Trumpets, or horns, or some weird Cantian musical instruments, started to sound, heralding something happening inside the amphitheatre. The Games were obviously about to start. I knew that if I didn't get back in, the doors of the amphitheatre would shut and I'd get shut out. Of course I felt very very frustrated that I couldn't find Mum, but I couldn't avoid the fact that right now, I knew that the best thing I could do was quickly get back to my seat in the *cubiculum*. At least there, I would see what was happening in the amphitheatre.

And then, when I got back to my seat, something happened that felt even worse than knowing that the Cantians had captured Mum.

54

Well, when I got back to my seat the first thing I saw was that everyone had changed places. Dora was sitting where I had, then Troy next to her, then Sam, then Lindsay, then Declan. The seat where Declan had been sitting was empty, but I hardly noticed that really.

What I really noticed was that Lindsay was sitting next to Declan, *AND THEY WERE HOLDING HANDS!*

I just stared at Lindsay and Declan.

I felt totally, totally sick.

I glanced at the others. Dora, Sam and Troy looked very uncomfortable. I actually expected Troy to make some comment, but for once that verbal cavalier was silent, as if even *he* was too amazed at what was happening to know what to do about it.

'What... what's happening?' I said to Lindsay, hardly able to force the words out.

'Don't worry, Moonford,' Declan said, calmly, and speaking for her apparently, 'these things happen in life. Your girlfriend has simply realised that I'm the guy she prefers.'

I could only think it was all some kind of joke. 'Listen,' I said, hoarsely, to him as much as to Lindsay, 'I wasn't able to find Mum. I'm not in the mood for silly games, so please, both of you, stop it.'

I wanted to raise my voice higher but of course I daren't in case any Cantians heard us, so actually I said it all pretty much in a sort of hissed whisper.

Lindsay turned to me. 'No-one's playing games, Josh,' she replied, speaking as calmly as Declan had and with horrible coldness. 'It's exactly what Declan said. I've just realised I really like him.'

'*Really like him?*' I returned, again in a hissed whisper. 'But you think he's a complete prat!'

'No, Josh,' Lindsay said, still horribly calmly, 'I've never actually thought Declan was a prat. It's just that I didn't realise what a great guy he was. I do now, thank goodness!' And she reached out her right hand and stroked the back of Declan's annoying long dark-brown hair, 'And he's such a handsome fellow...'

'Actually, mate,' said Troy with a glance at me, 'I reckon your girlfriend's gone completely bonkers.'

I just looked at Lindsay. 'How can you... how can you want to sit next to Declan and tell me you like him?'

'It's not only that I like Declan, Josh,' Lindsay said. 'It's much more than that. I'm very much in love with him.'

Now I felt faint as well as sick. '*In love with him?* Are you serious?'

'Do try to relax, Moonford,' Declan said, with incredibly annoying calmness. 'We can't draw attention to ourselves, you know perfectly well why, and it's dangerous you making such a fuss. Come and sit down and try and be calm. This is life, Moonford. It doesn't always go according to plan.'

'Not go according to plan?' I said, keeping my voice down as much as I could, which probably wasn't very much. 'You're telling me my girlfriend has suddenly fallen in love with you? I think saying that life doesn't always go to plan is a bit of an understatement, don't you?'

My heart was racing and my lungs were bursting with upset, and my stomach was hurting, and I felt my brain throbbing too.

You might have thought things couldn't have got any worse, but they did.

At this point... what happened now was that LINDSAY AND DECLAN ACTUALLY STARTED KISSING!

After about ten seconds of gawping, appalled, at this terrible, terrible sight, I forced myself to look away, out at the audience.

There were tears in my eyes. I hurried away from Lindsay and Declan and went to sit as far away from them as I could. Lindsay and Declan were still snogging. All I could think was *why's Lindsay being like this? What's happened?* I just couldn't believe that she really had suddenly, in the few minutes I'd been away, started to think she liked Declan more than me.

I also thought *where's Mum?* Because of course it wasn't only Lindsay who was upsetting me. Everything else was too. My eyes pathetically started to get wet with tears.

I knew it was pretty unlikely Mum and Carlo would be in the audience but, all the same, I had a good look. There were loads of Cantians in their coloured togas and dresses. Quite a few were children who looked about the same age as Dora and Sam, but there was no Mum, nor Carlo. Seeing Cantian kids there made me feel a tiny bit more hopeful for a moment that what we would see might not be too awful (though I still felt totally awful about Lindsay) but then I also thought: *this is a place where giant earwigs pull chariots, and where people are crucified, and where huge roast maggots are served for breakfast and where you can stick your fingers through windows, so how do I know what kids here are or aren't allowed to see?*

I wondered whether Marcus was among the audience. But I couldn't see him either.

Our *cubiculum* was near the end of the left arm of the horseshoe. To our left was the parapet where, in Roman amphitheatres, the people in charge of the event would've sat, but, right now, the only people on the parapet were three soldiers. Each was armed with an oblong shield and a sword, and dressed like the soldiers we found lying unconscious at the entrance to Cantia. They were standing to attention behind three large white seats that looked a bit like thrones. Other soldiers were standing at regular intervals in the aisles of the tiered seating.

And then there were the flags.

There were five altogether, on the parapet above the arena. Each flag had an extremely creepy design: a bright red letter 'C' against a white background. I supposed the 'C' stood for 'Cantia'. In the middle of the curve of the letter was a picture of a horizontal sword with the sharp point facing outwards. Above the 'C' at the top was the word *SEMPER* in capitals, and at the bottom there was another word: *SUPERIOR*.

Declan must've guessed what I was thinking, because he suddenly said, 'Those S's on *"SEMPER"* and *"SUPERIOR"* look exactly like the zigzag Nazi "SS" sign, don't they?'

I didn't know how I could speak to him but I knew I had to.

I nodded grimly. 'Yes.'

The *SEMPER SUPERIOR* flags were supported at the top by a horizontal bar - I suppose because there weren't any breezes down here. There were flags all round the stone wall surrounding the arena.

'What does *Semper Superior* mean, Josh?' Lindsay whispered.

I felt like telling her to get a Latin dictionary and stop asking me to translate Latin for her. But I didn't say that.

Instead, I said, my mouth very dry, 'It means "always on top. It must be the new Cantian government slogan.'

I just felt SO awful. The terrible thing was that now I'd seen the weird new relationship between Declan and Lindsay, I actually began to get sort of all nostalgic for the time, which had ended only a few minutes ago, when we were all down in Cantia and Lindsay was with me. This horrible feeling of homesickness for that time, if you see what I mean, felt absolutely dreadful. I couldn't believe what had happened. There I was, next to Declan, and now he had his arm around my girl. I felt bombarded by terrible feelings and terrible upset.

I was only sixteen, but I was growing up fast. I was only young, yes, but one thing I know, you grow up really quickly when your heart gets broken. Anyway, I can't keep telling you how awful I felt about what was happening or you're going to probably get fed up with this book and just do a rude one-star review on Amazon and even send it back to the bookshop and demand your money back, so I need to tell you what was happening in the amphitheatre, although you should factor into your thinking please that in everything I say now I was still devastated about what was happening between Lindsay and Declan, who, thank goodness, didn't do any more kissing, at least not for the time being.

The flags made me feel even more awful than I already did. They made me think of those documentaries you see of the Second World War on TV and on the internet, with black and white footage of Nazi tanks rolling over bleak Polish and Russian plains, and soldiers shooting people and letting them slump into mass graves. Mum didn't like me watching that kind of stuff, but I watched it anyway on my laptop when she was in the kitchen or when she was in her bedroom listening to music such as her favourite Beatles song *The Long and Winding Road* or doing yoga or pilates, both of which she loved. I used to call it Pontius Pilates.

A heavy-looking red tapestry, gripped by big black metal hooks, reached down to the floor of the arena in front of a *cubiculum* on the opposite side. I could see the same black hooks on our side, so I assumed there was a tapestry hanging in front of our *cubiculum* too. The tapestry opposite had the *SEMPER SUPERIOR* symbol on it in black, so I supposed the tapestry on our side did, too.

Where's Mum? I wondered.

Suddenly Sam hissed at me:

'Josh, I think I know why Carlo was kidnapped.'

The high walls around the *cubiculum* meant no-one else could hear us.

I stared at him. 'You do? Tell us.'

'Tiberius likes TV and movies, doesn't he? Carlo's a hero in *The Guardian of the Sword* and in *Raiders of Montego Bay*. I think Tiberius has seen the movies. I think that man Tiberius wants Carlo to do something heroic down here, for Cantia. That's the "important job" he was talking about.'

'But Sam,' I said, 'why would Tiberius imagine Carlo'd be happy to go along with their plan?'

Sam shrugged. 'I don't know.'

Declan glanced at me. 'Actually, after what your brother's said... I think I do.'

55

'What... what d'you mean, Declan?' I asked, though I was hardly able to talk to him; I still felt so awful about him and Lindsay.

'I can't believe I didn't work it out before,' he said, in the calm, relaxed, happy way of the well-loved and well-kissed. 'Maybe I would have, if I hadn't been concentrating so hard on keeping us all alive.'

'Work what out?' I said, deciding not to tell him what I thought of his attempts to 'keep us all alive'.

Declan said: 'It's to do with that TV presenter Carlo mentioned... he said her name was Emma Crucifus, didn't he?'

I nodded. 'Yes. She covers movie news, premieres in Leicester Square, that kind of thing. She hosts the movie programme *Show Reel* too.'

'Does she?' said Declan. 'I've never heard of it.'

'Oh, darling, you're very sensible not to watch an excessive amount of television,' Lindsay said to Declan boringly.

'Thank you, darling,' Declan replied.

'It's a pleasure,' Lindsay said, nauseatingly.

Declan looked around at us all. 'If that TV woman's name's Crucifus, it all makes sense.'

'Why?' I said, flatly, and still feeling sick and hopelessly heartbroken.

'Because,' said Declan, giving Lindsay a little private glance of love, 'like I said, there've always been some

Cantians who want to leave Cantia. Before they leave, they get a treatment which makes them think their memory of Cantia's just a dream. It's a bit like CAESAR's memory-wiping technique, only not as total. Of course, it prevents ex-Cantians giving away the secret of Cantia and, also, it stops them wanting to go back. The same procedure implants in their minds the desire to take the surname, "Crucifus", for their new lives in our world. After they take it, they think Crucifus has always been their name.'

'*Crucifus?*' I repeated.

Declan nodded. 'Yes. Maybe because the Cantians - many of them are very religious, like I said - feel that if anyone has to leave their beloved Cantia, it's as bad as being crucified, though having seen people crucified yesterday and today for the first time in my life, I doubt that.'

I tried to piece it all together. 'So... are you saying Emma Crucifus is a Cantian?'

Declan shook his head. 'No, I don't imagine she is, not if her English is good enough for her to be a TV presenter. Crucifans - that's what CAESAR calls them - basically have to learn English from scratch.'

I nodded slowly. Despite how awful Lindsay had made me feel, I knew I had to try to stay sane and coherent and not collapse into a hopeless pile of unloved lovesick uselessness. 'So... how does Emma Crucifus fit into this?'

'She'll have an ancestor who was originally from Cantia,' replied Lindsay's new boyfriend. 'Most descendants of Crucifus emigrants live here in Kent, as it's the county that contains Cantia, but some live farther away, even abroad. There are quite a few in Europe, and even some in America and in other countries. There are three in Japan and two in China. There's even a US lady senator with a Crucifus ancestor, but she's married so she has a different surname now. People who are called Crucifus have no idea why they have their surnames, any more than we usually know why we have *our* surnames.'

Declan drew a quick breath, then said: 'My hunch is Tiberius believes that, because Carlo's such a famous movie star, and plays heroes, he'd be willing to do something heroic down here, for Cantia?'

'An interesting idea,' I said, and not ironically, either. I had to admit that what Declan said made sense. 'You really think that's possible?'

'Yes, I do,' said Declan. 'And I think the reason why Tiberius believes that Carlo would go along with that plan is this: *Carlo has Cantian blood.* I've known it since we met him last night. Don't you remember what he said to us? About telling Emma Crucifus, during the interview, that his great-grandfather on his mother's side was a Crucifus? We know Tiberius watches TV, don't we? Well, what if Tiberius and his sidekicks were watching that interview?'

'But darling, Carlo said Tiberius's English isn't very good,' Lindsay put in.

'Yeah, I remember him saying that too,' said Declan. 'Well, maybe Custardface really is in league with Tiberius, and perhaps Custardface told Tiberius what Carlo had said.'

'How would that be possible,' I asked, glad to have found a chink in Declan's theory, 'when Custardface doesn't speak Latin?'

Declan shrugged. 'I don't know.'

'Also, darling,' Lindsay said, 'Carlo clearly doesn't know about his own Cantian blood, does he?'

'You're right, darling,' said Declan, 'he doesn't. But I bet you twenty kisses, that Tiberius and Custardface saw the interview Carlo had with Emma on TV: I mean the interview he told us about.'

'Oh, darling, you've worked it all out so very well, I think,' Lindsay said. 'But honestly, you don't need to *bet* me any kisses, you get them anyway!'

To avoid puking, I said, 'Declan, your theory's pretty crazy. But it just might make sense, in a crazy place like Cantia. Though if you're right, I don't think Tiberius would go to all the risk and trouble of kidnapping Carlo unless there was some... *incredibly* important reason behind it all.'

'What d'you mean, Josh?' Lindsay asked me.

'I mean,' I said, flatly, and avoiding most of her glance, 'I think Tiberius must be planning something very, *very* big.'

The crowd suddenly went quiet, and we looked to see what was happening. On the far side of the arena, the bars of the gateway had started to lift up. A dozen or so people wearing black armbands marched towards the centre of the arena. Some were in their twenties or thirties, but some about the same age as Lindsay and me, while a few were younger than the twins. They each carried long, grey musical instruments consisting of tubing that coiled within itself several times.

At the centre of the arena, they blew a deafening fanfare, which sounded like the whine of an ambulance or fire engine. I'd never seen such weird and spooky instruments. They reminded me of the whelks at the seafood stalls in the seaside town of Whitstable, about ten miles north of Canterbury, where Mum sometimes took the twins and me for a day out at the seaside.

I thought of those days, and how I missed them and wanted them to come back. Suddenly I missed them almost as much as I missed the time when Lindsay had really liked me and had enjoyed kissing me.

56

At the sound of the fanfare, the audience rose to its feet. To avoid looking out of place, we did the same. The spectators began to applaud in a very weird way: three sharp claps, then a pause, then three more sharp claps, and so on. We copied them. I suppose because we didn't have much choice.

Suddenly the fanfare and the applause stopped, so abruptly it would've been funny, if I'd been in the mood to laugh.

The audience sat down. Of course, that meant we did too.

Now the musicians turned in step and walked back through the gateway. A small army of acrobats - men, women, boys and girls, perhaps fifty people altogether - rushed out towards the centre of the arena, performing the most amazing acrobatics I'd ever seen.

If I hadn't been so not in the mood to watch it, and not so worried about Mum and so upset about Lindsay, I'd probably have enjoyed it. But when everything feels awful, you can't properly enjoy *anything*. Finally the acrobats ran out of the arena.

Next, two well-muscled Cantian men, wearing nothing but SS boxer shorts, strode side-by-side towards the middle of the arena, turned and bowed to each other before starting to wrestle.

For about half an hour, there was a stream of wrestling bouts, one after the other, featuring man against man, woman against woman, boy against boy and girl against girl. There were even some weird bouts where a man wrestled three women, or a boy wrestled three girls, the women or girls usually winning the fight - not surprisingly, it seemed to me, women and girls being dangerous enough by themselves, e.g. Dora, let alone when there were three of them.

Dora was so fascinated by it all she looked hypnotised. I guessed she was remembering all the moves to use in her next fight.

Then the wrestling bouts ended and some very different fights began.

These were weird, even by Cantian standards. These featured giant earwigs pitted against each other in one-to-one combat. The earwigs seemed to have the ability to survive any kind of injury, at least, up to a point. Once an earwig started getting beaten, it soon lost so many bits that, in the end, it often only consisted of a thorax with a leg and pincer attached, which was then finally reduced by the victor into a quivering thorax.

Things got even more violent after that. Half a dozen earwigs were set to fight against twenty giant maggots, which wasn't really a fight at all, because the poor maggots couldn't put up any resistance, and when the earwigs caught up with them they smashed their horrible rear pincers into the maggots and lots of white stuff shot out of the wounds - like if you'd stuck a fork into a blown-up balloon full of milk.

Every time a maggot got pincered, there was huge applause from the Cantians.

'Gross,' said Sam. He and Dora were both cringing in their seats by now, but I got the sense they were enjoying it, all the same.

I glanced at Declan. 'I thought you said the Cantians were a highly religious society?'

'Well, yes, Moonford, they are, or at least they were, before whatever's happening now, happened.'

I gave a nod, but didn't say anything back.

All I could hope was that, wherever Mum was, she wasn't looking at this. Mum hates violence.

After the last poor maggot had been pincered, earwigs were led off by Cantian men in hooded grey togas. It was interesting, in a weird way, that the earwigs obviously recognised their masters and were obedient to them. *Maybe the earwigs' brains get enlarged too*, I thought.

Then the remaining scraps of exploded maggots were dragged off like torn, oily white bedsheets. Silence fell throughout the amphitheatre.

57

Everyone in the audience, including us, was looking at the parapet.

And now three men emerged onto the parapet from a door at the back. They all wore black togas, with hoods, though they'd pushed the hoods back so we could see their horrible faces.

The one at the front had dark, curly black hair and a villainous-looking face. The one in the middle was hairy and heavily built. Even at that distance he looked like a large ape.

Declan leaned forwards to me. 'That guy at the front's Tiberius,' he explained, quietly. 'I don't know who the hairy guy is.'

'Oh, I see,' I grunted. I tensed, waiting for Lindsay to say something to him with 'darling' at the end. But mercifully she didn't.

The third man was almost completely bald, with bushy sideburns and he wore glasses with black frames...

'Look,' I said, in a hissed whisper. 'Him with the specs... *it's Custardface!*'

Right away I grabbed the front of my toga and hoisted it up to cover my face so that he wouldn't recognise me. I was quite far away, but for all I knew his glasses gave him sharp eyesight.

'Stop doing that, Moonford,' said Declan. 'You'll draw attention to us.'

All I wanted to say to Declan at that moment was: *you've*

stolen my girlfriend, isn't that enough? Don't think you can give me orders too. But I didn't say that, because despite all the hurt I was feeling, I obviously knew just how dangerous our situation was

I dropped the fabric of the toga, but put my hand up to cover some of my face.

There was a fourth man, too, though he stood some way apart from the others: as if he was aware he wasn't as powerful as they were.

'I know that guy over there, too,' I whispered to the others. 'He's a big-mouth called Antonius; the one I beat at chess and won the money from. He's a senator.'

'What are those things the soldiers are holding?' Sam said in a hissed whisper, pointing at two soldiers who had just appeared on the parapet. They were each carrying a long, silvery cylindrical object in both hands - it looked a bit like a high-tech machine-gun with complicated twists of metal running along both sides.

I leaned forwards towards Declan. 'D'you think that's the kind of gun we were shot with?'

'I don't know,' said Declan. 'Maybe.'

'I think it was one of those I saw in Custardface's holdall in the skeleton room in the museum,' I said.

The spectators suddenly burst into applause for some reason. We did too, to be safe. While the audience was clapping, Tiberius, who stood in front of the middle throne, lifted his hands above his head and began waving them in a boastful, mad way like a drunken football supporter. Custardface went to stand in front of the throne on Tiberius's right, and the ape-like man, who'd been in the middle, went to stand by the closest throne.

Declan glanced at Lindsay. 'Darling, I hope you're not

too scared. I know this must be frightening for you. But I'm here and I'll look after you.'

Lindsay smiled. 'Thanks, darling. I feel so much safer, knowing you're here.'

I noticed Troy giving Lindsay a seriously pitying look.

Well, at least no-one on the parapet seemed to have noticed us. Custardface turned to the soldier behind his seat, who handed him what looked like a white ball with a looped cord attached to it. Custardface took hold of the white ball, and slowly raised it high above his head. As he did, there was a massive roar from the crowd.

Only, now, I saw what I'd first thought to be a white ball was actually a *skull*. Custardface brought the skull down again and put the cord round his neck so that the skull hung down over his toga'd chest.

Was it the girl's skull from the Roman Museum? Tiberius stepped forward. The roar died down. He started to shout Latin in punchy phrases, which fortunately made my job of translating it for the others a lot easier.

'*Salvete, Cantia!*' Tiberius exclaimed. '*You knew me as your senator. I regret our former proconsul Augustus is seriously ill. I have taken over the government in Cantia with Maximus here on my right and Brutus on my left. Augustus has given the triumvirate his blessing! As for the other senators, they have paid on the crosses with their lives for their disloyalty and cowardice.*'

'The people who were crucified were other senators, just like Sam thought,' I hissed at the others. 'Augustus is ill and isn't proconsul any more.'

Declan nodded slowly.

'*Custardface calls himself Maximus down here*,' I whispered to them all.

As for Brutus, who could *he* be exactly?

'*These are great days for Cantia!*' Tiberius shouted. '*Today is the first of the Days of the Skull! Welcome to the days of the Godless Revolution!'*

I quickly whispered a translation to the others of this vile expression. Tiberius had used the Latin words *'profanus tumultus'* which means impious or unholy revolution, but I thought 'Godless revolution' a better translation.

Tiberius fell silent again and looked out over his audience. *'The days when we were given trifles in exchange for our Holy Wisdom are over. Now, we shall sell our Holy Wisdom... to whom we choose in the World Beyond, and take our rightful place in that world!'*

There was more applause. So the Cantians definitely did know about our world.

I whispered a translation to everyone of what Tiberius had just said. The applause died down. Then I turned to Declan again. I didn't want to speak to him, but I had to.

'Can Tiberius *do* this? I mean, can he sell Cantian science all over our own world? And what's this about a Godless Revolution? What about their religious beliefs?'

Declan shook his head slowly. 'I don't know what's going on at all, Moonford. Still, I should be safe enough here, as I'm an agnostic.'

'Well, I'm not,' I said.

Declan looked at me as if he'd never seen me before. 'No?'

'No,' I said. 'I'd say I believe in God. I accept there are many reasons *not* to believe in Him, but there are also plenty of reasons *to* believe in Him. Basically, though, I totally don't believe that the universe could have come into existence by itself. But right now I'm more bothered by what's going on here. We have to rescue Mum and Carlo, and then stop all this.'

Tiberius was shouting again:

'Citizens of Cantia! You will all benefit from our great

revolution! Our glorious new government shall take Cantia to the greatest heights ever achieved in our 1,500-year history! Cantia, Semper Superior! May God bless our revolution! May the Days of the Skull never end! Cantia has been reborn!'

The applause was now more or less total, though it didn't include everyone. Us, for example.

Another definite non-cheerer was an elderly, noble-looking black man sitting at the front of a tier of seats about twenty yards to our right. He wore a white toga, had short, curly grey hair and looked to me like someone of considerable importance. He was shaking his head slowly. I didn't think Tiberius had noticed him.

When the hubbub from the audience had died down, Tiberius went on:

'People of Cantia! Let me introduce to you my fellow triumvirs, Maximus and Brutus, who will help me lead Cantia to greatness! Now hear me, people of Cantia! Brutus has chosen a wife! The happy wedding will be held, today, on the Ides of September, the day we call the Celebration of Sanctuary! Yes, Brutus's wedding will take place today, here, now, in the amphitheatre, after the punishment of the criminals and traitors.'

'So you're telling us Brutus has chosen a wife,' Declan said. 'Lucky guy! Love certainly makes the world go round, doesn't it darling?' This with a glance at Lindsay.

'I've a horrible feeling who Brutus's wife might be,' I said.

Maximus/Custardface stepped forward. I wondered how he planned to address the crowd. What was he going to do: speak Cockney rhyming slang? After all, he couldn't talk Latin.

But when he did speak, it was perfect Latin, or at least as far as I could tell, anyway.

238

'*A revolution needs unity and strength,*' he said. '*Those who are not with us are against us.*'

'How can he speak Latin?' I gasped, to Lindsay, my treacherous ex. 'You remember how I heard him saying on his phone he couldn't understand their "crazy language", and now... he's speaking it!'

'Perhaps, when he spoke to that mysterious guy Stan, he was lying,' Lindsay suggested.

'Why would he lie to Stan?' I said.

'Maybe he knew you were listening to him,' Lindsay said.

I shook my head. 'If he'd known that, he'd've done something about it. No, I think somehow... he's learnt Latin in a week.'

As if to prove just how well he spoke the language of the Ancient Romans, Custardface started saying right away, in fluent Latin, that he and his brother Brutus were 'very pleased' to be two of the triumvirs of Cantia, and that they would be responsible 'for ensuring the people of Cantia support the revolution' and that if anyone didn't, they would 'soon regret it'. Custardface added that the 'Days of the Skull' would be the greatest in Cantia's history, and that all Cantians 'loyal to the revolution' would benefit.

Then, all at once, he stopped talking and stepped back. The horrible, hairy, ape-like Brutus stepped forward instead. In a voice like a barking dog - the way I'd expected him to speak - he shouted, '*Might is right! Victory to the strong! Power to the triumvirs! Death to traitors!*' before letting his sinister gaze sweep the entire assembly.

More applause rang out, though not from us. When this faded, a voice shouted '*Salvete, Cantia!*' to the right. It was the grey-haired elderly black man. He got to his feet, looking round out at the audience. As he stood up, the applause suddenly came to a stop. I felt sure this old man was an important man in Cantia.

'*My fellow Cantians, you know me as Senator Septimus. But I am not only your senator! I am your friend! Many of you have been guests in my house and have enjoyed excellent food and civilised conversation.*'

He looked at Tiberius. '*You yourself have been a guest in my house, Tiberius.*'

Tiberius said nothing.

Septimus went on: '*Tiberius, what is this terrible blasphemy about the "Godless Revolution"? Such a revolution is a disgrace for God-fearing and God-loving communities such as Cantia. And tell me, has anybody seen Augustus these past few weeks apart from you? I notice with relief he is not among the good brethren of the Senate, my fellow senators, whom you have seen fit to crucify. Ah yes, the crucifixions! Are you aware, Tiberius, that until yesterday, no Cantian has been crucified for more than a thousand years? Why have you brought that vile and barbaric punishment back into our midst?*'

Septimus raised his right hand and pointed directly across the parapet at Maximus and Brutus.

'*And, Tiberius, what exactly is the ancestry of Maximus and Brutus? I have only seen them before in the Senate. Are the rumours true that they are from the World Beyond, and that they have learned our beloved language through some new form of Holy Wisdom?*'

Septimus's eyes swept the audience as if he was confident many of them were on his side. Then he looked across the arena at Tiberius:

'*I think I need not remind you, Tiberius, that the rule in Cantia is made holy by our devotion to God and to the tradition of our great forefather, Aeneas of Troy, who founded the Roman*

Empire that gave us life, the empire destined to rule without limit. Here, in Cantia, we maintain the great and glorious tradition of pious religion of the Roman Empire, for we are the last of that empire and Cantia must therefore live forever, or there will be no Roman empire remaining. Hear me, Tiberius! You have brought evil into our world. I also command, as the true successor to Augustus, that there are to be no more crucifixions, do you understand? Now, answer my questions, Tiberius, in order that the citizens of Cantia may know the truth of what is happening in our world!'

Tiberius, Maximus and Brutus moved towards the edge of the parapet. I noticed Antonius leaning forward, too. The skull hanging down on Maximus's chest bounced a little as he moved.

'Septimus, be silent!' Tiberius shouted, *'you are old and foolish! The days when Cantians feared God are over. God is no longer necessary in our world, for we have great powers of our own, of which God Himself may be afraid. You do not even keep giant earwigs, as all true men should. You should not ask questions about matters you do not understand. As for the crucifixions, they were conducted to end the foolish lives of the weak senators. We only spared your life, because you were the deputy of Augustus and you are of the same dark race as he is. Hear me, Septimus! Today, the power in our world is in the hands of the triumvirs. The indecision of the Senate shall no longer prevent Cantia from taking its proper place in the World Beyond! You speak of rule without limit: that shall now be the rule of Cantia, using our Holy Wisdom. Sit down, Septimus, and be proud you are privileged to live in the new Cantia!'*

(By the way, I'd never heard the Latin word for 'earwig', *forficula*, before, but I guessed it from what he was saying.)

Septimus shook his head. *'No, Tiberius, I shall not still*

241

my tongue because you command me to do so. As for keeping giant earwigs, I do not wish to have anything to do with such dangerous beasts. Hear this, Tiberius: I DO NOT ACCEPT YOU AND YOUR FELLOW BLASPHEMOUS TRIUMVIRS AS OUR LEADERS! All Cantia deserves to know the truth about Maximus and Brutus. If you choose not to give me a satisfactory answer, Tiberius, I shall demand here, in front of our people and on behalf of our people, that you, Maximus and Brutus be expelled from office and arrested, and that the Senate shall once again assume power in Cantia!'

Septimus fell silent. I was just whispering to the others a translation of what Septimus had said, when two deafening bangs rang out.

I saw Septimus fall forwards against the low stone wall in front of him, topple over, fall headlong through the air and crash down onto the arena floor.

58

There were a few shouts from the audience, but mostly there was a complete, terrified, silence.

I was stunned. I mean, I'd never seen anyone shot before.

I didn't know for certain if Septimus was dead, but I thought he must be.

'*The bastards,*' Troy hissed. 'The old bloke didn't have a chance. He wasn't even armed. And with all these kids here watching, too.'

My eyes flashed back to Maximus and Brutus. They were both holding revolvers and grinning. Smoke curled from the barrels of their guns.

'I'm... really sorry you had to see this,' I whispered to the twins. 'I'm so sorry.'

Dora and Sam just stared at me. I didn't know what they were thinking. I mean, I couldn't tell whether they were horrified, exhilarated or maybe both. Instead of spending any more time trying to work this out, I looked out over the audience. I saw children crying, and adults crying too, which made me think that maybe the Cantians weren't as hard-hearted as I'd thought, and that maybe it was just their leaders who were.

Maximus pointed his revolver above him. He fired. I wondered if this shot would bring the entire Cantian sky crashing down onto the amphitheatre, but apart from a very loud bang, nothing happened.

Most of the wailing stopped abruptly. Maybe parents

had realised that putting their hands over their children's mouths was the best thing they could do at that moment.

The two soldiers with silvery guns advanced towards the wall and pointed the weapons threateningly in every direction. Now every spectator was in the line of fire.

Maximus and Brutus, still pointing their guns at the audience, began sweeping the guns slowly from side to side, as if to show that they would jolly well shoot *whoever* they wanted *when* they wanted. What a nightmare. This certainly was a Godless Revolution.

Tiberius, even, seemed momentarily unsteady on his feet and completely shocked. For a few seconds he didn't say a word, then he seemed to pull himself together.

'Oh people of Cantia...'

He gazed round at Maximus and Brutus, who returned his stare icily.

'You have all seen what happened to Septimus. In our new Cantia there is no room for compromise or weakness!'

He seemed to have fought some battle within himself and won . . . or lost.

'But, Cantians, hear me too when I say that the new Cantia will also be a place of joy! The triumvirate shall dispense justice to those who oppose us, but will also bring happiness to those who are on our side! So, fellow Cantians, I ask you to join with me today, on this great day that is so special for Cantia, in welcoming Brutus's bride to our Games!'

Tiberius clapped his hands twice. A few seconds later, two soldiers emerged from the top of the stairway leading to the parapet.

They were holding a woman between them, each of them holding her by one of her shoulders.

It was Mum.

59

Mum was staring down at the floor of the parapet.
'She must still be drugged,' Troy hissed at me.

I thought that must be the only explanation why Mum was the way she was. I just prayed none of these scumbags had been violent towards her.

'Yes,' I muttered. 'Perhaps she is.'

'There's no perhaps about it, mate,' Troy whispered back. 'Your ma's dosed up to the eyeballs.'

Tiberius started speaking again. I made a massive effort and managed to follow what the nutter was saying, or rather, shouting;

'People of Cantia! Before we can share the happiness of Brutus on his wedding day, there are debts to be settled! Septimus, a traitor to Cantia, has paid the price for high treason with his life! No longer shall he trouble our glorious revolution! In our old, weak world,' Tiberius went on, *'the worst punishment inflicted was for criminals to be fined, and sometime also mocked in public. But today, in the new Cantia, we shall be strong! Cantia, Semper Superior! Criminals who break our laws shall be executed!'*

Tiberius clapped his hands.

About twenty men and women in grey togas and dresses - I thought maybe these were prison clothes - were pushed into the arena through the open gateway by soldiers. The prisoners included four grey-haired elderly men, who reminded me of poor Septimus. All the prisoners were carrying swords, but the way they looked up at the audience made it obvious that they didn't want the swords and that the last place they wanted to be right now was here.

They moved away from the gateway as quickly as they could. And we could see why.

Now, six gladiators ran out through the gateway.

Two of them were dressed as *retiarii* - Roman fisherman-gladiators. Each one wore a black loincloth and carried a trident in his left hand. Their right arms were armoured from the shoulder down to the hand and held bedsheet-sized fishing-nets.

Two others I recognised as *provocatores*: I'd seen these in books about gladiators at school. They had heavy armour and bronze helmets with eyeholes that completely obscured their faces. They were carrying swords, and oblong shields with the Cantian symbol emblazoned on them.

The last two gladiators were dressed in Thracian style, with helmets a bit like the ones firemen wear. They carried small square shields in their left hands, had leg armour stretching above their knees down to their feet, and had short swords that had vicious, curved blades.

I blinked twice. 'Oh no...'

'*They're not real,*' Declan whispered.

'They look real enough to me,' said Troy.

'No, I mean they're artificial gladiators,' said Declan, leaning towards us and keeping his voice low. 'They're mentioned in my briefing file, but this is the first time I've seen them.'

I glanced at him. 'Artificial gladiators?'

'Yes,' said Declan. 'They're basically robots.'

'But how can the Cantians make robots if they don't have computers?' Sam hissed.

'They don't need computers to make robots,' Declan told

Sam. 'That's just how *we* think about technology. They've invented new types of materials they've trained to behave in certain ways.'

'How can materials be *trained*?' Sam persisted.

'Listen, Moonford Three, I don't actually know,' said Declan, 'but like I said, the Cantians have got their own materials technology, so they can do that sort of thing.'

I turned to Declan. 'Can we stop these artificial gladiators somehow?'

'I wish I could, Moonford. You don't think I was expecting any of this, do you?'

Maximus and Brutus were watching the scene in the arena with expressions of enormous enjoyment and anticipation on their faces, as if it was a particularly enjoyable Hollywood movie, or something you might see on 'the custard'.

The men and women were running as far away from the gladiators as they could, until they were lined up against the wall beneath the parapet.

Some of them dropped their weapons, and didn't bother to pick them up again. They knew that they didn't have a chance against the gladiators.

The gladiators moved slowly towards them in a really threatening way. They looked and moved realistically. If they were artificial, as Declan had said, they were amazingly advanced.

The hunted prisoners now turned and faced the gladiators.

'We have to do something to save them,' I hissed at Declan. 'We have to do something.'

'What, and get killed too?' he hissed back.

The gladiators came to a standstill and waited about ten yards away from their victims. The *retiarii* stood ready with their tridents, the *provocatores* with their swords and the Thracians with their curved swords. They stared up at the parapet.

Tiberius looked down at them.

Raising his right hand, he turned his thumb sharply downwards.

60

The two *retiarius* gladiators, each turning towards a victim, drew back their tridents and laughed in an eerie, robotic, high-pitched way.

Maximus and Brutus each grabbed hold of a silvery gun from the guard beside them, leaned over the wall and began firing lines of distorted air, the lines shimmering silver from the barrels of their guns towards the doomed prisoners. At the same time, the two gloating *retiarius* gladiators unleashed their tridents. The terrible three-pronged weapons shot through the air with horrible speed.

What can be happening? I wondered.

All I knew was that, by the time the tridents reached the place where the hunted men and women all stood, the victims had vanished. The tridents shot through the air, smashed into the wall with loud clangs and fell to the ground to join the discarded swords lying there.

The two gladiators who had hurled the tridents looked up at Maximus and Brutus, who both laughed very loudly, and very stupidly.

There was a strange silence throughout the amphitheatre, then Tiberius spoke again:

'People of Cantia! Witness the remarkable power of our new weapon. The traitors have been banished just one minute into the future! Observe, as they reappear!'

And we did. We waited. So did the gladiators.

It's strange: a minute isn't a very long time, and usually

you hardly notice a single minute passing, but we certainly noticed that one.

It seemed to take ages. There was no sound in the auditorium while it went on.

Then the minute was over, and the prisoners suddenly reappeared on the ground below the parapet. But because they'd been sent through time, just like we had, they were all weak, and they were all on the floor, trying to recover. While they were, those devilish gladiators launched their attack.

'Don't look,' I said to the twins, but they still ignored me completely. But Lindsay really didn't look; she buried her head in her hands. Troy, Declan and me looked; somehow I couldn't *not*.

It was completely awful and ghastly cruelty.

Was this what an audience in Ancient Rome used to watch? Were the Romans just bloodthirsty savages? Or was the ghastly spectacle in front of us what happened, I wondered, when people didn't have the chance to watch regular *pretend* horror and violence on TV?

I didn't think the prisoners would have been a match for the gladiators even if the prisoners hadn't been weakened by being shot with a time gun, but in this weakened state they had no chance at all. The gladiators didn't laugh - they were too robotic for that - but you could tell, from the enthusiastic way they did the killing, they were having a good time.

The *retiarius* gladiators seemed to take special delight in ensnaring their victims and wrapping their nets around them - like spiders wrap flies in webs - before delivering a frightful death-blow with their tridents. When they struck flesh, blood jetted out like a tap turned on full.

These were real deaths, not pretend deaths.

I looked at Mum. She didn't seem to have noticed any of it. She was still staring in front of her.

61

When every prisoner was dead, the gladiators threw the bodies onto a blood-soaked pile.

Tiberius looked down and shouted *'Gladiators! Return to your cells!'*

At once, in strange and silent unison, the gladiators marched back across the arena, heading for the wide gateway. As they did, Maximus and Brutus fired their time guns at the pile of dead bodies, which immediately vanished, leaving nothing behind but the blood-soaked ground.

Now Tiberius began shouting again:

'The traitors have been killed and their bodies sent a thousand years into the future, so their corpses shall not pollute Cantia!'

Tiberius's voice rang around the amphitheatre: *'This new and most remarkable weapon is called a Time Sword.'* What he said in Latin was *gladius temporis*: the sword of time, or a Time Sword.

'He says it's a "Time Sword",' I whispered to the others.

'That figures, here in Cantia,' said Troy.

'People of Cantia!' Tiberius went on, *'in our wisdom we, your triumvirs, have brought into Cantia someone of great fame in the World Beyond. He is a descendant of a Crucifus. We ask him to become our king, because he appeared in the fable of the Brave Raiders of the Sea. We planned to use his name and repute in the World Beyond, to advance our interests. But he has refused our kind offer! For this, he must be subjected to the Ordeal of the Beasts.'*

I translated all this.

'Declan,' I said, annoyed I had to rely on his knowledge but aware I didn't have any choice. 'What's the "Ordeal of the Beasts"?'

'I've no idea,' Declan muttered, 'but I don't like the sound of it.'

'Josh,' Lindsay hissed, '"the fable of the Brave Raiders of the Sea"... could that mean the movie *Pirates of Montego Bay?*'

I nodded. I didn't like Lindsay very much any more, but I didn't want to be rude to her, so I replied to her. Besides, I knew that our predicament, and Carlo's, was much more important than my own feelings.

'Yes,' I said. 'I think they did bring Carlo down here because he looks the part and they know he has Crucifus blood. Yes, now I understand. They wanted Carlo to agree to be king of Cantia, so Carlo would use his influence to help those creeps with all their evil schemes.'

'And they must have captured poor Carlo when he went to rescue Mum from Tiberius's house,' said Dora, sounding suddenly more grown up than I'd ever heard her sound, 'and Carlo must have told the tri-um-weirdoes he'd never want to be their king, *and now he's going to be killed.*'

Then I saw Carlo.

He was emerging from the gateway into the area, wearing only a white loincloth and sandals. He carried a bow and quiverful of arrows strapped round his bare back.

'God, no,' muttered Declan.

I was stunned. Carlo - in the arena! I glanced at Mum. Surely seeing Carlo would snap Mum out of whatever strange state she was in? But her face remained expressionless.

Then I heard the most blood-curdling roar I'd ever heard.

Carlo obviously heard it too. He ran out of the gateway at full pelt.

And then, as we watched, two enormous lions, lions out of a nightmare or a horror story, lions longer, taller, more massive than any I'd ever seen on TV or in movies - male lions with great black manes, massive, vicious jaws, huge muscled paws and golden-brown bodies, with muscles that rippled like the arms of a heavyweight boxer - padded out into the arena.

'Augustus had two pet lions, descended from lions that once fought in Cantia's amphitheatre centuries ago,' Declan murmured to me. 'Maybe Tiberius and those two oafs have put Augustus's pet lions into the Bio-Amplificator.'

The enormous lions roared so loudly, the whole amphitheatre shook.

62

So it was all now just like I said right back at the start of all this.

I wanted it to be a dream, but it wasn't.

The two giant lions were scanning the arena with glowing green eyes, the spectators in the amphitheatre stomping their feet and hurling bloodthirsty shouts.

Have the Cantians always been like this, I wondered, *or only since their Godless Revolution started?*

My heart thumping in my chest, I turned to Troy. '*I'm going to try to save Carlo.* I've got my sword. That big tapestry down there that's hanging from those hooks: maybe I could use it to lower myself down.'

Troy glanced down at the tapestry and the hooks. 'You're right. It might work. You go, and I'll follow you.'

Declan stared at Troy and then at me. 'What about me? Where do I fit in?'

'Nowhere,' said Troy, 'you're superfluous to requirements, just like you said I was.'

'OK, OK,' Declan replied. 'I admit I shouldn't have said that. Listen, I'm armed and I'm coming down into the arena with you both.'

'I'm coming too,' piped up Dora, 'and so is Sam.'

I turned to her. 'No, you're not. You and Sam stay here. It's much too dangerous.'

'Oh, yes,' Dora retorted, 'and watch the coolest man

in the world get EATEN ALIVE when we could try to save him?'

The giant lions roared again.

I glanced down at the tapestry, wondering if my weight would rip it. But I knew the tapestry was our only chance.

One of the huge lions, screaming and roaring, started rushing towards Carlo. Carlo quickly put an arrow in his bow and shot at the charging lion, but missed. The lion jerked to a standstill, then roared even more loudly.

I turned to Lindsay and kissed her quickly on the lips. She looked astonished, and taken aback, but maybe, just maybe, she didn't actually look cross.

'I... I need to say something to you,' I said.

'What, Josh?'

'I may get killed down there in the arena. Yes, that's very likely going to happen. But I want you to know that I really love you and I think what's happening between us - that you prefer Declan to me now - is a total nightmare.'

But she didn't even reply.

I couldn't bear to see how little Lindsay cared about me. I turned round and looked down at the floor of the arena.

Suddenly, the idea of dying didn't seem so bad after all.

It was much farther down than I'd thought it was.

Could I save Carlo? Could I kill a giant lion?

Seizing hold of the edge of the tapestry, I carefully climbed over the top of the wall. Then I lowered myself down. Even then, as I did it, I was amazed I did. I must have been running on hyperness and adrenalin, or maybe I was just so upset about Lindsay that I didn't care very much any more whether I lived or died. I hadn't decided what to do if one of the lions came to get me, though. I just kept on lowering myself down, supporting my weight by scrambling with my right foot against the wall and my left foot against the tapestry.

I let myself down as far as I could go, but the gap between the bottom of the tapestry and the ground was still taller than me. Bending my knees, I jumped the rest of the way hoping that, when I hit the floor, I wouldn't break an ankle.

Landing safely on the gravel, I quickly got to my feet.

The shouts of the crowd sounded even louder down in the arena.

Troy had kept his promise. He was about a quarter of the way down the tapestry now and... there was Declan, too, at the top, looking down.

But I'd been spotted. Lots of spectators were pointing at me, and there were even a few cheers. I unpinned my toga and let it fall to the ground, leaving me in just my red Greenpeace tee-shirt and my Chinos, which must have been quite a surprise for the spectators.

Then I took my gladius out of my trousers, where it had been ever since I'd picked it up from beside the unconscious soldiers. I threw off the horrible SS armband, too.

I ran as fast as I could towards Carlo. I didn't have time to think about things, even what might happen to Mum, I was just too much caught up in the moment.

Carlo fired another arrow at one of the lions, but missed again. Suddenly I remembered something Carlo's character, Salogel, said in the book *The Brotherhood* when he was asked how he could shoot so accurately. *"When I let loose an arrow,"* Salogel explained, *"my yearning soul shepherds it to its target."* The characters in fantasy books always talk like that. I wondered why, right now, Carlo's own soul wasn't 'shepherding' the arrow to its target.

I saw the giant lion farthest from me break away from the other one and run towards Carlo.

Carlo shot an arrow, and this time it struck home. The lion let out a mighty howl, jerked to a standstill and began pawing at the arrow, shrieking with pain as it did. The arrow had hit the lion just next to its left eye.

The other lion began to rush towards Carlo like a psychotic high-speed train. Carlo put another arrow into his bow and fired, but missed again. The lion went on running, so I screamed *'Here!'* at it, and, *'Come and get me!'* - completely forgetting we weren't supposed to be speaking English in Cantia.

The lion came to a scraping standstill like that same high-speed train doing an emergency stop, sending up giant clouds of dust. Then it turned and fixed me with its fiery orange eyes.

Suddenly I realised I didn't feel quite so brave after all, and wasn't quite so willing to die.

I knew if I tried to run away from the lion, I'd have no chance. But if I tried to stare it down, maybe... well, I was about to find out, because a moment later the giant lion started bounding towards *me*.

Its weight made the ground shake. I held the sword so tightly my hands hurt. I loved how the sword seemed part of me. I caught a glimpse of the spectators; they were on their feet, cheering.

Then I heard a shout. *'I'm here, man!'* It was Troy's voice. I didn't look behind me; I knew I needed to keep really focused on the lion. But it made me feel so much better Troy was there too, even though the terrible lion just kept on running at me, and even though, right now, Troy was too far away to help.

I lifted the sword with both hands. The giant lion opened its great vicious jaws; its roar seemed to split the earth and nearly knocked me over with its force.

My heart felt about to explode. The lion roared again. Its jaw must've measured a yard from top to bottom. Its front teeth were like four yellow daggers.

If I'm going to die here in the amphitheatre in front of all these people, I thought, *at least I'll fight.*

The huge lion fixed me with its orange eyes. Then it sprang.

63

The giant lion landed with an enormous thud about ten yards in front of me. The next moment, holding the handle of my sword ultra-tightly with both hands, I ran towards the huge beast. I don't know how I plucked up the courage to do that, but somehow I did.

The lion swiped at me with its ghastly giant paws, each claw at the end like a ferocious curved dagger. I kept low, trying to dodge them, weaving and searching for some weak point on the beast, and trying not to be scared to death. But the lion moved just too fast. It smacked at me again with one of its paws, and I felt the wind rush past my face, but the paw missed me by a few inches.

Then I saw one tiny chance, and I made the most of it. Glimpsing the lion's underbelly, I jumped up and used every bit of my strength to stab upwards into its belly with my sword, which sank deep into the lion's flesh.

Even as I stabbed, I couldn't help thinking that this wasn't quite what someone wearing a Greenpeace tee-shirt should be doing. But what could I do? I needed to protect us all. It was self-defense. So I gave the sword a final push, then let go, burying half the blade in the lion. It raced past me, roaring with pain, and smashed into the wall, making the ground tremble. It lay on its side, panting, blood streaming from the wound.

I felt a chill over me at having hurt it. It was an innocent creature being used by bad men. But all the same, I couldn't help feeling proud and triumphant, too.

I've just fought a giant lion, and won!

But were Lindsay and the twins still safe in the *cubiculum?* I looked up to see.

They weren't there.

Oh no, they've been captured.

But then I saw Lindsay standing in the arena, looking across at us in terror.

Wow. Lindsay's come down the tapestry. She was brave enough to do that. She doesn't even have a weapon. That makes her braver than Declan, Troy and me.

I felt a bit sick though when I wondered if her love for Declan had made her brave.

There were still a couple of swords on the floor of the arena. Obviously, no matter how I felt about Lindsay, I wanted to run to her and give her one of the swords. But there wasn't time. The lion which Carlo had shot was still pawing at his arrow, and watched us with its fiendish orange eyes as it prepared to charge again.

Then I noticed the twins coming down the tapestry, too, side by side, and they were about to drop onto the ground. They landed safely and began racing towards the swords lying on the ground.

But the lion had fixed its eyes on Dora and Sam. Troy yelled and waved his sword to distract it, and I did the same. Then - as Carlo, Troy and me were running to the twins to protect them - the beast reared up on its massive hind-legs and sprang at the twins, a solid mass of muscle, fur and claws. As it landed, it seemed to swallow up the twins as if they'd been squashed by a falling mountain.

64

Another terrible howl filled the air.

I realised it wasn't the twins who'd made the noise, but the giant lion.

It stumbled backwards, then fell over. Howling and roaring, it picked itself up. Only now did I see the three-pronged head of a trident buried in the lion's belly.

The twins! The twins have done it! I hadn't seen them grab one of the tridents that had clanged against the wall earlier, but obviously they had.

I was out of breath. Dora and Sam were lying on the ground near the wall, motionless.

I sprinted towards them. As I did, Carlo shot two arrows at the lion that had the trident in its belly. Shooting two arrows simultaneously was a trick Salogel had performed in *The Brotherhood:* I'd never realised Carlo could do it in reality. Maybe, until that moment, *he* hadn't either.

One arrow missed, the other scored a hit. The lion backed farther away, roaring. The roar from the spectators was almost as loud. And then the lion spotted me and I thought it was going to pounce again.

Troy ran towards me, sword in hand, as the lion let out another diabolical roar and rolled over on its side. And another tremendous roar, as it writhed in a mass of claws, muscle and jaws. One more roar, the most sorrowful I'd ever heard... and it collapsed with a massive thud.

I ran over to the twins.

Dora was conscious, but dizzy. She didn't look as if she was injured. Sam was groaning and pointing to a gash in his left thigh. I quickly ripped off my shirt, made a tourniquet and tied it round the top of his left leg.

Now I saw Declan on the arena floor. I wondered whether maybe winning Lindsay's love had given him enormous courage, or maybe he was actually braver inside than I'd ever imagined. He seemed to be really into the battle, and behaving like a hero, instead of the arrogant wimp he'd been so far.

Carlo, Troy and Declan were rushing towards the remaining lion, the one that had my sword still in its chest. The beast had got back up on its feet and looked warily at the three of them.

Then I saw a purple toga, with someone in it, tumble down from the parapet towards the lion. With amazing speed, the lion rose onto its forelegs, opened its huge jaws and sank its teeth into the person in the toga.

There was an utterly horrendous scream.

Then I saw the person in the toga was Tiberius, and he was the one who'd screamed.

The giant lion rose to its feet, shaking its mighty head. Tiberius shrieked... and then the only sound I could hear was a dreadful wrenching as the lion's jaws bit clean through him.

The lion shook its head again, and with a horrible ripping sound, Tiberius's body basically broke into two ragged pieces. His head, torso and arms fell on the floor of the arena in a shower of blood.

Why did Tiberius fall from the parapet? I wondered.

The lion stood where it was, staring at us. It was breathing in fast, thick gasps. I expected Maximus and Brutus to fire their revolvers at it, or for them to shoot the wounded beast with the Time Sword. But Maximus and Brutus didn't move and didn't fire.

Then I saw Lindsay.

She wasn't carrying her sword. She walked slowly up to me then, after lightly touching my hand, she went on walking forwards.

Towards the lion.

I was too paralysed with amazement and horror to do anything to stop her, and by the time I stopped being paralysed she was so close to the lion, I knew if I ran towards it to try to protect her I'd only put her in more danger.

Lindsay lifted her hands up towards the lion. I suddenly realised she was somehow trying to communicate with it.

The lion simply stared at Lindsay with its great orange eyes.

My heart thumped in my chest.

Lindsay, her arms still raised, walked right up to the lion. She didn't stop, but my heart nearly did.

The lion twisted its head to watch her.

Now, Lindsay took a few more strides until she was under the lion's belly. She reached up her right hand and took hold of the handle of my sword, which dangled from the lion's body. Carefully, gently, she eased the sword out and threw it away to her left. It landed on the ground some way from the animal. I expected loads of lion blood to come out, but the wound released only a trickle of blood.

The lion slowly sank to the ground whimpering and laid the left side of its great head on the floor of the arena.

I wondered if it would recover. I hoped it would, though obviously not now. I didn't want it to chase after us anymore. But it just lay there on its side, breathing slowly.

An enormous cheer rang round the amphitheatre.

I wanted so much to hug her and kiss her. But of course I couldn't do that.

I hurried towards her, but kept my distance.

'How... how did you know the lion wouldn't kill you?' I asked her.

'I just had a feeling it wouldn't,' she gasped.

Maximus and Brutus were standing, looking out over the parapet, surveying the scene. I watched those two scumbags draw their revolvers, but then they looked round at the cheering crowd and stuffed the guns back inside their togas.

I caught a glimpse of Mum, but couldn't tell if she was still spaced out, or just stunned by what she had seen.

The cheering went on.

It's finished, we've won, it's over.

But then I saw the robot gladiators emerging from the gateway on the opposite side of the arena.

They were heading towards us.

65

Carlo, Troy and Declan had seen the robot gladiators too. I ran to pick up my sword from where Lindsay had tossed it down. Then I hurried towards the men.

As I neared Carlo, I saw that he still had a dozen arrows in his quiver. Now he turned towards the gladiators. Both the *retiarii* had re-armed themselves with tridents.

Troy and Declan rushed to Carlo's side. Carlo was already firing; he really was as accurate as Salogel now. He picked off two gladiators - a *retiarius* and a Thracian - even before they came face to face. Both arrows struck the gladiators deep in their unarmoured faces. They made weird jerking movements, then collapsed on the ground.

So now there were four left: a *retiarius*, a Thracian and two *provocatores*. Carlo wounded the Thracian with another arrow in the chest. The gladiator looked shaken, but kept on coming.

As I ran to be with Carlo, Troy and Declan, I felt drunk with excitement at having the chance to fight, and perhaps die, alongside them. I was just so hyper, and so happy Troy was on our side. And even Declan, the more-brains-than-brawn literary genius, was completely mental with battle-lust now. He dodged the wounded Thracian's lunging attack and plunged his sword into the Thracian's chest, bringing the gladiator to his knees.

Declan tore the sword out of the gladiator's chest, then began hacking at the Thracian's neck with the side of his sword.

I knew the gladius wasn't too sharp on the sides of its blades, and Declan needed four or five blows before he managed to behead the Thracian. There wasn't any blood, so I supposed he must've been right about them being robots. I didn't feel bad about them being killed because they weren't really alive, just horrible sinister sort of machines.

Troy, meanwhile, stabbed the *provocator* in the neck and chest. The gladiator collapsed.

A massive roar erupted from the crowd.

The other *provocator* charged. I held hard onto my sword with both hands and ran forward to meet him.

And then excitement surged up from deep in me and I became faster and more agile than the nasty artificial scumbag of a creature I was up against. Cantian 'Holy Wisdom' was clearly advanced stuff, but making artificial gladiators, who were truly effective against warriors like us who could fight back, seemed too tough a job even for the Cantians. I stabbed the *provocator* under his breast-plate, dodging his blade, but the handle struck me hard on the front of my head, knocking me to the ground and making me see stars.

When I got to my feet again, I saw the *provocator* lying on the ground. I raced towards him, meaning to stick my sword through his robotic throat, but he no longer moved. His eyes were staring upward into nothingness. He was dead - or whatever the robotic equivalent of death is.

Only one *retiarius* was left now, edging nervously back from us. *Is it scared?* It lifted the trident in its right hand and the net in its left. We marched towards it, full of blood-lust. Carlo fired an arrow that, amazingly, pinned the net to the ground. The *retiarius*, still holding the net, stumbled and fell over.

Troy and Declan moved in, wrestled the trident from the

robot, used the trident to pin it to the ground by its neck, then chopped off its head with their swords, each striking a blow in turn like two woodmen chopping down a tree.

66

Ear-bashing yells and foot-stomping reverberated round the arena. The noise was deafening.

I glanced at the giant lion, the one Lindsay had 'tamed'. It still lay on its side, breathing slowly. I had a feeling it would recover, though I was pretty sure its fighting days were over.

But the other lion was certainly dead. It lay without moving, like a great toppled statue. Carlo, Troy, Declan and I ran back across the arena to the twins and Lindsay.

Dora was on her feet, but Sam still lay on the ground, his leg slowly bleeding through the tourniquet I'd made.

The crowd went on cheering. Carlo pointed towards a door on the far side of the arena. I followed his finger. Mum was on the parapet. And suddenly I saw her break away from the soldiers, race towards the front of the parapet, and jump.

For a terrible moment I thought Mum wanted to commit suicide to avoid marrying the ape-like Brutus. But then I realised what she really had in mind.

She's trying to cushion her fall by landing on the dead lion. As I realised this, I saw that Mum's face was alert and wide awake again. She was looking all around her, obviously amazed at where she was, and what was happening. Yet somehow, I didn't know how, she'd managed to keep control and work out a plan.

And now Mum put the plan into action, jumping and landing on the back of the dead beast. The lion's muscles were obviously springy enough, even in death, to break her fall.

Mum grabbed the lion's fur to slow the fall, and quickly lowered herself onto the ground. Dora gave a quiet cheer: the roaring of the crowd drowned her out. Not for the first time, I realised what a totally amazing Mum I had.

I ran over to her. 'We've got to get out of here! We could be shot at any moment with a revolver or the Time Sword!'

All of us, including Mum, ran as fast as we could towards the gateway, with Carlo and Mum supporting Sam between them.

The spectators were still cheering. I expected Maximus and Brutus to fire their guns or the Time Sword at us at any moment.

But they didn't fire any shots. I wasn't sure why, but maybe they thought we were all giving the citizens of Cantia too much good entertainment to want to shoot us. The two scumbags who ran Cantia now were into entertainment, weren't they? After all, the very first time I'd met Custardface he'd talked about the Roman Museum being even better than the TV.

Within half a minute we were all through the gateway and into a glowing yellow corridor that seemed to stretch a long way. Behind us we could still hear the cheering of the crowd.

Troy, Declan and me, our swords still drawn and dripping, led the way. Our shirts, shorts and bodies were covered in lion blood. I called out to everyone behind me to see what weapons they had. The twins had left their trident in the lion. Carlo had left his sword in the arena. But he still had his bow and quiver and a couple of arrows left.

More Cantian soldiers might appear at any time. My forehead was really sore and a bruise was swelling up.

271

'We have to get medical help for Sam,' panted Carlo.

'He's losing a lot of blood,' said Mum.

'Declan can help us,' Dora told him.

'Why d'you say that?' asked Carlo.

'Because he knows all about Cantia,' explained Dora.

'Really?' said Mum.

Dora nodded. Mum turned to me. 'What *on earth* are you, Dora and Sam doing here? And what's Carlo Clancy doing here'

'Well, at least you recognise him this time, Mum,' Dora said.

'Of course I recognise him, Dora,' said Mum.

'But Carlo once came to the shop and bought some things and you *didn't* recognise him,' Dora said.

'I did,' said Mum, 'but I could tell he didn't want to be recognised, so I didn't give him any sign that I had.'

Well, that was a surprise.

Mum glanced at Lindsay, 'are you Lindsay Penhaligon?'

'Yes, Mrs Moonford, I am.'

'And I suppose this boy is Troy Wilson?'

'That's right, Mum,' I said.

'Hello, Mrs Moonford,' said Troy.

'Dr Penhaligon was on the TV news,' Mum said. 'I met him and Mrs Penhaligon and Mr Wilson every evening... until I was kidnapped.'

'You met my dad?' Troy sounded stunned.

'Yes,' said Mum, 'He's a jolly nice chap. So you're Troy! I recognise you from the newspapers and the TV. Yes, Troy, we've all been worried sick.'

She looked hard at our very own Salogel. 'Hello, Carlo. I was woozy, but I saw you in the corridor.'

Carlo smiled. 'I saw you too.'

'Mum, listen,' said Dora. 'We missed a whole week!'

'What do you mean, darling... I mean, Dora?'

'We'll tell you later,' I said, 'assuming we make it out of here alive and there is a later.'

'All right,' said Mum.

Then we moved as fast as we could. Sam, being the most badly injured, was slowing us down, but no-one pointed that out.

The corridor, with its glowing yellow walls, seemed endless, and then it went round a corner to the left, and maybe ten yards after we'd turned the corner we found ourselves passing a small room with vertical bars on it, and no door.

In the room, which was basically an empty cell except for one of the Cantians' stumpy little chairs, was Marcus. He was sitting on the chair. His arms were folded in front of him and he looked utterly miserable.

He stared up at us and we stared at him.

'What are you doing there?' I asked him, in Latin.

'Senator Antonius has become friends with Tiberius,' Marcus said. *'Antonius hates my mother and father and has sent them into the arena. He hates me too. He's going to feed me to the bio-amplified lions.'*

'Who is he, Josh, and what's he saying?' Mum asked.

'This is Marcus, who taught me Cantian chess. It sounds like his parents were among the people we saw get killed.' I knew I wasn't being insensitive in saying this in front of Marcus, as Marcus didn't speak English. 'Marcus says they're planning to feed him to the giant lions.'

'Not any more,' Troy put in.

'Dead right,' I said. I glanced at Troy and then at Declan. 'Can you see if your swords can do anything to the bars?'

Troy and Declan didn't need persuading. They started chopping at the bars with all their might. I took my sword and joined in. It was like chopping very hard wood. Marcus got off his seat and stood back. A minute or so later, we'd cut away enough of the bars for Marcus to squeeze through.

'Sally Vetty,' Dora said to him, after he had.

Marcus gave her a Roman salute. *'Salvete, puella pulchra.'*

Dora glanced at me. 'What's he saying about poo?'

I shook my head. 'He didn't mention poo, Dora. He just said "Hello, beautiful girl" in Latin.'

'Hey, listen,' said Troy. 'I've not just about pulled my arms out of their sockets to cut these bars to free this guy so he can chat Dora up!'

'I shouldn't worry, Troy,' I said. 'Dora only knows about two words of Latin, and Marcus can't speak a word of English.'

'Yet!' exclaimed Sam.

Troy glanced at Sam, but said nothing.

'Thanks to you all for rescuing me,' said Marcus. *'Now I must go and find my parents.'*

I shook my head slowly. *'I think your parents are dead, Marcus. I'm really sorry.'*

He just stared at me. *'Dead?'*

'I think so. I'm so sorry.' What else could I say? Of course, I didn't know for certain that his parents had been among the prisoners, but it seemed pretty likely they were.

Tearfully, Marcus said: *'Then I must go to see Septimus, my grandfather who is a senator. He will take care of me.'*

All of a sudden my throat felt lumpy again.

'That old guy who got shot is his grandad,' I told the others.

'Josh, don't tell him about the old man,' said Declan. 'The kid'll probably have a nervous breakdown.'

'What choice do I have?' I said. 'If I don't tell him the

truth, he'll try and find Septimus, and probably get himself killed too.'

I turned to Marcus. *'Your grandfather Septimus is dead, too. I'm very sorry. But you don't need to worry about the lions any more. They can't hurt anyone now. Come with us.'*

Marcus still looked too shocked to speak.

At last he managed to say: *'Who are these people with you?'*

'They're from the World Beyond,' I told him. *'We all are.'*

'Does the World Beyond truly exist?' Marcus asked, in Latin of course. 'I have heard of it, but I thought it was only a legend.'

'Yes, Marcus, the World Beyond does exist,' I said.

Marcus nodded slowly.

Now we all ran, though there was a limit to how fast we could go, because of Sam. I kept expecting to meet Cantian soldiers with instructions to kill us. We raced a couple of hundred yards down the corridor, which started to veer to the right. We went on down it.

'So you're in on all this?' Carlo said to Declan, as we hurried along.

'Yes, I'm afraid I am.'

'Why didn't you tell us before?'

'Er... um...' said Declan.

'It didn't suit his purposes,' I said.

'Well, Declan,' Carlo told him, 'maybe, in that case, you should change your purposes.'

'Yes, sir,' said Declan, 'I already have.'

'I'm glad to hear it,' said Carlo.

'Mum, did they drug you?' I asked her.

Mum nodded. 'I'm afraid so.'

'They're devils,' I said.

'Well, yes they are, but the drug's worn off now,' Mum said.

'Thank goodness for that, Isabella,' Carlo put in.

Mum looked bewildered. 'How do you know my name, Carlo?'

'Because,' said Carlo, 'I remembered you from your shop, and Josh told me who you were. I know the name of everyone here, Isabella. They're like old friends now.' He looked round at me, Dora, Sam, Lindsay, Troy and Declan. 'Thanks for coming to my rescue, and saving my life.'

'It was a pleasure,' said Dora.

'Carlo,' said Mum, 'what are you doing down here anyway?'

'That's a long story, too,' Carlo told her, 'and this definitely isn't the time to explain.'

'What language are you all speaking?' Marcus asked me.

'The language of the World Beyond,' I said. *'Actually, there's quite a lot of your language in it, to be honest.'*

'How is that possible?'

'That's a long story too,' I said.

There was something on my mind and I just had to ask Mum about it.

'Mum, nothing . . . nothing else happened to you, did it?'

She shook her head. 'No, Josh. My ghastly prospective husband didn't go anywhere near me, thank goodness. Their real names are Vincent and Dinsdale Stokes. I found that out before they drugged me. They're brothers.'

I just stared at Mum. *'Dinsdale?'* I said.

67

'Yes,' said Mum, 'Dinsdale. That's his name.'

'It didn't mean dinner at all,' said Sam. 'It was a nickname.'

'Maybe Dinsdale was in prison and "Stan" got him out,' Lindsay suggested.

'What are you talking about?' Mum asked them.

'I'll tell you if we ever get safer,' I said 'Mum, did anyone push Tiberius?'

'Yes, Dinsdale did. I don't know if anyone else noticed, except of course his ghastly brother. I had to have breakfast with the three of them this morning. Tiberius obviously completely misjudged Vincent and Dinsdale. He thought he was in charge.'

At that moment I heard the patter of footsteps coming towards us - they sounded like rather small ones - from the part of the corridor we couldn't see. Declan and Troy held their swords at the ready, but I'd put mine back into my shorts. Now I drew it out and stood next to the others. We were a wall of swords.

Who, or what, were we about to meet next?

68

It was a person rather than a thing - which made a pleasant change.

He was a very small man in a short white toga, with fair hair and clear bright sky-blue eyes.

He nearly collided with Troy, but just managed to stop running in time. The tiny man stared at my sword, but didn't seem too bothered by it.

I decided to put it back in its sheath; the tiny man didn't appear to be a threat.

'This is the guy who brought me my horrible meal,' Carlo said.

The little chap looked at Carlo for a few seconds, smiled faintly and maybe also guiltily, then began to speak so quickly, I only just managed to follow his Latin.

'Hooloo's master Tiberius is dead! Brutus... such an evil man he is!... pushed master off the parapet and into the jaws of the great lion. They thought Hooloo did not see. They are making Cantia into a place of nightmares! They call it the Godless Revolution. They are wicked, wicked, wicked men! But they do not know that Hooloo has from his master much authority here in the amphitheatre. Follow me. Hooloo will do all he can to help you, and perhaps you will not die.'

'He wants to help us,' I told the others, and quickly told them what he'd said. I'd worked out that he liked talking about himself in the third person.

I glanced at Hooloo. *'Do you speak the language of the World Beyond?'*

I thought he might have been into TV, like Tiberius seemed to be.

'Indeed no, young Saxon warrior,' Hooloo said, with a shake of his head.

I was disappointed he didn't speak English. I thought 'young Saxon warrior' was a pretty cool thing to be called, though. But all I said to the others was: 'He says he doesn't speak English.'

Declan nodded. 'I imagine he'll only speak Latin, and his own language.'

'Own language?' Lindsay repeated.

'These tiny Cantians are all members of the Ileik people,' Declan said. 'They descend from the original Neolithic Britons, who built Stonehenge. In our world they've all died out and we know almost nothing about them, but a hundred or so of them survive in Cantia. I guess there were lots of them working to carve and then transport Stonehenge. They have their own language, called Ileik. Of course, that's died out in our world too.'

I suddenly wondered if some of the people in the audience, who I'd thought were kids, were really Ileik.

'Come! You must hurry!' Hooloo called.

We quickly followed him. After maybe twenty or thirty yards Hooloo stopped at the outline of a door in the strange yellow glowing wall. He looked at the outline intensely for a few seconds. The top of the door slid upward, giving an opening we could run through into a room that was about twice the size of our sitting-room at Prospect Place. This room didn't have any windows, though.

Hanging up on a wall, from grey hooks, were clothes and armour which wrestlers, gladiators or soldiers would wear:

breast-plates, loin-cloths, leg-armour, black boots, belts, tunics and helmets. Leaning against the opposite wall were weapons: swords in scabbards, and short curved swords like the ones the Thracian-style gladiators had used, and vicious-looking spears and tridents. There were fishing-nets, too. It was strange to see all these old-fashioned weapons after watching the Time Sword in action.

'*Refresh yourselves,*' Hooloo told us, pointing to a stumpy table on the far side of the room with a grey metal jug on it, and some grey cups.

'*What's in there, Hooloo?*' I asked him.

'*Water. Drink. You must all dress in whatever you wish and arm yourselves. Hurry. We have little time.*'

'He wants us to drink if we're thirsty,' I told the others.

'*If* we're thirsty?' said Dora. 'I'm *incredibly* thirsty.'

'I could drink a lake,' said Troy.

'OK, so we'll all drink,' I said. 'And he says, put on whatever you want to wear and take weapons. And *hurry.*'

Carlo nodded. 'I think everyone should put some armour on, too.'

'We need a doctor for Sam,' Mum said.

'Will Hooly find us a doctor, Declan?' Dora asked.

'Actually... it's H-U-L-L-U,' said Declan.

'I can't get dressed,' moaned Sam. 'My leg hurts too much.'

'I'll take care of you,' Dora told him.

My bruised head was hurting too, but I decided not to mention it. Hullu ran up to Sam and looked intently at the nasty gash in Sam's left thigh. Then he turned round in a graceful fashion, walked over to me, reached up and touched my head. I winced. Hullu's beautiful, clear blue eyes were full of thought.

He went over to a drawer in a little cupboard under the weapon-rack and pulled it open.

'*Get dressed, quickly!*' he called out to us in Latin.

But we all watched him instead because, by now, we'd all noticed a small, gold-coloured, glowing sphere, about the size of a tennis ball, that he was holding in the tiny fingers of his right hand.

69

I was sure Marcus must've known about some of the weird Cantian technology, but he'd obviously never seen this glowing sphere thing before. He was as amazed as the rest of us were.

Hullu hurried back to Sam and moved the glowing sphere back and forth over Sam's wound for a few seconds, then came over to me and did the same to the front of my head. Right away, my head felt much better.

Sam's wound stopped bleeding, and seemed to have healed a bit, but it still looked red.

I turned to Hullu. '*Thank you. What is that?*'

'*The Ball of Wellness,*' Hullu replied. '*It helps to heal, but only God can cure completely. If we use doctors here, the evil men will find you. The boy can now continue travelling with you.*'

'Thanks, Hullu,' I murmured, and told the others what Hullu had said.

'Can you ask titch if we can take that golden thing with us?' said Troy. 'We might need it.'

'Yes, good call,' I said. I turned to Hullu and asked him.

But Hullu shook his head. '*Hullu is sorry. It only has healing powers when used in this room.*'

'He says it doesn't work anywhere else,' I told Troy.

'It must use some special force-field to alter biochemical structures,' said Sam.

'Well, Sam, whatever it does,' Mum put in, 'I'm still worried about you.'

I turned to Hullu. *The boy has lost much blood.*

'Tell him to drink water now,' said Hullu. *'If he does, the power of the Ball of Wellness will give him more blood.'*

'Is that really possible, Josh?' Mum asked, once I'd translated.

'I think, in Cantia, anything's possible.'

'Then Sam must drink,' said Mum.

'We all must,' added Carlo.

Sam drank some water. Then we took turns and drank lots. Fortunately there was plenty of water in the jugs. As I drank, my whole body started to feel much better after everything we'd gone through.

Some colour had come back into Sam's cheeks, although he still didn't seem himself; and he looked really anxious. I saw Sam glance at Dora. 'How are you feeling?' I asked him.

'A bit better. I'm terribly worried about Bruce, though.'

'I'm sure he'll be all right, Sam,' I said. I wanted to add *and we'll be back home soon, anyway*, but I didn't, because I think if you hope too much for something great to happen, very likely it won't.

Dora glanced at Sam. *'Tell them,'* she hissed at him.

70

S am looked at me, Dora, Mum, and back to me again.
'Tell us what?' I asked.

Sam went red. He undid the zipper of his shorts and reached down into them. I could see the white elastic of his underpants.

He tugged out the small blue plastic food container he keeps Bruce in when he takes him on an outing. There were air holes in the top that Sam had made so Bruce could breathe.

'You... brought Bruce with you?' I gasped at Sam.

Sam nodded. 'The container fitted quite well in my pants. And obviously there was no danger of it falling out, because...'

'... why did you bring him?' I asked him.

'Because Sam's *mental*,' Dora put in.

'Well, last week, when I knew Dora and I were going to the Roman Museum with Troy,' said Sam, 'I didn't want to be left out, so I came with Bruce.'

He paused for a moment, and looked sorrowful. 'I suppose Bruce is dead now, though, from all the running round we've been doing. I've been too scared to look to see if he is.'

'I will,' I said. I eased off the lid. Sam gave a yelp, turned away and buried his head in his hands.

Bruce was curled up into a little tyre of black coils close to some bark-chips. There was no lettuce or cucumber in the container. Sam would have put some food into the container, so I supposed Bruce had already eaten it.

I lifted Bruce out of the food container and put him into the palm of my hand. He felt cold to my touch, but then he was cold-blooded, so he would have done anyway.

Bruce didn't move on my hand.

'Well?' asked Sam in a stressed, high-pitched voice.

'I'm sorry, Sam,' I said. 'I think he's...'

But then I felt something, a wriggling, leggy tickle on my palm.

'He's alive!' I yelled.

Sam opened his eyes, stared at Bruce and broke into a beaming smile. Bruce began to unwind, and strolled over my palm, which I had to keep turning, to keep him horizontal, so he wouldn't fall off.

Dora clapped her hands. Marcus smiled too, obviously very happy seeing Bruce alive.

'Dora, you knew about Sam bringing Bruce down here, didn't you?'

'Not to start with. Only since last night in the holy house. I'm really glad Bruce is OK, but Sam's *so stupid* for bringing him.'

Declan came over to inspect Bruce, then gave Sam a puzzled look. 'What exactly is it?'

'My giant millipede,' Sam explained. 'I love him.'

Dora sighed loudly.

'I hope Bruce won't bite Josh's hand,' Lindsay said.

'No, he only bites if he gets cross,' said Sam.

Bruce began walking up my arm.

'He must curl himself up tightly if he gets jolted about,' I said. 'In that little hard ball, he'd be safe.'

Hullu broke into a bright smile, and started jabbing his little right forefinger at Bruce without actually touching him.

'*Vermiculus! Vermiculus!*' he exclaimed excitedly.

'Cantians, living underground as they do, have a deep cultural attachment to worms and other creepy-crawlies,' Declan explained.

'I can't imagine why,' I said.

'Bruce *isn't* a creepy-crawly,' protested Sam.

'Sorry,' said Declan.

I put Bruce into the container and gave it back to Sam.

'*We must leave now,*' Hullu said.

'*Hullu, where are you taking us?*'

'*Young Saxon warrior, I know of two paths upward from Cantia to your world. The evil men know of the paths too. They will place guards there so you cannot use those paths to escape.*'

Hullu fell quiet, then raised his small right hand and, speaking much more calmly now, extended the same finger that, a minute or so ago, had jabbed excitedly at Bruce.

'*But there is a much older path, that lies deep in Terra Horridissima.*'

I glanced at Declan. 'What's *Terra Horridissima?* One of those badlands you told us about?'

'Yes. Just about the worst, according to the Cantians. I wasn't even sure *Terra Horridissima* really existed. I've always thought it was a legend.'

'*Are you sure there's a path to the World Beyond through Terra Horridissima?*' I asked Hullu.

'*Why would Hullu tell you of the path if it did not exist? Do you not know that a stultus always speaks the truth? Some believe there is a great sea above near where it begins, but Hullu thinks such a sea above our heads cannot possibly exist.*'

'*Yes, Hullu,*' I told him, '*there is such a sea. I've often swum in it in the summer.*'

'*What is summer?*'

'*Maybe I'll tell you one day,*' I said, feeling a bit tearful inside. Hullu suddenly turned and glanced at Marcus. *'You are a Cantian?'*

'Yes. I am Marcus, son of Tertius and Fulvia.'

'They are dead,' Hullu said, with a sorrowful nod. *'And Septimus, father of your father Tertius, is dead too, I regret to inform you.'*

'I know,' said Marcus. *'I no longer wish to live in Cantia. I wish to see the World Beyond, where my new friends live.'*

Hullu shook his head. *'The World Beyond does not exist.'*

'Josea told me it does, and I believe him,' Marcus said.

Hullu just looked bewildered.

I glanced at the others. 'Marcus wants to come back with us.'

'Great!' Dora exclaimed.

'I wonder if he'll like burgers?' Sam put in.

'After what the Cantians eat,' said Declan, 'I should think that's very likely.'

'Assuming we get home,' I said. I quickly translated the rest of what Hullu had said.

'What does Terror Whatsit mean, anyway?' Troy asked.

'It's Latin for "Most Horrible Land",' I said.

'Oh, that's just *great*,' said Troy.

'But if the path back up to our world is close to where the overhead sea is,' I said, 'the path can't be far away. After all, Whitstable - which is by the sea - is only five miles north of Canterbury. But we can't go home yet.'

'I agree,' said Lindsay. 'We need to stop what's happening here in Cantia.'

I nodded. 'You bet we do. We can't have Vincent and "Dins" selling Time Swords throughout the world. Somehow we need to stop this ghastly Godless revolution, because if we don't... and if we don't make it home, no-one will ever know what's happening down here ... or what's happened

287

to us, apart from CAESAR. We know what Vincent and Dinsdale are planning: to sell Time Swords in our world to every bunch of criminals or terrorists that'll buy them.'

Carlo nodded, then looked at us all. 'OK, listen. I agree with Lindsay and Josh. We can't leave here until we've done what we can to stop the revolution and deal with the bad guys.'

'I completely agree with Carlo,' said Mum.

I was puzzled she didn't find Cantia more shocking and terrifying. I could only suppose she was too hyped up about everything to bother much with where we were. She sounded really determined, which surprised me a bit, as I'd have thought she'd have been more interested in getting the twins home.

Hullu looked at me. *'What is it you are all saying?'*

I quickly translated what we'd been talking about.

Hullu shook his head slowly. I could tell at once he didn't agree with our plan. *'But if you do not leave very soon the evil men will come for you, capture you and kill you all, except the woman of great beauty, who will be married even if she does not wish it!'*

'Hullu,' I said, *'we know the risks, but we don't have any choice. What's between here and the entrance to Terra Horridissima?'*

'There are fields used for growing food,' Hullu said, *'and then there is the Hall of Holy Wisdom.'*

I glanced at Declan. 'Do you know what the Hall of Holy Wisdom is?'

He nodded. 'Yes, it's where the Cantians develop their technology, their "Holy Wisdom".'

'Do you know if we can find any weapons there?' I asked,
'I don't know. I've never actually been there. But if we go

to the Hall of Holy Wisdom,' Declan said, 'don't expect to understand anything you see there.'

'Declan,' I said, 'I'm more interested in finding useful weapons than worrying about not understanding Cantian technology. Will there be Time Swords there?'

'I don't know,' said Declan. 'I certainly hope so.'

'We wouldn't know how to operate a Time Sword anyway,' Sam said.

I turned to Hullu and asked him, in Latin, the same question I'd just asked Declan.

I do not think so, young Saxon warrior. Only two Time Swords have been made so far, and the evil men have them.'

After I'd reported this very very bad news to the others, I said:

'I think we should let Hullu take us to the Hall of Holy Wisdom. That's where we'll make a stand against them. Maybe there'll be some other weapons, and besides... we have to make a stand *somewhere*. In the meantime we should take all the conventional weapons we can. They won't be much use against the Time Swords and revolvers that Maximus and Brutus have, but they'll be better than nothing.'

'Yeah, and if we do manage to stop the revolution and beat them all,' Troy said, 'we'll probably need weapons to get through this Terror place which titch told us about. Right, so Josh and Dec and me have got our swords, but we could all take spears as well.' Troy pronounced it 'Deck'.

'Good thinking, Troy,' Declan said.

Lindsay stared at Declan. 'Darling, since when did you call him Troy and he call you Dec?'

Declan smiled. 'Ever since risking our lives together, fighting giant lions and robot gladiators, that kind of everyday stuff one does.'

'Right, Dec,' said Troy.

Declan transferred the sword he was carrying to his left hand, walked up to Troy, made his right hand into a fist and stuck it out at Troy, who did the same. Their knuckles smacked together.

'To victory!' Declan shouted.

'Yes!' Lindsay shouted.

'To victory!' cried Troy.

The twins dashed in and touched knuckles with Troy and Declan too, shouting 'To victory!' I had a serious impulse to join in, but I was already thinking of the dangers that lay ahead, and decided not to jinx us.

'I want to carry a trident,' said Dora, hurrying over to where several of the fearsome three-pronged weapons were stacked in vertical racks.

'I'm going to carry a trident too,' said Sam. He grabbed one with his right hand, and as soon as he did he started to use it as a crutch, though of course the end without the trident on it reached up several feet above Sam.

Marcus grabbed hold of a sword and held it confidently, I wondered if sword-play was something taught at Cantian schools.

I decided my bloodstained sword would be enough for me. I did find a scabbard, though, and attached to a belt.

I looked at Carlo. 'You should get as many arrows as you can. Your bow is the best weapon we have.'

'I'm not so sure about that, having seen you, Troy and Declan in action,' said Carlo. 'But listen, each of these quivers has at least twenty arrows in it. I could do with a bit of help getting the second one on me.'

I helped him on with the second quiver. He really had become Salogel now.

We all put on breast-plates over our shirts, then all of us, except Mum this time, put on soldiers' breeches, Roman armour and tunics. This meant that all of us, apart from Mum, finally had to abandon all our own clothes except for underwear, as the Roman uniforms didn't look right on top of our normal clothes. I won't bother going into the details of how all this undressing and getting dressed worked, except to say there was a lot of back-turning and eyes shutting so Lindsay and Dora could dress in privacy. Mum supervised things bossily, the way mums do. She still had her yellow Cantian dress on, that she'd have been forcibly married in *and still might be,* I thought, with a sudden fresh stab of alarm, *if Maximus and Brutus catch us.*

'Quickly now, people of the World Beyond,' said Hullu.

He led us out of the room. The corridor soon began sloping sharply downwards, then turned to the right in a tight bend. After a few minutes we reached another outline in a gently glowing wall. Hullu stopped in front of the outline. The door opened. Hullu, leading the way, beckoned us inside.

71

This new room was completely different from anything we'd ever seen before.

It was hexagon-shaped, for one thing, and the walls, ceiling and floor were brilliant white. The ceiling consisted of six panels, which sloped upwards to a point, and matched the hexagonal wall panels.

Hullu looked back at the door. It shut instantly.

'Perhaps this is a trap,' said Sam.

'It'd better not be,' Troy muttered.

I was worried it was, though. Marcus looked pretty worried too. He'd obviously never been here before either.

I turned to Hullu. *'Where are we?'*

'In a Traveller's Chamber,' Hullu replied.

'He calls it a Traveller's Chamber,' I said to Declan. 'What's that?'

'I give up,' said Declan with a shrug.

Hullu gestured to us to spread out to all sides of the chamber. He directed everyone to a different place until we were all positioned evenly round the sides. Hullu let Dora and Sam stand close by each other with the trident, which they held with the three-pronged head resting on the floor. Then Hullu, stepping over the trident, advanced to the centre of the room.

He looked up above him at the point of the ceiling where the tops of the panels met. He stretched his arms upwards, touching the tips of his fingers together to make a kind of roof above his head, then began speaking quietly in a language I couldn't understand at all. I could only suppose it was Ileik.

A moment later the room went pitch-black. Dora whimpered. For a few seconds I was conscious of a gentle shaking sensation, but it stopped as quickly as it had begun. Then the room was flooded with light again.

Hullu, who was still making the roof-shape above his head, now brought his hands down. He ran over to the hexagonal panel of the room where I thought the door had been. Right away, a door-shaped outline appeared. The door opened, sliding to one side. Hullu went up to it and beckoned us through.

'Tell your friends we are in the Hall of Holy Wisdom,' Hullu said to me.

'He's just told me we've arrived in the Hall of Holy Wisdom.' I translated this.

'He's crazy,' Troy said. 'We must be still in the amphitheatre.'

But as we left the white room, the walls of the corridors outside weren't glowing yellow any more, but seemed to be made of a strange material that kept changing its colour. This made walking through the corridor a bit surreal.

'I suppose the Traveller's Chamber contains some mechanism that distorts the space-time continuum and enables the transport of matter through waves of energy,' Sam said.

'Hold it,' I said. 'Are you saying we've all just been broken up into molecules, transported through energy waves and reassembled here? I really don't think that's happened.'

'If the system was highly efficient, you wouldn't even be aware of it,' Sam told us.

'This place is so strange,' said Mum.

'On the other hand,' said Declan, 'it might just be a very quick and vibration-free pneumatic railway.'

'Whichever way it works,' I said, 'we've travelled without actually travelling.'

'Well, that's Cantian technology for you,' Declan said.

The new corridor continued for some time, then opened out into a wide hall, a sort of atrium that seemed like a larger version of the Traveller's Chamber. The hall was hexagonal, had a similar-shaped sloping roof and was brilliant white. One of the wall panels, on the far side, had the words *Bio-Amplificator* on it in black letters.

There was something else too - small holes in the walls all round the atrium, about a yard from the ground.

'Look,' I said, 'I know what they are. The Cantians call them "Wisdom Mouths". These're like the ones in the tables the Cantians played chess on. They catapulted me into a strange virtual world where my chess army was a real army.' I looked at Declan. 'What do you think these Wisdom Mouths do?'

'I can't imagine. So that's what happened when you played Cantian chess?'

'Perhaps we should try putting our fingers in the Wisdom Mouths to see if that helps us,' said Troy.

'I think we should leave them alone,' I said. 'All I know about them is they give you a really strange virtual experience - right now, we need to stay as real as we can.'

'We certainly mustn't let Bruce near one,' said Sam.

'Why not?' I asked him.

'Well, he might get stuck,' said Sam.

That was when I had my idea.

72

I suppose it was a fairly obvious idea really. But like all good ideas - e.g. *1) let's try kissing girls and see if it's nice, or 2) how about making a machine so we can talk to people who are too far away to hear us shouting at them, or 3) let's make something we can use to fly through the air from one country to another, or 4) Let's share stuff about our crazy lives with each other on the internet;* - someone had to have the idea in the first place. At that particular moment, that person was me.

Though perhaps not. I mean, you've probably had the idea too, even before I did.

Maybe you had it because you're a genius. Me, I needed a prompt.

So how had I got my idea? Well, what Sam just said made me imagine Bruce getting stuck in a Wisdom Mouth, and then I suddenly thought how Bruce wouldn't get stuck if he was... well, bigger.

I turned to Sam. 'Give me the container with Bruce in, would you?'

Without asking me why, Sam let go of the trident, letting Dora take its weight, then brought the container over to me.

'Why d'you want that, Josh?' Lindsay asked.

I looked at her and then at everyone else, and explained.

73

'*Oh... my... God,*' said Dora.

Sam just stared at me. 'But Josh, what if Bruce explodes?'

'Why should he?' I said. 'The maggots in the amphitheatre didn't.'

'They did when the giant earwigs got them,' Sam pointed out.

'Only because they were pincered,' I said. 'And the lions didn't die when *they* were enlarged. The earwigs didn't explode either.'

'Josh,' Lindsay put in, 'I really think you need to focus on the consequences here. Even if your plan works, the results'll be... well, really unpredictable.'

Just like you, you mean? I nearly said, but didn't, because I realised that Lindsay and I had by now sort of agreed on an unspoken basis that we wouldn't let Mum know that we'd split up, or at least not yet.

'Bruce is an invertebrate, after all,' Lindsay went on, uninterrupted by me. 'His brain is efficient, but very simple: sleep, eat, sleep, eat.'

'Sounds OK to me,' said Troy.

'Please, Troy, I'm being serious,' Lindsay said. She looked round at us all. 'If Bruce gets big enough to be dangerous, he'll be really merciless, and utterly ruthless, worse than even the most dangerous warm-blooded creature could be. His brain will get bigger too.'

'Yes, that's true,' I said, remembering how the earwigs in the arena had recognised the hooded men who seemed to be their masters.

I turned to Carlo. 'Maybe, if things go wrong, and Bruce gets really out of control, you could... you know, with your arrows...'

Carlo nodded.

'That won't work, he's armoured,' said Sam. 'I don't want to think about it.'

'Well... I'm hoping that won't be necessary,' I said. 'Sam, I think you'll really be proud of Bruce.'

'I'm proud of Bruce *already*.'

'Well, it's a crazy plan,' said Declan, 'but it's the only one we've got. And Cantia's a crazy place, so maybe it'll make sense down here. Ask Hullu if he'll show us where they do the bio-enlargement. I'm coming along too. I wouldn't miss it for the world.'

'Me neither,' said Carlo. 'Usually I only get to see the special effects at the premiere.'

'I'm certainly going along,' said Troy.

'Dora and Sam, you stay here with me,' Mum said.

'No way, Mum,' said the twins.

'I really want to you to,' Mum said.

'How can I?' Sam replied. 'I need to be with Bruce.'

'And I need to be with Sam,' said Dora.

'Well,' I said, 'I'm not going to go, as at least one of us needs to stay here to see if those creepy guys come here.'

'I'm not having you staying here by yourself, Josh,' Mum said. 'And, after all, I know Vincent and Dinsdale. If they do come I know what to say to them.'

I nodded. 'Yes, I suppose that makes sense, although I can look after myself.'

I knew Lindsay would go with Declan. I looked at Marcus. *'Have you ever seen the Bio-Amplificator working?'*

'Never, Josea.'

'Well, do you want to see it now?'

He nodded.

'Then would you like to go with them?'

'Yes, Josea.'

'Then you go with them.'

Marcus smiled. *'Thank you, Josea.'*

A few moments later, everyone except Mum and me followed Hullu. They took their weapons with them, except for the trident. Sam carefully held Bruce's container in both hands.

Hullu led the others towards the strange white hexagonal wall panel with the words *Bio-Amplificator* on it. When Hullu and the others were within a few yards of it, a door-shaped outline appeared in the wall. Hullu, determined, went up to the outline and the door opened. He was followed by Sam carrying the container as if it were an offering for the high priest of Cantian technology, which I suppose in a way it was.

The door closed behind them.

There was just Mum and me now. I looked at her and she looked at me.

'You know that skull they kept going on about, Josh? Before they drugged me... that man, Dinsdale - he really is a *terrible* person - boasted about it. He told me it's from the Roman Museum. He smashed the glass cabinet where the skull was kept, and took it.'

'His brother must have told him about the skull. The very first time I saw Vincent Stokes was at the Roman Museum, at the open evening last week. I think somehow Dinsdale, or maybe Vincent, must've been on their way to Cantia yesterday - a week later, that is - met the guards and knocked them all out, just for fun.'

'Josh, that's exactly what happened,' Mum said, 'except it didn't happen yesterday - Saturday - but on Friday evening, two days ago. Dinsdale brought me down... or rather dragged me down, when I was in the museum. That dreadful man seemed to come out of nowhere and grabbed me. I'd been just so worried about you all, and where you were, and the director of the Roman Museum gave me permission to explore the museum myself, to see if I could find any clues to your disappearance that the police hadn't found. I was pretty persuasive, I can tell you. The three Cantian soldiers who guarded the entrance said things in Latin to Dinsdale. I imagine they wanted to take over my custody - and he let go of me for a moment and knocked all three of them out with his horrible hairy fists. Dinsdale understands Latin, by the way - though I don't know how.'

'Me neither,' I said. 'Also, he must've hit those soldiers pretty hard, if they stayed knocked out for a night and day. I just hope they're OK.'

'So do I,' said Mum.

Again, I wondered why Mum wasn't more surprised by being in Cantia; somehow she didn't seem to be. And it was funny she suspected we'd disappeared in the museum when nobody else did.

'Dinsdale's more like an animal than a human being,' said Mum. 'And to think he wants to *marry* me.'

'I won't let Dinsdale marry you, Mum. None of us will.'

But I wasn't sure how we would stop it happening, if it came to that. Also, I thought what a terrible enemy Dinsdale would be, if he could knock out three armed Cantian soldiers.

Then I had an even worse thought, which was: *with*

Tiberius dead, they could capture and kill us all except Mum, and she could be stuck down here for the rest of her life as Dinsdale's slave-wife, and no-one would ever know she was down here.

That was the last thought I had before I was suddenly engulfed in a mind-blowing white flash and billowing white clouds.

By now, though, I knew what had happened to us.

74

After I don't know how long... maybe a few minutes, maybe longer, I came round to find myself lying groggily on the floor beside Mum, surrounded by a dozen Cantian soldiers, mostly armed with spears, though a few had bows and arrows strapped to their backs.

The soldiers with spears were pointing them at us. Their other hands held shields bearing the horrible *Semper Superior* logo of revolutionary Cantia.

But one soldier didn't have a spear or a bow. Instead, he had a Time Sword, which was making a weird humming sound that slowly grew quieter, as if it were cooling down.

There were five very sinister-looking men there too, with nasty scowls and wearing grey togas with the hoods up, like evil friars gathered to watch someone burn to death. Each of these creeps was carrying a *sword* in one hand and, in the other, a chain leading to a studded collar. And wearing each studded collar was a giant earwig. The earwigs were looking at Mum and me with huge jet-black eyes each at least six inches across. I thought these must be the policemonks.

I hadn't seen giant earwigs up close before. They looked totally gross and disgusting. Their antennae were about a yard long; their bodies dark brown, shiny and scaly. From end to end, the creatures were as long as racing cars. Every earwig was clacking its pincers as if desperate to use them on us.

Keeping an eye on the soldiers, and making no quick movements, I stumbled to my feet and helped Mum up.

Then, suddenly, Vincent and Dinsdale Stokes emerged, like evil spirits, from round the corner. They wore hooded purple togas, but their hoods were down. I wished they'd kept the hoods up - at least, that way, I wouldn't have had to look at their faces.

A couple of the earwigs' masters moved out of the way so Maximus and Brutus could come and look at Mum and me up close.

The skull of the poor girl from the Roman Museum, who'd died so young, was dangling from Vincent's neck.

Vincent pointed his revolver at us. It was a big, grey gun and looked even scarier now I was seeing it close up. Vincent was grinning, showing his brownish teeth. Dinsdale was beside him.

Vincent, aka Custardface, stood admiring his two tattoos, one of a red snake with yellow fangs on the back of his left hand, and the other of a roaring male lion with a golden mane on his right. Then he looked at Mum. He grinned evilly.

'Hello, gorgeous,' he said to Mum.

75

It was the first time I'd had the privilege - if you could call it that - of seeing Dinsdale up close.

He wasn't quite as tall as his almost equally psychotic brother, but what Dinsdale lacked in height, he made up for in muscles, hairiness and smelliness. His bare arms were as broad as bollards, his hands as hairy as a monkey's. His legs were concealed by his toga, but I didn't exactly think they'd be wimpish, either.

Dinsdale had a few days' beard growth. The corners of his mouth were turned down in a way I'd never seen before on a human being. He smelt very strongly of sweat. He had short black hair growing low on his forehead, and his eyes were small, black, and looked evil. He reminded me of a mad gorilla. Not that I want to insult mad gorillas.

'The great thing about a Time Sword, you see, Bella,' explained Vincent Stokes, or Maximus, as he called himself down here in Cantia, 'is that they make it easy to catch people what are trying to run away from you. All you got to do, when you see them from a long way away, is shoot them a bit into the future - in the case of you and this kid, just five minutes - and when they reach the future, you can be there waiting for them.' He grinned again. 'I used it before on this little brat and his friends when they was in the Roman Museum, trying to find me. They went a thousand years into the future, and then ended up a week later than they started out.'

'Yes,' I said, 'I know.'

'You do, do you?'

'Yes.'

'I saw you in the room where the skull was, didn't I, you little bastard? I'd just come back from Stinker Watson's funeral.' Vincent smiled at me with his brown teeth. 'I s'pose it were only fair I went to his funeral, seeing as it were me what shot him.'

'Yeah, Vincent, it were only fair,' growled Dinsdale.

I glanced at Dinsdale. He glared back at me. 'What you lookin' at me for?' he demanded, pointing his revolver at my forehead. I was totally scared.

'Leave him alone, Dinsdale,' Mum said.

Dinsdale glanced at Mum, then gave a wild, braying cackle, like the sound a psychotic billy-goat might make in the mating season. He backed away from me a bit, though he still kept his gun pointed at Mum and me.

'It's cute how he does what you say, ain't it, Bella?' said Vincent, approvingly. 'You can tell he loves yer, can't yer? That's why I didn't send you and this kid far into the future just now. Dins wants you to be his wife.'

'*I will never be your brother's wife, under any circumstances,*' Mum retorted. 'I'd rather kill myself than marry him!'

'Aw, don't come over all coy, Bella,' Vincent said. 'You know you and Dins are made for each other. He's a real man. Not like Mr Movie Star. Gor blimey, if it hadn't been for them kids, he'd've been swallowed by them lions as quick as Dins downs a pint of beer.'

'It was cowardly of you to put Carlo in there against those beasts you so cruelly enlarged,' Mum said. I could hardly believe how brave she was being, what with the guns trained on her, the Cantian soldiers with their spears, and the strange hooded men with their giant earwigs. But then

I thought, suddenly: Of course *Mum's brave, bringing us up with no dad for most of the time and struggling to make Food for Thought work.*

An obnoxious smile came onto Vincent's hideous face. 'That little girl with the curly hair: she's a sweetie. Good fighter, too.' He smiled even more revoltingly. 'I might let her live. She can be one of my servants, bring me my dinner and pour me my drinks.'

His horrible grin broadened. 'Gor blimey,' he said, when he finally spoke again, 'you seen how she and that other little kid stuck the trident in the giant lion's guts? Now, that's what I call entertainment. It were a pity that cute girl with the golden hair saved the other lion's life with her witchcraft stuff. Yeah, it were bleedin' marvellous. Even better than the custard. Them two girls are cuties. That's why, back in the museum a week ago yesterday, I didn't let this little bastard and his chums stay a thousand years in the future. It seemed a shame to fire those two cute girls a thousand years in the future. As for today, in the arena, well of course, Dins and me could've shot everyone, but why spoil the fun?'

'How is it you can speak Latin?' I asked Vincent.

He just glared at me. 'None of your business, you little horror. Shut yer gob or I'll shut it for yer, and crucify you into the bargain.'

That seemed to set the social tone of the conversation. Then Dinsdale started grunting and looking at Mum really creepily. 'Hello, darling,' he said, 'how about a kiss?' and he reached out his hairy paw towards her. Mum shrank backwards, as any sane woman would've done. I'd have had a go at Dinsdale, if it hadn't been obvious my reward would've been to be shot, speared, earwigged, crucified and very likely Time-Sworded, too.

I wondered how everyone else was getting on with my Bruce plan.

Dinsdale stared at me. 'I was dying for one of them lions to bite you in 'alf,' he said, charmingly.

Vincent laughed. 'But since that didn't happen, that stupid bastard Tiberius had to oblige us instead. Now, you little brat, where are the rest of you?'

'They're not here,' I said.

'Well, of course they ain't,' Vincent replied, 'or I wouldn't be asking you where they are, would I, you little prat?' He pointed his gun at me again. *Where are they?*'

'Leave him alone, Vincent,' Mum said. 'He's only a boy.'

And then I realised Mum didn't want Vincent or Dinsdale to know I was her son. She probably hadn't told them she had any children.

I still said nothing.

'OK, Bella,' said Vincent, '*you* tell me.'

'They'll be back soon, Vincent, don't you worry,' Mum said. 'So what will you do then, kill us all? How long do you think you and your brother can get away with this?'

Vincent took a step back from us, admired his tattoos for a few moments and smiled down at them like they were his best friends.

Then he looked back at Mum. 'Actually, Bella, I reckon the answer to that is: *as long as we want.* Cantia ain't part of Britain, and British laws don't apply. We knew that before we came 'ere. The Geneva Convention don't count down 'ere neither. And anyway,' he gave a sinister snigger, 'Cantia's a long way from Geneva. You see, Bella, the only laws what matter down here are the ones me and Dins makes.'

'For the moment, perhaps,' said Mum.

'For ever,' said Vincent. 'And once we've dealt with these stupid kids, Dins and me can get on with running the place

without any interruptions, and you'll marry Dins and have kids wiv him. But as you ask, Bella, there *is* another reason why it was you what we kidnapped. You see, someone we know, someone we listen to, someone high up, told us we had to capture you, so we did.'

'Who?' Mum said.

Vincent gave one of his obnoxious smiles. 'That would be telling, wouldn't it? What really matters is, now Dins and me are in charge of Cantia, the Cantians will have a good, strong leadership.'

'Yeah,' growled Dinsdale.

'*Strong leadership,*' Mum echoed. 'I suppose, what you mean by that is, murdering everyone you don't like.'

I was incredibly impressed by how she stood up to those two violent thugs, in front of the soldiers and the hooded creeps with their giant earwigs.

'The truth is,' I said, determined to support Mum, 'you've made Cantia a Nazi nightmare.'

'Listen, you little prat,' Vincent snarled at me, 'Dins and me, we love Hitler and what he did in Germany. When we met Tiberius, we got talking about the custard and it turns out he liked watching Nartzi history stuff on it, just like me and Dins do. He couldn't understand much of what he saw about the Nartziz on the custard, specially when they talked German, and as for English, he don't speak it proper like what we do. Anyhow, we pretended to be friendly with him, till it was time to feed him to the lions.'

Vincent thrust his bottom jaw out and laughed, which made him look even more horrible than ever, if that was possible. 'Yeah, Hitler and the Nartziz was the people what ran Europe proper. That's why we're making Cantia into a Nartzi place. We'll run it with fists of steel, and it'll be all the better for it.'

'*Somebody will stop you,*' insisted Mum.

'And who'd that be, Bella?' asked Vincent. 'We got the soldiers on our side and the policemonks too.'

'The policemonks?' I said.

'Yeah,' Vincent said, 'these men 'ere with the earwigs. They're monks and cops at the same time, so they don't cost much to use, and their earwigs help to keep law and order. This place... it's a paradise for me and Dins.' It was like as if he was talking to himself rather than to Mum and me. 'Who'd have imagined it,' the scumbag went on, 'a Roman town under Canterbury? 'Course, the food and drink needs improving, but we'll get reg'lar supplies of burgers, chips, onion rings, beer and southern fried chicken sent down by the British Government. They want to keep us happy, don't they? It'll be great. The British Government don't even know who we really are. For all they know, we're just Cantian people like everyone else down here.'

He smiled again. 'It's even better than our summer holiday last year in Majorca when Dins and I were both out of the clink at the same time. And the women down here, they're gorgeous ...' He cackled. 'Yeah, it'll be great being in Cantia. As for Dins... well, Bella, like I say, he wants to get married and start a family. Which is where you come in.'

'*I've told you, I'll never marry your brother,*' Mum said.

'Oh, I think you will, Bella, love,' Vincent replied.

As he spoke, I saw the doorway, where the twins and everyone else had disappeared with Hullu, was opening again. My heart started to thump.

Dora rushed out of the doorway. She gave me a look I couldn't fathom, then she saw Vincent and Dinsdale, the soldiers and the policemonks with their earwigs. She cried 'Mum!' and ran to her, wriggling in among the soldiers and somehow avoiding the earwigs. She hugged Mum, then

308

stood defiantly in front of her, as if she wanted to shield Mum from being shot, speared, earwigged or sent off into time oblivion by the Time Sword.

'So... this little girl's your daughter then is she?' sneered Vincent.

Mum didn't say a word.

'Yes, I am,' returned Dora. 'And I love my mum very much, so don't you dare hurt her!'

At that point, Lindsay, Troy, Declan and Marcus streamed out from the door. I signalled Lindsay frantically. When her eyes met mine, I saw how scared she was.

There was no sign of Sam, Carlo or Hullu... or Bruce.

Five of the soldiers suddenly broke away and in a rattle of boots, shields and weapons, surrounded Troy, Lindsay, Declan and Marcus.

Vincent stared at Declan. 'I still don't understand what you're doing here, you stupid ponce. But being as you've got so friendly with this bunch of losers, you can die with them. Except for Bella, of course. We've got other plans for her. No sense killing *her*.' He smiled. 'What a waste that would be, 'specially as Dins likes her so much.'

He pointed his gun at me. 'Any more of these kids yours, are they, Bella? This little bastard, for example?'

Again Mum didn't say a word.

'Never mind,' said Vincent. 'One's enough.' And he stuck his gun against Dora's left cheek, digging into it and making her wince. I wanted to hit it out of his hands, but if it went off, Dora was right in front of it. 'Bella, go and be with Dins, unless you want me to shoot your pretty little girl's head off.'

Dinsdale leered at Mum, who gave a great sigh then walked slowly towards him. He put his horrible hairy bollard-like arms round her.

Vincent gave a satisfied nod, as if everything was going to plan. Then he turned to me.

'Right, you little worm, where's the movie star?'

'How should I know,' I replied.

As I spoke, I heard one of the strangest sounds I'd ever heard in my life.

It made me think of the wailing *maaairr* of a sheep or lamb, except that the sound was much deeper and had a kind of metallic clang, as if it might've been made by a music synthesizer. I turned to see where it was coming from.

Sam, the grimmest of expressions on his face, came through the doorway and stared hard at the triumvirs and soldiers. To Sam's right was Hullu, his little fists clenched, glaring at Vincent and Dinsdale and, despite being so small, looking really, really angry, like an avenging angel.

But there was still no sign of Carlo.

Then I saw something else.

76

The something else walked between Sam and Hullu, on what looked like never-ending legs.

I knew at once what - or who - it was.

Bruce had been enlarged into an enormous black cylindrical monster about three feet in diameter, with a round head, no visible eyes, incredibly sharp-looking mandibles, two long antennae, large black circular scales on his back like dinner-plates... and 184 legs. Sam and Hullu had come through the door by now, but the monster was still coming in, and making the same strange sound over and over again.

'What... what's that?' cried Vincent.

The Cantian soldiers, and the policemonks, all stared horrified. The earwigs, maybe sensing a kindred spirit from the realm of the cold-blooded, started clicking their rear pincers together noisily.

I could see now that Bruce was at least fifteen feet long. He finally finished emerging from the doorway, then suddenly reared up on several dozen of his back legs and gave a terrible, deafening shriek, the top of his massive head at least twice as high from the ground than the height of a man.

The Cantian soldiers yelled *'Pinguis vermiculus! Pinguis vermiculus!'* and backed away from Bruce who was, I couldn't help thinking, a fair amount bigger than the *pinguis vermiculuses* they were used to having for Sunday lunch.

Some of the soldiers were so scared they dropped their weapons and shields and raced out of the hall down the corridor. But the soldier holding the Time Sword gritted his teeth. He seemed more determined of his staying power. I wondered if he was about to fire at Bruce, and if he did whether the Time Sword's beam would be strong enough to be effective on him.

Whatever the soldier was thinking, panic got the better of him, because he dropped the Time Sword onto the floor, which it hit with a loud clang. The soldier sped off down the corridor screaming.

Half a dozen Cantian soldiers remained, however, along with the policemonks, who didn't seem as easily flustered as the soldiers, though even they were wide-eyed.

Some of the soldiers hurled their spears at Bruce, but they were about as effective against him as lollipop sticks against a tank.

Then one of the policemonks shouted, in Latin of course, '*Giant earwigs, attack!*'

Could the earwigs understand? I wondered.

Unlike the Cantian soldiers, the giant earwigs weren't scared of Bruce. I suppose, in a way, they saw him as one of them. They just went for him, and I couldn't help admiring the ghastly skanky earwigs for their courage because it seemed, just about anything that attacked Bruce had as much chance of staying alive as a toad under a steamroller.

I wanted to help Bruce, but I knew Vincent or Dinsdale would have shot me in a second.

Bruce didn't care about the guns. All *he* cared about was zapping the earwigs.

He killed three of them using his massive mandibles, chopping them into a non-edible sushi of legs, chunks of thorax, smashed pincers and obliterated heads. It wasn't a pretty sight. One of the earwigs, using what neurones it had in its not-so-stupid earwigoid brain, scuttled out of the way and down the corridor. The other two put up more resistance, and pincered Bruce's body viciously.

All this did, though, was make Bruce even angrier and more vicious: his armour protected him against the pincers. He slammed himself down on one earwig, flattening it so that, when he moved away, it seemed quite funny - unless you were the earwig - like a diagram of a giant earwig in a biology book. The other earwig leapt onto Bruce's back and went on pincering him but Bruce writhed with mad power and whacked the earwig off him with his tail, then terminated the horrible creature's military career by biting its head off and gobbling down the head as a tasty snack.

The rest of the soldiers, seeing what happened to the earwigs, fired arrows at Bruce, but they just bounced harmlessly off his armour.

Carlo came running towards Bruce from the doorway, with his bow drawn. Carlo leapt on the back of the rearing Bruce, who didn't seem to mind, like a faithful horse with its master on it. Lindsay, Troy, Declan and Marcus pressed themselves against a hexagonal panel of the atrium, determined not to get in Bruce's way - and who could blame them?

Bruce brought the front part of his massive body down to the ground in a thud, making the floor shake. The shaking and the din seemed to catapult the two remaining Cantian soldiers out of their paralysis. They lifted their spears back and aimed them at Bruce but even before they threw them, Carlo shot simultaneous arrows, two at a time, so fast it was like he'd not only become Salogel again, but was now miles better than Salogel had ever been.

Both arrows struck their targets. But I realised now that Carlo hadn't been aiming at death spots like the forehead or chest; he'd aimed for the soldiers' spear-arms.

He doesn't want to kill them, I thought, *just put them out of action.*

And it worked, because the soldiers dropped their spears with cries of agony then, before they had time to react, Carlo fired with brilliant accuracy at those policemonks and shot their sword arms, too, and they stumbled away, shouting with pain, but alive.

Only now, Vincent and Dinsdale started firing their guns at Bruce, but the bullets bounced off his thick scales and hit the walls. I yelled to everyone to get down; I knew the ricocheting bullets would be deadly. Everyone flung themselves to the ground, except Carlo up on Bruce's back, who took aim at Vincent, but before he could shoot an arrow, Vincent shot Carlo. The bullet hit him in the upper part of his right arm. Carlo gave a shriek of pain and dropped his bow.

'*Carlo!*' Dora cried, rushing towards him.

Sam sprang to his feet, too, gave Bruce a big push in the direction of Vincent and Dinsdale and cried '*Attack!*'

Bruce rolled forwards on all his legs towards the two triumvirs (or maybe they were bi-umvirs now as there were only two of them) and Bruce's enormous sharp mandibles operating with a sound of a thousand scissors snapping open and shut.

Vincent and Dinsdale kept shooting at Bruce, both of them swearing as they did, but the bullets thudded uselessly off Bruce's body.

'*Dora, Sam, get down!*' I yelled. For once, they listened and did as they were told. They slammed themselves down to the floor. Carlo tried to get to his feet. Blood trickled from the wound in his right arm. He stumbled in a daze. Dora, who was close by him, reached up, grabbed him round the shoulders and pulled him to the ground with an impressive strength I didn't know she had.

I prayed that the bullet Carlo had taken hadn't hit a vein or artery.

Suddenly Vincent dropped his revolver and dashed towards the Time Sword.

'Bruce!' shouted Sam. 'Get him before he Time Swords us!

Maybe Bruce understood or not, but he wasn't quick enough. A few seconds later, Vincent reached the Time Sword. In a flash, he adjusted its settings, and then, to my amazement *pointed it at himself.* He activated it, and the Time Sword hit him with its stream of strange silvery distorted air.

Vincent disappeared. The last thing I saw him do before he vanished was hurl the Time Sword towards Dinsdale. Then he was gone.

The Time Sword bounced and rattled along the ground.

Dinsdale went on pressing the trigger of his revolver. But he saw how close Bruce was getting, and with a cry of terror he dashed to the Time Sword. Bruce was nearly on him, and Dinsdale didn't have time to check the weapon's settings; he just pointed it at Bruce and fired, letting the beam play on Bruce's entire vast body for a few seconds.

Bruce vanished.

Dinsdale fired at Carlo, who vanished too.

'*You devil!*' I shouted at Dinsdale. 'He was wounded already!'

I ran towards Dinsdale trying to barge him down, but he was too quick for me, though I did crash into the Time Sword, which dropped to the floor with a clang. Dinsdale grabbed my hair and punched me in the gut, which really winded me. He flung me to the floor. I lay there, trying to catch my breath.

'He's only sixteen, you monster!' Mum shrieked at Dinsdale and launched herself at him, her arms reaching out to strangle the hideous psycho, but he just batted his unloving potential bride away with his left hand as if she was a moth.

I was still winded and helpless on the floor, but now Declan and Troy were in the fray too and Lindsay, as well as Troy, aimed rabbit punches at Dinsdale's neck but missed completely.

Dinsdale clouted Troy on the side of the head, knocking him to the ground. I began to get my breath back. Declan and my ex Lindsay and even Sam, all battle-crazy, went for Dinsdale too, and Dora did as well, then a few seconds later I joined in. But it was hopeless, Dinsdale was as strong as a grizzly bear. We kept attacking him, and he yelled unholy words, and terrible growling insults, and panted his ghastly smelly breath at us all.

Declan got punched on the nose. Well, he deserved it, but I was sorry to see it anyway. It's true he'd stolen my girl from me, but I suppose if your girl wants to go off with someone else, there's not much you can do about it and you just have to try to make the best of a bad situation. Declan felt more like a friend now, anyway, even though I still felt totally heartbroken about Lindsay. Troy received a mighty kick on his bottom and Dinsdale grabbed Lindsay's right arm and flung her about three yards - and despite everything I was terrified she was going to be badly hurt - but she somehow landed on her feet, set her jaw in a fierce frown and looked *really* cheesed off. Dora and Sam got kicked and clouted, and I was hit more times than I'd like to admit, but when you're in pain already, and the adrenalin's shooting into you, there comes a point where you can't feel anything much more.

Even with all of us trying to attack Dinsdale, and despite the punishment we were taking, I thought we were wearing him down, but not enough. *What'll happen when we get tired, and can't resist any more? He'll simply kill us all with his bare fists.*

I had no idea where Bruce was, or Vincent. But then, suddenly, a strange whooshing sound, made me jump . . . Bruce reappeared in the hall. But where was Vincent?

A second or so later, Carlo re-materialised in front of us. He looked really groggy. His right arm was bleeding everywhere. He arrived on top of Bruce, and immediately slid down from Bruce's back and collapsed onto the floor, breathing heavily.

I raced to help Carlo. Dinsdale gave an understandably terrified shriek at seeing Bruce again, and began running down the corridor to escape.

I wondered just how fast Bruce could run.

The answer was: *very fast*. Bruce shot, on his 184 highly co-ordinated legs, after 'Dins'. I thought maybe Bruce was interested in his own dins. Bruce's speed was at least twice that of the soon-to-be-pensioned-off biumvir, whose animalistic howls echoed round the hall. I remembered how being Time-Sworded exhausted people for a while, but Bruce - perhaps because he was only an invertebrate - didn't seem affected. Maybe only primates were.

Dinsdale was still shrieking and fleeing down the corridor as fast as his hairy legs would carry him, but it was no use. A few seconds later Bruce caught up with him, grabbed Dinsdale's legs from behind and gobbled up the bottom parts. Dinsdale shrieked and crawled for a few yards before Bruce attacked him again.

Bruce's gigantic black scaly body completely covered Dinsdale. There were horrible grinding and gnashing noises, accompanied by frightful moans from Dinsdale, and then nothing but the terrible sound of mandibles munching, slicing and filleting human flesh, and the slurp of Bruce's hungry jaws, as he ate Dinsdale alive.

Once Bruce had finished his meal, he turned round in a beautiful multi-legged movement, then he ran back up the corridor towards us, leaving a trail of blood and bits of torn flesh, some of which still quivered a bit.

Would he attack *us* now? But Sam smiled at him and said, 'good boy, good boy,' and Bruce slowed down and made his way slowly towards Sam, and Sam went to meet him, his right hand ready to pat Bruce on the head.

It was then the earwig struck.

77

I'd forgotten about that particular earwig. It was the only earwig left alive. It was the one that had scampered in terror down the corridor when it saw Bruce. Now, it raced like a tornado back towards Bruce, as if the horrible pincery creature had sensed in its enlarged brain that, in Bruce's moment of triumph, he was off guard.

The giant earwig raced so quickly towards Bruce, there was absolutely no time for any of us to do anything to stop it. The earwig - in an incredible kamikaze effort - leapt up on Bruce's head and smashed its rear pincers into him. One pincer went into Bruce's hard scales and did no damage at all, but the other pincer dug deep into Bruce's head, just beside his right eye, where his armour must have been less tough.

Half a yard of the left-hand pincer plunged into Bruce's head. The pincer dug deep and stayed there. The earwig had ghastly strength.

Bruce gave an ear-splitting shriek. He reared up on his hind legs, flung the earwig off him with a mighty shake of his head, gave another shriek, and stumbled over to where the earwig lay stunned on the ground. Bruce slammed his upper body down on the giant earwig, smashing it into pulp.

Bruce stumbled back towards Sam. A thick brown liquid started to seep out of the open wound. Sam, seeing this, began to cry.

I felt like crying myself.

Carlo was up and on his feet now. He had our tourniquet on him and his wound didn't seem to be bleeding so much.

'How... how are you, Carlo?' I managed to get out.

'I'm OK for the moment, Josh, but I need to get to a hospital soon if we can get out of here, unless we have one of those healing balls around.'

That was all he said. He seemed far more concerned about Bruce, and rushed to see how he was. In fact, we all did.

Bruce was obviously too weak now to be a threat to us or to anyone else. We all gathered round him. He was still moving, but . . . everything about him seemed to be happening in slow motion.

'*Oh, no,*' Sam murmured. '*Oh, no.*'

'Oh, I do hope he won't die,' Dora said, voicing what I knew we were all thinking. She was rubbing various punched or kicked parts of her body as she spoke. She glanced at Sam. 'Bruce *ate* the hairy tri-um-weirdo. But... I thought Bruce was a vegetarian.'

Sam was too upset to reply. He patted Bruce gently on the head, murmuring words of affection to him.

'I don't think giant, giant millipedes are vegetarians, Dora,' I said.

'I dink, in view of wad'z happened, dat'z a fairly zafe azumption,' Declan muttered, holding a sleeve of his toga to his bleeding nose, and pinching the bridge of his nose with his left hand.

We all stared at Declan.

'Look, I hope you don't all dink I'm being inzenzitive,' Declan said. 'I'm really zorry Bruze haz been injured. He zaved our livez. But he'z an invertebrate, and... well, we zaw in de arena dat dey're more dolerant of injury dan mammalz like uz, aren't dey? I dink he zhould be OK.'

It took me a few seconds to work out what Declan had said, but I managed to.

Now I glanced at Hullu. *'Can we take Bruce to the room where you keep the Ball of Wellness, and use it on him?'*

But Hullu shook his head slowly.

'It will not work on a vermiculus, for their blood is cold.'

I reported this back to the others.

'We should at least try,' said Sam. He sounded miserable.

'Sam, he's Hullu, he knows,' I said. 'But listen, I think Declan's right. If we can get Bruce home somehow . . . we can get treatment for him.' I turned to Hullu. *'Can you make Bruce small again?'*

Hullu shook his head sadly. *'That is not possible.'*

'Josea, why do you want to make the giant worm small again?' Marcus asked.

'Because in our world, such a creature does not exist and everyone would be afraid of him,' I explained.

I glanced at the others. 'Hullu says the process doesn't work in reverse. I'm afraid Bruce can't be made small again. We'll just have to try to get him home as he is. There's a vet in Canterbury on St Dunstan's, near the Westgate Tower. We could take him there.'

'I think that might cause a bit of a commotion, Josh,' said Lindsay.

I nodded. 'Yes, you're probably right.' I imagined us escorting poor, wounded, enlarged Bruce up St Dunstans to the vet, with crowds of terrified Canterbury people running away shrieking, and the traffic jammed up to well past the level crossing, and a beautiful dark blue streamlined high-speed Javelin train stopped on the crossing and passengers gaping at Bruce, and police helicopters going *whirlywhirlywhirly* overhead and an SAS team arriving in an armoured personnel carrier and all pointing their assault rifles at poor Bruce, and tanks on their way.

'Listen,' I said, looking at the others, 'We don't know where Vincent is. The revolution might not be over yet.'

'I think Vincent shot himself some way into the future,' said Sam, 'so as to escape Bruce, and then when the Time Sword banged onto the floor, it jolted the settings and changed them, and so when Dinsdale shot Bruce and Carlo he only shot them a few *minutes* into the future. Vincent must have gone farther into the future, because he hasn't come back yet.'

'But we don't know when he might reappear,' I said.

'No, we don't,' Sam agreed.

Mum looked round at all of us, then said: 'We've been lucky, and Bruce has saved our lives, but if we stay here, I think we really are going to be killed, and I can't allow that to happen to any of you. I have to report back to CAESAR's leadership - well, assuming we get out of here alive, anyway. The important thing is, thanks to all of you, we now have a Time Sword, CAESAR's scientists can investigate it and see if anything can be done to neutralise its effects. Also, I now know who sent the Cockneys down into Cantia. Vincent let it slip out this morning, when they'd forced me to have breakfast with them. Vincent had a hangover. That didn't surprise me. He told me that down here in Cantia, he gets drunk on Cantian wine every evening.'

'He muzt be a glutton vor bunishment,' Declan said.

I stared at Mum. 'What's going on, Mum? Why are you talking about CAESAR like this? What d'you mean, you have to report back to CAESAR leadership?'

Declan glanced at Mum. 'Hello, Mrz Moonford.'

Mum smiled faintly. 'Hello, Declan.'

I just stared at them. 'Do you two... do you know two *know each other?*'

'Yes, darling, I mean Josh, we do,' Mum said. 'You see, there's something I need to tell you.'

'What's that, Mum?' I asked.

'I'm Declan's controller.' Mum said.

'But... how.... why... when...?' I stammered.

'In that case, Mrs Moonford, you must have known about Josh becoming a candidate for CAESAR!' Lindsay gasped.

'Yes, Lindsay, I did,' Mum said. 'I recommended Josh personally.'

'Oh my God,' said Dora.

'I should have guessed it,' said Sam.

I just stared at Mum, as I started adjusting everything in my mind that I knew about Mum, and really about everything else in my life.

'Vincent and Dinsdale always knew who I was,' said Mum. 'Sir Stanley Templeton-Greene must have told them.'

'Sir Stanley Templeton-Greene?' I gasped. 'The *politician?* The government's Minister for Technology? *He's* involved with this?'

'Yes, I think he is,' Mum said, with a nod, 'though I don't know how exactly. He's not in CAESAR; but I'm pretty sure he somehow got wind of what CAESAR does and sent Vincent and Dinsdale down to get hold of the Time Swords. They did what he wanted, but as we've seen, the whole power thing went to their heads and so they also thought they'd set themselves up as the new rulers of Cantia at the same time.'

'Sir Stanley Templeton-Greene must be Stan!' I exclaimed.

'What d'you mean, Josh?' asked Mum.

I quickly told her how I'd overhead Vincent on his phone the previous evening in the Roman Museum, and how he'd been talking to someone called Stan. I also told Mum as much as I remembered of what Vincent had said to Stan. I remembered most of it and Sam filled in the gaps.

After we'd explained all this to Mum I glanced at Declan. 'Did you know who Stan was all the time?'

'No, diz iz de firzt time I've heard of diz,' Declan told her, and I knew him well enough by now to know he was telling the truth.

I stared at Mum again 'So what exactly are you at CAESAR?'

'Regional Officer, reporting to the Deputy Director. But enough of me. I'm more interested in what Declan's been doing.' She turned to him. 'I think you've done very well, Declan. After all, the Cantian revolution wasn't your fault.'

'Dank you, Mrz Moonford.'

'He's a complete darling,' Lindsay commented.

'What Lindsay means is,' I said, despondently, 'is that basically Lindsay has left me for Declan.'

'Really?' said Mum, with a glance at Lindsay.

'Well, yes, Isabella,' Lindsay said, 'I have fallen for Declan. In fact, I love him to bits. I haven't mentioned it since we met you here as I didn't want Josh to feel awkward in front of you.' She glanced at me. 'I'm sorry, Josh.'

I just gave a shrug. What was there to say?

'I'm very sorry about you and Lindsay, Josh,' said Mum, 'and I very much hope you'll stay good friends. As for me, Josh, surely you must sometimes have wondered how I've managed to support you all, when the shop has always done so badly? It's because of my secret job with CAESAR.'

I noticed Dora and Sam were still in the staring-open-mouthed stage of shock at Mum, as if half a minute ago *she'd* turned into a giant giant *giant* female millipede.

'We need to get home,' Mum said. 'We have to get Sam

325

and Carlo to a hospital, Bruce to a vet, and the Time Sword to CAESAR.'

'But Mum,' I said, 'the revolution's still going on.'

'I know,' Mum said, 'but think of the humiliation you all inflicted on Vincent and Dinsdale when you dealt with the giant lions and the robot gladiators in the arena. Reputation is everything in Cantia, which is such a small community. Tiberius and Dinsdale are both dead, and Vincent has been made to look very stupid. I'm hoping that this awful unholy revolution has come to an end. When Vincent reappears - and I tend to think it won't be for some time to come - I don't think the Cantians will take him seriously any more, especially once they know it was Dinsdale who threw Tiberius into the arena. Right, now we have to go.'

'Do you speak Latin, Mum?' I asked her.

'No, darling, hardly a word. You're the Latin wizard, not me.'

'Can Marcus come with us?' asked Dora.

'I'm happy with that,' Mum said, 'but really I need to ask Declan, as in a sense this is to some extent his project.'

Declan shrugged. 'Yez, ov courze he can join uz and come back with uz… if we can get back.'

I hurried over to Marcus. Speaking Latin now of course, I said, *Marcus, you can come home with us. Would you like that? You can come up with us to the world above?'*

Marcus suddenly clapped his hands together in delight. *'I'd like that very much. I want to know your world better.'*

I looked round at the others. 'He wants to come, and he says he wants to know our world better and that he wants there to be friendship between Cantia and our world.'

'He'z a good jhap,' Declan said. 'And by de way,' he added, 'I'm not going to recommend dat Marcuz has the dreedmend which'll make him dink dat hiz memory of

326

Cantia is all juzt a dream. Vortunately, I'm high up enough in CAEZAR, although of course not az high up as Mrz Moonford, to be able to make a decision about diz.'

Hullu looked extremely excited. He glanced at me and then at Marcus and then back at me. '*Hullu is so pleased that Marcus will be visiting the mysterious and no doubt wonderful World Above!*' Hullu exclaimed. '*But Hullu is sad, too, because he would like to go there himself!*'

'*Well, maybe one day you will.*' I said to Hullu. I smiled at him, then said:

'*We have to go.*'

Hullu nodded. '*Follow me.*'

'*Where?*' I asked him.

'*To Terra Horridissima,*' replied Hullu.

I glanced at Mum. 'He says we have to go through *Terra Horridissima*. Do we need to, though? Can't we go back to our world by the way we came? It'll be easier.'

'Hullu's right, Josh,' Mum said. 'We have to go that way. The revolution might've been weakened, but we can't assume it's all over yet.'

'Just what d'you know about *Terra Horridissima*, Mum?' I asked her.

'Very little,' Mum said. 'Let's just hope it doesn't live up to its name too much.'

Declan cleared his throat. He glanced at Mum. 'Before we zet off, I need to confezz zomeding, Mrz Moonford. I dink it'z only fair I do. After all, Moonford'z your zon, and I veel a bit awkward about dis.'

'About what, Declan?' Mum asked.

Declan scratched the back of his head with his left hand and then cleared his throat. 'Well, az we've won against the baddiez and dingz are looking a bit more bromizing for us,

I subboze it'z time I came clean about zomething I've done which I subbose I really zhouldn't have.'

'What on earth do you mean, Declan?' Mum said.

Declan glanced at Lindsay.

'What is it, darling?' Lindsay asked.

Declan cleared his throat again. 'Err…err…would you mind butting your right hand into your bocked?'

'Yes, of course, darling,' Lindsay said. 'But which pocket do you mean?'

Declan went red and looked around really shamefacedly at Mum and me, and then turned to Lindsay again. 'De bocked on your right.'

Lindsay put her right hand below her toga and into her right trouser pocket.

'I can't find anything there, darling,' she said to Declan.

'Juzt but your hand right deeb down into it,' Declan instructed.

So Lindsay did. This time she obviously found something and she retrieved it and pulled it out and held it up.

What it was, was one of those little red heart-shaped toy things I'd seen in the toy shop.

'What's that?' I said to Declan.

'Yes, Declan, what is it?' Lindsay asked. She said 'Declan' now rather than 'darling'.

'I know what it is,' Mum said.

'What is it?' Dora asked.

'It's a Cantian Love Heart,' Mum said.

Mum looked hard at Declan. 'I think you should explain.'

'Yeah, explain, Dec,' Troy commanded his new best friend.

'Well, er…er…' said Declan, 'well, bazically if you but diz into zomeone'z bocked den dey vall in love automatically with the berson who but it in their bocked until it'z daken oud,' Declan said.

328

'Yes,' Mum said. 'That's basically it. And so what you did was find a way of putting a Cantian Love Heart into Lindsay's pocket, is that it, Declan?'

Declan didn't reply, but just went very red.

Lindsay glared at him. '*You mean you used this Love Heart thing to make me fall in love with you?*'

'Bazically, yez,' Declan replied. 'Oh, don'd look so accuzingly ad me, you liddle Cornizh bixie. I didn'd nodice you comblaining when we were having thad big kizz at the amphitheatre. You're a zuperb kizzer, by the way. You zeemed to really enjoy it.'

'*Only because you tricked me into loving you!*' Lindsay retorted.

I felt in a daze. Was it possible that Lindsay still liked me after all? I could hardly believe it.

'Anyway, I think Declan's been very silly, and I'm afraid I'm going to have to mention it in the report I make to my superiors,' Mum said. 'But, in all fairness, Declan, you've at least confessed, which will I suppose reduce whatever punishment they see fit to give you.'

Only now I realised why Declan had confessed, unless he'd also done it out of kindness to me, which was I suppose at least possible, or bozzible as Declan would have said.

I glanced at Lindsay. 'Does that mean you don't think you and I are history after all?'

'Josh, darling,' Lindsay said, 'I don't seem to have a very good memory of how my feelings were different for a while but they're certainly the way they always were. I like you very much. I'm very fond of you indeed. As for you, Declan, you've shown how brave you are and you're not such an idiot as I thought you were, but I have to say, you're really not my type. And besides, you're a bit old for me, in all fairness.'

Declan looked definitely upset, which I could imagine,

after all, *he'd* just been dumped by Lindsay now. Beautiful women have too much power, really.

Troy went over to him and patted him gently on the back. 'Don't worry, Dec. You're a hero now. I know we can't talk about Cantia if we ever manage to get out of here, but the fact you know you're a hero will change everything once we get back up to our world, if we do. Women will fall at your feet.'

'Dad'z very kind ov you, Droy, made,' Declan said. 'But acdually I do have a girlfriend. Only zhe's in London and I haven'd zeen her for a couble ov weekz.'

'*You mean you tricked me into loving you when all the time you had a girlfriend anyway?*' Lindsay demanded.

Declan gave a shrug. 'Zorry, bud yez.'

Lindsay gave a loud sigh.

'How does the Love Heart work?' Dora asked.

'Oh, I suppose it does something clever with pheromones and hormones,' Sam said, in his usual authoritative way.

'And how did you get it into my pocket, Declan?' Lindsay demanded.

'It waz when we were all hungry and waiding to zee wheder Jozh could win uz some money. Dere was one momend when you happened to have de right zide of your doga lifted ub a bid and you were dodally engrozzed in what Jozh was doing and you weren'd dinking about anyding else, you boor liddle devoded love-ztruck bixie. Dad was when I managed to zlip de Cantian Love Heart indo your right-hand bocked.'

'Now, that's what I call devious,' Troy said, but with a smile, as if now that Declan had done something like this, he really was one of the gang.

I had so many emotions swirling within me that I didn't really know what to do. But what was really amazing at this point is that Lindsay came over to me and gave me a kiss on the lips. Not a really long sexy kind of kiss but just a really lovely kiss as if to say *we're back together now.*

I wanted the kiss to go on longer, but we could hardly do that, not there in front of everyone. Lindsay and I broke the kiss, smiled at each other, and then joined the others in running to pick up our weapons. There was an additional high-tech one lying on the floor. Hullu pointed to it. *'The treasures of battle go to the victor,'* he said, solemnly. *'That is your prize.'*

'Thank you,' I said, glad we didn't have to insist.

'What did Hullu just say?' Mum asked.

'We can have the Time Sword.'

'Good,' she said.

'Iv we can ged id home,' said Declan, 'id'll be de very firzd alpha dechnology CAEZAR'z ever god from Candia.'

Troy nodded. 'The way I see it, we've all risked our lives to get this. Marcus has suffered even more. He's lost his mum, dad and grandad. I know CAESAR needs the Time Sword so that they can investigate it like Mrs Moonford said, but if we manage to get out of here and back to our world, I don't see why we should give the Time Sword to CAESAR for nothing.'

'I never said we had to, Troy,' Mum said.

'I want to carry the Time Sword,' said Dora.

'But you're bringing the trident with Sam,' I pointed out.

'We'll leave the trident here,' said Dora.

'No,' I said, 'we might need it.'

'I'll carry the Time Sword,' Mum said. 'But there's something else you *can* carry, Dora.'

'What's that?' Dora asked.

Mum glanced at me. 'What's "skull" in Latin, darling?'

'*Calvaria,*' I told her. 'The poor girl... she was only fourteen when she died.'

Mum nodded. 'Poor thing. Dora, you go and pick up the *calvaria*, and carry it proudly, because it's the skull of a girl who was only two years older than you. She never had the chance to become a woman. Yes, carry her skull with pride, and respect it.'

'But how shall I carry it, Mum?' Dora asked.

'Well, Dora,' Mum said, 'I suppose I think for the time being the easiest way to carry it would be to carry it round your neck.'

We were all very sad already because of Bruce, and what Mum had said about the girl made us even sadder. Dora, sniffling, went over to retrieve the skull, carefully put the cord round her neck, and let the girl's skull hang down in front of her. This made Dora look strangely scary.

'I dink Mrs Moonford is right and dat de Days of the Skull are over,' said Declan.

'But Vincent will still be a threat and a troublemaker when he gets back,' Mum said.

'I hope he's been sent thousand years into the future,' said Sam.

'Well, if he haz,' said Declan. 'I bity bosterity.'

I nodded my agreement, then looked at Carlo. 'How's your arm?'

'It hurts a lot,' he said, 'but the tourniquet seems to have helped. Tourniquets mustn't be kept on for too long, though. They cut off the blood and can cause gangrene. I just hope we can get home soon.' He glanced at Sam. 'How are you?'

'OK,' said Sam. 'It still hurts, but it stopped bleeding when Hullu held that strange golden ball over it. I'm more worried about Bruce.'

'You're brave,' Carlo said. He looked round at the rest of us. 'You all are.'

'If we get the skull home safe and sound,' I said, 'I don't think it - *she* - should be put on display again. She deserves a proper burial.'

'I agree,' said Carlo.

I glanced at Mum. 'Please be really careful with the Time Sword, and don't accidentally push any buttons or tweak any levers.'

'It's all right, Josh,' Mum said. 'I'm not completely hopeless with technology, even if I do run a health-food shop when I'm not working for CAESAR.'

'The Time Sword might be useful in *Terra Horridissima*,' Troy put in.

'If we can work out how to use it,' Declan said.

'Either way,' Mum said, 'We have to get Carlo to hospital and Bruce to a vet just as soon as we can.'

'If we can make it out of here,' said Troy.

78

Hullu led the way. Carlo looked pale. As for Sam, he was hanging in there, but he kept wincing, which I knew meant he was in more pain than he said he was. I wished the Ball of Wellness cured you more completely.

Bruce was only moving slowly. The flow of horrible brown stuff from his wound had stopped, but a great grey tiredness seemed to have fallen upon him, and I swear some of his scales had changed colour in places.

We followed Hullu down a corridor that ended in a white wall. But I wasn't too surprised to see the outline of a door appear in the wall as we got closer and for the door to open as Hullu reached it.

I was right behind Hullu, then came Marcus, Carlo, Troy and Declan, and Mum, Dora and Sam behind them. Bruce was keeping up with Sam, but only just. Hullu led us outside - or at least to the Cantian version of outside. The light was a lot dimmer than it had been earlier. The Cantian day was obviously heading for its end.

Ahead was a big field, where hundreds of enormous reddish-brown mushrooms - their tops at least a yard wide - were growing. The field stretched a long way on both sides. Beyond it, maybe a mile away, the top of a grey hill emerged from foggy mist.

Looking back, I saw the Hall of Holy Wisdom was an even bigger building than I'd imagined: vast, gleaming, silvery, windowless.

'I think Bruce is dying,' said Sam, almost in tears.

'No, no, he's OK, I'm sure,' I said.

'Follow me,' Hullu urged.

'We're coming,' I said. *'Hullu, what are these mushrooms?'*

'Boletus,' Hullu replied. *'A most expensive delicacy in Cantia. They are almost as expensive as the black elixir.'*

I wondered if Hullu meant Marmite.

He led us along a narrow path that ended about halfway across the field. We tried to avoid the large mushroom plants, and not to sink too deep into the soft brown earth. That wasn't easy, and everyone's feet and sandals got muddy. Poor Bruce, injured as he was, did the best of all of us, as his long body and scores of legs allowed him to spread his weight. But he was crawling along really slowly now.

At last we reached the end of the field, with the grey hill increasingly filling the horizon, its top now disappeared in the mist.

'Terra Horridissima is on the other side of the mountain,' Hullu explained. *'I must go no farther.'*

'Hullu,' I said, 'How dangerous is Terra Horridissima?'

'Hullu fears that it is very dangerous indeed, young Saxon warrior. But approach it with courage, make use of all your weapons and wit, and you may survive.'

We all put our weapons down so we could shake Hullu's tiny hand and bid him farewell.

'Goodbye, dear Hullu,' said Dora.

'Farewell, girl of much courage,' Hullu said.

I told my excellent sister what Hullu had just said. Dora leaned forwards, bent down and kissed Hullu on the forehead.

Hullu went bright red. He looked at us all and raised his tiny right hand, his palm vertical in salute.

'Hullu,' I said, *'is Augustus still alive?'*

'Yes, he is, young Saxon warrior.'

'How do you know?'

'Because, young Saxon warrior, Hullu must confess that he wickedly and foolishly helped his poor dead master Tiberius to deliver Augustus into the shades of sleep. But Augustus still lives.'

I gave a nod. 'Well, Hullu, you've helped us get out of here so I suppose that makes up for what you did. Listen, I think the people of Cantia will be much happier than they are now if Augustus is restored as proconsul.'

'Hullu listens and understands, young Saxon warrior. Hullu shall do what needs to be done.'

He waved at us and scampered away. His little form was soon lost from sight among the mushrooms.

Dora began to sniffle. 'I hope we see him again one day.'

I nodded. 'So do I.'

The hill, or mountain as Hullu had called it, blocked our view. There was no way round: it stretched as high and as far as I could see, and its extremities seemed to fade into mist in the distance.

'Time to climb,' said Carlo.

'Bruce will find this very difficult,' said Sam.

He was right. Bruce was terribly weak. All of us, including Declan, did our best to help him along by pushing him gently, or at least as much as we could, given that we needed to keep hold of our weapons. But he was so enormous and so heavy, we couldn't really make much difference. Bruce managed to struggle up the hill, but you could tell from the way his sides were heaving he was finding the climb really tough.

Yet somehow we slowly climbed the hill, which was pretty steep, maybe (I thought) about forty degrees. We were helped a little, and I suppose this applied to Bruce too, by the hillside being mostly rough, grey rock, which made it easier to grip.

It was about an hour before we started to approach the misty peak. Bruce was still doing his best. Mum was so eager to help push Bruce, she kept dropping the Time Sword. Every time she did I was worried it might suddenly activate and send some of us to some remote future time, where girls are even bossier than they are now, or worse still, might not exist.

But finally, we reached the summit.

It was really foggy up there, and we had to stay close to see each other at all.

Bruce was in a very bad way, his sides were heaving more than ever and for the last ten minutes or so he'd gone so slowly we'd had to wait for him several times.

'*He's dying,*' Sam said again, and now he was in tears.

'We have to keep going, if we're going to have a chance of saving him, Sam. We can't carry him,' I said.

'I don't think Bruce can go on much more,' Lindsay said.

'Come on, Bruce, come on,' Dora urged.

'Yes, do your best, Bruce,' Carlo said, patting him lovingly with his uninjured left arm.

Bruce made a sort of supermillipede effort, and got going again, and we all pushed him. Dora was in tears now and I felt pretty sad myself, but tried not to show it.

The mist grew thicker.

'I'm just so nervous about *Terra Horridissima,*' said Dora.

'We have to be brave,' said Troy. 'We've done pretty well so far, I reckon.'

We silently agreed, and carried on helping Bruce.

Slowly the mist began to clear.

Suddenly I called out: 'I feel… grass under my feet!'

The moment I felt that, I felt something else, too.

There was a strange blast of warm air on my face, as if a great mass of energy was pulsating all round us. A moment later, Bruce's body, which I was pushing against, suddenly vanished, and I fell over, dropping my sword as I did.

I picked up my sword. 'Where's Bruce gone?' I said.

We all stopped walking.

Then I saw him.

Bruce was a couple of yards in front of me, caught in some long tufts of grass.

He was small again.

Sam went and gently and lovingly picked Bruce up.

He looked hard at Bruce, then glanced round at us all. *'He's dead,'* Sam whispered, then began to cry.

We crowded round, and stroked Bruce, and took turns to hold him. I put down my sword and cupped Bruce in my hands, desperately hoping that at any moment I'd feel a leggy sensation like I did before.

But this time I didn't.

79

'I don't *understand*,' Sam muttered, wiping his eyes with the sleeve of his toga. 'Why did Bruce have to die? He'd beaten everyone. But that last horrible earwig... it just ran up and got him. That was the only way Bruce could be killed, by something sneaky and evil.'

'Sam,' I said, 'Bruce... he was our hero. He saved us all. He gave his life for us.'

'Well said,' murmured Carlo.

'*Why did Bruce get smaller again?*' said Sam. 'The lion didn't when we killed it.'

'I think I know why,' Declan said. '*Look.*'

And he pointed ahead of us, to where the mist was thinner. I saw grass ahead, and the open sky.

We were back in our own world.

I know I should've felt glad we were back in 'the World Above' again, but I was too sad about Bruce to feel happy. I still cupped poor Bruce in my hands. Lindsay had picked up my sword.

And then... we were in the open air, and stumbling through thick grass on a green hill. At the top we looked out over a town beside a bright blue sea that stretched to the horizon, with the evening light slowly fading overhead.

'What I dink,' Declan said, 'is dat zomehow bio-amblivicazhun can't be maintained outzide Cantia.'

'You could be right,' I said. 'I felt a great gust of warm air back then.'

'I felt it, too,' said Sam. 'Perhaps... perhaps that was when the energy the bio-amplification uses left Bruce. And by then, he was dead.'

'I think you must be right,' Mum said to him.

She gave the Time Sword to Dora, who was still wearing the girl's skull round her neck. Then Mum went and put her arms round Sam. After all, despite his genius at understanding what was happening to us and how Cantian technology works, he was only a tiddler really.

I looked round at them all.

There was Mum, no longer just our Mum, but, amazingly, quite high up in CAESAR, and who'd been paid by CAESAR all this time, which is why there'd always been enough money, even though the shop did so badly.

There was Sam, who was still holding poor dead Bruce in his cupped hands.

There was Dora, carrying the Time Sword and with the skull.

There was Lindsay, leaning on my sword. Lindsay, who liked me again.

There was Carlo, with his tourniquet and with his bow and two quivers.

There were Troy and Declan - big mates now - with their spears and swords.

And there was Marcus, holding a sword in his right hand and a shield in his left. I'd forgotten about him. His eyes were like stars, they were so wide they caught the setting sun, and his mouth hung open, at his first sight of the World Beyond. I knew that feeling.

Our world.

Somehow, we'd all managed to survive.

But not Bruce.
Bruce was dead.

I looked back to see where we'd come from, but... and this was very strange, I couldn't see any mist behind us, let alone any grey hill that might have led back down to Cantia. I saw that we were on a hilltop, in thick green grass, and that the hilltop sloped gradually down behind us, until it merged with another, smaller hill which wasn't, however, the hill we'd come up. Cantia was gone.

'I love our world,' said Lindsay.

I knew what she meant. But in many ways, she's a deeper person than me. She probably thought deeper things about it. I was just glad to be back.

It was a beautiful evening. It was still summer, after all, and while maybe the Cantians didn't know what summer was, we did.

Dora turned round and looked at the view of the town and the sea. 'Where exactly *are* we?'

'Back in our own world,' Declan said. 'Dat town's Whitztable.'

'Whitstable?' echoed Dora.

'We've been here a few times,' said Mum, with a smile as she glanced at me and the twins.

'Dere'z de Old Nebtune bub over in de distance, on de beach,' Declan put in. 'I've often gone to gigz dere with Bamela.'

'Pamela, you mean?' I said.

'Yes, Bamela. My girlfriend. I don'd zee her az often az I'd like to, unvortunately, becauze zhe livez in London.'

'Declan, does Pamela know you're in CAESAR?' I asked.

'No, Jozh,' and it suddenly seemed to me that he really

was going to call me only "Josh" from now on. 'I can'd led her know, eider,' Declan added.

'Carlo, we need to get you and Sam to hospital,' Lindsay said.

Carlo nodded. He glanced at Mum. 'I need to phone Frankie . . . she's my producer... to tell her I'm OK and to arrange a people-carrier for us. The way everyone's dressed, we obviously have to keep out of people's way and hide the Time Sword. Unfortunately, with my arm like this I can't drive. Do you drive, Isabella?'

'I'm afraid not,' Mum said.

'I can,' said Declan.

'You *can*?' I said.

He gave a quick nod. 'Yeah. What'z the broblem? You dink intellectualz can't drive?'

'No, he just thought *you* couldn't, Dec,' said Troy.

Declan grinned at him. 'I'll have you know I bassed my dest last zpring, youngster.'

'What did you bribe the examiner with?' said Troy, with a smile.

Declan grinned at that, but didn't say anything. I must say I felt pretty surprised myself; I mean, at the thought of Declan driving. It didn't seem to me like a Declan type of thing to do.

'Excellent,' said Carlo. 'The movie company vehicles all have comprehensive insurance for any driver, so that won't be a problem.'

'Good job it's insured, if Dec's going to be driving it,' said Troy, though he was still smiling.

Carlo used my phone to call Frankie, and told her how to find him. Obviously he didn't say a word about us and we all stayed completely silent while he made the call. He asked her to come in a Galaxy Pictures people-carrier, and not to bring anyone with her.

He also asked Frankie to bring two changes of clothes for him. I realised Carlo cunningly wasn't asking Frankie to bring clothes that would fit someone of Sam's height, as Carlo wouldn't want Frankie to know he was with any other people.

I could tell from Carlo's sudden silence on the phone that Frankie had started asking him what had happened to him, where he'd been, but he said it was a 'long story' and that now wasn't the time to tell it. He also told her he didn't want any news going out to the media for the time being, but would she tell his mum and dad he was OK?

Carlo ended the call, then glanced at us all. 'When Frankie comes I'll meet her alone and commandeer the people-carrier,' he said.

'What are you going to tell her about your clothes?' I asked him.

Carlo shrugged. 'I'll say I was kidnapped by a crazy fan who forced me at gunpoint to put these clothes on, but I managed to escape. That story has the advantage of being more or less true, after all. Frankie mustn't see any of you, let alone the Time Sword. When I'm in the people-carrier I'll ask her to get a cab back to Canterbury - I think I'll tell her I'm waiting for a friend who'll drive me back and that I need to report what happened to me to the police before I can leave, and that, in any case, I want to get changed by myself. I'm her boss, so she won't ask any unhelpful questions.'

'Let's hope not,' said Mum.

'Don't worry, Isabella. Frankie won't cause any problems.' He smiled at mum. 'Once Frankie's gone I'll use the people-carrier's onboard phone to call Josh and you can all come down to the vehicle.'

'What if we get spotted while we're waiting for you, Carlo?' asked Dora.

Carlo shrugged. 'Just say you're rehearsing a Roman play outdoors. As soon as I'm back we'll go to hospital so Sam and I can get our wounds seen to.'

I nodded.

We said goodbye to Carlo, who went off. He looked like the star of *Gladiator 2*. Dora gave Bruce back to Sam to hold. Then, one by one, we collapsed down onto the long grass and just lay there looking at the sky. It was hard to know how I felt. I mean, I was so, so sad about Bruce's death. Without him, we wouldn't have made it. I was very glad to be home, yet I missed Cantia already.

'I suppose the Cantians call it *Terra Horridissima* to put people off trying to get out and exploring our world,' I said.

Lindsay shrugged. 'Or perhaps they think our world *is* a terrifying place.'

'Yes, perhaps they do,' Mum said. 'But it's a beautiful place too. And it's all we have.'

'Apart from Cantia,' said Dora.

80

Once I heard from Carlo on my phone, we hurried down the hill to the people-carrier. Carlo was there by himself, wearing a pair of blue jeans and a black tee-shirt with *The Archbishop's Anagram* on it in spidery white lettering.

As I got into the people-carrier, I noticed that up at the front of the vehicle, above the windscreen, there was what looked like a flat TV screen probably about two feet wide and one foot deep. As I sat down I asked Carlo what this was for. 'Oh,' he said, 'we sometimes need to watch rushes of movies - that's the raw footage after a shoot - while we're on location. It's also got a microphone and a loudspeaker built into it so that we can Skype with other movie industry people and executives of the company whenever we want to.'

I nodded.

'Frankie's phoned the Chaucer Hospital,' he said. 'They're expecting me, and they know I'm bringing someone else, too. OK, Declan, let's go.'

Carlo quickly showed Declan the way round the people-carrier's control panel. While he did this, Dora emptied some junk out of a cardboard box she found in the back, then took the skull and its cord from around her neck and carefully placed it in the box.

Once Declan had worked out how to use the controls, which involved only three jerking stalls, a few accidental swishes of the windscreen wipers, an accidental spurt of the windscreen washer, and then a deliberate swish of the windscreen wipers to clean the window, we set off.

The last thing Declan did by mistake before driving off was switch on the radio. It was playing some Golden Oldies channel, and we joined it in the middle of that excellent song 'We are the Champions' by Queen, which seemed to me very appropriate at that moment.

The next song was 'The Long and Winding Road' by the Beatles.

Carlo said, 'I love this song!' the moment he heard it start to play.

Mum gave a little cough. 'So did my husband. So do I.'

I wondered if she was going to start to cry.

We all listened.

> *The long and winding road*
> *That leads to your door.*
> *Will never disappear*
> *I've seen that road before.*
>
> *Many times I've been alone*
> *And many times I've cried*
> *All the same you'll never know*
> *The many ways I've tried.*

None of us said anything until the song ended. Then Mum began to cry a bit, so I gave her a hug. I really wished Dad was still around, so he could hug her too.

We got to the Chaucer Hospital, which is on the south side of Canterbury, on the outskirts, about half an hour's drive from Whitstable. In the hospital car park, Declan drove the people-carrier to a lurching standstill.

It was dark, and everything was quiet.

Carlo gave Sam the clothes he'd got for him, as Sam's were all bloody. Sam changed behind the people-carrier after asking us all not to look. When we were allowed to, I saw he'd rolled up the bottom of the trousers so they'd fit. The shirt looked pretty baggy on him, of course, but Sam, little hero as he was, didn't look as silly in it as you might've expected.

Once Sam was dressed, Carlo quickly changed behind the people-carrier too.

Sam gave me the food container with poor Bruce in it, then Carlo and Sam headed into the hospital together.

Now there was nothing else for us to do but wait.

Lindsay and I held hands - well, my hand that wasn't holding the food container with Bruce's little body in it, anyway.

I was glad of a chance to sit and think about everything for a while and just sort of absorb it.

Dora and Troy chatted quietly to each other about Cantia. I got the sense they were more interested in chatting to each other than in what they were saying. Marcus sat in the back seat, looking spaced-out at being in the World Beyond. I suppose, for him, it was like when we'd first discovered Cantia. And of course he didn't understand any of what we were saying either. But I was sure we could teach him English before long, and that Dora and Sam would teach him some rude words and how to use computers and phones etc.

Suddenly I wanted to be in Cantia again. Even the times when Lindsay had upset me didn't seem to matter as much as they had when we were in Cantia.

81

It was quite dark in the people-carrier, as the interior light wasn't on and the only lights, which were from the hospital some way away, didn't really reach us. Lindsay and I were already sitting close to each other. I put the food container down on the empty seat next to me. Now Lindsay and I snuggled up closer, and then we were so close and (I think) feeling so excited by our Cantian adventure that we just had to kiss, and we did. And we really liked it (well, I did, and I hope Lindsay did too), so we just went on kissing.

If the others noticed they didn't say anything. I thought Declan might make a cutting comment, but he didn't, perhaps because he was dinking of Bamela.

It must have been about half an hour before Carlo and Sam came back. Lindsay and I had kissed almost all that time. Of course it was dark in the people carrier, which was quite spacious, so it was quite easy to be private in there. The half hour seemed to go *incredibly* fast.

I thought kissing Lindsay was even more amazing than being in Cantia.

When Carlo and Sam came back, Carlo had a white bandage over his left forearm, Sam, who had a dressing on his leg, was holding a bottle of tablets.

'How did things go?' Mum asked Carlo.

'Sam's had his wound cleaned and bandaged, Isabella,' Carlo said. 'He's been given painkillers, but luckily didn't need any stitches: I presume we've Hullu's golden ball to thank for that.'

'What about you, Carlo?' Mum asked.

Carlo smiled at Mum again. 'The bullet was quite near the surface. Thank God it was an ordinary metal bullet and not a hollowpoint. I told the hospital there'd been an accident at the studio's shooting-range. Oh, and I said Sam had fallen over. That was sort of true, I suppose. They were able to take my bullet out with just a local anaesthetic. I need to go back tomorrow for a check-up, but they said I'm all right to go now.'

Now Carlo smiled one of his bright movie-star smiles at all of us with his white teeth.

'Let's go home,' he said.

82

Declan started the people-carrier again, this time without stalling it even once and without accidentally putting the radio on.

As the people-carrier headed out of the car-park, I looked through the window across a gloomy, dusky field that led into the heart of the even gloomier countryside.

Dusk had settled in now. I remembered a line from *Macbeth*, which we'd done in English the previous term. The line I remembered was about light thickening and 'the crow making wing to the rooky wood'. Macbeth said it when he was going mental because his life was starting to get too dark and devilish.

As I thought this, an amazing thing happened.

The screen suddenly gave a beep and came on. At once, the screen was filled with a large face whose features I recognised at once from the TV news. The podgy cheeks, the stringy black hair, the fleshy ears, the big red nose and the large mouth: there was no mistaking them.

'Sir Stanley Templeton-Greene!' I gasped, wondering how on earth he'd managed to make the screen come on.

'Yes, indeed,' he bellowed. 'Can you all hear me?'

Declan quickly brought the people-carrier to a stop at the edge of the car-park. He switched the engine off.

'You're that politician bloke Sir Stanley Templeton-Greene, aren't you?' Carlo said, then turned to us all and, shaking his head, mouthed more than whispered, *'I've not put the camera on. He can't see us.'*

'"Politician bloke"?' Sir Stanley echoed, in his booming voice. He obviously hadn't heard what Carlo had mouthed, though. 'If you mean, the most able and talented politician in Britain, yes. You must be Carlo Clancy, the actor. I recognise your voice from a DVD I once saw of a stupid movie about some elves. I've been following the media coverage of your disappearance.'

'How did you get my phone number?' Carlo demanded. 'Or make the screen come on?'

'Listen, Clancy,' replied Sir Stanley, 'I'm Britain's Minister for Technology. Do you seriously imagine there's any telephone number in the United Kingdom, or indeed anywhere in the world, I can't obtain if I need it? As for activating the screen in your car remotely, it was a piece of cake for someone of my technological talent.'

'Yes,' said Mum, 'and apparently so was arranging for Vincent and Dinsdale Stokes to be sent down to Cantia.'

'I wish I could see you,' said Sir Stanley to Mum. 'You've a nice voice. What are you doing next Saturday? How about a romantic weekend with me in Monte Carlo on my yacht?'

'Thanks, but no thanks,' said Mum.

'Somehow, Stan,' said Carlo, 'I don't think you're her type. She doesn't like villains.'

'Why do you assume I'm a villain?' Sir Stanley retorted. 'Because I'm a little overweight? Is that the basis of your morality?'

I cleared my throat. 'No,' I said, 'actually it isn't because of that. It's because Vincent Stokes boasted to me that you sent him down to where you sent him, and that you arranged for his brother Dinsdale to be released from prison so he could be there too. Oh, and Vincent also told us you've some friends abroad who'll pay you a fortune for each Time Sword you supply to them.'

Sir Stanley's charming face flushed red with fury. 'That stupid Cockney half-wit! He should have kept his mouth shut! I should never have involved Vincent and his brother!'

'Oh, by the way,' I said, really doing my best to stay calm, 'Vincent Stokes didn't actually tell me anything about you. But just now, you did.'

Sir Stanley's face became even more contorted with rage. 'You little devil! Who are you? What's your name? I can't see you, but I'll remember your voice! You'll regret this!'

'No,' said Carlo. '*You'll* regret this.'

'Oh, shut up, Clancy, you overpaid Thespian,' retorted Sir Stanley. 'Your movies are all nonsense, and you are utterly overrated.'

Sir Stanley drew a few large, loud, breaths then looked at us all, his invisible adversaries. 'Listen, all of you. You think you've won, don't you? Trust me, my friends: *the game has only just started.* Shall I let you all into a little secret? It's this: *I've already got a Time Sword, and I know how it works.*'

I said nothing. Nor did anyone else in the car.

'Yes, that's shut you all up, hasn't it?' said Sir Stanley. 'How did I find out about Cantia and get hold of a Time Sword? We'll meet again, make no mistake. You may think you've won, but you haven't. I always win in the end. I shall return. *Oh yes, I shall return!*'

He began to cackle in the most terrible of ways. After a few seconds of his cackling and us having to look at Sir Stanley's ghastly gloating and boasting face, the screen suddenly went black and, somehow, switched itself off with a dull pinging sound.

'He's finished,' Carlo said. 'He's just bluster and hot air, that's all.'

'But he said he's got a Time Sword,' I said.

'He must be lying,' said Carlo.

Everyone, including me, gave a grunt or murmur of agreement. After all, who was going to argue with Carlo? I couldn't help wondering, though, how Sir Stanley knew about Time Swords at all.

83

What I knew for certain was that life would never be the same again.

There was so much I was still wondering about, of course. How was Sir Stanley Templeton-Greene connected with CAESAR... if he was? How had Vincent and Dinsdale Stokes got involved? How had they learnt Latin in a week when they were so dim? What was happening in Cantia now? What would it be like to work with CAESAR, that is, if they allowed us to? Would Lindsay, Troy, Marcus and the twins be allowed to join CAESAR as well? What other amazing technology were the Cantians inventing? What would CAESAR do with the Time Sword?

And what would happen to Lindsay and me?

Then I had another thought.

Wasn't it weird that Dad had suddenly disappeared without trace?

Over the past eight years I'd got so used to the idea of Dad vanishing, that by now it seemed almost normal. But of course it wasn't normal for your dad suddenly to disappear for no particular reason.

And the point was, our time in Cantia had been so weird too. And that was what set me thinking...

Was it possible, I wondered, was it just possible, that somehow the two biggest mysteries of my life were connected?

Declan drove Troy home and they did a high-five when they said goodbye. Troy said it was a great shame it was so dark, because he really would have liked his neighbours to have seen him leaving a car 'which Carlo Clancy was in'.

Declan then drove Lindsay back to her house. I gave her a hug outside the car and then she went into her house. I knew that Troy and Lindsay would have a lot of explaining to do to their parents but Mum had of course already spoken to their parents about the mystery of their disappearance before she'd been abducted and taken down to Cantia. Mum promised that later that evening she would phone Lindsay's mum and dad and also Troy's dad and explain as much as she could explain what was going on. Of course Lindsay and Troy knew they couldn't tell their parents anything about Cantia.

As for Lindsay's mother, I was pretty sure her affair would be ending now because of course Lindsay was able to tell her mum and dad what Declan had told her about the man Lindsay's mum was seeing, although of course Lindsay knew she couldn't say what the source was.

Declan drove Mum, Dora, Sam, Marcus and me to our house on Prospect Place, then we said goodbye to him and he drove off to his own house. I was sure he'd enjoy, in the morning, his neighbours seeing the Galaxy Pictures people-carrier parked outside his home.

The rest of that evening was really really amazing. Of course, it was great to see CAESAR again… I mean Caesar my pet parrot. Mum had only been kidnapped and taken to Cantia the previous Friday evening - unlike us, Mum hadn't gone forward in time a week, and Caesar had been OK, as he'd had enough food and water for two days in his cage.

After I'd replenished Caesar's water container (it wasn't

completely empty anyway) and filled his food container to the brim with the birdseed he liked, we all spent the evening playing Monopoly, at least after Mum had made us a very nice vegetable stir-fry.

Marcus was pretty much in a complete daze, which wasn't surprising. Declan, who of course was and is an expert in helping Cantian people come to our world, had told me not to hesitate to give him a call (he gave me his phone number of course) if Marcus showed any signs of going into meltdown. But Marcus didn't.

Marcus would be sleeping in the spare room just inside the hallway that leads to the main living room and while the spare room is, as I think I've mentioned, fairly full of Mum's stock it was actually quite easy for me to get a futon from Mum's bedroom that she didn't need and which had been at the back of a cupboard for some time and to make it into a bed with the help of Dora, Sam and me lugging it around and getting blankets down so that Marcus would have somewhere to stay.

It was amazing, really, having a Cantian boy staying with us.

I wondered what Marcus would think of our world.

He loved the stir-fry and he helped us all wash up afterwards. I suppose the truth is that young people like us are much more adaptable about coming to a completely strange world rather than older people who must have a lot more problems adapting.

Also, Marcus enjoyed playing Monopoly with us, though he didn't do too well; he kept getting sent to jail. It was very sad to be playing without Bruce and I noticed that there were often tears in Sam's eyes. Mum won, needless to say, and this time, because Marcus was there, she didn't do her usual complex lending and showing mercy that she normally did because it would have seemed a bit silly if she'd done it just for us. I suppose that was a private thing and not something she would do while Marcus was there with us.

I asked Mum, during Monopoly, whether I was going to get made part of CAESAR and whether Dora and Sam were. Mum said she couldn't talk about it because she had to discuss it with 'her superiors,' whatever that meant.

She also said she had to discuss it with Declan. I didn't really like the idea that my future career in CAESAR would be subject to what Declan thought: the guy who had tricked me and Lindsay so horribly really with the Cantian Love Heart, but all the same, I suppose when you're part of an organisation or when you want to join an exciting organisation anyway, you need to accept things the way they are.

'What shall we do with Marcus tomorrow?' Sam asked Mum, after we'd finished the game of Monopoly and were all having bedtime cocoa.

'Again, I need to talk to my superiors,' Mum said. 'But for the time being, I think Marcus should simply come to school with you. How old is he, by the way?'

'Fifteen,' I said, 'at least as far as I've been able to work it out from what he told me about how the Cantian calendar works.'

'Well,' said Mum, 'schools are usually all right about pen-pals from abroad spending a few days or even a week with the person whose pen-pal they are, so I think you should just take him to school tomorrow and if any teachers ask they can always phone me during break and I can explain the situation.'

Marcus was extremely excited about this plan after I told him what a school in the World Above was. They had them in Cantia too, apparently, but the schools there were much smaller and they were strictly segregated between girls and boys, which of course our school, the Joseph Conrad High School, isn't. Dora and Sam were really excited that Marcus was coming to school with us.

84

That week was pretty amazing. Of course Marcus had a tough time at school because he couldn't basically understand any of the lessons at all, but he sat next to me and I gave him all the help I could and in any classes which I was sharing with Lindsay, she gave him help too. Marcus began to learn English from the very first evening he was with us and by the end of that week he spoke a surprising amount.

It wasn't going to be easy to help him learn English because after all you can't exactly just go into a book shop and buy a Latin-language book called, in Latin, *Teach Yourself English* but all the same Lindsay and I gave him all the help we could and in the evenings the twins helped too. Mum suggested that Marcus get a notebook and write down all the English words he knew and he did this - Sam supplied him with the notebook. Sam's always got stationery among his things.

Marcus was at least lucky that Latin and English use the same alphabet. It seemed weird realising this. I mean, I'd always known this, but it suddenly seemed weird because the idea of Cantia being the last bastion of the Roman Empire was a really strange idea that I was still trying to assimilate and yet it didn't seem so far-fetched when I realised that our alphabet was basically the same, although of course we have some letter combinations e.g. 'th' for the beginning of the word 'thin' or 'the' which the Romans didn't because they didn't have the sounds at the beginnings of those two words. Or at least if they used those letters they didn't have the sounds. Somehow, being at school with Marcus that week made me realise how close in many ways the Roman culture still is to ours even *now*.

Marcus was fascinated by everything. He looked around with awe at the school, the classrooms, the other people.

He found it really amazing that girls were in the class with us. Apparantly in Cantia boys and girls went to separate schools. Marcus did his homework as well as he could: Sam, Dora and I all helped him and none of the teachers seemed to mind or object.

The only difficulty, needless to say, was when we had Latin with Mr Kinder, our Latin teacher.

Marcus came with me to the Latin lesson. Naturally, I'd briefed him very carefully beforehand that he simply mustn't speak too much Latin in the class and mustn't give the impression that he found the exercises too easy. He complied with this to some extent, although not really very well and at one point when Mr Kinder asked us a question in Latin, Marcus replied in what was sounding like horribly good Latin until I gave him a nudge under the table and he fell silent. Mr Kinder seemed a bit bewildered by him but fortunately didn't have any suspicions after I explained that Marcus had been studying Latin since he was very young. Well, that was true enough.

Of course that evening when I got my Latin homework, Marcus helped me and it was really a doddle.

What was also interesting was that all throughout the week Marcus was asking me more and more questions about the Ancient Romans.

I'd have thought he would have known a lot about them from school in Cantia but apparently the Cantians themselves didn't have a great deal of knowledge about the Ancient Romans: their knowledge about them was mostly legendary.

Marcus kept asking me questions about Ancient Rome and of course I did know quite a lot about it and I felt in a really weird way that I was giving him information which all was completely central to Cantian culture because of course as far as they were concerned ancient Rome was absolutely their cultural and social origins even though for them those origins were lost in the mists of time and legend.

To change the subject from Ancient Rome, at least for the moment, Dora, Sam and I took Marcus to McFarlanes burger restaurant - the twenty-four-hour McFarlanes on Canterbury High Street, on Tuesday evening for a feast of fast food.

Marcus found McFarlanes fascinating. He had a King Mac, large chips, an orange juice and he poured himself three of those little cardboard pots of tomato sauce.

I've never in my life seen a human being enjoy a meal as much as Marcus enjoyed his first visit to McFarlanes.

I wasn't completely sure whether this was because after all, fast-food burgers can taste quite nice as long as you don't have them too often, or simply whether because compared with eating giant maggots and all the other weird stuff they eat in Cantia he must have felt like being in McFarlanes was like paradise.

And then on the Friday evening, at about six o'clock, after that week with Marcus, which was the first week back at school after our experience in Cantia, we got a visit from Declan.

Mum only gave us a few minutes' notice to say that he'd be arriving. When he did, he and Mum spoke together quietly in the kitchen, with the kitchen door shut, and with

Dora, Sam, Marcus and me all desperate to know what Declan was talking about. Finally, after about half an hour, Mum and Declan emerged.

'What's happening Mum?' I asked.

'Quite a lot of exciting things, actually, Josh,' Mum said. 'Apparently CAESAR has accepted the recommendation Declan and I have made that you, Dora, Sam, Lindsay and Troy are all to be given probationary periods as CAESAR members.'

'Brilliant!' shouted Sam.

'Great!' said Dora.

'What about Marcus?' Sam asked.

'He's included too,' Mum replied carefully, 'but because he's a Cantian there have to be some things which are kept secret from him for the foreseeable future. Anyway, what I need to tell you all is that tomorrow morning, Saturday, we're all going on a flight.'

'What do you mean, "all of us"?' I asked Mum.

'I mean everybody,' Mum replied. Declan gave a solemn nod. 'I mean you, the twins, Marcus, Declan, Lindsay and Troy.'

'What about Carlo?' Dora asked.

'I don't know about Carlo,' Mum said. 'I'm going to Whatsapp him later this evening and tell him what's going on. I know he's very busy with his movie preparations here in Canterbury but maybe he'll be able to get the weekend off, I just don't know.'

'Where are we going, Mum?' I asked.

She smiled. 'Rome.'

'*Rome?* Why?'

'Josh, darling, you're on your probationary period for CAESAR now and one thing you need to learn when you're on a probationary period for an important organisation like CAESAR, is not to ask questions all the time. There is a reason why we're all going to Rome but I'm not allowed to tell you yet. I don't know when I can tell you. You just have to trust us.'

'Your Mum's right, Josh,' Declan said.

He only called me Josh nowadays, not Moonford.

'Are you OK about coming with us?' I asked Declan. 'I mean, I'm only thinking of you. You haven't seen Pamela for a while.'

'That's very thoughtful of you,' Declan said. His nose had apparently recovered. 'In fact,' he went on, 'I'm going to go and stay with Pamela in London next weekend, I mean the one after this one, but a lot might happen between now and then so I'd better not talk too soon.'

'What do you mean?' I asked Declan.

'I can't tell you any more at the moment, Josh,' he replied.

Well, we hadn't had our dinner yet but we did have dinner though as we all had to do our packing, Mum gave me the money and I went to the Jasmine Garden Chinese take-away on nearby Zealand Road. I bought a take-away for us all including Declan who stayed with us that evening until about ten o'clock, when he walked home.

The plan was that we would be picked up by Declan driving some vehicle CAESAR was supplying at nine o'clock in the morning and he'd drive us to Heathrow and we'd get a plane to Rome at two o'clock on Saturday afternoon. I didn't know how long we were supposed to stay in Rome, or whether we'd be going back to school on Monday or indeed any time during the following week. I just knew I had to be quiet and let things unfold.

I still couldn't imagine why we were going to Rome, but it seemed very fortunate for us because of course Marcus had been fascinated by the place all week and he was extremely excited we were going there. In fact, he seemed to think the whole idea of us going there was just for his benefit, and I had to gently explain that that wasn't really the case. He told us all over our Chinese take-aways, which we had in the living room sitting on the sofas and armchairs, that he was really excited that the following day he would be seeing, as he put it in Latin, *'Ultra Caelum Patet Mundus,'* that is, 'The World Above the Sky'.

85

Well, that was that. It had all been arranged. I still didn't know why we were going to Rome, but I didn't ask about that any more. Carlo, to Dora's enormous disappointment, wouldn't be coming with us but Mum and he had agreed to keep him closely in touch by Whatsapp. I didn't know how much she'd be telling him about what happened to us in Rome. I did know that Carlo had promised Mum not to tell anyone about CAESAR. What I really hoped is that when we were in Rome, Mum might ask Carlo to come and see us.

The following day, the Saturday morning, we all got up really early and in a very excited frame of mind, Declan came and picked us up in a white minibus with no writing on the sides and about ten seats inside. Declan had a passport for Marcus with him. I'd completely forgotten that Marcus would need a passport (the rest of us already had them). It was pretty obvious CAESAR could do pretty much everything.

Declan drove us to Heathrow airport without any accidents, and parked in the long-stay car park. After going through the laborious security procedures, which of course nowadays means pretty much taking off all your clothes at the security check to make sure that you're free of horrible devices which could interfere with the flight or blow people up, we went to the boarding gate and caught a British Airways flight at 14:05 to Rome.

As the plane climbed into the sky from Heathrow airport, I held Lindsay's right hand tightly in my left. She had the window seat and was looking thrilled at taking off. I was thrilled too, but what was really on my mind *was why we* were going to Rome.

Yet deep down, I think I knew.

Deep down, I think I knew, or at least suspected, even then, that it was something to do with Dad.

THE END

ACKNOWLEDGEMENTS

Josh Moonford and the Lost City of Cantia is not an extremely long novel, but it has had an extremely long gestation.

I wrote the first words for it on a night in early April in 2006. That first draft was written in the third-person and I made the draft far too long: Josh and his friends didn't even go down into Cantia until about page 400 and the book itself had 774 pages long and was more than 150,000 words long. Inexplicably to me now, I had become too interested in describing their lives at school and in Canterbury before the actual Cantia adventure began.

The problem was that I thought I was writing a kind of *Lord of the Rings*-type epic when in fact I was writing nothing of the kind: I was simply trying to produce a thriller about some young people - three of whom, Josh, Sam and Dora were based on people I actually knew - and what happened when they went into Cantia.

Also, because I did write the first draft in the third-person, it was horribly full of my own judgments and opinions about my characters and the world of Cantia. In short, it didn't work, though when I look at that early draft - I still have it - there are some things in it which I think are quite amusing and some plot ideas which I want to develop if I ever write a sequel.

Unfortunately, I am one of those writers who when they write in the third-person, tend to bring themselves too much into the story. I have written one published novel in the third-person - I wrote it as a ghost writer so I can't mention its name here - where I didn't intrude into the story too much and the novel worked reasonably well as a result. But I was always passionately interested in the idea of an underground world underneath Canterbury, and in the end I discovered that I could only have any chance of writing the book successfully viz. by eliminating myself from it, if I told it in the first person from Josh's point of view. Sometime in 2008, after spending untold hours over revising the third-person version, I decided to rewrite the book completely into a first draft of the book that became *Josh Moonford and the Lost City of Cantia*.

But that was still a long time ago and the book went through literally dozens of edits and revisions as I changed my mind about what needed emphasising and as I gradually got to know Josh, Lindsay, Dora, Sam, Troy and Declan much better. Eventually I was able to do what any novelist should be able to do, which is basically to let his or her characters in effect be the story themselves and do the job with minimal interference from the author.

Incidentally, the plot idea that Declan (who I admit is my favourite character and loosely based on my favourite Shakespearian character - Jacques in *As You Like It*) was in fact part of CAESAR, only came to me quite late in the creative process, perhaps in 2009 though I don't remember the exact year. I do, however, remember exactly when the idea came to me: I was walking down Nunnery Fields in Canterbury, where I live, and crossing the pavement on the railway bridge close to my home when the idea suddenly occurred to me. Once it had and I had put it into the story, the overall plot became much more complex and, I hope, more interesting.

During my journey with *Josh Moonford and the Lost City of Cantia* (whose original title was, simply, *Cantia* but that seemed too vague to me and didn't give enough idea of what the book was really about), I've had encouragement and advice from many people, especially my good friend the writer Jo Bavington-Jones, who suggested the title under which the book was published. Thanks also to you, Jo, for your careful proof-reading, but any mistakes that remain in the book are my fault, not Jo's.

My great gratitude to New York literary agent Russell Galen, who gave me absolutely loads of advice about the early draft of the book and how I needed to make it better, in particular that I had to learn how to show rather than tell. Russ wrote me a 6,000-word email about my writing which changed my attitude to writing fiction and frankly inspired me to write much better than I had before.

Other people whose help I've greatly appreciated, in alphabetical order of surname, are: Lee Butcher, Mollie Cheek, Annelisa Christensen, Stuart Conquest GM, Sally Day, David Davies, Rupert Essinger, Sandra Glover, Emily Green, Dr Laurence Green, Michael Green, Andrew Greet IM, Francesca Garratt, Uschi Grounds, Stephen Gillatt, Fiona Godfrey, Jovanka Houska IM, Briony Kapoor, Helen Komatsu, Caspar Latham, Maurice Lyon, Jacqueline McBride, Nicole Roberts, Rupert Simonian, Joanna Simons CBE, Clair-Marie Slater, Malcolm Smith, Bruce Todd, Mike Waddington, Yvonne Whiteman, Jane Young and Gina Zahn. Many thanks to you all for your help and insight. A big thank-you also to Cheryl Periton for her help and especially for reminding me that Marcus would need a passport for the trip to Rome.

My sincere gratitude to Mike Kinder, my former Latin teacher at Wyggeston Boys' School, Leicester, for his generous help with the Latin. The book has less Latin in it that it did initially, but I greatly enjoyed working with Mike. Gratias tibi ago, magister. You'll have noticed that Mike is the Latin teacher in Cantia.

Thanks to Paul Twivy and Tim Cassidy for the joke about the distance between Cantia and Geneva, though in Paul and Tim's version the joke referred to the distance between Geneva and Oxford, which is admittedly even farther.

Additionally, I'm very grateful to my precious friend the late Barbara Elsie Lammers (1954-2016). Barbara tolerated my reading aloud to her several of the early chapters of the first, third-person, draft of the book in 2006, and gave me many useful comments, especially when she thought I should change something. I very much miss Barbara, who was a deeply creative, talented, beautiful and kind lady and a wonderful mother too. I wish she could have seen this published version.

The three people who are the originals for Josh, Sam and Dora are all now grown-up and the original of Dora has a daughter of her own. Writing this, I can only echo what C.S. Lewis said in his introduction to *The Lion, the Witch and the Wardrobe* in which he observed to the real-life model for the character of Lucy:

I wrote this story for you, but when I began it I had not realised that girls grow quicker than books. As a result you are already too old for fairy tales, and by the time it is printed and bound you will be older still. But some day you will be old enough to start reading fairy tales again. You can then take it down from some upper shelf, dust it, and tell me what you think of it...

And that, perhaps, is one of the ironies of writing a book for young people and basing it on the characters of young people one knows: by the time the book is published the young people are not young any more and may indeed have young people themselves, which is one way of saying that life is greater than art but also perhaps the observation indicates that there is a sense in which art is even greater than life.

At any rate, I feel greatly privileged to know the originals of Josh, Sam and Dora, and Isabella, and I hope they will see at least some of their themselves in their counterparts in this story which ultimately derives not only out of my friendship for them, but also out of my deep love for Canterbury and its resonating historical wonders and mysteries.

Anyone who has walked through Canterbury at night, or for that matter in the day, feels very close to Cantia at least in their imagination.

As for me, a child of the Midland city of Leicester where I was born in 1957, I had my first glimpse of Canterbury in 1964 when as a six-year-old boy my parents and my younger brother and I stopped in Canterbury for the night when driving from Leicester to Germany for our summer holiday. This, incidentally, was the first time my late father Ted Essinger (1922-2005) had returned to Germany since he fled the country as a Jewish refugee in July 1939, just six weeks before World War II broke out.

That sight of Canterbury in 1964 was my first; I never forgot how much I loved the city and in 1977 I lived there for a few months between school and university. In August 1986, only a few weeks after a most enjoyable day trip to Canterbury in the late spring of 1986 with my much-missed late friend Roger Taylor, I decided to come to live in Canterbury, this city of literal and imaginative wonders. I plan to stay here for the rest of my life.

Finally, I want to acknowledge my great admiration of

Sir Ridley Scott's masterly *Gladiator* (2000). I feel I owe a considerable debt to that magnificent movie, with its wondrously convincing portrayal of Ancient Rome. *Gladiator* has been both a great inspiration to me while I was working on *Josh Moonford and the Lost City of Cantia*, and also kept up my belief that Josh's story was worth telling, during times when - like all writers I imagine - I wondered if I'd bitten off more than I could chew.

James Essinger
Canterbury
January 2019